DERMOT SOMERS
COLLECTED SHORT STORIES

for Maeve

DERMOT SOMERS

COLLECTED SHORT STORIES

Incorporating *Mountains and Other Ghosts* and *At the Rising of the Moon*

BÂTON WICKS · LONDON

Copyright © by Dermot Somers
Published in Great Britain in 2004
by Bâton Wicks, London

Trade enquiries: Cordee, 3a De Montfort Street, Leicester LE1 7HD

British Cataloging-in-Publication Data
A catalogue record for this book is available in the British Library
ISBN 1-898573-50-6

Printed and bound in Great Britain by
T.J. International, Padstow

CONTENTS

MOUNTAINS AND OTHER GHOSTS

First published in 1990 by Diadem Books, London

THE ISLAND

It seems extraordinary now that all three could end up on a rope together. Yes, I let it happen. I suppose it was partly stupidity and partly a hope that sharing would resolve their problem; mostly though it came about because beyond a certain tension relationships dictate their own events. If Tommo needed to destroy Brian then they'd end up on a ledge together somehow. And if both had an obsession with a third, then sure as hell he'd be there too. When that level of passion is reached the cogs of the inevitable grind into gear.

Even so, given that *something* had to happen, did it have to be on my time? Not that that's the important question. There are bigger issues involved here. A shocking laugh echoes in my ears – confuses me more than the scream that preceded it.

An ideal decision is impossible. If I do not report what happened on the island, if I conceal an attempt on one boy's life by another, then I am an accessory of sorts. In itself that wouldn't bother me too much, if it ended there. How can I conceal the fact that Tommo is capable – still capable – of that sort of desperation? Next time it might really come to a fatal conclusion. And yet, even more insistent than the screech of pain and the laugh that followed it, is the terrible memory of Tommo's tears.

'He – was – *my* – friend!'

I'd never have known it was possible to cry like that: to have held so much pain, rage, grief as he released in that adolescent damburst. The intensity increased and he was shaken by convulsions, weeping solid memories, fragments of friendship, debris of broken homes – harsh shapes dissolving in a flood of acid tears – prams and shattered chairs, torn bedding, a naked doll big as a baby, life-size wads of skirts and coats, linen grey as drowned skin, all the wreckage of a young life spilling out.

He crouched beside me on a ledge above the calm, clean sea, consolation useless. The convulsions quietened. Close as he was, his voice when it came was a long way off, muffled in some internal distance where his heart crouched by the flood before it slipped in forever. Grown up now, he could never cry again. Unbearable to renew that pain. I kept a hand on his shoulder; the denim might have covered a thin flake of rock.

Below us the sea swayed between the boulders, its grey indifference full of restless burial. It was just as if Tommo's rope was cut and he slipped with his new manhood into the water a hundred feet below.

What good will it do to report his act? I have no faith at all in detention. And they won't find Tommo anyway to put him away: he is drowned deep in his own life.

Instead they'll use the incident to shut down my programme and deprive all the others of the brief freedom we can teach them. For that reason – because this is a pilot scheme, an experiment – my instinct is for concealment. You may think I'm protecting my job, but that isn't it. There are easier jobs than taking screwed-up kids out into the wilds on rehab programmes. I don't expect to transform anyone, and there's no moral involved in mountain navigation or in paddling a straight line; it's enough for me to get them out – water, wind, rock, challenge, courage, achievement – out from under cover of deprivation to meet themselves not as we, but as nature, sees them.

I can't get away from it though: he could have killed someone.

And Brian's laugh! What goes on in a mind like that? Laughing on the edge of the void. Is Brian so far removed from the ordinary, so subtly displaced he makes a virtue of his alienation? Could that be what Tommo and the group saw in him, an otherness that had them fascinated but quivering on edge? It wasn't just sex – that was only an expression of something more extreme, something that came through in that cruel laughter, a private strength, immune to loneliness, that Tommo understood ... and envied?

I had them on a sea-crag. They'd paddled out to the island and camped there, the culmination of a three-week course in 'adventure skills'. There were six of them and, to help me, one officer from their detention-centre, a skilled canoeist, I'll give him that, but not strong on the human side. And that was a pity with this first group. I could have done with support, because they were *bastards*!

That was the basic problem; as a group, a gang, they were totally unsuited to an experience meant for individuals. It was as if they'd been hand-picked to destroy the programme right from the start.

Mr. Tuohy, the staff-man, muscular, impatient, kept rubbing them the wrong way. He couldn't relate on common terms – his accent, interests, humour were all wrong, and he didn't know how to lie low and get on with his job. He had to keep imposing his well-meaning but superior manner, either pointedly ignoring their behaviour as if it was beneath contempt, or else over-reacting to vulgarity. He'd have suited well-brought up boy-scouts, and I couldn't understand how the mistake had happened. As a result the unruly group couldn't relax and be free of authority for a while; they were forever reacting against the kind of irksome order he represented. In his frustration he tried to draw me in on his side over their heads, incriminating me in the exercise of authority. He couldn't see that the more superior he felt the more absolute was their scorn. Like all boys they would at least have admired him for his skills, but he used canoeing as a means of assertion – they called it showing off – and that finished him altogether.

I suspect Dr. Farrell, director of the detention centre, chose Tuohy for me specially. Farrell (Doctor of what? I still don't know) didn't care much for innovation. He splashed liberal rhetoric about and the centre was full of pool-tables and colour televisions, but there was nothing personal, nothing from the heart. Behind the chrome and plastic the place was as homely as a fun-palace. Radical measures were being forced on him from above by some political initiative (of even briefer duration if I submit this report). But behind it all, detention to Farrell meant what it said. Tuohy told me his boss believed he was training young misfits for a life in prison and the best he could do was get them used to it early. That kind of belief is self-fulfilling.

That's the other reason why I want to save this programme at all costs: to confound his expectations.

'I can guarantee you one thing with these fellows …' Farrell promised as we left his centre, the blue minibus heaped up with ropes, helmets, rucksacks, paddles, boys. I awaited the wise word of experience; 'They'll always let you down. Always.'

Such a failure of inspiration seemed funny at first; I almost laughed. Did he think I understood him, shared his cynicism, this paunchy warder with his pseudo-doctorate, the collar of his wrinkled business suit faintly sprinkled with dandruff, grey hair smeared to his scalp and the shine of a leather chair all over his life?

What did he think of my beard and jeans, adventure-jargon, liberation of the spirit, diplomas in Mountain-this and Outdoor-that? I know what he thought. Another fool with no experience of the ineducable, a few weeks with Tuohy and the incorrigibles would sort me out!

And yet – I still come back to it – there was almost a deliberate death.

When I call them a gang, it wasn't just leadership, the kind of thing you can isolate; they were going through all kinds of collective responses too. They had gestures, chants, private slang: but by far the most obvious feature was the pseudo-homosexual phase they were in. No girls in their lives and they were making a ritual of it. It was mostly harmless talk and exhibition – planned as a protest against sexual segregation in the hope that someone would throw them a few girls while radical gestures were in. Smart thinking in itself, and it might have worked – a different kind of hunger strike – except they got hauled out on crags and rivers instead. Cold-water treatment. No wonder they resented me. Mainly though, they were just acting out provocative ideas, teenagers with a primary mission in life: to defy!

But Brian was different. He wasn't the leader. Tommo was – more or less – at first. Tommo wasn't tough at all, but he looked savage which goes a long way. He made a convincing act of his instability too. He had to be doing something crazy all the time to feel important, and to make you see he was important.

I saw his file: separated parents, alcoholic mother, juvenile crime, institutions – textbook start – but unluckiest of all in the need to make an impression. He would always be rebuffed because he was short, thin and vicious-looking. His sharp, blue eyes were much too close together, he had spikes of aggressive ginger hair and a mouthful of rotten teeth. I saw how he tried to make an impact on adults the same way he ran his gang – with fast, funny, dirty talk – but all that came over was his head-butting, frontal style and those scaly teeth leering at you. For a day or two I kept him at bay, until I found there was no harm in him. His unfortunate appearance seemed made up of ill-fitting bits and pieces from different faces, not all of the same age or temperament. At first I saw it as a symptom of a fragmented personality until I realised that his experience hadn't disintegrated Tommo at all: it had compacted him with need. He was wholly and inconsolably himself, cemented together by the kind of craving for attention that is inevitably the first phase of pain.

He lived on sugar as far as I could see: sweets, minerals, tomato-sauce, chocolate. Tuohy was disgusted by the boy's teeth, forever trying to bully him off sugar and onto toothpaste, but Tommo didn't believe it was the sugar did the damage; it was the craving for sweetness, the addiction itself that caused the rot, like a solitary blight inside him that made him different from normal people and would poison him eventually. While he waited, he issued conflicting orders, set things on fire, stole anything mobile, and sucked cheap sweets, baring his gums with an appallingly ruminative thoroughness at Mr. Tuohy all the while. He was entertaining company when you learned to look slightly to one side of him, the way you treat headlights in the dark.

He was only a puppet when it came to leadership. I was surprised the centre hadn't briefed me on group-dynamics; either they didn't notice – which is quite possible – or else it was part of the conspiracy to sink the outdoor scheme.

Joe Curran was the brains, not Tommo at all. It took me a while to spot because he was discreet. Unlike Tommo, Joe wanted control, not attention. He orchestrated the whole obstinate atmosphere and subverted any success we had, carrying out his will through Tommo while their partnership lasted. And that was the reason for the partnership too, not the fact that they were both from Dublin – bloodbrothers, as Tommo thought, among rednecks.

Joe was cautious, intelligent, never capsized his canoe. He was the boy who spends his time on the dodgems avoiding collision while the others are hellbent on it, but his manner concealed a blade-sharp edge that was exposed sometimes between a bitter word and a soft smile. That edge would never soften because it was the rim of his true self. He was the Director on the other side of the fence, the other half of Tuohy's 'them and us', the one who would always let you down, because that was his mission; you were the enemy and he was going to make you pay. The kind too who always uses a front-man to take the friction.

Tommo didn't know he was being used. At first Joe conversed pleasantly, sensibly about discomfort and the value of risk so that I had innocent hopes for him, while Tommo foulmouthed me openly, grinning all the time, not meaning the abuse but proud of his ability to provoke. It occurred to me later that it was poor Tommo, trying to communicate the only way he knew how, who gave the abuse; but it was Joe, polite and cold, who meant it.

They weren't bad at the sports – they'd done a bit before and thought they knew everything. Climbing was about abseiling, you canoed on flat water, and hill walking happened when you got lost. They lacked self-confidence though and bravado was no substitute. The principle of the whole thing eluded them. They had a totally different concept of adventure: theirs was urban, illicit, subversive. I had to make a real effort to realise that mine was just as odd to them.

They ruled out the sea at first with an absolute sense of their own rights that you never get among ordinary schoolboys of the same age – a stubborn sense of the self, concerned only with resistance and demand. Swimming was out because it was too close to washing – hygiene was under protest back at the detention centre. But when the masks, snorkels, and huge, black fins were unpacked the 'dirty protest' collapsed. They wanted spear-guns: it had to be about hunting. They assigned Tommo his own snorkel and warned him to stick to it.

Every shadow underwater was 'Jaws!' and they leapt for the beach. When they conquered that terror Tommo would swim up from below and bite them through the wetsuit. When it wasn't 'Jaws!' it was 'Aids!' Their world was full of four-letter sensation.

Orienteering made no sense to them at all; they dealt with it by throwing away maps and compasses as fast as they were handed out. Privately that was alright by me; I'd rather stick to the hills and crags and the programme was all about 'choice' anyway – educated choice. i.e. you have to do it first before you decide you don't want to.

As I say, they made sense of things according to their own priorities, so hill walking was learning to survive on the run, or after a bomb. I had to recall a lot of primitive stuff about snares, and edible weeds, although in the long run we had to agree the only realistic thing was to raid the homesteads. Rock-climbing, up and over … well, obviously a handy skill.

Maybe they forgot these theories in the boredom or excitement of the action, but I despaired at first, because they would never let me think for a moment they were enjoying something for its own sake. As soon as there was any danger of that concession they began to complain or criticise, because if they got satisfaction from the experience then they owed me something and they couldn't have that, yet. It irritated the bristly thorns of independence that detention had given them.

One day I brought them underwater to a submerged car off the end of a Connemara pier, an old Mercedes stripped of its emblem and grille. In its murky interior a big lobster flexed his claws behind the windscreen. While Brian distracted him by hanging motionless near the glass I reached in through the passenger window, grabbed the lobster behind the pincers and brought him to the surface, a steel spring coiled in my hands. When I lifted him above the water to show how easily disarmed he was they scattered in – disgust? Puzzled and foolish I swam back down with the outraged creature and replaced him in his car.

Back on the pier they got hysterical satisfaction from a crumpled cigarette Tommo found in his pocket. The lobster was consigned to an oblivion deepened by the fear they'd shown and the excessive effort I was making to win them over. And yet, later on he would surface in their drifting night-talk, a new shape in the imagination, that outlandish crustacean, his claws like Tommo's teeth, piloting his stolen Mercedes out to sea. Sometimes too, as if I'd closed in downwind of a deer or a hare I saw a boy completely lost in profound, unguarded freedom. The slightest move, even a glance or a smile from me and the moment vanished. It might have lasted longer and longer with sunshine and practise but for the constant interruption by that other powerful experience of the self – or the mimicry of it. No one could emerge from a wet-suit or bend to tie a lace without one of the others leaping into a lascivious posture behind him, eyes rolling, tongue lolling.

It was a joke of course, and you had to laugh, it was so absurd; despite sloppy wetsuits, flapping cagoules, scrawny pimpled flesh and faces blotched with cold they never missed a cue. It became a reflex action; stacked together on nervous belays, eyes wide with apprehension they would begin to thrust at one another with idiot-automatism while calculating the drop below and the knots involved in their safety.

Yes, it was impossible not to laugh, though sometimes – tired and replete, mock-dancing to music on the radio, the thing contained a languid affection, and I wondered if they found the pathos in each other poignant … if that was it?

In the group of six there were two who didn't play-act. They made the gestures but in a deeper sense Brian and Joe were serious. And the others didn't tackle them so much either except for Tommo: he even tried it on me once – and regretted it when he was picked up and hurled fully-dressed into the sea.

Brian, quiet, self-absorbed, was older than the others – not in age – so old in outrage that they could never catch up. Tuohy told me about Brian, my star pupil, with the self-importance of one who knows the bad news, the inside story. Subject to violent abuse from infancy, Brian had stabbed his common-law step-father at the age of twelve. Tuohy said 'stabbed to death!' but that wasn't quite true. When taken into care there was said to be something sinister in his docility at first, as if the truth were incubating and must explode some day. Outbreaks of silent delinquency had begun to occur recently, more enigmatic than serious. Tuohy thought that was why Brian was assigned to me, to see if the dynamics of adventure would release some spring, for good or bad. I began to feel very much alone, trying to hem them in with action and exhaustion.

After a week it was obvious that Brian was the focus of the group-sexuality that undermined all we did. During every bout of exhibitionism – trouser-dropping, mooning through the minibus window (as if the public could tell the difference between their faces and arses anyway!) they referred to him with sidelong glances at his soft features, dark eyes unmoved behind cream-skinned, half-shut lids. He had some dubious power, an effect I never saw, something that came out in the night perhaps – if it came out at all. If it was present during the day it was only a pale reflection of itself and manifested to the ones who knew what to look for.

Tommo didn't get on with him. He was actively resentful of Brian. I noticed it quickly, but didn't know what to make of it. Then, in the second week, a crucial change of allegiance occurred. Joe Curran began to drop Tommo, his friend and fellow Dubliner and Tommo fell very awkwardly indeed. Things were difficult now in a different way. Just when I thought I understood the group and could get the most out of them, everything had changed.

Brian and Joe moved obliquely towards each other on the edge of chaos, not quite looking at anyone, their gazes sometimes tangling, sliding apart like surreptitious torch beams. And the other three, who would have been fine on their own, grew giddy with tension and regressed into a hectic childhood from which they sometimes emerged for a single frame to show a startling flash of skill, an instinctive hand-jam or a perfect paddle-stroke, only to flounder off balance immediately and disappear under.

Tuohy got into a terrible state of excitement one night – claimed he caught them 'at it' in the hostel showers, Tommo and two of the others. And maybe he did, but it wouldn't have been what he thought, an orgy of perversion. They were always setting him up, in the same way that Tommo stripped his gums at him. It's possible they picked up a few thrills in the process, but that wasn't the point.

The same when they mimed drugs, peeling back a sleeve on a tattooed arm, thumb braced against an imaginary syringe, initial grimace of desire and pain, then the face suffused with idiotic ecstasy subtly different from the sex-expression – while all the time a sharply-amused eye was peering out behind the act to see how you were taking it. From the start I refused to react; you don't lecture a boy on pacifism when he squeezes a toy trigger at you. It was interesting that Joe and Brian weren't in the showers that time. Tuohy thought they were the innocent ones. But whatever Brian and Joe got up to, was done for themselves, not for show; it would be a celebration of otherness, a private pact between them.

I discovered that first on the night of the whiskey. We were on a two-day hill walk with an overnight camp near Mám Eidhneach high in the Twelve Bens. Strenuous walking on steep, rocky ground, stunning views. Three tents: Tuohy (he snored) and I in one, the group divided between the other two. At midnight a row erupted. I awoke through a nightmare: Apaches attacking the wagons. The nearest tent, torchlit from within, throbbed with raucous fury – a bedlam of rage, nausea, tears, and a maudlin slur, 'One Day at a Time, Sweet Jesus …'

Sweet Jesus, indeed. Whiskey! Tommo was incoherent with drink, fury and betrayal. No sign of Joe though he'd started off in that tent. There were four in it now, fighting bitterly. As far as I could interpret, Joe had left with the bottle and gone to the other tent – Brian's – to give them a drink. Instead of coming back he'd ordered the other two boys over to Tommo. The shift was complete. Joe and Brian were too drunk to stand up, they lay silent and inward as stones, unblinking in Tuohy's relentless torchlight. He dragged them all out in the night wind, shivering and puking. Torches strafed the dark, showing rubber limbs, toppling bodies and ghastly faces askew like masks. Tears; you could see how much closer one or two were to childhood than manhood and would remain so all their lives.

I couldn't interfere on their behalf. This time Tuohy's anger was official, institutional. We knew who'd brought the whiskey: all he wanted to know was who had bought it. He was prepared to keep them stumbling on the wet mountainside till dawn if necessary. They wouldn't tell him anything at all, even the babies, and yet it was obvious from the disclosures minutes earlier – when I'd asked no questions at all and they were only too keen to betray – that Joe was the culprit.

Tuohy wouldn't believe it: he was determined that Tommo was

responsible, and of course it suited Tommo to take the rap, seeing himself with drunken pride as leader of the pack still. Basic to Tuohy's fury and my own sense of foolishness was the fact that they'd insisted the previous day that he and I should carry the provisions since they were the most important loads. We'd been set up – made clowns of. Even I couldn't let it pass.

I asked Tuohy to call off the bizarre inquisition (though it had its funny side) and promised we'd punish them in kind next day. I got out the map and head torch and, over a half mug of whiskey, devised a forced march.

In the morning, an hour after dawn, we stripped the polluted tents around them and tumbled them from their sleeping bags. Packing was done in silence, and if they ate it was only in queasy defiance. Joe, I noted with satisfaction, was particularly rough, but now that his role was out in the open he carried himself with the hardened aloofness of a convict. The rift between himself and Tommo was final from his side, though Tommo – who looked as though he'd been robbed from his grave – was still trying to patch things up. He fried Joe a slimy egg along with his own, and when the offering was ignored he slithered it soft and flabby as a wound into a plastic bag for lunch.

Brian was the only one in control of himself. He was eating thoroughly as if he knew what was in store with the usual self-absorbed air through which he seemed to look out on the landscape. Quiet stream, grey rock, mountains, drifting clouds: it was as if the world contained his own secret reflection and he would not care to disturb the surface.

It was a superb punishment – saved from sadism by the amount we suffered ourselves. Gradually, horribly, it dawned on them that we were not returning to the bus the quick way as Tuohy had led them to believe. I said nothing, hoping to load the consequences onto him, and this silence gave me an unexpected air of menace. They had to follow me for protection from the wilderness ... but they had no idea whether I was leading them out, or further in. On the grim slopes of Binn Bhán (the first time: we would cross it later in the day from the north) they had threatened to mutiny, but the Connemara sky closed down on cue and I took a gamble, stalking upwards into the mist. They followed like frightened sheep.

Secretly I was astounded by their performance, hungover and shattered, heavy-loaded over eighteen miles of steep, rocky mountain in bad weather. Maybe they could only respond to coercion, but three weeks ago it seemed they could hardly walk a sea-level mile.

Now they endured it in their own distinctive ways. Joe was stoic but you could tell he would never forgive. Brian, dreamy absent, had set his body in motion and vacated it. Tommo was stunned at first, withdrawn and grieving, but every now and then a flash of himself broke through. 'Sir! Sir!' (he deliberately called me Sir because I was trendy enough to prefer first names and he reckoned I hadn't earned that yet.) He stood at the side of a high, desolate pass, rain running down his baggy anorak, as I prepared to contour down Binn Chorr and sneak back around the other side. He gestured urgently up the ridge rising steep and fierce above, 'Sir, sir, can we go up that one sir? Can we sir?' And the friendly, evil grin to let me know he understood just what was going on and could always go one step further than he was pushed. I liked him.

He began to look after the three weaker lads as well, not from compassion at all but with a great show of protecting them from my viciousness. He played this card so well – brave, young refugees victimised by cruel oppressor – that I was forced at last to swing guiltily back towards the road. At one stage in the afternoon we were skirting slopes within a mile of the minibus but they couldn't see it in the rain, and they were going so well that we spent a further two hours treading rocky humps and hollows in the immediate area. Even Tuohy didn't fully realise what was going on, and finally he more than anyone was pleading for release. To a great extent I was punishing them for my own mistake, for trusting them. And further, it shocked me to realise how little they understood me after a week of sustained effort, how readily they accepted ruthlessness from me as if that was all they had expected.

I gave in at last, sat them down, passed round my flask and learned an incidental truth: no matter how famished they were, their own personal tastes – tea or coffee, sugar or not – took precedence. I chatted for the first time all day, commiserating on blisters, lamenting the sorry decline of our 'adventure holiday' and the great distance still to walk. We were nearly halfway I said. There might be a way out …

Joe smelled compromise, came straight out in the open, negotiating. I could see him in the future trading territory with the law in some city of blackmailed ghettoes. With the instinct of a dealer he seized my delicate drift. No further incidents in exchange for a short-cut …

The deal concluded, he sat back; I think he expected a taxi to arrive. Tommo hadn't sat down at all. There were no cigarettes left and he was smoking a biro or something, chewing imaginary gum. He'd eaten the cold, fried egg and guzzled most of the flask; I couldn't bring myself to drink from it after him.

I marched them tactfully away from the bus for twenty minutes, contoured around in driving rain and in three quarters of an hour they saw it – fortunately, because I had begun to spot our previous tracks with embarrassing frequency. Even Brian joined the stampede and I had to restrain Tuohy.

No further incidents; but an error had been committed. I should never have made a deal, however tacit. It brought me out of detachment and into their style. I was one of Them now – along with Tuohy and the Director.

For the final week the weather improved. Connemara steamed and shimmered, lakes evaporating in a heat wave. We paddled out to an uninhabited island for the last few days; the real thing, self-sufficiency, Survival! We brought an astounding amount of food. They preferred to leave nothing to their own resources, just in case. I won't say which island – I'd prefer to reserve that crag in case the programme survives.

It's a big, rambling cliff on the seaward side, sheltered from Atlantic swells by a high reef that juts out into the ocean, half-encircling the cliff to take the brunt of the weather. Even on wild days there is a pool of calm water, wide and deep, below the crag. When the sun shines the pool is a glossy, green lagoon full of cool, weedy mystery, its inward eye rimmed by the shadow of the reef. Smooth caverns burrow into the rock floored with shells and sliding shingle. An underwater archway tunnels under the reef out to the open sea, requiring a cool head and a very deep breath to traverse.

On our first day we abseiled down the cliff on two hundred feet of rope, swam out across the lagoon to the reef, the water so warm the wetsuits were irksome. We scrambled up and over the reef, down to a ledge on the seaward side. The unbridled ocean swelled and sucked a long way below.

One by one they took deep breaths, faces tight with excited appre-hension, screamed Death to a chosen enemy and leapt onto a rising wave. A long way down, the yell strung out behind, water lifting solid as glass shattered in a cold crash, down through foaming light, breath clenched, mask clamped to the face, streaming through the water, wild emerald – then lunge for the surface, blinding light, cheering faces ...

One by one I led them back underwater through the tunnel. To get enough depth we climbed up high on the reef and plunged again. Far below, wet light shone through a green door in the rock. Kick hard with the fins, dive towards it. Enter the arch. Cool cavern, open at both ends. A roof of rock above, dark and sinister, the rubber body rises bubbling towards it. Blow out air to sink, keep kicking – pinned underwater against the underbelly of the earth. Surging up through the inner pool of warm, calm water, the world bursting with light and silence, fish flicking, plankton thick as midges, the cold ocean far behind. Lungs full of rich, golden air.

I ducked back through the arch for the next initiate. All but Brian recoiled at the entry where the dark rock pressed down like a tomb. I had each one by the wrist as if to steer, and at that point a subtle jerk overcame the hesitation and we were down, through, out before they knew it.

Yes, I thought about rebirth –

Only Tommo and Brian would follow me back through the tunnel and then return on their own. But when they broke the surface and threw up their masks in triumph, recognition clamped down like a visor and they swam apart ...

And yet, more than anything before, the tunnel seemed to unite us in a real sense of adventure. Even Tuohy didn't try to be superior but yelled and screeched along with them – told how terrified he'd been until the thrill took over, and they laughed and made no attempt to cash in on his admission. I thought we had it made; peace and harmony.

They got their wetsuits off without molesting anybody and then grabbed harnesses and ropes. We were going to climb two hundred feet to the top along the steep, easy ridge formed by the junction of the reef and the main cliff-face.

I was quietly astonished again by the way they accepted everything now without question, not even as a conscious challenge, but simply the next thing to be done. They accepted the progression of 'adventures' as if it was the natural course of events; they'd jump from a plane tomorrow or climb steep ice if those options were ordained. Is this how armies get trained? At the heart of elation I felt unease: where does choice stop and programming begin?

They wouldn't dress though, insisting on climbing in togs in case they fell in, though a parachute would have been a better precaution in that event. By now they were relaxed about ropes and belays, able to protect each other while I soloed along beside them and supervised. Soloing –

unroped climbing, normal for an instructor – shocked them and they had more difficulty with the apparent folly of this than with their own climbing. 'Sir, sir, if you farted you'd be dead, sir!' But now they'd accumulated confident experience and I found it amusing to see how smoothly they swung into gear, accepting things they had thought outrageous at first. Climbing the ridge safely, competently, I saw that – without even knowing it they were thoroughly enjoying themselves. The warm rock bristled with good holds, but it was steep enough to require technique and attention too, for the sea fell away below us and the rock seemed excitingly undercut and exposed, as if it overhung the water, an optical illusion not uncommon on sea-crags. People, the mainland, the law, seemed to belong to another life – a drab, unappealing existence, the wrong side of parole.

I saw the tunnel-mouth, a pale outline under the sunken reef, but I knew better now than to point it out. Wait till they saw it themselves. Likewise, if I pointed out they were enjoying themselves, or even asked, their faces might still close and the innocence evaporate. So I said nothing and sure enough they spotted the tunnel and were very smug indeed that I couldn't see it. Tommo went a step further and recognised a lobster in it from a hundred feet up. When Joe reckoned the tunnel wasn't wide enough for the car and the lobster had to come in on foot like the entry to a particular block of flats, I thought they were back on the old footing again and I felt a blaze of relief for Tommo. Weeks of sun, wind and hard going had taken the pinched look off their bodies, even if some of the faces could never be rescued from deprivation. They were fit and tanned, red anyway, as they swarmed up the cliff, clad only in swimming togs, climbing belts and shoes. We must have looked extraordinary – if he saw us at all; often the unexpected is invisible – to the small fishing-boat that chugged past the cove picking up lobster-pots. The group turned around on the rock waving fists, yelling obscenities, in case he took 'our' lobster. Fortunately the boat was out of earshot. I was afraid he might misinterpret the gestures and call out a rescue. I was about to point out the new line to be climbed tomorrow, a system of steep cracks wrinkling the centre of the face, but I remembered what I'd learned, waited till we stood on top where it appeared the most attractive choice, and casually suggested they pick something themselves. Sharp eyes narrowing on the options, Joe Curran picked the cracks immediately. He nominated himself and Brian for the first ascent. He made no mention of a third. The rebuff needled through the sunny afternoon. Tommo caught my eye as the others jostled, uncertain of priority.

'Me!' His face was raw, like a creature stripped of feathers.

'Every climb has a name ...'

'What'll we call it?' Joe raised the matter next morning. He had a strong sense of ritual.

'*The Jacks are back!*' Tommo whooped irrepressibly. Joe cut his sausages in silent sections.

'Call it *Penal Colony*,' Tuohy gibed; he was reading Kafka, 'Apt in every sense.'

'Why not *Metamorphosis* so?' I was stung to foolishness, 'There's a change going on, you know!'

He grinned at me pityingly, 'You don't know the story, do you? They're dung-beetles already.'

No sun that day. A relief; sunburn and salty backs made painful paddling. We were half-camped, half-resident in a deserted cottage, split into two groups of three, one to kayak around the island with Tuohy, in and out of sea-caves, land on inaccessible beaches, observe birds and seals, throw stones at them – no, we'd eliminated that. And my group, bound for the new climb. On the way to the crag Tommo stayed close to me relating rough snatches of his life while Joe and Brian hurried ahead.

'Sir –' he interrupted himself abruptly, 'will it be hard?'

I stopped, examined him in detail, close up. Yesterday's glimpse had given me an insight far behind the bony nose, thin, anxious mouth, crooked eyes. His skull vibrated slightly as he focused on me. I stared harder, the way you examine someone sleeping, and know without doubt what you really think. He returned the scrutiny, attempting some painful exchange, his chin raised, the sad teeth jutting and the slight vibration continuing all the time. Was it the reason, I wondered, for that sense of jittering motion – his body chasing round to keep up with those eyes?

Climbing was not his strength, he didn't have precision skills either, couldn't hit a dartboard or a cue-ball. An optical problem?

What to say? I understood the power of the simple, universal fantasy, how he hoped to shine, to triumph, to reinstate himself.

I couldn't help him with it. The exchange faltered.

'No harder than what you've done, Tommo. But doing something new

is always special. For yourself! For yourself, Tommo! Do you understand?'
He broke away. All he'd heard was the special promise.

He withered on the rock. Turned his head and shot me a look of anger and despair. We both knew I shouldn't have let him try.

'Steady up, Tommo! Get a grip on yourself!'

Joe mimed my advice with a vulgar snigger. Dung-beetle is right.

All Tommo had to do was reach up, grasp a pointed flake above his head, pull hard, and swing his left foot up to a large, flat hold. After that the crack leaned back again. The position was intimidating, not technical. He would have lunged awkwardly up without a second thought if the rope was above him, me anchored on a ledge taking it in as fast as he came. Now, with the rope below – leading – he couldn't climb. He knew immediately he couldn't do it, so the time he spent there had no forward motion at all. The day thickened around him, waiting. The sea rested against the foot of the cliff, the tide ceased to go in or out. Even the sun wasn't going anywhere until Tommo made his decision.

Standing on similar holds, five feet away, I saw how simple the moves were – easy for me, impossible for him. I felt a stab of impatience, angry that his big moment could collapse so simply, become such a trite catastrophe.

'Come on, Tommo ... Do it!'

He found it difficult even to remain straddled where he was, his limbs wilting towards the belay-ledge. He shot me another stark glance, not angry, not imploring either; in his need he measured me for help. I failed him again.

On the ledge below, silence. They would not sneer at climbing-failure. Too close to the common bone. But he had thrust himself to the fore to lead the crux, 'the glory-bit' he called it, brushing aside their furious objections with my support – given against my better judgement, suspecting as I did that he'd been cultivating it on the way across under the guise of intimacy.

Joe and Brian stood braced against the belay, feet planted firmly on the rock. Joe held Tommo's rope in a belay-plate, there was no danger, even if he fell – and yet, in their cold silence, the refusal to console, something awful was occurring, like a deliberate accident. I guided Tommo's heels back down an awkward move to the ledge. Through the suede I felt sharp bones tremble. I smelled failure on his clothes, a stale, distasteful whiff – cigarette smoke and nervous sweat. Hard not to avert my face. I chatted with hollow levity, patted shoulders, clipped and unclipped ropes. No response.

Brian was next. Too late to call it off, the inevitable was launched. He was animated, anticipation on his flushed cheeks. He had a fit, springy look today. Clothes always fitted him well, which is a quality of the body, not the clothes. His hair seemed to belong neatly to his head too; the others were all lank or shock-headed as if a casual scalp had been grafted to the skull. Joe kept his sleek and sharp, which wasn't the same thing at all either. He held Brian's rope with the cold concentration of a boxing-manager; someone else takes the punches, he takes a profit. Tommo hunched against the rock, staring blindly at the sea.

Brian reached up for two handholds, launched from the ledge; like grasping the handlebars of a bike and coasting smoothly away – reflexive as that. The holds conformed fluidly to his needs, a smooth climber with skill and balance. He took the hard move first try, not lunging or swinging, a delicate step.

I leaned across discreetly, placed a chock in the crack above him, He disdained the interference, lifted out the nut, jammed it in another position more to his satisfaction and clipped the rope into the karabiner. Independence. If he fell the chock would hold the rope and Joe could take the force below. Above the crux he paused in mid-move, giggled down at the belay. I moved up the crack beside him, ready to place another runner to continue his protection. I realised I was watching something new, blatant, exposed. Behind us the day was quiet; the sigh of the sea and the crying of birds underlined a tense, cinematic silence. Slither of soles on rock, hiss of breath. Faces below. I barely existed for these three; they were in an elemental, adolescent world. I sensed its secret, ugly terms making a parallel ascent along lines of tension that must not overlap ours.

Brian was showing off. I handed him another runner. He snatched it without a glance, placed it properly, clipped in. His moves were exaggerated now, made for effect, expressing his ability, celebrating himself and his exposure. I glanced down at the ledge; Joe smirked, Tommo's face was knotted.

I knew there would be another rope length of easier climbing up above. Tommo could lead that, I thought, be first to the top of the cliff – a hollow satisfaction, having failed on the glory-bit. But the hardest part of growing up is coming to terms with hollow satisfactions.

Brian performed an intricate series of moves in his private, smiling dance – wide bridges and high steps, leaning out on handholds, posing instinctively. I warned him sharply.

Fifty feet above the belay, with three good runners on the rope below, he pulled up on a steep flake, leaned far out in silhouette. The surge of movement stalled. He tugged sharply, grunting with annoyance, fingers whitening on the rock. The rope strained; 'Slack!' I yelled at Joe, and then I saw the problem. The rope had slipped into a sharp crack above the belay and jammed solid. Joe – it was actually his fault – tried to flick it out from below without success. I was reluctant to climb down and leave Brian alone.

'Tommo! Reach up and pull it out! Tommo!' I called confidently on the kinship of the rope. He stood still a moment, his face a white blotch, then he obeyed. Reached up high, gripped the rope below the pinch, and tugged it sharply outwards. A few jerks and it came free. I turned back to Brian. Time for another runner. He was swinging nonchalantly on the flake, showing off again. Below him the rope still flicked. Angry, hissing voices, a scuffle. I thought Tommo mistook the runners for constrictions on the rope. He whipped it savagely. The first nut lifted out.

'Stop it, Tommo! Stop …'

The second runner lifted. Joe's knuckles lashed. He knew how to hurt, the pain far sharper than the blow.

Tommo shrieked. Like an electric shock the sound whipped up along the rope, the last nut popped, the rope stretched tight as wire.

If Brian fell he'd hit the sea.

I clawed across to place a runner. Another blow, a shriek.

Pulled from below, Brian's waist jerked suddenly, arms shock loaded, one foot torn free, hands hooked tight. I clung to the rock – as if the whole crag moved.

'Tommo! Tommo – !' Shuddering, jolting, he clenched the rope. Then Brian laughed, sharp and shocking as a blade. Tommo slumped below, misshapen, adrift.

Brian swung smoothly up the flake, sauntered towards a ledge. I vaulted after him, threw in a nut and clamped him roughly to it.

Safe! Safe! I tried to shake him, to yell with nervous tension, but he looked right through me, indifference in his eye. I did not exist.

I couldn't bring Tommo up to the same ledge as Brian, neither could I leave him alone below; he might untie. He had the look of exhausted options.

'Brian, bring Joe up here – then wait!' I shook him with violent satisfaction, 'WAIT! Do you hear?'

I climbed down to Tommo while Joe came up. It was chilling to see them, Joe moving coldly past me, while above him Brian fished tranquilly with the rope as if there were no vicious shadows darting for hooks under the surface. But I knew Joe wasn't going that way for long – no longer than he needed the rope to get him off the alien angle of the cliff.

Joe was through with Brian – afraid of his unpredictability. Like myself, Joe understood he couldn't hope to control the source of that laugh. And just as he'd dropped Tommo, for being arbitrary, now he would drop Brian for an even deeper inconsistency, a private anarchy that could not be resolved. But in their totally different world neither Brian nor Joe would ever be lonely: each was sufficient to himself.

As soon as I reached him Tommo broke down. Not a response to me as a person; more as if a witness, any witness, confirmed what he felt.

Misery, betrayal convulsed him. 'He – was – *my* – friend!' More than a friend; blood-brother, tribesman.

There was violent anger in him still.

'The bastard!! I'll get him –' he swore. For a moment I thought he meant Brian, then I understood again. And I knew what Tommo must do to survive; turn his pain into hatred, and freeze the wound.

THE OLD STORY

As soon as the three men climbed above the shelter of the lower slopes the wind hardened against them. It ripped through the falling snow, flung a bitter flurry in their faces, then swept the hillside clear.

Another mountain was revealed.

We saw their tiny figures, high above us, as we escaped down the valley out of the smothered hills. We said nothing, unwilling to trip the rhythm of descent.

Farmers, we uneasily supposed. Going up for stranded sheep. But there were no dogs. And it was too late.

Where the snowbound bogs began a rough, upward curve we saw them halt in a straggling line. Three black dots printed on the white slope. They were a poignant Morse S ... an abbreviated stammer of distress.

Above them the mountain grew and grew into the sour murk of the evening, the snow shower lifting steadily up the slopes, yet never clearing the horizon. It seemed there was no top to this mountain.

We shuffled downhill towards the distant car, casting anxious glances back.

There was a morbid sense of dislocation in the scene, like a landmark exposed in the wrong context; a row of familiar rocks shrouded in snow. But our boots were cold and wet; we had defied the taboo of Christmas Day and struggled high into the snowy hills. Condensation soaked our clothes inside the windproof anoraks. Delay was impossible. We might have tried a warning, if we'd been near enough to shout to them, three black dots dwindling towards obscure conclusion across the grey page of the evening. All around, the language of outrage was snowed under, leaving only that last …

There was nothing we could do. The remorseless snow began again, cold ash of time drifting down between us. They disappeared slowly behind the weather. Into the past, one by one.

Darkness thickened across the mountains.

Hugh stared up into the appalling gloom. Rory, the guide, had abandoned them finally. Vanished without a shout or a backward glance. His surging footprints grimly rejected the funeral pace.

Hugh staggered forward another step. A swirl of wind whipped up snow and scoured his face. His legs were numb from the hips to the toes. He dragged a foot out of the flat powder and lurched forward, hit rising ground, no momentum. He was going uphill again.

His feet clubbed through the steepening surface and sank between tufts of buried heather. Loose snow piled into the clogs and wadded around his ankles. Tilting forward he saw his shinbone scrape against the frozen crust of the footprint. A cold, bloodless wound, ivory-white, bracketed each shin.

He concentrated on placing his feet in the deep holes Rory had kicked in the snow, but the gaps were too great for a boy. Air rasping in his throat he fought for the energy to match that rhythm, the powerful stride of survival, but he stumbled at every step and was forced to plunge his cringing foot again in a fresh trail.

Higher up there were heavy drifts of snow banked in rolling waves with miniature cornices, blue-shadowed and blade-sharp. Feathered patterns of snow ice, bitterly frozen, encrusted the humps of hidden heather.

A steep, sliding step up a bank, his foot skidded, a fierce gust wrestled him back a pace. The tips of his broken teeth sang bitterly in his skull in a mouthful of icy wind.

Slumped in shivering defeat memory assaulted him with a rage of loss. He remembered the speed of his thin bones flying; legs leaping and hurtling, racing over sand hills in sea-storms; eyes, teeth, every inch of skin flogged by sand and salt spray; skimming the wind-lashed reeds that thatched the dunes, bare heels thudding and plunging in solid banks of sand, their scalloped edges blade-sharp and smoking wildly in Atlantic gales.

Battered beaches in Donegal, Hugh racing the hounds of Castle Doe through the endless dunes, his wild red hair streaming on the sea-wind.

Fierce disciplines of his beleaguered culture and its medieval wars. Elizabethan intrigue squeezing the North-west chieftaincy. At fourteen he was ripped from fosterage, kidnapped from impending leadership, four years held to hostage in the imperial stronghold of Dublin Castle …

Now he was out; on the run.

In a stupor of exhaustion Hugh swayed in his footsteps facing the barrier of snow. Thin garments were stiffening ominously against his skin. He trembled convulsively, the blue of his hands shading to bone-white towards the fingertips. Old scars ringed his ankles, the marks of manacles that bound him to the Castle walls since his last escape. A jagged cut to the bone where the rough file slipped in haste last night.

Down at the car, darkness drifting in like a lapse of memory, we dropped our rucksacks. We had Cicatrin in First Aid boxes and enough bandages to cover a body whole. But we dared not linger, looking back. We must escape before the roads were buried.

The car skidded precariously out of the hills and back to the city. We could not be responsible for the consequences of the past. We are only guilty of the repetition of events, the endless failure to correct.

History comes round and around like winter.

The soldiers get there first. The stretcher-bearers are always last.

And the vice-regal soldiers, bounty-hunters on horseback with sword and halberd, they are out there too, combing the frozen hills for the fugitives.

If they dragged Hugh back from the jaws of winter he would hang for his liberty by the starved neck; red head and white face preserved in a skull-cap of black pitch, a weathered lump on a flag staff above the battlements.

And if he eluded them too he would survive to suffer heaped up tragedy in a brief future, traditions erased, a whole history unhinged at Kinsale. And death handed down for centuries.

Hugh dared not look back down the slope, refused even to turn his head.

If Art O'Neill had fallen behind he was beyond help now in this fatal half-light. That was why Rory had finally forged ahead. He was leaving Art to fate. If they dragged him any further they would all die.

Images of his friend and fellow-hostage tormented Hugh's imagination. Art O'Neill had been larger than life. In prison he loomed over Hugh's wretched spirit, sustaining him, subtly tempering his passion for escape.

But while Hugh paced the cage of the jail Art rotted, as if all the strength of his will was being absorbed by the younger boy. Hugh could not clear his mind of the round face that had swollen slowly in front of his eyes twenty-four hours a day during four bitter years of hostage.

He saw Art again and again slump belly down in deep snow, a bloated carcass bulging in a thin silk shirt. He saw the heavy head strain hopelessly, imploring uphill after Hugh's disappearing back. Brutally he blinked away the image, clubbed the snow from his face with frozen fingers, and stumbled on. He must catch Rory. The guide was strong and knew the way. Nothing else mattered. Art would drag himself along behind, crawl out of the Pale on his belly if need be. Art O Neill would not yield to a blind mountain in Wicklow. This was his second flight too. There would not be another. Again Hugh imagined him sprawled on the white slope below, arms out-flung in desolation, embracing a curve of snow, lacerated feet helpless in his small, tight clogs.

An open wound tore Art's forehead above one staring eye. Thin blood trickled from the wound into the eye and down the creased cheek.

The watery blood arrested Hugh. Stopped him in stumbling flight. He knew if he turned back he would tumble downhill, down the steep slope of his own will. He stopped in despairing resignation and shuffled slowly around.

Art was staggering grotesquely towards him, huge body swaying on buckling legs.

Soft flesh quivered on his great bones, fattened on the flour and grease of prison. Heavy thighs shuddered in his sagging hose. No exercise in years but the daily shamble to a closet squat, and still he had covered twenty-five miles of wintry Wicklow in a night and day, clad in sodden indoor clothes. He had hung between their shoulders until Hugh and Rory could no longer support him, and he was left reeling forward alone.

It was too cold for blood to flow, but a rusty stain caked his forehead, matted with wisps of hair and masonry grit.

Hugh shuddered in the sickening grip of the accident descending the rope. Art's gross body squeezing down the shaft from the high prison-closet.

Art was violently opposed to that escape-route, but at the end of all the arguments he had no choice. If he remained behind he would be hanged for his friend's escape. His power had wasted away, he had lost control of Hugh.

It was a tight fit, even for the boy's wiry form, sliding down the knotted tapestries, a hundred feet down the loose shaft cringing at every touch of the slimy walls.

Hugh had plugged his nostrils and filled his mouth with wine-soaked wool before he gripped the twisted cloth, but by the time he lowered into the main sewer that ran into the moat he was retching violently.

Art couldn't possibly squirm down that filthy constriction. In a guilty panic Hugh thought of swarming back up again, but that was impossible.

He crouched shivering and sweating in the dark sewer, the anal canal of Elizabethan imperialism. Upstairs the raucous soldiers celebrated Christmas.

The tiny circle of light at the top of the shaft was suddenly obscured. A shower of debris rained down, then bigger stones and broken bricks came ricocheting fiercely down the tunnel.

Art was struggling and wrestling inside the wall of the tower. His kicking feet and hoarse breath were audible below through the rattle of rotten masonry. Inch by inch he squirmed downwards, and every rumbling, stinking second Hugh awaited the clamour of pursuit. The knots in the cloth rope had been tied in a frantic hurry, with the minimum overlap to increase the length. If a knot slipped under Art's enormous weight...

Hugh understood that this was Hell he had chosen; not escape any more, but descent into Hell.

At last Art's legs kicked out of the shaft through the roof of the horizontal culvert. The forked shadow of a monstrous delivery fought across the roof in the light of the taper Hugh held aloft to burn the vapours.

Hugh turned his face away in revolted pity.

The emerging body was beyond recognition. Art had become the shape and substance of his own decay.

His feet touched down and he crouched to enter the culvert. A spray of dirt and splinters rained down on his shoulders as he released his grip on the cloth rope.

Then a vicious, whining rattle, thud of stone on bone and Art toppled limply forward into Hugh's arms.

The taper fell from nerveless fingers but in the last second of sizzling light Hugh saw the dirty, dizzy blood spurt from Art's open forehead.

Across the whipping snow Art came toppling towards Hugh. His glazed eyes were fixed on the stalk of support outlined in the shifting wilderness, a streak of lank, red hair glowing against the sky. Art's body was finished. He felt neither cold, nor tired, nor hungry. A vast numbness stirred fitfully by sparks of reason; Rory running to Glenmalure. Hugh … Hugh waiting.

His knees folded without resistance, tumbled him forward against an unbearable bank of snow. Hugh waiting.

He whispered, sinking 'Ní thig liom … dhul … níos faid.' Confession of defeat.

As he fell he saw Hugh move.

But no touch on the shoulder. No tugging hand. When he opened his eyes and raised his head Hugh was gone.

Two rows of overlapping footprints marched away into the dark. Art levered himself to his hands and knees, and crawled towards the steep bank. Origin and destination meant nothing now. Continuity …

The mountain levelled out. Hugh was traversing a dark plateau. Less snow here. The fierce wind scoured it off, the air stinging with icy powder. Rory's tracks half-obscured already.

Round clumps of mountain-grass grew clear of the hard crust. As coarse as sedge the rusty tufts resembled wild scalps of warrior-hair.

Head after head marched in mourning ranks beside Hugh's stumbling feet, an army of Gallowglasses buried on a hopeless mission, the rough red hair blown down in fringes over the frozen faces beneath.

Hugh realised the entire mountain was the treacherous crust of a burial ground. He was lost, sinking deeper in the grip of the cold; ankle-deep, knee-deep, wading into the deadly snow, down among the ranks of buried soldiers.

He dragged himself out of delirium; hallucinations dissolved behind his eyes, reverted to shapes in the blowing snow. Night already, and he was nowhere. A wasteland of ice and pain and hunger. Christmas Day darkening and he knew he was treading a deadly frontier; light and dark, hope and despair. Life and death.

Through the early hours of the escape Hugh had fiercely sustained the fantasy of a last gentle ridge somewhere on the rim of the Wicklow sky. Midday, the sun high and healing, pouring benediction into a deep, green valley. Bowing sentries step silently aside, a tumult of cheering faces, reaching hands, powerful arms bearing him aloft into the unsubdued sanctuary of the Gael.

He peopled his illusion with aching felicities. His own mother, queen of the north, standing shoulder to shoulder with Fiach O Broin, warrior of Wicklow, at the heart of the valley stronghold to welcome him home to freedom.

A banquet, a bed, fast horses, north to chieftainship and then years and years of vengeful victory, reversing the tide of empire. Replacing it with his own?

As the day wore on, and the agony increased, and Art began to die slowly, Hugh's paradise dimmed hour by hour, until finally he would have traded freedom for a hint of food and rest. He was gone too far and too far gone, and there was not the faintest dream flickering in the savage arena of the night.

Hugh stood rooted in the vacant tracks. The footprints were old and obscure already. He trembled at the ultimate isolation.

His body knotted suddenly with shock, then doubled over on itself in rigid, empty shudders. He was pitched abruptly to his knees weeping in convulsive terror.

Tears flooded from his eyes, slid without sensation down his numb cheeks, over the frozen knuckles clenched against his mouth.

And with the clarity of despair Hugh understood that his face and fingers felt no trace of the hot tears, felt nothing at all. And his feet too were lost, victims of a frost creeping steadily towards the core, feeling for the frantic heart.

A movement behind him. He jerked round, at bay. Saw the huge silhouette swaying again in the dark.

Art's features were sunken holes in the flesh of his face. His feet ploughed through the snow, every movement a last refusal to lie down and die. Grey all over, bleached bloodless.

Arms folded across his chest; lifting himself bodily across the snow.

Hugh crouched, open-mouthed, transfixed by the apparition, tears congealing on his cheeks. He saw Art stumble, the arms slid loosely apart, limp hands tumbled down by his side.

There was no hint of life in the gesture. The collapse of motion itself.

Hugh was close enough to see the blind glazing of the eyes and the loosening skin, as the will finally released its grip.

Hugh's arms lifted in desolate supplication. He grappled the toppling body to him and shook it savagely. Not to be alone ... the only one ...

He begged Art's folding flesh to go on enduring, to survive. A mute, massive weight leaned upon him.

Feverishly pleading, Hugh dragged an inert arm over his own shoulders, around his thin neck and staggered forward in the frozen embrace. Rory's prints had vanished. Art's feet were anchored in the snow. On the wind-swept side of the mountain Red Hugh O Donnell wrestled with death.

We knew them of course ... just as you did. They moved vividly against the background of their history, so vividly we sometimes reached to touch, fingers faltering in confusion against the tracked white of the page.

There was nothing there. Twinges of memory and premonition.

But they were part of us, because the story refused to end in a hole on a hillside, a shallow grave.

Rory brought help from Glenmalure the following day. And Red Hugh rose from the dead. He transcended time.

They dug him, barely alive, from under the snow, gave him back to history with the irresistible force of resurrection.

He tore the country asunder for the last ten years of his short life. Envenomed with frostbite and fury he drove us violently towards the penal centuries.

But Art was dead. His death underlines the miracle of Hugh's survival. He is the victim history and faith teach us to need.

We could never arrive soon enough to save him. Not from Glenmalure or any other point in terrain or time.

We are cursed with a need for human sacrifice.

FACELIFT

kkkrrRRRUUMPPP.

The front of the buttress lifted clean away from the crag.

BOOOOOMM!

It vanished.

Ex-SAS man Willard grinned over his detonator. Knocked up Sheffield that little lot did! Gritstone fragments crashed around him in the violated dawn. He prised the helmet from his skull and rose to his feet. A shocked pall of dust quivered over Stanage. Ducking low, he ran towards it, weaving from force of habit.

The explosion reverberated through air and earth; down on North Lees campsite stunned climbers struggled into their clothes; an unattended word-processor in the office of *High* magazine hiccupped acknowledgement; and in Chesterfield cemetery, freshly interred, the corpse of Captain Robert Bennett felt the seismic shock and turned in its grave. Twelve days earlier, in a Belfast back street, the captain had been shot in the back. Accidentally, by one of his own men. But his tragic conclusion is not the point here.

Dave Willard had picked up some funny habits in Ireland. *kkkrrUUMPP!* – that sort of thing. Of course the Special Services had taught him a few tricks too – *BaBOOOOOOMM* and all that. Brought up in Brixton, Dave adapted quickly to undercover work in Ulster. His small brain and powerful body were linked by a short fuse and there was plenty of scope for self-expression. And he was learning techniques to take home to London when the crackdown started there. He need never be unemployed. At first the excitement of Northern Ireland compensated for the loss of climbing, but eventually he grew bored with peace-keeping in Belfast and Armagh and craved again the brutal simplicity of rock.

Home on leave it was next-to-top priority. Down to London first for the prostitutes, then he hit Wales, the Lakes and the Peak as hard and fast as he knew how. But he found no satisfaction. Flesh or rock it was all frustration – second-hand, third-rate. All the good stuff was gobbled up in his absence.

Everything he touched felt used; classic rock with its polished holds and initials carved around the belays; when he rang Vanessa from Euston

Station she was booked out, but she slotted him in between nine and ten. 'Ta-ta, Dyve, give my love to the regiment. See yer next time.'

Dave wanted to break fresh ground, climb new routes, see his own unique achievement signed in bold lines upon the landscape and the record. But there was no hidden fruit waiting to be plucked, no innocent gems left for the right man. If it hadn't been done already it was impossible – except for punkish ponces in ballet tights. He suppressed an urge to rape a few of those, and went back to Belfast to settle simpler scores.

Dave knew now he had missed out, given up a great career in climbing to be dumped forever in Paddyland where a soldier couldn't even get sex. The lucky bastards that went to the Falklands got an ocean cruise out and back and hero mugshots in the *Sun*. Dave imagined his own picture facing Page Three with the paper closed tight on the pair of them and a rasp of stubble on his jaws. Desperation growled in his throat.

He got all the comics through the post – *Penthouse, Mountain, High*, and bulletins from his old club, the National Front Climbing Squad. His narrow-eyed skull throbbed with news. Nancy-boys and pimps making names for themselves every month while the only place Dave Willard's name featured was in the hit lists of the North. He grew meaner with deprivation, more ruthless in his work. He made it on to the most exclusive hit-lists. One week he may have been Number One on the Wanted charts for an operation blamed on the IRA which dropped their political wing two per cent in the opinion polls. But it wouldn't have ranked with a first ascent in Derbyshire.

Dave was thirty-three, the panic year. The present was septic and the past poisoned. He was unmarried. Unmarriageable. No one wanted an ugly soldier with pig-iron bones, a concrete skull and a career in violence. He had no illusions about his charm. Whores sometimes turned him down although they could use the work. He reckoned the army was the right place for him on that score. Where else could he see dozens of blokes even uglier than himself every day? Then suddenly, at thirty-three, he was terrified it mightn't be as simple as that. Maybe he was queer? Those new harnesses in the magazines were doing it to him. And the ballet tights. No one could ever lust after the contents of an old fashioned Whillans! Not without a fetish for surgical appliances!

Dave badly needed a change. He'd seen a lot of hard men break down in Ulster. That was why some outfits were called crack units. His hands shook and sweated when he trained his gun on suspects. He made a last ditch effort to assert priorities. Captain Bennett had been a climber – only a public school climber, it's true, but he must know which way was up. And there was a couple of geezers in another unit who used to do peg routes on Malham.

Dave proposed a trip to Fair Head in Antrim. Captain Bennett was reluctant. He smelt the black rot of psychosis on the soldier. What Willard didn't know was that the captain was one of a small group of superiors who blocked promotion for trigger-happy soldiers. On the other hand he welcomed the opportunity to assess the man in a neutral situation.

'That's a nationalist strip,' he warned Dave, 'We'll stick out like sore pricks up there, Willard. Play cricket in Crossmaglen if you want a high profile. Anyway I haven't climbed for – oh, years.' Dave hinted that it might be the the crag that – ah, frightened the captain, and soon they were speeding north from Belfast. The captain recalled that it had always been thus in climbing – ego overpowering acumen.

The trip had the atmosphere of an ill-judged mission, Captain Bennett thin, terse and aloof, Nick Grimes and Roger Wilson, grizzled, taciturn veterans sitting warily behind. Willard bulked in the front beside the officer boasting obsessively about his climbing. There was nothing much to boast about – classic trade-routes on British rock, a couple of alpine seasons in which the Aiguilles Rouges loomed larger than the other side. They listened to him with the inscrutability of interrogators as a suspect hangs himself.

The cluster of cottages at Culanlough and the hidden car park smelled like a trap to the captain. In the normal course of duty this would be a stake-out. Imagine coming here for pleasure and walking away from the car! He shook his head in amazement. He glanced at Grimes and Wilson: hard faces, old ropes, canvas rucksacks – *The Guns of Navarone* – and he was reassured.

Half a mile of bleak moorland stretched north to the rim of the crag, a sudden horizon. The sky shone bright with the reflection of the sea below. The rough land wore the sleepy look that screams ambush to the eye trained in paranoia.

'For Christ's sake, men,' the captain urged unnecessarily, 'let's keep our mouths shut. And cover that haircut, Willard, this isn't Bosigran with John Barry!' Dave grunted, his hand hovering near his cagoule pocket. He was tempted to park his gun in the hammer-holster of his Whillans but he refrained.

As they approached the rim, and leaned forward to look, Dave's lip curled in preconceived contempt. A spit squirted like gull-shit from his mouth. Stringing out it drifted down fifty, a hundred, two hundred and ten, twenty, thirty, forty, fifty feet of – *splatt!* – perfect dolerite, dark and clear, cracked and cornered, hard and huge. A boulder-field as big as a beach with every grain of sand a boulder shelved half-a-mile down to the sea.

Dave gulped, swallowed space. 'Not like Cloggy! Ain't much beside ol' Clog is it? Or Gogarth.'

'For God's sake man, Fair Head's about three miles long. Without a break!'

'Stanage is four.'

'And Three Hundred Feet High!' The Captain's voice rose in anger, 'What do you want, Willard? The Verdon?'

'Lose this little lot in the Verdon,' Dave babbled. 'Wouldn't even notice it.'

'Don't know much about geology, do you son?' Nick interrupted. He spat too, but carefully behind him. There was something solid stuck in his throat, something to do with the vertical vacancy below, and he was afraid he might remain attached and follow it over the edge. 'Let's have a look at the guidebook then.'

'We'll WRITE the flamin' guidebook!'

'Obviously summat's been done.'

Dave spat again. 'Nuffin' done 'ere, me old cock! Paddy don't climb. Only just stopped crawlin' abaht on all fours.' He cackled raucously. Captain Bennett closed his eyes wearily in repudiation. He reached into his rucksack and pulled out a guidebook.

'This one is years out of date now. Bought it first time I was posted here. Very keen in those days, very keen. Always meant to get to Fair Head.' He looked around him sadly and flicked through pages packed with routes, 'Paddy's a bit more advanced than you think, Willard.'

Dave shrugged. 'Easy stuff. Gullies an' that! Go up 'em after sheep don't they! Plum lines ain't been touched. Been waitin' for this all my life. This is where D. Willard carves 'is name in bleedin' great letters into the 'istory of British rock. Let's go!'

'WILLARD!' The captain was shaking a rat between his teeth, 'I give the orders! This is Antrim. We're not climbers here. We're the British Army! Don't you forget it because no one else will!' He turned to the others, 'If you men have no objection we'll climb within sight of each other. Two recommended routes here in the centre of the crag – An Go Ban Sore', he read it out in his clipped bark, 'and something beside it, maybe Beal ack Runda, or this other one.' He pointed to it on the page, 'Slí na Fírinne.'

E1 (5b), 280ft. Four pitches, only one, the second one, hard. He liked the look of the name, slender, sharp, sensible, like a clean crack leading somewhere definite. Some of the other routes were unintelligible thickets of diphthongs and consonants. Peacadh Mairfeach he saw overleaf, and Conchubhar and Aoife. Surely they must be clogged with something horribly viscous to have names like that? For a strange moment he visualised off-widths choked with catarrh and phlegm.

'It's Gaelic of course,' he explained, peering at the names, An Gobán Saor E1 (5b) 280ft. 'I've seen that word before' s-a-o-r, Sore Eire I think it was, on a gable in Armagh.'

'Bleedin' code-names,' Dave burst out. 'Subversive shit-house talk. Another way of sayin' BRITS OUT innit? You know wot them fackin routes are?' He challenged the captain, 'They're fackin graffiti, that's wot!'

Again Captain Bennett's thin mouth snapped, but this time he said nothing. He understood that climbing was a young man's sport and that Willard was mourning his youth and independence in his own violent way. He was not the only mourner. For a variety of reasons no one had seen the captain smile since he was posted to Northern Ireland. Gradually his lips had shrivelled up against his teeth and now his cheeks were folding bitterly in the same direction. Shedding hair and features his unhappy head was turning into a middle-aged skull. He was growing old too fast. Flying milk-churns, hunger-strikes, bombs, bullets, budget-slashes, ambushes, assassins, mutinies, murders, civilian slaughter, white-washes and cover-ups had strained his Sandhurst resources, but now Willard was stretching his personal reserves beyond the limit. Rank was no use to the captain here. Rock, the old leveller, had stripped him of advantage right down to his nervous system. He had to climb better than Willard to regain his status – and after that he could kick the bastard out of the unit with a clean conscience.

They found the Greyman's Path, a narrow break in the crag guarded by a huge, natural statue, staring blindly out to sea. Before passing under a slender column jammed across the head of the gully the captain examined it for trip-wires. The place hummed with tension, like a stairwell in the Divis Flats. He gave the signal to proceed with caution, and dark, enormous walls opened before them. Like a patrol of skin-germs straying into the oral cavity they marched awe-struck along the gums, gaping up at the magnificent molars and the great clefts, crannies and crevices between them filled with fabulous pickings.

Dave ran in berserk circles laying claim to every line. His small eyes bulged with passion and veins throbbed in his low forehead. He would climb them all, ALL, ALL. First ascents every one. The captain found them in the book, Burn Up, Creeper, Kraken …

'Lies!' Dave howled. 'Forgery.'

The crag stretched inexhaustibly ahead. The scale was beyond imagination, and the captain was somehow aware that between them, pooling all their Anglo-Saxon resources and discounting Willard's hallucinations, they possessed virtually no imagination at all. Furthermore, as he stumbled through the labyrinthine boulder-field he was conscious of the prime target they presented to enemy trundlers high on the ramparts. With startling clarity he imagined men in black balaclavas lining up overhead with buckets of bubbling pitch. He would be even more exposed while climbing. A man splayed out on a crux-move looked as if he had been shot already. Often felt like that too, the captain remembered ruefully. But nothing happened and every step he took calmed his nerves and enriched his awe. He paused at the foot of a curling ribbon of rock 250ft high, flanked by two impossible chimneys and capped by an overhang big as a tank parked under another overhang the size of an army lorry – and he was suddenly overwhelmed by a sweet sense of insignificance and peace.

There was no one up there watching him, no ambush, nothing but rock and sky and the purely private choice of success or defeat. People were too small to crowd a stage as big as this; a place for ancient giants! The captain realised moreover that the whole of Northern Ireland was inhabited not by tribal warriors but by ordinary people who were smaller than the places and events surrounding them, decent people who worked for prosperity and earned adversity instead. Peace could never be imposed upon them. It was a condition of the heart and the habitat. By right, everyone should have a choice between happiness and hatred and all their choices would add up to the future. But for too many the choice was ordained by history. It was not easy to understand all that inside an imposed uniform and the captain knew he might forget again as soon as he dressed in barracks. He too was misunderstood in the province.

He tried to think the idea through, but he raised his head and his tight thoughts burst like a flock of pigeons towards the enormous corner of An Gobán Saor. The two Yorkshire-men wheeled to their allotted route and the pigeons scattered in disarray. Dave Willard attempted to solo, in passing, a 150ft direct start to the route. Only the hard move off the ground defeated him.

Not far to the right they found Slí na Fírinne. A set of perfect columns clean and pure as organ-pipes formed the lower half of the crag. Jamming-cracks divided them and the geometric facets presented offset bridging surfaces. But which groove? Several were perfect. Now he understood the cryptic footnote in the guide:

Do not confuse with An Bealach Rúnda ... Pitch 2 From the top of the fifth column climb a circular flake (the dot on the i) to gain a deceptive wall, an exposed hand-traverse, a sensational layback and a furtive finger-crack.

He saw the flake first. A hundred feet up there was a dark wheel of rock as if something huge had parked on the pillar and all but one wheel had toppled off. Nonsense! He struggled for the scale. Big as a millstone? ... no, that would be invisible from here like a lost tiddly-wink on a shelf. He flipped that childish image from his confused brain. Once, in barracks he had consented to throw a coin in a pitch-and-toss school played by some soldiers, off-duty of course. His coin had flipped erratically across the concrete, rolled in a silly circle and then, against all the odds, had come to rest on edge against the end-wall, just like the flake (leaving the pillar aside for a second). He had strolled away to a round of applause. Now he had to climb straight up to the damn thing in front of the soldiers. Pitch! And Toss?

He had forgotten how to climb. He flexed his shoulder-blades wanting wings. The angle was impossible. Had he sauntered up such steepness in his youth? Pretend he was lying on his belly and crawl along the concrete to the coin? Look damn silly ... Call the whole thing off, spot a sniper? He glanced back at An Gobán Saor. Nick was already climbing. Like a good soldier on patrol he checked each move for hostile intent, disarmed it briskly and proceeded to the next suspect. It looked so smooth – so disciplined.

Captain Bennett, here at the foot of Fair Head, down among the roots of Ulster with the wild Sea of Moyle at his back and Britain an obscure smudge on the skyline, was discovering a hectic imagination. It wanted him to climb. Somewhere far back in his mind the hand-traverse, the layback and the furtive finger-crack tickled the hairs on his neck – from the inside. Dave Willard peered up the vertical chute of the first pitch and his tongue rasped across dry lips; 'Not ... not like gritstone, is it?' he whispered.

The captain selected his strategy. Despite its awesome architecture the first pitch was only HVS (5a). He sacrificed that one to Willard. Ideally he would have sent him down a cave, sealed the entrance and gone climbing himself, but while it was acceptable to lose soldiers in combat one couldn't just take them out in the country and bury them in holes.

On close inspection the first pitch was formed by a pair of parallel pillars two feet apart with the front facet of a third inset behind. The enormous columns were fitted together with the precision of Inca construction, except that volcanic contraction had arranged sufficient space between the blocks to accommodate human hands. And ergonomics had wisely advised that the cracks should open and taper periodically to form handy pods and slots, and furthermore that the edges of these slots should be slightly rounded to minimise discomfort. Footholds were provided also for a short distance: neat grey incuts for an initial boost. Dave had no excuse to dawdle and the captain was left to resume meditation. He watched Nick overpower a bulge on the first pitch of An Gobán Saor. Some would call it cheating, but in military terms efficiency was everything. It justified the means. And knotted slings were a damn sight fairer than grappling hooks! Still, he felt embarrassed; not quite the thing. On the other hand, suppose they were invading this coast – he allowed himself a boyish thrill of conjecture – a quartet of commandos scaling Fair Head to take the enemy by surprise. No need for melodramatics, he rebuked himself, the invasion was long over. And the army was staying put. Nowhere else to put it anyway. The captain amused himself for a moment wondering what on earth the government would do with the army if it had to withdraw from Ireland. Put it on the dole? He listened to Willard being employed in the pitch overhead. The rope ran out in jerks. Just as he had expected, no talent. Willard climbed like a successful invasion: brute force and inability to retreat. A cracked cry of triumph cut short the political analysis. Willard was up and almost immediately the captain was climbing.

He was struck at once by the unexpected ease, the upward thrust, the sense of muscle-memory as if the revival of adolescent joy had erased his age. He savoured the friction, the clean, dry rock, the monumental shapes that curved around his hands, reviving his gritstone skills in this smooth, stately, adult context. He recognised the cold, unequivocal smell of rock, the thrilling tension in the nerves, the concentration of the senses and the self. There were red smears where Willard had bludgeoned and he avoided them fastidiously. The fellow had already fouled the crag with saliva and blood and the captain hoped fervently there would be no worse secretions. He intended to stay in front – in case.

Twenty, thirty, forty hand-jams. It was as if the ideal sequence of moves had been drawn from his memory, expanded, repeated and extended until it exhausted the desire for continuity, and then at ninety-nine feet the rhythm broke – a knuckled bulge and flared finger-slot punished ecstasy with excess – and then the belay. Willard squatted, rooster-like, skinned elbows flapping. 'Wot a cracker! Wot a fackin cracker! Wot'll we call it, Cap?'

'I TOLD you! It's done already. It's called ...'

'I won't say nuffink if you don't. We'll send it to *Mountain* tomorrow. Needs a good strong name, eh. Touch o'class. Wot d'yer reckon to *The British Empire*? Always fancied that for a route.'

A retro-thrust of revulsion took the Captain to the top of the circular flake. He hadn't even noticed it. He was about to leap lightly onto the headwall when something pushed him sharply in the chest in the manner of a school bully. He staggered clockwise down along the wheel and stared up in surprise. The devious wall above swaggered.

The captain snorted, wrenched himself some slack and charged again. The bulge shouldered him off. He stumbled up and down, up and down, as if the circular flake was revolving stiffly under him. Now he knew that shape: it was a bloody treadmill!

Above the bulge the wall slabbed back. There must be something up there? The dark rock was blotched with pale lichen, all colour and no substance, losing the holds in its piebald confusion. Hanging his head for balance he swung one arm in a swimming stroke across the slab. A hopeful edge. The other hand came up and found another. Tiny pasted petals, he was bound to rip them off and take to the air like a detonated butterfly. Opposing side-pulls only, but he was committed now, too late to change, hanging out of balance. Old muscles crushed the gristle in his shoulder-blades, hauled him across the bulge, neck and head vibrating, feet flailing onto friction. He leaned into a shallow scoop to rest and his body was temporarily out of focus, distorted by effort. It didn't fit his clothes, as if his jeans and shirt were back to front, climbing shoes on the wrong feet. He shook himself into shape and swallowed harsh breath. Hand-traverse ... layback ... finger-crack ... God!

Despite the lichen-stains the rock was meticulously clean. On his left the headwall rose in an enormous pillar, thick and ill-defined with a blunt arête, unlike the sculptured columns down below. A faint groove continued overhead into inconceivable surroundings, grotesque variations on the vertical. His jaw sagged with shock and then he saw the rising fracture running left across the pillar to the arête. The hasty hand-traverse ... He looked for footholds first. Not a single centimetre of support. Instead a long dark stain where rubber skated.

He reached out into the crack. The edge curved smoothly downwards like the underlip of a massive, pouting statue. Nothing for it but to reach right in and hope she had her bottom teeth. He plunged in to the elbows, spittle-smooth rock, he rummaged fiercely and the toothless gums closed around his wrists chewing the skin in horizontal jams. He prayed, paddled in space and thirteen stone of flesh and bone dragged dangling from the elbows. The jams were solid – almost suction – and he lurched towards the profile. His breath hissed through gritted teeth and he heard grunting in the atavistic air. It seemed to come from a long way off, as if it was someone else, some unrestrained vulgarian pumping towards the same arête from the other side. Someone like Willard about to smash through the back of the mirror ... the Captain was climbing atrociously but he would not be the one to retreat before collision.

Around the arête everything changed, slipped back under control. A massive foothold appeared, as if it had been hacked out with a well-judged axe. And the old witch's mouth had a single tooth after all – a jagged spike ideal for a handhold and a sling. Above it and a little to the side a sharp inverted V showed how the pillar had cracked and sheared. The captain was struck by the notion that Fair Head could choose this very moment to grind back into shape. He almost withdrew his hands. He was reducing the universe to the clockwork of the human time scale, and the idea amused him suddenly. He heard a sound from his own mouth somewhere between a giggle and a guffaw. This was good climbing, great climbing. Willard was out of sight below and the captain realised he was happy. God, how happy he was to be doing this! And two and a half pitches still to come!

Opposite him, at mid-height on their route, Nick and Ian were beginning a sinuous corner. He promised himself that one next time. Where to now? A thin flake-crack darted directly overhead. He dismissed it, the traverse must continue left. Captain Bennett swung out confidently to look. The stance was undercut. Instantly the whole world fell away from beneath his body as if a stairway had collapsed and he was left hanging by his fingertips from the landing. Down, down, down he looked, down the pit behind the pillar, down the empty stairwell to an alcove in the basement, and for one terrible second he imagined his own skeleton in that shoe-cupboard far, far below.

He shuddered back on to the foothold and raised his eyes to the layback overhead.

'E1, my arse!' he thought profoundly.

He concentrated on placing protection. Suppose – fumbling for psychology now – suppose this was at ground level, a standard layback, say the Right Unconquerable, the ultimate classic. That had been no problem once with a bit of nerve, and this couldn't be half as hard, or long? Putting myself on the line for this, he thought resentfully – the first ascent had it easy, knew what to expect. Wish it could be my route – all this effort for nothing. He flexed his fingers and his will, grasped the fine-edged flake, thrust one foot high against the wall. A dry sting in his thigh where the varicose knot lurked. He hung out on white hands. Don't look, he ordered Nick and Ian silently, Don't look now. Trust the protection, that was essential. The solid wired nut in a slot, the sling around the tooth. But the rope ran diagonally across the arête and straight up the crack, so that drag was now a problem. Fingers trembling with doubt – run for it! The reality of the Right Unconquerable returned. Someone had shouted a warning as he fumbled for that final hold. He had looked down and his innocent partner – face a blank now – had strolled far back to observe the move. The rope ran in at 45 degrees, tight as a guyline, the first nut popped and the rope unzipped the layback neatly from below. As his top nut swung towards the shoulder-belay in the boulders he found the hidden handhold in a hurry and stern words startled Stanage.

He was racing up the layback now hand over hand, hoisting an anchor up a flagpole. He made twenty feet in a single burst, then bridging holds appeared and took the strain out of the final steepness. But the flake was growing thick and blunt, the crack behind it shallow. At the end of tenacity he reached another foothold. The whole crag was quivering. The layback done and still no belay-ledge!

Captain Bennett wobbled weakly, fingers throbbing, his last protection thirty feet below. The only weakness in this blank rock was an off-width crack – continuation of the layback – leaning to his right. It dragged him out of balance when he tried to lock numb hands between its flaring jaws. No purchase. Futile fists. Where was that damned finger-crack?

Punch-drunk he felt his body fade and fold... And then the wiry reassertion of the will. Twist the wrist and fist. Screw into the groove. Dynamic jamming. Keep rooting, something has to hold? Torsion: the very act of twisting. Sweat leaked into his mouth. He spat salt spray.

Torque, the Twisting Force. He needed Torque!

I'll call it *Torquemada*. Sod whether it's done or not! The Spanish torturer. Willard won't like it. Prefer an English name here. Half-Nelson? His foot jigged without mercy on the hold, and his body began to sag...

One hundred and twenty feet below Willard stood up on the belay to ease a cramp. Bored with looking at the sea. Bennett should be on easy ground by now. He relaxed his grip on the rope and stretched his fingers. Leaning out he glimpsed a sudden movement on a distant section of the crag. There was a roof midway on a vertical skyline, a square-cut overhang – and Willard saw a... a climber swinging out beneath it, reaching over the lip, moving up. It was happening hundreds of yards away but he knew instinctively it was a *first ascent*, that sense of breathless hush about the body as of a substance entering a new dimension. There it was, the ecstasy of virgin flight, the pioneering consummation Willard desired and dreamed. He imagined it as triumphant self-projection, a sustained ejaculation of the ego. Seeing others at it, was like glimpsing an orgy from a passing train.

Willard unclipped from the belay and leaned far back for a hungry look. Limned in sunlight the usurper clung to the front of the overhang, graceful as a gecko. With baleful, expert eye Willard measured up. Ten pounds of plastic properly placed would land the bastard in the sea with an armful of overhang to keep him down...

Overhead, Captain Bennett slowly folded backwards. His fists uncurled. Fingers scrabbled in the groove, scraped towards the rim, found a thin, deep slit... and held. Incredible! A finger-crack where he had fought for off-width jams! He tried to see what saved him, peering around into the groove. No matter how he craned it was invisible, tucked away in secret. It nibbled at his fingertips with furtive generosity.

It was early evening when they rejoined Nick and Ian at the car. 'Well?' beamed Captain Bennett. 'What was it like, chaps? Looked jolly good!'

Nick grinned, 'Best bloody route in the world, sir,' and he winked. Driving to Ballycastle Nick suggested beer. The captain hesitated. His initial desire was to get as far from Willard as possible. Not knowing how the brute would behave in a pub. He was no longer a cold professional soldier but a victim of climbing dementia such as the captain had not witnessed since the days of his college-club. Still he was reluctant to pull rank and spoil the occasion for the others. There were traditions to be observed, not only military but a cragging code as well.

And wasn't it strange, he recognised it now, how the peculiar aftertaste of climbing absolutely demanded beer! If they could get that flavour into bags it would make great crisps, the captain thought. He was no longer surprised by his own ideas.

'Just one,' he agreed.

He was trapped by the oldest trick. He should have got in and bought the one and only round, a gesture – to be cut short at that. But crafty Nick got the first one in and the captain was doomed to four.

They sat in a dark corner of the lounge and immediately a cordon of wary space was thrown around them. Captain Bennett felt himself dissolve eerily in the shadows; the elation of strenuous success was giving way to a numb exhaustion. Roger and Ian were affected too. The pints of creamy Guinness drenched them in sentiment. Memories of British climbing: finest in the world – Cemetery Gates, Cenotaph Corner, Valkyrie, the Unconquerables – caressing each beloved bead in the rosary of rock.

'Bleedin' trade-routes,' Willard scoffed, 'played out all that lot is …'

Nick flared, ''Ow many 'ave you done then? 'Ow many? You won't find them on 'Arrisons bloody Rocks!' He elbowed Roger to get the next round in as the captain was looking edgy. 'If you can show me better routes bein' done today than Joe an' Don was doin' twenty years ago I shall give thee best …' His chest puffed and veins swelled in his forehead in that distasteful manner the captain always associated with patriotism.

'Rubbish! Lot of ol' cobblers that is, livin' in the past. There's better right 'ere for starters. An' I'll be back to sort it aht. Ol' Paddy's not keepin' this little lot to 'isself. Right sir? Me an' the cap'n 'ere's comin' back to Fair 'Ead to clean up.'

Captain Bennett shook his head and sighed. Fair Head deserved better than this. He imagined the courteous pace of development to date, isolated from corruption, no hype, no back-stabbing, no cheating, no crowds and – he cringed at the sound of Willard's egomania – no noise. He recalled Stanage on a summer Sunday; like the terraces at a football-match. No peace or healing, no escape from conflict there, no respect for the sanctity of place. The climbing today at Fair Head, once he had cleared colonial paranoia from his mind, had been a virtual communion of geology, space and the human spirit. Admittedly human spirit had suffered a stormy passage, but he hoped he had accepted the prolonged pain and the fleeting joy and learned from them.

Not Willard though. Willard – the captain fumbled towards the start of philosophy – Willard was the … the rage to conquer, the presumption of power. Willard, the captain realised painfully, in all his caricatured awfulness was peculiarly British, a throw-back, the dregs of Empire. For one microsecond the captain thought he had perceived the role of the entire army. Mercifully it was a brief exposure, then he was back to the singular again. As long as Willard remained in the North he was part of the intransigence, the fortifications. Something must be done.

Captain Bennett drained his third beer dizzily and as Willard strutted to the bar he left his chair with a confused excuse. He went into the Gents and out the other side through the Public Bar, into the street.

When they returned to the car there was a folded note under the windscreen-wiper. The captain read it out in a toneless voice, then passed it round:

GOOD CLIMBERS DON'T USE THEIR KNEES. YOU WON'T HAVE ANY KNEES IF YOU COME BACK. SEE YOU NEXT TIME.

Willard cursed scornfully, and Captain Bennett understood how much of courage is ignorance.

'It's a bleedin' con this is! The IRA know nuffin' about craggin'. It's local climbers tryin' to scare us off.' He wheeled towards the pub. 'There's a bastard in there looked familiar. Seen 'im on Snell's Field I reckon. Lets take 'im out.'

The captain issued a curt order and Willard was dragged hastily into the car.

An hour later as they sped along the motorway through Belfast Ian opened the captain's guidebook to Fair Head and broke the brooding silence.

'I'd like to copy down the route we done, sir. Mind if I borrow your pen?'

He wrote it out in careful capitals, AN GOBAN SAOR, with details, then lips pursed and head back he stared thoughtfully at the result. 'Can I see your note again sir? The one from the windscreen'.

Willard was transferred. He couldn't believe the irony. Just when he'd got his hooks into Fair Head he was shifted back to bleedin' Blighty. They said he had been marked down for terrorist reprisal after sustained service. He was awarded a non-committal decoration and a posting to a Midlands plain to protect plutonium against a women's camp. He had plenty of free time for climbing too.

Willard hit the gritstone hard. Every weekend he prowled the edges probing for opportunity. Every new route was rejected, '... done before, meathead. Check guidebooks before submitting claims.' *Climber & Rambler* sent him 'Notes for Contributors' and asked hopefully for an article.

One clear and simple day at Stanage, as he threaded his way through the strident queues, the answer dawned on Dave Willard. The virgin rock he sought was there alright, miles and miles of it, buried under all this hackneyed stuff that was being pawed and mauled by the multitudes. It was time to dig deep, clear away the rubbish and begin the New Era.

He approached a buttress and crouched breathlessly before it. This altar of gritstone climbing was only a block about forty feet high, set four-square into the hillside and separated from similar, less sacred blocks by chimneys and gullies. It was not only horizontally stratified in the usual manner of gritstone, it also had a vertically layered effect. There was a great flake – narrow at the base, wide at the top – pasted to the front. The edges were worn by countless sweaty caresses.

Dave scraped his jaw and pondered. Just behind that brittle flake there was only a blank and unprotected wall. No use to him! Dave sensed rather than knew his own limits. He moved a little to the right and everything fell into place. A deep, narrow chimney split the side of the buttress from top to bottom. X-raying with his mind's eye he felt a classic fault-line weaving right through the rock. All it needed was a touch of surgery, a simple facelift.

Down at his van Dave unpacked the toolkit. There was a false bottom where he kept his emergency rations, the special Northern Ireland kit; four half-kilo packs of plastic explosive, a long-life power-pack, coil of electrical wire and two steel screwdrivers.

In the morning Stanage opened to the dawn like an irritated flower. There was a parasite burrowing among its petals. Squirming inside Curving Chimney (Diff. 40ft) Dave Willard poked his putty deep into place. He ran out the spool of wire to a natural bunker among the boulders. Working with practised skill he dug the plus and minus poles out of the battery and wound his cable-ends around the screwdrivers. He pushed one deep into the battery, and held the other like a dagger in his hand.

The rampart lay silent in the rising light. The road below ran empty beneath the trees of North Lees farm. Deserted moorland purple in the distance. About to be stabbed in the heart, the Peak lay sleeping peacefully. The screwdriver plunged. *kkkrrRRRUUMPPP!!!*

Overbleeding-kill indeed! The Right Unconquerable and the Left had disappeared and most of the rock behind them.

Dave scrambled up the smoking stairway of rubble to the top of the crag. Diff. Maybe. Not quite the sculptured classic he'd planned, but a start anyway. Gritstone was too soft, rotten really. Better luck tomorrow with Cenotaph Corner.

NIGHTFALL

Even in the hour of the wolf the Eigerwand was blacker than the surrounding night.

Before he stepped across the bergschrund onto the lowest footholds of the North Face he switched off his radio with deliberate finality. The crisp catastrophe in the tiny headset died and the war preparations were silenced for the first time in weeks. The vacancy of the mountain night drained him of everything but fear, and frost. There were no stars above or below; all the lights of Kleine Scheidegg and Grindelwald were shrouded in the blackout, and clouds masked the sky.

All over Europe the lights were out.

Swearing and scrabbling L arrived on the ledge beside him. His radio stammered armies, missiles, conferences, nuclear fronts, within the dreadful dome of his helmet.

'Where are we?' L whispered in panic. He stank of fear and sweat. A muscular reluctance.

'At the start,' R hissed. 'The First Pillar starts here.'

He almost shouted to release the tension, as if the furtive whispers were its only source. But caution clamped his throat. They could still be stopped.

R knew history and precedent as instinctively as he knew the grammar of speech. The village policeman sweating up the lower slopes towards the still-unknown Diemberger in 1958, not to prohibit his ascent, but to relieve him of his passport so that his body could be identified later. The sweating policeman was a whole platoon of trained fighters now, with a range of technical weaponry that could drop a man off the North Face as easily as the old policeman dropped the passport in his pocket.

After a decade of alpine seasons R knew a little about the intricacy of the Swiss defence preparations. If they had the materials they would have built a transparent dome over the country when the nuclear threat became a promise, but failing that there was an infrastructure of underground shelters ready to gulp the entire population into the earth.

As a student in 1984 R had spent his first season above Grindelwald, camping within the shadow of the Eigerwand. Nothing cataclysmic happened in world affairs that year. It was all occurring quietly of course, but in the circus of the public imagination there had been a failure to perform. Orwell was relegated to a side-show, a suspected charlatan like Nostradamus and the clairvoyant hermaphrodite.

R didn't take much notice of security-effects in Switzerland on that first visit, travel was unrestricted, and anyway he was dazzled by the extravaganza of the Oberland, all those mountains crowding into his nervous ambitions, shouldering each other for space – the Mönch, Jungfrau, Eiger.

But he did notice, in passing, some of those great, camouflaged doors set into tree-clad mountainsides, their keys in the care of computers. And he heard how new roads were designed to double as runways in war, and motorway tunnels as hangars for jetfighters already stored away within the rocky core of the country waiting for the inevitable collision of east and west in the air-space around the cockpit of Europe.

But in particular he noted what the American general had said, hawking it up from his chest like phlegm to be spat in the face of an ardent continent, 'We fought the first World War in Europe; we fought the second World War in Europe; and if you dummies let us, we'll fight the third World War in Europe too.'

The ardent continent turned the other cheek, not in peace but in indifference. That was a long time ago. People didn't want to know. And now the nightmare had hatched out of sleep and apathy; the rape of reality had begun.

R and L were trapped in Switzerland by the crisis. The border-posts were sealed absolutely.

The air-waves of Europe were choked with variants of a trigger-incident. A British ship blown out of the Mediterranean by a nuclear strike, presumed Russian. But it seemed the ship was transporting American missiles into proscribed waters, and the fall-out from the encounter was threatening the Yugoslav and Albanian coastline.

Washington and Moscow issued cryptic statements and an hysterical rumour revived in the European media that Russia and the US would ally to confront China. Unaccountable detonations in areas sensitive to conflict all over the world were being traced to launches within Chinese territory. But this propaganda had in turn been fired from behind equally suspect borders.

At the beginning of the crisis R and L had their Irish passports confiscated, and were ordered to report to the military police every day. Fearing internment they ignored the order and hid in their discreet tent up on the high meadows of Alpiglen, listening in shifts to the news bulletins.

It was obvious that censorship and deliberate confusion were rampant. The BBC was the most apparent offender with its jingoistic hero-worship of NATO. Ever since the new king took over in England the BBC had become known for its propaganda as Big Brother Charlie. Ireland was an associate member of NATO, proposing a kind of Florence Nightingale image for itself in the present crisis, but in craven reality the country was being used for base purposes by the Americans and the British.

R tuned in to the Swiss stations every hour for the weather reports. He got them in French, German and Italian, and they were in succinct, multi-lingual agreement. A depression was storming in from the Atlantic, bad weather rolling relentlessly towards the Alps. The Bernese Oberland, the collective north wall of the Alps, was the frontline obstacle to that trough.

For two days R had sat in seclusion, demented by ambition. He was there for the third year in a row to attempt the North Face of the Eiger. Bad weather and shortage of time foiled the previous attempts. Now there was no lack of time: he was a prisoner in the country, but the weather was going to rob him again. He could not focus seriously on the other holo-caust preparing outside the bubble of Switzerland. It was unthinkable. A media exaggeration of a media creation. Humanity was gathering speed on the slippery slope, but it would pull off a self-arrest before the brink.

There had been several Irish ascents of the face in recent years, even an ascent by the Japanese route, but always in the company of a foreign climber. No Irish pair had climbed it yet. A fine distinction people scoffed, but R coveted it. Speed was a competitive issue too. He remembered a remark by the ageing climber who had spread the disputed first Irish ascent out over three days; 'I don't know whether it was the first Irish ascent or the second, but I guarantee it was the *slowest* Irish ascent.'

R checked his watch in the streaming rattling dark. 3.30 a.m. More than an hour until dawn. The freeze had been insufficient to tighten up conditions on the mountain. The weather was changing already. They had eighteen hours at the very most to reach the summit before storms broke.

But as long ago as 1950, making the fourth ascent, Waschak and Forstenlechner had climbed the face within that time, and one-day ascents were a normal feature of the seventies and eighties, Messner and Habeler in ten hours, Boivin solo in seven and a half. Ignoring the part conditions played in these figures R felt a gambler's sudden confidence.

Inching up the initial groove, clinging to steep, wet limestone, he was relieved to find the climbing sound and reasonably easy. Reaching high the fingers hooked good handholds, and the probing boot found solid purchase every time. It was traditional to climb this section unroped by the light of a headtorch to get as high as possible before sunlight, snowfall, any disturbance on the summit turned the ice-fields into lethal ambushes.

His head torch was tuned to a mere spark to avoid detection. He was climbing blind, and a sudden loss of faith in an awkward move made him pause in fear and almost turn back. But he heard L cursing just below him, and remembered the secret attempts of the thirties, when men who were publicly branded as fascist lunatics launched their destinies on this face without the security of any previous ascent, determined to force the limits of the impossible.

They were ill-equipped then, and carried crippling packs. Eight men died before the first success. These were in the front row (kneeling) in R's mental picture of heroes. There was no excuse for turning back, and nowhere to go.

The wet grooves led to sloping, scree-laden terraces where the whoosh and detonation of stone-fall brought a rush of sweat to every inch of skin. The transition from dark to daylight failed to produce the spectrum of a fair-weather dawn. Grey, watery light strained through the heavy clouds clinging to the horizon. R waited on a small, sheltered ledge for L to catch up. They were still on the rough plinth that forms the lower third of the climb.

He switched on the headset and flicked feverishly from station to station, accumulating horror as he went. An unspecified town in Germany crippled by the bombing of a military base. No mention of casualties or reaction, just the stark obliteration.

In England a power plant and a notorious research station devastated by sabotage. Radioactivity leaking. This information from a French bulletin while the BBC delivered a tight-lipped account of summit conferences and diplomatic meetings. When L arrived his radio was off. It was too distracting to climb and listen simultaneously. He was gasping for breath and could not speak, but he looked with desperate interrogation at R.

'It's okay. Things have quietened down. There's a United Nations conference. Nothing's happened,' R lied.

L craned his head to look up at the climbing above, and his head remained tilted in awe. Tier upon tier of blank, impenetrable walls lifted into the confusion of the sky lit by the sullen dawn.

It had taken a masterpiece of persuasion to lure L on to the climb at all, but R had played it with all the expertise of an unattractive man used to bending reluctant women to his will. It was done by subtle association, conjuring up heroic figures and romantic images until the victims felt they were falling for some great mountain explorer instead of a man who had simply observed the originals and borrowed their style.

He had begun to work on L the previous morning as they lay festering in uncertainty within the bubble of fabric camouflaged on the slope below the face.

They had a small electronic dictionary to which they referred for clarification of the news bulletins, but its vocabulary was irritatingly limited, and they were in constant doubt as to the accuracy of their interpretation.

L wanted them to surrender to the police. He had naive dreams of repatriation based on neutrality.

'Are we going down or not?' he demanded. 'We've about two hours left to check in. After that we're outlaws or refugees, or something.'

Hulking, overdeveloped shoulders made his cropped head look small and immature, but he had the trusting eyes and biddable expression of a youth who could be led if his imagination was enlisted.

R was considerably smaller and older. A conservative in many ways he maintained the traditional Irish style of mountaineering beard, sandy and unkempt, the high-altitude look.

'If we go down now,' he said with convincing assurance, 'they'll lock us up for the duration. We won't be left wandering around in case we're spying or something. And if we stay here someone is going to spot us, and report us anyway ... maybe even take a shot at us.'

He giggled unexpectedly. 'I feel a bit like Heckmair,' he confided. 'You know, in '37.'

'Heck – who?' L looked blank.

'Anderl Heckmair,' R told him encouragingly. 'One of the greatest climbers of all time. Very good on rock,' he added hastily, emphasising L's narrow speciality.

'He led the first ascent of the Eiger North Face in 1938 with Ludwig Vörg. They took Harrer and Kasparek along with them for the ride. Harrer didn't have a ghost of a chance without Heckmair, even if it was him who did all the writing afterwards.'

Secretly it was a colossal shock to R that his partner had never heard of Heckmair. He had never been in the Bernese Oberland before, and he simply didn't have that traditional obsession with the Eiger, which seemed to have run its course with R's generation. L had done some impressive rock climbs in other areas, the kind of thing that was technically way out of R's old fashioned reach, but he had limited experience of ice and mixed climbing.

'Heckmair was here in '37 too, for a reconnaissance,' R resumed the theme.

'The Swiss made it illegal that year to attempt the face, on the grounds it was suicide. But Heckmair, a sort of Robin Hood character, couldn't be kept down. He hid in a bathing hut down in Interlaken for a while, and then moved up here secretly. He had to stay incognito because he was so well known, so the Alpenhorn player who was laid on for the tourists kept him hidden in his hut and used to give a toot on the big bugle if anyone was poking around.'

'Pretty good.' said L admiringly. 'I like the sound of old Heckmair.'

'Doesn't look too hard though,' he added, craning up at the colossal triangle of limestone and ice that loomed above them, and consequently could not be seen in true perspective. The massive tilted ice-fields appeared meagre and foreshortened from below, while the high, bulging forehead of the face seemed to merge insignificantly with the prominent cheekbones. The notorious Ramp, a huge groove-system leading to the upper face, looked like a frowning rock-wrinkle offering easy escape to the Mittellegi Ridge.

'Oh, it's not hard nowadays with modern gear,' R hastened to assure him.

He needed to convince himself too, for he knew all the disturbing facts and figures. The 1938 route consisted of 10,000 feet of intricate zig-zag climbing threading its way to the summit 6,000 feet above the buttercups and gentians of Alpiglen. At every crucial stage of the climb a key passage to the next section had to be located accurately.

He could recite by heart the worn litany of tragedies caused by sudden storms rendering the White Spider and the Exit Cracks impassable.

But on the other hand, to those who hit the right weather and the right route, the climb presented few problems. There had always been Eiger-aspirants who coached themselves exclusively on that gambling prescription.

'They were fantastic characters in the early days,' R yearned. 'They stopped for nothing and nobody.' His voice conveyed the grandeur of participation.

'Well, the bugle player has a bazooka now,' L answered, as a barrage of explosions resounded among the distant hills. 'And he's changed his tune. That doesn't sound like *Edelweiss.*'

'Just target practise. They've been at it all morning.'

Sometimes it was impossible to distinguish between the reverberations in the distant valley, and the rattling volleys of ice and stone on the melting face.

'Listen,' cajoled R, beginning again when the echoes had died away, 'did you ever read a book called *No Picnic on Mount Kenya*?'

L who had read half a dozen books in his life and hadn't thought much of any of them, shook his head.

'Well, it's a true story, set in Africa in the last war, an absolutely incredible story but true all the same.'

R began with that sense of munching at a story, peculiar to small-mouthed men with beards. But he had a reputation among the younger climbers for a certain kind of anecdotal experience; he was a mythmaker who had been somewhere in the vicinity of many major occurrences in the mountaineering past. But he had never pulled off a coup himself, so he was obliged to trade in other people's legends. That was the principal source of his urge to contrive a first on the Eiger.

'There were thousands of Italian prisoners of war locked up in a British camp in Kenya. One of them was a dedicated mountaineer, and he had this dream of escaping to climb Mount Kenya He had never seen the mountain, except a diagram of it on a tin of corned-beef, but it was only thirty or forty miles away. There was no question of escaping back to Italy or anything like that; it was impossible to get out of Africa even if a man could survive long enough in the bush to get anywhere.

'So he and a couple of mates secretly made up crampons and pitons in the camp workshop, the same way prisoners in an ordinary jail cook up tools and weapons to escape. The difference was that the Italians went and tackled one of the finest mountains in the world for the sheer independence of it ... and then *escaped back* into the camp again. There was nowhere else for them to go, you see.

'They were missing for weeks, maybe months, incredible adventures of every kind, wild animals, giant plants, glaciers, you name it. And then getting back in without being shot was another adventure. But the camp commandant turned out to be one of those all-round British types, jolly good show, blind eye and all that, and it appears he was impressed by what they had done.

'It's a fantastic book. You must read it. I'll lend it to you when we get home.'

L turned away moodily. 'If we get home.'

His lower lip protruded like that of a sulky boy and he rippled his muscles impotently, staring at the hostile mountains all round the horizon.

'Of course we'll get back home,' R laughed, thumping him jovially on the back. 'But we may as well do something useful while we're waiting.'

L doubled over on the small stance with a stomach-cramp, forcing R to lean out over space a thousand feet above the start of the route.

'Relax,' R advised him roughly. 'It's only tension knotting your guts.'

'The weather doesn't look too good.'

L's nervous chatter was getting to him. 'What's wrong with it?' he snapped, then made an effort to control himself. 'It's only a bit of cloud blowing around in the bowl of the face. You've seen that yourself on a fine day from below. This face has its own private climate, all to itself.'

'Christ, a big rock only just missed me down there!' L continued miserably, 'I don't fancy this at all. How far up are we? It isn't even good climbing.'

'It'll get better soon,' R soothed. 'We're near the Difficult Crack now, so we'll be sheltered from stone fall by that big, red wall above. The crack is a really famous pitch, just your style.

'We're as well off to keep going now. You don't want to have to descend all that crap down there when the sun starts melting the loose stuff off the top.'

From where they stood, below the bulging red rock of the Rote Fluh, the big ice-fields were invisible, recessed into the rock, and R dismissed them with a wave of foreshortened illusion, persuading L, and himself too for a moment, that all that livid, white scar tissue – streaming with water and rattling with stones – hardly existed at all.

L looked round in panic as the mist broke up into whipping streamers of misery, revealing the appalling scree-laden desolation of the level where they stood, and the dark wings of the face unfolding above to receive them.

R was moving on already. Accustomed to this kind of scrappy climbing he could see little difficulty in reaching the summit that day. The weather should hold, and the face was a lot less steep than he had imagined. It was even going to be quite easy, he cheered himself with a thrill of relief, the attitude of a man who desired climbing not for its own sake, but for achievement; and if it turned out to be a soft touch so much the better. Lack of quality would not disappoint R, so long as the reputation was there.

He checked his watch.

The BBC news caused a sickening kick of disbelief in his stomach.

Conciliation had broken down irretrievably due to undefined shifts in the alliances comprising the Superpowers. 'Confrontation seems inevitable,' a tight-lipped British observer threatened.

R shook his head frantically at the failure to specify, as if a blockage in the headset might be withholding the vital information.

Then an excited, almost hysterical announcer described Germany as an 'Holocaust of anti-American sabotage', whereupon the station simply gave up and played Elgar.

France was a gabble of incoherence ...

On Radio Geneva, one strong, uninterrupted, military voice alerted the Swiss nation over and over again to Emergency Action.

The voice, toneless as a tannoy, insisted at ten-second intervals in the stunned silence of R's brain:

Attention! Attention! Crise Internationale! Crise Internationale!
Attention! Attention! Aux Abris! Aux Abris!

To the Shelters!

Stupefied by shock R stared out into the blind mist.

For a moment he felt a phantom hunger devour his senses. Then utter isolation. He visualised streams of humanity pouring down from the hillsides, spilling out of the buildings, melting off the streets and draining through the ground into great concrete silos, human reservoirs – or mass graves. The army would stay close to the surface, gun muzzles bristling from every aperture in the surface of the country. He stood paralysed for so long at the vision of a whole population sucked into holes in the ground that L almost caught up with him. He was shrieking some hideous warning and waving frantically.

R looked up and saw, silhouetted against the brightening sky, a spatter of rocks spewing over the rim of the Rote Fluh, and arching towards him in casual slow motion, so that there was plenty of time to dive under the cover of an overhang and watch the huge chunks thunder onto the terraces hundreds of feet below, then bound outwards with increasing speed as if volleyed on vigorously by the ledges.

No going back down that rubbish-chute. The face was sloughing like an avalanche-slope.

The tiny voice vibrated in his ears *Aux Abris! Aux Abris!*

He shook his head as if he were being stung.

How could he explain to L what had happened, and cope with the boy's panic, despair, his fury even if he guessed deception?

He tried to frame in simple words the idea that life on the planet might have degenerated into chaos while they were climbing a mountain, but the words jammed far back in the mind, like L's electronic dictionary stunned by an untranslatable idea.

He couldn't face a moment of truth of such monumental magnitude that human history crashed into it at express speed and stopped dead with the impact.

The people in the valleys, running through the streets, down the concrete subways all over Europe weren't facing up to it either. They were taking the first step blindly, and then the next one into the dark.

Better keep going, and keep quiet, and maybe it would go away like the Cuban flash-point and all the other crises.

For a fraction of a second his mind was suffused by radiant relief while he imagined it all to be an hysterical fraud by the media, like the notorious hoax Orson Welles pulled off in the thirties when millions of Americans panicked out of all control, convinced by radio-bulletins that New York was being invaded by aliens from outer space.

But, as if awakening from a nightmare, past the blissful moment of relief to the realisation that reality is even grimmer than the dream, he remembered the soldiers in the streets, the confiscation of passports, and the barred compounds, and he knew no hoax could be that elaborate.

It was easier to keep stumbling sickly ahead of L, saying nothing. If he spoke he would have to believe what he heard himself say.

There was something doomed about L, he thought dumbly, as if recognising an indicative smell or a sound, something vulnerable about the way the small head sat on the bulky shoulders. He thought of the youth lured to extinction in the old film *Mort d'un Guide*, and shuddered.

R was finally brought to a halt by a steep, unavoidable groove, slick with water. A frayed remnant of old rope dangled down beside the problem, its dubious point of attachment hidden from view. Recklessly he grabbed the rope in both hands like an enraged bell-ringer and began to pull up hand over hand. What did it matter whether it broke or not?

But a sudden sense of survival jolted his body, and he shot a hand and foot securely into the crack.

Arriving on a straggle of bleak and tilted terraces at the foot of a huge, overhanging wall of uncracked limestone R was on top of the introductory plinth, and at the foot of the real North Face.

He gazed around. This desolate spot was one of the most intense deposits of mountaineering memory in the world. The Wet Cave Bivouac was here, and the Stollenloch exit from the rail-tunnel. The pulverised ledges, wreathed in tatters of mist, were crowded with ghosts. Buhl, with his shapeless, hillbilly hat; Heckmair, with a homely shin of pork in his sack, staring out of a measured silence at Harrer, so jaunty with one ice hammer and not a single crampon-point to his name. Bonatti too, going up and then quietly coming down, not just a hero but a survivor; Hinterstoisser and Toni Kurz tiptoeing past the trap in the gallows floor. … Mingling with the myths he had mouthed so many times, R stumbled in the stage door of history, through the deserted wings and onto the empty stage.

All he saw was a dribbling backdrop of uncouth wet rock and the swirling emptiness in front of his feet into which both audience and the earth had disappeared. Headset switched off he heard only the scree-chips grinding under his boots, water dripping on worn rock, and the whine of falling stones.

At the foot of the Difficult Crack, below the Hinterstoisser Traverse, the Swallow's Nest, Death Bivouac, the Traverse of the Gods, and the White Spider, the most poetic route in the world, R felt the responses of that revered chant sound in the void without an echo.

L scarcely knew them, any more than he knew the Stations of the Cross. He was just at the foot of the fixed rope now. R heard him grunting below, but the rope never twitched or tightened. L was climbing free. He found R sitting on the dripping terrace like some tragedy unveiled by a thaw, his shoulders slumped under the weight of his pack and the weariness of total desertion.

L was talking at him, but the words didn't register. A break in the swirling mist and he saw distant slate-grey ridges swathed in ugly cloud.

A storm was threatening, his brain measured instinctively, coming to pour destruction into the shattered bowl of the face.

L fiddled impatiently with his headset. He jerked R's arm.

'What does *abree* mean?' he demanded. '*Abree*! What's *abree* mean?'

R shook his head dumbly. The motion was too much for his self-control. Tears broke loose and trickled down into his beard.

L noticed something of his condition and took it for the dejection of fatigue. Competition stirred in his muscles. He had been slighted by the ease with which R stayed ahead on the unfamiliar mixed scrambling below.

'I'll lead for a start,' he volunteered. 'It'll get the weight of the ropes off our backs. Where's that crack you were talking about?'

The mist closed in again, but R knew the way as clearly as if he had been there before. The photographs and descriptions were printed in his mind.

L flexed his sturdy arms, and the pack settled between his shoulders. He scrambled awkwardly up easy, wet rock and ball-bearing scree, but when he reached the foot of the difficulties and began to move up on steep, black rock he entered his own element.

When R's turn came to follow he found the initial moves strenuous and unbalanced. He had climbed much easier grade fives than this notorious four. He was wading through a numb grief that clogged his will and dulled his senses like the aftermath of a broken heart. L swarmed on in the lead, the rope running out eagerly behind him, until he came to a halt at the foot of a solid wall that impended above him like the hull of a ship.

It was a mark of their different traditions that L was peering inquisitively up the overhanging wall while R never even glanced upwards but faced immediately out to the left. Even without foreknowledge of the Hinterstoisser Traverse that skirted the obstacle he would automatically look for avoidance rather than head-on challenge.

He had command of himself now. There was nothing to do but go on, even if only to avoid descent.

He felt he was getting close to a basic truth of mountaineering, now that it no longer mattered. Draining Mallory's catch phrase to the dregs, he realised that when it came down to the very bitter end of experience, a man continued climbing a mountain, not because it was there, but because he himself was there.

R suffered the cruel contradictions of absurdity and compulsion at the heart of climbing.

Once over the Hinterstoisser there could be no return, psychologically at least, because that was how it was in the early myths of the mountain and famous men had died terrible deaths trying to undo that step. Of course it was only a myth. Climbers could descend from any part of the lower face and often did, though the exposure to danger was considerable.

But L wouldn't know the facts and now it was necessary to ensure that he continued upwards.

'Out there is the Hinterstoisser Traverse,' R spoke slowly. The saliva in his mouth felt as thick and warm as blood. 'Anderl Hinterstoisser and Toni Kurz found a way out there across that slab in 1936. Hinterstoisser spent the rest of his life trying to reverse it in a storm. He abseiled down over there, and fell to his death.

'Toni Kurz survived for a night and day, hanging on a rope, injured, frost-bitten, and slowly dying of exposure. He lived ten times as long as Christ on the cross, and the only thing missing was the crown of thorns. All the time he thought he could be saved.

'He made up a makeshift line from bits and scraps and hauled up a safety-rope from rescuers on the ledges a hundred and thirty feet below. He slid down the rope until he jammed on a knot just a few feet out of reach of rescue.

'He died of exhaustion hanging there, although they could practically touch his feet from below.'

R stopped, overcome. That legendary body had dangled for a long time over the abyss of his memory on its old frayed rope, a thick crop of icicles growing longer and longer on the crampon-points.

There was nothing to see but the wet and vacant slab, and some disconnected snatches of the mountain breaking through the mist like phrases from a torn description.

In the disturbed pools of L's eyes R watched the shapeless bundle ripple and rotate with the deliberately ugly motion of fear, an empty spider on a long thread having spun all its substance into support until there was nothing left to survive.

L hesitated, weighing the hollow image. Then he added it to his load, and moved out on the near-vertical slab.

A rail of old rope looped out into the mist, but L didn't touch it. He clipped his own rope for protection into the pitons and traversed delicately on rounded holds and curved edges until he reached the upward crack. A veil of mist was ripped away and he stood exposed in clear silhouette on the other side of a clean divide. The intervening rock gleamed in the light with the bland polish of perfection.

R reached for his camera. Then he remembered, and the motion faltered and fell away.

When the rope came tight and it was his turn to move, he entered the pitch as if it were a wave of cold water, screwing up his features, holding his breath. Jumping in, he immediately grabbed the fixed rope and clipped his harness to it. He crossed the slab with the aid of the slender banister, climbed the steep crack at the end, and at 10 a.m. arrived in a bleak fanfare of sunlight at the Swallow's Nest.

The small bivouac niche was heaped over with old snow, and a large turd tumbled carelessly to one side, a signpost to humanity.

L was measuring dumbly the enormous expanse of face visible above them now; they had only rounded the lower jaw-line and still the huge, hollow cheeks of ice, and the bulging forehead glowered in repudiation.

R's limbs weakened at the prospect and the brittle heart in his chest crumpled under a fresh onslaught of pain.

'Jesus Christ!' wailed L, as a flurry of stones pumped down the first ice-field. 'How're we going to tackle that lot? It's like the Battle of the Somme up there.'

'Just take it step by step,' R muttered savagely. 'We'll get there. And if we don't, it doesn't make much difference.'

The hopeless abandon of the tone struck L with the force of revelation; appalled by some unspeakable understanding he asked no questions.

R snapped on crampons and grasped ice axe and ice hammer in either hand.

The ice was angled at about forty-five to fifty degrees and it was wet and rubbery after a warm night of thaw. The axes and crampon-points gouged lumps and flakes out of the insecure surface. Pebbles drummed an advance warning on their helmets, but nothing bigger came down until they reached the shelter of the next rock-barrier, where the Ice Hose bulged a continuation and they looked up to see the sky studded with rocks like stampeding hooves.

Bitter bravery rose in R's throat like bile, and he silently took the lead, kicking and axing his way up the steep tongue of ice that led to the massive Second Ice-field. When the ice ran out on bare rock he stubbed and trembled up the grit-sliding, nerve-wracking slabs without grace or pro-tection. The Second Ice-field was so enormous they felt paradoxically safe emerging on to its murderous slope, as if they were too insignificant in all that vast expanse to be hit by any of the random debris that came down; and yet every screaming missile seemed to home in on their position and when the first impact missed the ricochet made a second attempt.

Their tools flailed the grit-encrusted ice as if they were trying to burrow rather than climb, but finally, after hours of bombarded exposure they scrabbled out of the target-area into the relative safety of Death Bivouac.

Again dreams and the dead were pervasive, and R merged with the frozen memories of Sedlmayer and Mehringer. In 1935 they were the first men ever to attempt the face, driving a hard and direct line into a five-day storm and oblivion in this savage spot.

R was not much more real than Sedlmayer, whose ice-statue was seen, by observers circling the face, to guard the bivouac until winter carried him down.

As he stared out into the shallow clearance of the afternoon at the storm clouds bulging on the horizon R heard – not the mournful prowling of the old spotter-plane droning a farewell among the pillars of the face – but the venom of a jetfighter slashing the sky.

During the traverse of the Third Ice-field towards the Ramp, hands slotted between the steep, wafery ice and rock, R felt a deep, crumbling detonation filling, suffusing, swallowing the void behind his back. It swelled over thunder, beyond avalanche, to a pulsating explosion so heavy and ponderous that it extended beyond sound into a physical disintegration of distance, a brain-bruising shock that squeezed off perception from the senses so that he could not judge whether the mountain was moving or still, whether it was wind or heat that sucked at his stunned body; and though the entire face was alive and quivering with disruption nothing was more apparent than a great central stillness of ruin within the growing heart of the sound, a core of silent aftermath devouring the explosion from within. The swollen masses of cloud were closer now, not having drifted in, but as if some mighty force had warped and buckled the space in which they hung.

Consciousness began to filter through R's numb brain, and he stumbled forward into the rocky gully of the Ramp. L was there already. He had lost the power of speech and was retching convulsively, deep sobbing gasps torn by the roots from his lungs and stomach.

R anchored himself instantly.

The rope seared across his shoulders whipping him awake.

L landed heavily on a sloping ledge a few feet below, and the rope held him. He was dazed, but the effort of scrambling back up controlled his hysteria.

Neither said a word. Sobbing breath and dripping sweat spoke the language of desperation.

R lurched up the easy gully in the lead, realising helplessly that the hard, steep bottleneck at the top of the Ramp would by now be in waterfall condition. All the climbing in his life had led insistently to this moment, but now that he needed overpowering skill and endurance he knew with a stark sense of failure that the ability was not there.

If it depended on him to prolong his own life, then he would die here.

The exit of the gully was blocked by a steep, narrow chimney. Water gushed and swirled down the dark, polished rock, submerging the line of the climb. On the right and left overhanging rock bulged ponderously.

R belayed with slow, dull care, attaching himself to five different anchor-points. L was heavy and there was not much protection on that right-hand wall where Lachenal had fought out his rock-variation to the waterfall on the second ascent in 1947.

He threaded L's rope through a friction belay-plate, checked the anchors again and then pointed at the bulging pitch overhead.

Now, he said, You wanted rock. Climb that, you bastard.

But no sound emerged.

L barely lifted his eyes. He stepped up to a ledge with the heavy, tread of a man on the gallows and laid hands on the rock.

'Get in some protection,' R ordered sharply.

L fumbled a nut into a crack.

'Clip that peg out on the left.'

L attached his rope to the old piton, and resumed his position, breathing heavily.

'Get on with it.'

His arms tightened obediently, fingers closing on the flaky rock as if he were gouging handholds in it. His feet came up and the boots bridged wide apart on small holds.

He began to pull up. A foothold snapped off, his body plunged, and R was dragged against his anchors by the rope. L stood up again, and shook himself.

Failure was good for him.

This time he examined the problem, and braced himself.

He pulled up powerfully again, but didn't rest or hang on the holds. He used them dynamically, following through on each move, and reaching up fast for the next invisible edge.

He was fifteen feet above the last piton, arched out around the bulge.

His legs vibrated and the muscles knotted in his arms. To his left a big crumbling flake jutted.

L's left hand blurred away from a hold, left foot lashed out on the wall for balance. As his body slewed into a fall his hand clamped the edge of the flake.

He swung violently out from the wall, and the other hand smacked around the shuddering shield of rock.

Feet kicked up against the flake, arching his body out, and then he was lay-backing fiercely. A hand grappled over the top of the flake, feet and body swung free, and then, with the irresistible savagery of survival, he wrenched himself up onto the ledge above.

Climbing the ice overhead to the Brittle Ledges they did not know each other – frail forms weaving through a superhuman world, particles of rock and ice whirling like molecules, the air itself relentless friction.

A disease of darkness setting in.

Freezing cloud flailed them, stinging skin from bone with the leaded whipcord of hail.

L flapped across the brittle, broken ledges like a bundle of empty rags catching and dragging on spikes and projections. R was fumbling again among the sheltered ironies of history ... that old overcoat cast off high on the White Spider by Albrecht and Derungs, a black chrysalis that panicked the Scheidegg observers into thinking there was a body in it.

L fluttered against the cracked pillar at the end of the ledges as if he were blown involuntarily upwards, a moth in an up-draught, ragged and torn against the steep rock.

The wind hammered and howled. There was no more thought of release. No feel of another fate. Born into this, and the conclusion obvious. But not immediate. They staggered around a corner, out of the funnel, to a sheltered terrace.

The wind streamed past, faltered, dropped to a whisper.

Unbearably heavy in the sudden vacancy they slumped together on the little ledge, an irreducible heap.

Here was the Götterquergang, Traverse of the Gods, beginning of the end.

The ledge ran on, sloping and tilting in the gathering gloom. Utterly bleak and forsaken, it was no gangway but a riddle of steep, icy terraces crossing a buttress to a gleaming notch hundreds of feet away.

The notch was bright because, just beyond it, the White Spider was frothing furiously with avalanche.

R laid his head down in the dark peace of indifference.

The first storm-squall had passed over; there was a lull, the sky cleared briefly overhead baring jagged stars and cold promise.

Time drifted, disarranged.

On the hulking fin of the Eiger, R prowled the cataclysms of prehistory, ploughed the tidal glaciers of ice ages, and towered over a flurry of peopled time, farms and fields creeping like contagion through the foothills, fading into the immunity of the mountains.

Then the great iceberg of the Eiger, adrift in time, sliced into the densest century: tunnels, trains, tourism, and swarming men like lice or lemmings; and R felt the entire mountain shudder under his back.

Waking, the vibration was real, and he understood that the roaring in his ears was a total collapse of some monstrous balance in the world, a balance as singular as the molecular bondage below the skin of things, tumbling surfaces into the void like graves when the bones and the boxes implode and the wild soil falls askew in pits and craters. It was a collapse of time too, that tumbled cultures down like castles and burned the debris of paint, gold, and poetry to the smoky ash of centuries in a searing second, while the unrepeatable thunder of destruction rolled and reverberated in the empty perpetuity of a history and future all undone.

He looked out into the dark and saw the mushrooming storm-clouds glowing red, as if he were projecting a bloodshot vision on the night.

A jagged flash of lightning slashed the sky, and then again and again, spreading and catching, igniting particles of flaky fire in the abrasive atmosphere. His skin burned and seared.

R stared at the face inches from his own. The skin was rising in bubbles, hanging in shreds. The lips were black, and deeply cracked. L was dead.

The lightning stopped and the hot wind gathered.

Slowly, and without any fuss, cloud closed the sky, quenching the nine billion names of God.

R had time to understand, he was making the last ascent.

THE BOY WHO SHOT JOHN WAYNE

I

My cousin Tom was right about one thing: I was an outright cissy. A thin, pasty child, not so much from malnutrition as from some kind of emotional hunger, I was afraid to fight, no use at football. I slouched around, soaked in the misery of a masculine world. I wanted to grow up as different from everything around me on the farm as was humanly possible. A spiritual life seemed the obvious alternative. Not here of course. Kilnamon or anywhere like it in the Midlands would have been impossible. I knew the place too well to rise above it. There was nothing I wouldn't wish to forget; Uncle Joe's wet farm outside the town, the house unpainted and the hay-sheds rusting; bony cattle in the fields, briar and blackthorn and the rampant yellow ragwort. Tom was a year younger, but it seemed the other way round. Even at the age of twelve he was doing a man's work.

My father sent me down from Dublin every summer. I was his link with the land. He grew up here in Kilnamon in the spare forties. When Joe inherited the farm my father shifted to Dublin to better himself, but the only improvement existed in his own mind, I'm afraid. He was riddled with notions of status and failure all his life. Pride suffocated his humour and affection. He was a salesman in a hardware shop, a hardworking, honest man. He used to describe himself painfully to strangers as 'in a commercial way of business.'

The holidays on the farm were supposed to toughen me with manly values. My father can't have remembered his own brother very well. The only values Uncle Joe professed were muscle and money. He had no sympathy at all for me, a pale hostage from the city. And Tom too, poor Tom, uncouth and graceless, with strength to compensate for skill, understood what I never realised: that I was a usurper.

His brief boyhood was animated by two passions; fishing and films.

Both had a strain of violence.

When all my pocket money was spent and he could steal no change from his father for the cinema he went fishing in the river. Without a word from me, condemned to sit by his side, he flogged the sulky water with hook and line. Later he gutted the bony perch and fried them over the kitchen fire. Scraping fish from a burnt pan is the only act of sharing I recall in the house. I don't know what poison was in our fathers but Tom and I were both motherless.

The Royal in Kilnamon was no more than a mile from the farm. A draughty hall with wooden benches at the front below the screen, lines of chairs behind and two rows of cushioned seats at the very back. Tom went to see every new picture. He was a cowboy fanatic, war films in second place. Love stories were a source of jeering speculation about sex. Life, as Tom projected it, was explicitly basic. Everything led either to battle or to bed.

I couldn't escape him. He trailed me with him to show his power over an older city boy. And I had been conditioned to accept humiliation, almost to expect it as a right. The only people I ever got to know in Kilnamon were those who could tolerate the company I was forced to keep, Tom and the bullies who hung around with him. I'm sure there were decent people there too who didn't sneer and curse and steal, but they must have had somewhere else to spend their time.

They haven't come out to welcome me back either. I suppose they'll see how the glasshouses get on first. They've lived near cow-shit too long to get excited about an organic farm. It's the only one in these parts. Clean fruit and vegetables for an imaginary market. We're surrounded by tired farmers waiting to sell out to land-dealers; meanwhile they breed pharmaceutical beef and sneer at my pretensions. I've one gardener – farmer, I suppose you'd call him – a self-professed itinerant with a bad leg and a genius for growth. He's an unusual traveller: he's never left Kilnamon in his life. If the farm fails his days will be numbered. He will have backed the loser once too often.

II

When Uncle Joe died last winter I got the news by telegram. I almost missed it. It came to the college months after I had left. Father Boyle brought it round to the flat. I didn't realise they had my address since I'd moved a second time. It was embarrassing to find Boyle standing on the doorstep with the opened telegram. He shook my hand gravely, offered help if required, and took himself off. I resolved to move again.

The telegram was signed J.J. Gorman (Solicitor). The name seemed at once ridiculous and right, though I couldn't grasp the contradiction then. The news itself was no surprise. When I arrived in Kilnamon for the funeral a heavy figure stepped from the church-porch to greet me. I looked away. The last thing I wanted was to meet anyone. I had no connections here. This final visit was a cold duty to the past.

'Sorry for your trouble, Pat! Glad you could make it.' With a shock of displacement I saw Tom's former friend, a coarse hulk of a boy, distorted into an adult. John Joe Gorman (Solicitor). His face was folded in rolls of closely shaven fat. Heavy lips and eyes drooped with professional sympathy. A whisper in the flat accent: 'I'm lookin' after your uncle's affairs. We'll have a chat after the funeral.'

Things were beginning to come home to me in a conspiracy of understanding. I must have been blind till now. There were no mourners in the front seats. I knew there wouldn't be, of course, but... Thought stalled, my eyes veering around the gloomy church. So much smaller than I recalled. The seats dotted with the same old women in scarves and belted raincoats, as patient as the statues. I knew now they were heavier with fatigue than piety, their weariness was a holier condition than prayer.

The stained glass window above the altar was crudely made. More lead than colour. How had it spangled my boyhood prayers with such dull glory? I used to see blood in red glass and sanctity in stone cold shadows, a dangerous innocence seduced by sermons and sacrifice.

Uncle Joe's coffin rested on trestles before the altar, so transient it was already sliding through the candlelight into the dark. I knew no comfort to offer. John Joe tiptoed exaggeratedly forward, took a mass card from his inside pocket and propped it on the lid. He genuflected reverently and returned to kneel beside me in the front seat.

Uncle Joe had never entered the church before to my knowledge. Once, when we were loading hay into the loft I felt his coldness momentarily abate. I knew I had a religious duty to perform. Stuttering, I asked if he would come to mass with us next morning. He spat into the cart very close to my sandals. His speed increased and very soon he was pulling hay from under my feet. I was forced to jump aside to avoid the flying needles of his fork.

And Tom would only come to watch the women and make a nuisance of himself. He used to sit beside me, silently breaking wind, and then slide away leaving me stranded in guilt. John Joe Gorman also had some kind of anal obsession in those days. Loud, tearing eruptions were his style under cover of the gospel shuffle. All the boys were reduced to hysterical mirth and he was an immediate hero. His father was an important man anyway, a leading solicitor. John Joe always had a summer job in a garage on Church Street.

I looked at him now to measure the change. His face had the same sure sense of life as a source of profit. There was aggression in the bluntness of his head. His jacket was hand-tailored to accommodate hulking shoulders. The trousers were ponderously charged where the heavy thighs met the curve of his belly. How could this solid adult ever have been a boy? He was so absolutely established in his manhood. That confidence had never come to me. No matter how desperately I tried I could not remember growing up.

We drove behind the hearse to the graveyard. There was no other car. John Joe told me he had gone into his father's business years before. He had taken it over now. He was well used to dead farmers and their wills.

'Well, the old place is yours, Pat, and good luck to you. You'll be wanting to sell up I suppose.'

The blood was singing under my skin with excitement and appal. I had no idea what to think.

The hearse speeded up. No one wished to linger over Uncle Joe.

Independence must take years of practise and I had no experience of it at all.

It was drizzling heavily in the cemetery. I had seen all this before, my life whittled down to a cold solitude by this ritual. A figure tended a plot in a far corner. Under a wool cap a straggle of yellow hair. He straightened and turned towards us in respect as the coffin went down. I saw the crooked angle of one leg against the handle of a rake and suffered that shock of displacement again. The thud of soil on hollow timber, and memory jerked in a new direction. Uncle Joe cutting turf in the bog. He stood in the bottom of the bog hole hurling the heavy sods up faster then I could catch and carry them. Every sod punched the breath out of my chest. He never let up the pace. Christian training forbade harsh thoughts about the dead but I kept a voice in my head to think them for me: Now you swine the phrase formed involuntarily – throw this lot up... if you can.

After the burial I shook the hands of a few old men. They knew who I was, of course. A sliding glance into my eyes, murmur of condolence, and the attention shifted to my shabby lay clothes, the collar and tie around my neck.

I was branded with my own mistake. The only reason I had entered the seminary in the first place was to escape from home and Kilnamon. I traded one sense of claustrophobia for another, deeper kind. But my father was happy. University was out of the question, and if I couldn't be a doctor I had better be a priest. He invested a lot of anxiety in my prospects and I began to see that a spiritual life could be subject to the same values as any commercial way of business.

If I had come from an easier background I wouldn't have entered the Church at all. I'd have gone to England and disappeared into the army or the building trade. That was what Tom did when he fell out with Uncle Joe.

III

Tom started to drink in a determined way when he was about seventeen. He ran up debts on his father's credit and sold off lambs for drinking money. Apparently it was a sudden thing, an explosion, total loss of control. Later, he compromised a girl in Kilnamon, a maid in the doctor's house. He offered to marry her but Uncle Joe refused to let them live on the farm.

Tom came home drunk one night and Uncle Joe threw him out. There was a fight and Tom broke his father's arm. He might have killed him only someone interfered.

That fight had been brewing a long time. Tom told me about it on his way to England. He only called on me to borrow a few pounds to see him through till he got a start. The novitiate made him laugh. It reminded him of the County Home. I asked him where his girlfriend was. He sneered at my innocence.

'No shortage of women where I'm going Pat. No need to bring your own.'

My father was in Luke's hospital at the time for the first of many tests. I asked him if he could persuade Uncle Joe to relent towards Tom. He refused to interfere. Apparently he had fallen out finally with Joe himself over some inheritance that was never shared.

I had my own problems to distract me. Study was absolutely joyless and the vocation a fading echo. Dogma and discipline grew increasingly arbitrary but I had neither the courage, or, I suppose, the freedom to leave the seminary. Illness had forced my father to retire from work and he had everything pinned on me then.

My superiors battled for my integrity and submission. In frustration I thwarted their every effort. I turned vegetarian, an unthinkable thing in the Church, choking on the fatty bacon and stewed gristle. Father Boyle argued that the animal world was created for man's sustenance. The least I could do was allow it to fulfil its God-given function. He preached the Body and Blood of Christ almost as a dietary injunction. Curiously some of my classmates saw my ideas as an insult to themselves and what they stood for. It was like attacking their religion. They were the sons of farmers and they believed in red meat with a passion.

I was summoned to Boyle's office one morning. I expected an ultimatum but was introduced instead to a priest, home on holiday from England. He made me sit down and brace myself for bad news. I had never known there was any other kind.

He informed me that Tom had died in an accident in London. I made a show of grief and began to feel its effects. Attempts had been made to contact Uncle Joe without response, and the priest in Kilnamon had directed them to me. Father Murtagh wasn't sure of any details – he had simply brought the message in passing – but at last he admitted having heard that Tom fell from the balcony of a dancehall during a brawl. Whether he had fallen or been thrown was another matter, but he was a ganger with McAlpine's at the time and sudden death was not unknown.

Father Murtagh insisted that this report was probably a myth. He had come across the same story before and it had been the same dancehall in Camden Town, the one they called the Buffalo. Apocryphal, he called it.

He promised to send me details on his return.

Almost immediately I received a letter from Uncle Joe. I had never known him to write a word before, but it was strangely articulate. First he informed me coldly of my cousin's death, as if it was no more than his duty to let me know.

And yet in spite of the tone it seemed a personal letter. That 'Dear Pat' must have cost a mighty effort to a man whose voice was shaped by anger. I felt he was reaching towards me in friendship or despair. He explained that having fallen out with my father and lost his own son he was considering the question of his soul now that time was getting short. He doubted that he had such a thing as a soul though, and what did I think of that?

I panicked at the thought of responding to real human need. I knew exactly what he meant for I doubted that he had a soul either. He said he knew my father was dying. It was the first time I had seen it put so bluntly but I agreed with him on that too. Uncle Joe was a man of few words and no illusions. He expressed neither sympathy nor regret, and I interpreted this hardness as a refusal to ask for help. I went down to see him in Kilnamon.

The house looked as if it had been deserted for years. I found him down at the bottom of the farm mending a wall. There was a tractor ploughing behind him where the river used to swamp the land. But it was all drained now, the best of rich, black soil folding over behind the plough. He saw me alright though he didn't show it till I was halfway along the headland. Then he left the stones and came slowly to meet me.

It was one of those rare moments when I realised I was a man to other men. As a boy he never acknowledged me at all. He took my hand briefly now as if I had passed him something casual. The roar of the tractor absolved us from small talk. I felt the curiosity of the driver as he swung into another furrow and moved away. I thought it was an aimless stroll we were taking then, a refusal to sit down and meet each other's eyes. Now I know that we were 'walking the land', measuring me against it.

Uncle Joe was no longer the big man I remembered. I had grown tall myself and he was stooped with rheumatism. He shuffled beside me in a pair of blue overalls and wellingtons, an old tweed jacket, a shirt without a collar. The corded hollows of his throat shocked me with their frail tension. Shaving must be near suicide, I thought. His face was lined and angular, grey hair combed severely forward onto a bony forehead.

The farm was neglected. Broken walls and rotting bales of hay. But good land and plenty of it. Drainage had doubled the arable acres. Perversely I regretted the loss of the wet-lands that had depressed me so much as a fretful boy. The succulent flags were gone from the riverbank where poor Tom used to trail his line in anger and frustration. There was no habitat now for the heron that used to flap away at our approach. Tom had vowed to kill it for stealing fish.

We tramped for an hour almost in silence. Eventually, with desperate delicacy I asked him if there were any ... any problems I could help him with. He snorted, as close to laughter as I ever heard.

'You're not cut out for the confession box,' he grated. He looked at my cheap black suit and sandals sarcastically, 'whatever else might be in store for you!'

But he talked briefly about his son. He had never forgiven the broken arm. I mentioned the story I had heard. I wanted to know if Tom's death was accidental or deliberate. The old man spat.

'The way I heard it, he took pneumonia sleepin' rough. He was on a drunken batter, and he took pneumonia out of it. That's how I heard it.'

He left me to take my pick of the stories.

All of a sudden he seemed unbearably vulnerable in his hardness. He had missed everything that mattered, and so had I. I saw him pared down to the loneliness of the bone and was moved almost to tears.

My tongue was somehow loosened. I told him he had read me right, I hadn't the makings of a priest and never would have.

'What does your father say to that?' was all he wanted to know. His lack of any interest in me at all made me feel a fool for having confided in him.

'I haven't told him,' I replied. 'The least I can do is stick it out for the few months he has left. There's no point breaking his heart.'

There was no response. His pale eyes were screwed up, staring into the corner of a field.

I visited my father in hospital almost every day. Part of his skull was shaved and the blue marks of radium treatment were spread across his scalp. He was shrivelling into the old striped pyjamas. One day his condition had deteriorated visibly. There was a letter in his hands. The paper was crushed. He plucked at it with gaunt fingers as if he wanted to shred it and didn't have the strength.

'Read that!' He tried to throw it at me.

The letter was from Uncle Joe. I hoped it was reconciliation, but there was an ugly dread in the pit of my stomach. There, at the bottom of the page, was the kick in the belly.

'... It must be a hard blow to see Pat leaving the priesthood. He told me about it himself and maybe it's all for the best. My own blackguard let me down worse ...'

I raised my eyes from the page and tried to catch my father's dull stare. There was nothing I could say, no lie I could tell. He had turned his face to the wall in more ways than one.

Uncle Joe died a year after my father. I had long quit the college and thought they had let me go. In a flat in Harold's Cross I tried to organise a future for myself. I put in for jobs but my past was a problem. I didn't want anything that would take a spoiled priest as a guarantee of humility.

Somehow it seemed I must end up in Australia sooner or later. There was something doomed about me that demanded exile. I was thinking of London for a start when Father Boyle brought the telegram around.

IV

After the funeral John Joe brought me to the Imperial Hotel for a drink. There was no legal ritual in the Castle Street office. He produced the will in a corner of the hotel lounge. It came out of his inside pocket. I wondered how many more wills and mass cards were stored away in there like obituaries in a newspaper file. Without stirring a hand I owned fifty acres, a house, and assorted sheds. The very piece of ground I least wanted to see again on the surface of the earth was entirely mine. The sense of possession was impossible to grasp. They might as well have made me a bishop after I turned my back on the church.

To add to my confusion I got a whiff of John Joe's business style. I understood now why we hadn't gone to his office. We were in it.

This dark corner of the lounge was his by recognition. There were several people at the bar anxious for his attention, but when they saw him with a client they kept their distance. Two brandies arrived unordered. I was used to minerals and the occasional glass of beer. The first sip staggered me.

John Joe was spreading papers on the table.

'I'll have to eat something,' I mumbled. 'I got nothing on the train.'

'Easy now, Pat. Easy. We'll fix you up with lunch as soon as we settle this bit of business.'

'I'll get a sandwich or something...' I escaped to the bar. In the long mirror I could have sworn I saw John Joe shaking his head at the barman.

'Any chance of a cheese sandwich?' I was trembling with hunger. He shot a glance over my shoulder. 'Ham!' he grunted reluctantly.

'No. No meat thanks. Have you nothing else?'

He hesitated and then relaxed. 'I'll see what I can do for you. Pat isn't it? Sorry for your trouble. I'd have been there this morning only I had to open up here.'

I went back to my seat warmed by recognition.

John Joe seemed thoroughly familiar with the farm. He had all the values at the tips of his fingers. He estimated a potential price. To me it was a lot of money. He could drop a nought and it was still a lot of money to me.

Uncle Joe left no debts. That was why the farm didn't look prosperous. He never borrowed for development.

John Joe was into his second brandy. It had been cold in the graveyard. The flesh of his hands was pudgy, unused.

'I don't want to jump the gun right after a bereavement, Pat,' he said, 'but I think I know the score here.'

I could imagine him intimidating widows.

'You'll want to sell, Pat, isn't that right? You've had your own troubles by all accounts, but that's no business of mine. There'll be a tidy sum here to invest in something steady for the future.'

The implication that my position was common knowledge and even a source of shame infuriated me.

'I have a local client interested in the property already.'

'Who?' I asked, startled.

John Joe's mouth tightened. He couldn't snarl at me to mind my own business like he used to.

'Tim Brophy,' he said after a pause.

Tim Brophy! I was amazed. Uncle Joe had mentioned the name with the usual dismissive spit the day we walked the land. Brophy was the fellow who farmed the scraggy patch to the west. I didn't think he'd have the kind of money Gorman was proposing for Uncle Joe's – for my farm.

I was in no doubt about selling. And I wanted the money as quickly as possible. Dreams were reeling through my mind already. But I'd make sure John Joe didn't get a penny more than the minimum commission. I wouldn't give him the satisfaction of instant assent either, although it was hard to imagine anyone buying a farm near Kilnamon.

There was a lot of petty revenge to catch up on. So I said I'd think about it and let him know.

His mouth tightened again, and then formed a professional smile. Ah sure, he knew well how upset I was after my uncle. Wasn't oul' Joe like a father to me when I was a kid. And all the rest of it! I rose abruptly to leave. The sandwich hadn't come. John Joe circled my shoulders with a heavy arm and drew me towards the bar.

'We'll have a drink out of respect for the dead,' he decided, 'and the other fellah too, God rest him I always knew he'd come to a bad end.' He chuckled.

'Ah you wouldn't understand, Pat. You were always a nice quiet sort of a fellah. But Tom was a real hard chaw. Jasus, man, he was one tough fucker ...'

We sat on high stools in front of the bar. This was a new occupation for me and I wasn't too sure how to handle myself. The dizzy feeling could be due to the change of fortune as well as hunger, but it seemed best not to aggravate it with alcohol.

I asked for coffee. Again the barman looked to John Joe for advice and I insisted.

'Maybe you'll take a drop of something in it so.' he wheedled. 'On the house.'

'I will,' I said. 'A drop of milk if you have it.'

From where we sat I could see through an open hatch into the public bar. While John Joe reminisced I stared at a startling face beyond.

The man in the bar had his elbows propped on the counter. A glass of Guinness stood in front of him. His chin was cupped in his two hands. The shoulders of his donkey jacket were still soaked. I had seen him an hour ago standing to attention in the rain

At first he seemed in a trance, lids hooded over wide-set eyes. Heavy strands of straw-coloured hair hung down both sides of a broad forehead and high cheekbones. His skin was dark: the colour of freckles all run together into a single brown.

With a shock I realised his eyes were not closed at all. He was looking back at me from under the lowered lids. It was the stare of a horse dealer into a tourist's lens. I felt my face flush from the neck upwards. I knew I would have to wrench my eyes away in defeat. Then, as if a statue moved, he dropped his hands and his dark face dissolved in a confusing grin. He moved abruptly away, long hair swinging just above his shoulders. I heard a sing-song voice address the barman.

John Joe leaned across and followed my eyes.

'Tinker Ned!' he grunted. His face screwed up in contempt. 'You never met that fellah, did you? He'd be after your time ...'

He called the barman back. 'What did you let him in for?' He indicated with his head, 'I thought I ...'

The barman protested mildly, 'Ned is it? Sure I can't bar him for nothing. He's no bother.'

There was a growing suspicion in my mind about John Joe, but I was too absorbed to pursue it now.

Of course I knew Ned!

He was only a boy of twelve when I was fifteen, but he was very much of my time in Kilnamon. I couldn't believe John Joe had forgotten. He was leaving for another appointment.

'Ring this number tonight when you know your mind better. Don't leave it any later, Pat. Strike while the iron is hot.' Would he never go? He was whispering close to my ear. I felt the hot brandy breath on my skin. The huge hand was drawing a chequebook from an inside pocket.

'If you need an advance now for anything Pat ...'

I brushed him away with barely concealed disgust. I could still hear Ned's voice in the public bar.

I delved for his surname without success. Had he been refused one?

He lived with his mother in a council cottage outside the town when I was there. Tom had stories of the travelling man she married. He didn't stay around long enough to see his son. On another occasion he told me Ned's father was a black-haired local who got suspicious of his son's colouring and took off for London in protest. I didn't understand the implications, but I'm sure I sniggered anyway. A lot of people took the calamity of his origins out on Ned himself. Those who didn't blame him kept their sympathy very quiet. He was a handy scapegoat for every tool or farmyard fowl that disappeared. I took his guilt for granted because he was so untamed, forever blazing in the fields and streets with crazy energy.

He understood his heritage and flaunted it. His yellow hair grew long and the cheekbones and flattened nose were fiercely tribal.

He refused the drab accent of the Midlands and adopted the tone of the Connaught tinkers who passed our way with covered wagons and hooped tents. But Ned was a lot more colourful than these originals.

Tom had a strange bond of hunter and victim with him. They played out rituals of cruelty and pain from time to time, determined perhaps by the moon or the river floods. I was miserably grateful when these distractions took the pressure off me. But nothing could break Ned's resilience. His scrawny body bristled with belligerence after every beating. He was the kind of mongrel pup that takes on a pack of terriers because it knows nothing but resistance.

Ned and his mother lived off the back and front gardens of the cottage. They hardly ever bought food. That was akin to an admission of crime in Kilnamon. There were stories of stolen food hidden in the house, huge heaps of bones ground into powder to fertilise the garden. And it was true that strange vegetables grew everywhere. Even in winter there was growth. People said there were herbs for poisoning dogs when Ned went stealing chickens at night.

During the dull summer days Ned reminded me of a character in a film I saw; a young Apache kicking around a white settlement without a tribe of his own to go to. He was an outsider. The only one besides myself. But I knew how to keep my Dublin mouth shut while Ned was always in danger of being lynched for open subversion.

He resisted all the rituals of Church and sport that bound the people together in blunt solidarity.

In the middle of a football match when Kilnamon Juniors were trouncing the opposition for once, Ned raced across the pitch and stole the ball under the eyes of the population. It was his answer to the constant accusations of theft. The ball came back later in a shower of glass through the window of the pub where the team was drinking.

Ned went on the run for a week after that. He only returned when word went out that his mother would be taken into care in the County Home. A truce was declared to stop her becoming a burden on the ratepayers. That was the reason too why Ned was never committed to Letterfrack or Daingean – even after he joined a Corpus Christi procession with a pair of knickers on his head and an expression of such childlike piety on his face that no one could possibly stomach the insult. Grown men thrashed him out of the parade with sticks torn from the ditch, and his yells of defiance drowned out the hymn-singing children.

I asked Tom once if Tinker Ned was 'mental.' He considered the question seriously. Madness in its various forms was his favourite subject. He admitted that Ned was as smart as anyone else in the school. He could read, write, and do sums. He even liked Irish. But this intelligence was taken as definitive proof of Ned's cunning insanity. I was curious about his knowledge but I could hardly understand a word he said to me. His voice went up and down in wild bursts of fluency, like birdsong or a foreign language.

V

Ned, too, was obsessed with the cinema. He got in, in exchange for cleaning out the hall afterwards. The boys competed with each other in leaving disgusting surprises under the chairs. He carried subversion into the dark hall. Ned cheered whenever a cavalry officer got an arrow in his throat, or the great white hope was beaten to a pulp in the ring. He was fiercely dedicated to the wrong side, up for every renegade and snake-eyed redskin.

There was a cult of John Wayne in Kilnamon during my second-to-last summer. His films were coming through in batches. The local accent was ideal for adopting his coarse drawl. Tom, John Joe, and all the boys swaggered loosely from the hips as if they had artificial legs. Ned filtered through the shadows like an Apache scout.

He was twelve the year of John Wayne. Tom and John Joe were fourteen. And I was a craven fifteen.

The poster for *Pony Soldiers* went up midweek. Showing Friday and Saturday. Wayne wore US cavalry uniform in the poster. He rode a white horse and brandished a sabre. In case anyone thought he had gone soft there was a Winchester Carbine stuffed down beside the saddle and a six-shooter in a holster on his hip. He was all things to all men.

Tom and John Joe were broke on Friday night. They were in trouble over some vicious misdemeanour and couldn't raise a penny anywhere. I had the price of a single seat but for once I couldn't be bullied into giving it away. Yet with the loyalty of the victim I waited till they could go with me the second night.

The reports of the film were spectacular. The entire Friday audience was sworn to go again. Tom and John Joe got the cash together on Saturday. They had ten Woodbines as well, and made up in thick smoke and loud farts for the humiliation of the night before.

I remember nothing of *Pony Soldiers* until the moment John Wayne stood in his stirrups to lead the assault on the Indians. The sword flashed high above his bare head. His voice spat gravel as he ordered the attack. The camera stayed low and held him centre-screen, his arm raised in a salute to action, body outlined against the sun, the whole world shuddering with the thunder of a white crusade.

In the breathless silence an object whizzed over the audience and shattered against the screen. A violent stain exploded across John Wayne's chest, red blood drenching the Arizona sky.

John Wayne went galloping, galloping into attack, his great heart bursting across the screen. The wild laugh of the assassin rang out at the back of the cinema. The projectionist in his fright grabbed the film and ripped it out of its reel. We watched John Wayne and his white horse jerk backwards into oblivion, as if Tinker Ned's shot had blasted them off the screen.

The lights came on for interrogation. The screen was savagely bright and bare, red ink dribbling down the centre. Blood on a blank wall. Evidence of execution.

Tom and John Joe were the first away. Chairs went over backwards as they led the chase. Violence was about to build upon sacrilege, and I followed. The street was quivering with cold light. We caught Ned so easily he must have waited for us. At the end of a closed alley he stood crying in the shadows.

Tom, John Joe, and I closed in silently.

He was dragged to the garage where John Joe worked. The crime called for a secret court and a dark punishment. We knew Ned's act was an attack on everything we believed in.

There were a dozen boys crowded in the store-room, seated on tyres, a row of grim faces under a naked bulb. The windows were covered with flattened sheets of tin. The store was full of cold steel and dirty rubber, the tool-room of an ugly dream. I sweated and shivered. Ned, pinioned in Tom's grip, gaped like a wild bird, a goldfinch or a yellow-hammer.

John Joe uncoiled the air-hose from a hook inside the door. He kicked a switch and a shuddering hum filled the room. When he squeezed the trigger a jet of air hissed from the nozzle. A black needle shivered in judgement on a cracked dial. The glass was a star of pain.

'It's the treatment, Ned,' John Joe promised quietly. 'You know the treatment don't you, Ned.'

The boys leaned forward in their seats. My legs trembled beyond control. I was going to be sick.

John Joe smeared the silver nozzle with axle grease. He squeezed out another jet of air.

I did not understand. The atmosphere was sacramental.

Tom had one arm clamped around the victim's chest. The other hand was fumbling with Ned's belt. Ned began to laugh. Hopeless and high pitched it had nothing to do with humour or defiance. The walls were throbbing with the rhythm of the compressor. I heaved myself towards the door. No one looked around. John Joe was closing in with the hose.

When the heavy shutter swung behind me I stumbled forward into the cool night. The sound of Ned's hysteria receded into another world, faraway and skin-deep.

I didn't see him again that summer. The holidays were over. During the winter he had an accident with a tractor. His leg was badly broken and it mended crookedly. The next time I met him he had a severe limp. He was slow and shy, easier to talk to.

Obstinately, despite the facts, I blamed the twisted leg on the punishment.

VI

The barman was clearing his throat to catch my attention. He jerked his head expressionlessly at the hatch.

'He wants to buy you a drink.'

I hesitated, then slid off my stool and went through to the dingy bar.

'No use paying lounge-prices for it, Ned. How are you?' His handshake was hard and dry. Under the abundant hair his creased forehead and old eyes made a disturbing contradiction. My eyes dropped to his awkward leg. It occurred to me suddenly Ned might be thinking of my twisted vocation in the same way.

There was a silence. We needed some foundation in the past, something free of pain.

'I never thought you'd stick this place, Ned!'

'Ah, it's not too bad. Where else would I go?'

'Are you still out beyond …?' I tipped my head vaguely.

'Still there, Pat. I'm on me own now this last few year.'

I nodded, 'That's hard luck …' So hers was the well-kept plot in the corner by the wall.

'Sorry about your uncle, Pat.' It sounded awkward as if he wasn't sure it was the right thing to say. I raised my eyebrows sceptically. Ned grinned. 'Ah, Joe wasn't a bad oul' skin. He kept me goin' the last few year anyway. When work was hard to get.'

'You worked for Uncle Joe?' I said incredulously.

'Well, nothin' much like. We only kept the place tickin' over. He was always fair with the few bob though. I'll give him that.'

I was staggered by this revelation of a secret side to Kilnamon. I would have expected Joe to class Ned as thieving scum.

The ploughed field flashed through my mind. Last year, by the river! I thumped the counter in recognition:

'That was you! On the tractor! Right?' Ned grinned self-consciously and changed the subject.

'I saw you inside with J.J. Will you take a drink Pat?'

I looked at his own glass. 'I'll have a bottle of stout, so. Thanks Ned.'

Then I said slowly, as it dawned on me that he wouldn't have been gardening in the rain, 'You were there today too, weren't you Ned? At Joe's funeral, I mean ...'

Ned shifted on his stool and looked away. He wouldn't be drawn on his allegiances.

I persisted, on a new tack. I needed knowledge badly.

'What do you think of J.J. now?' I asked cautiously. I had to know if my version of the past was real. Ned rolled up admiring eyes. Under the yellow hair the flesh of his face was flat and hard.

'Oh J.J. is top dog now Pat, fair play to him. There's no holdin' him. He has it all stitched up.' He recited this proudly, as if we were all riding the wave of J.J.'s success. Then he winked, and muttered from the corner of his mouth, 'I only come in here to annoy him.'

I was lost again. 'How d'you mean?' He gave a start of comic surprise. The way he used to look years ago when I was ignorant of something he thought was common knowledge.

'Sure, he owns this place!' he said wonderingly. 'Did you not know that?'

The nods and hints. Hushed respect. I knew it alright. I just hadn't realised I knew it.

I took a long pull on the bitter stout, swallowing my innocence.

'He's looking after the ... the arrangements for me.' Ned was non-committal, pouring his bottle. I knew he was taking it in. My tongue was loosening.

'I believe Tim Brophy wants to enlarge his own farm.' I began. Ned choked over the rim of his glass and began to wheeze with mirth.

'What's the matter?' I demanded angrily. I was feeling foolish again.

'Brophy hasn't an inch of land to his name. He leases them few acres along the river.'

'Who owns it then?' I asked hotly, although I knew the answer now.

Ned looked at me again in wonder and pity.

'Who do you think?'

We moved to another pub where we could talk, and Ned told me of the factories promised to Kilnamon. Development was on the way. John Joe was buying up land to build houses in the expected boom. He reckoned he'd be building suburbs along the river in five years time. He'd be into national politics by then too. Uncle Joe wouldn't sell him an inch although John Joe bought all round him.

'I suppose you'll sell, Pat?' Ned asked gloomily. 'Why wouldn't you. There's nothin' doin' around here.'

I knew then I was going to dig my heels in. Obstruction was the best weapon against power. Perhaps it was the alcohol but I felt a sweet lump of obstinacy where my soul should have been.

I wanted to see my farm again. I stood in a new relation to it now; there was freedom as well as fear. I couldn't stay in the old borstal of a house though. I hadn't the nerve for that yet. But I could take a room here in town and go out tomorrow … early.

The thought of booking a room in a hotel, just like that, suffused me with the real, intoxicating taste of possession.

PURE NATURAL HONEY

He fell off her old bike near Luggala. No damage done, it was at a standstill anyway. A lady's model, a rusty, black high-Nelly without gears. Mike was trying to cycle it up the ferociously steep road above the Guinness Estate.

Síle stood leaning on slightly more modern handlebars and watched him with delight. She mopped perspiration and drowning midges from her face, shook back a sunlit mass of curly, brown hair. She looked like an ad for healthy living. Mike was much too vivid to be wholesome as he wrestled with the hill, so black-haired, blue-eyed, young and alive that there had to be badness in him somewhere.

His old Volvo had taken these Wicklow hills without strain the day he picked her up hitching to Dublin a month ago. He wore a neat, grey business suit then, white shirt and tie and serious leather shoes. At first glance he so resembled a solicitor that Síle felt like a throwback to the hippies. There were sinister objects, vague plastic torsos, on the back seat. He produced a smile so unexpectedly bright that she tingled with shock. The farmers and businessmen who gave lifts to Síle – she was tall, tangle-headed with clear skin, full lips and a striking wide-eyed face – were always predictable in their manner. Never objectionable, just shades of ordinary. But this one radiated a magnetic sense of energy and humour, barely suppressed; a lively actor playing an accountant.

Síle had her stylised country clothes on against the weather as she hitched; black broad-brimmed hat, brown hand-knit scarf, tweed waist-coat, lumberjack shirt, jeans and boots, and a good deal of her own handmade jewellery too. She knew she'd overdone it a bit but she felt pleasantly exotic in an old-fashioned way as his neatly cuffed wrist with a severely digital watch changed gears beside her knee.

He looked fit and slim to her appraising eye, no rugby or gaelic brawn; if he played football he'd score quick, clean soccer-goals. For the first time in months Síle was sharply aware of her own singleness. She searched for space to stretch long legs. He glanced in approval, 'Pull back the seat.' She saw plenty of strong, white teeth, an intelligent mouth – and he hadn't dived across her to find her seat-belt.

'Scenery or speed?' The car hesitated slightly at the junction before choosing the mountain road to Dublin.

'Do you live around here?' He began to be predictable, 'You don't sound local.'

'Quite close.' Careful, against her instinct, not to give too much information. 'You don't sound local either.'

'Just moved down! I love it though it's a long drive to Dublin, but I don't go every day.'

'Neither do I – I work at home mostly.'

'Me too! I've a terrific house. I'm modernising it.' Their eager information overlapped, broke off in laughter.

'What do you do? No let me guess. You're ...' he studied her quizzically and the car wandered, '... you're a potter!' He slapped the steering wheel straight and laughed, not unkindly, as if he knew her well already. 'Or a poet! You could easily be a poet, all that hair – and dressed for the imagination, as well as the road.'

'If that's how it works, you must be a computer-programmer,' she put him in his place. 'No, I'm not a poet – though I wouldn't mind. I'm not a weaver either, by the way. It's my turn to guess. You're some kind of engineer; or is it pharmaceuticals?'

'Pretty good, you must be a gypsy! I design special projects for the countryside,' he ad-libbed gleefully. 'Jails, abattoirs, schools, morgues.'

'Oh God, I'll walk, so.' The car breasted the ugly tree line and she stared entranced as the mountains flooded the morning with banked-up waves of colour. 'This is why I live in Wicklow.'

'Me too!' he agreed. 'I love all that space. The imagination can breathe ... and I'm not an engineer. I'm a kind of' – he pretended to wince 'well, a sculptor actually. You'd hate my work though; it's all plastic and steel, and viciously modern.'

He was full of self-mocking relish, 'Anyone who weaves or knits or hurls pots hates me!'

'Sculpture? Is that it in the back?'

'God no! Display-models for fashion-shops! That's just business. They're always looking for something different, so I sell them squares and cubes and it seems to suit them. Clothes aren't made for human beings anymore.'

'Neither is your sculpture by the sound of it. I work in fashion-design by the way. For people, not robots. No, don't apologise, I know the sector you mean – though I don't think I'd care to cater for something I didn't approve of!' She looked at him sternly, amazed to be so intimate, and then smiled at the consternation on his face. 'All my work is traditional,' she explained. 'At least, the materials are. Though I try to do something original with them – if I think it's an improvement that is. I'm still a student, so I'm working at various things – fabric, fashion jewellery. At the moment I'm designing furniture for a diploma-project; I'm bringing the chair designs up to town today, and I'll be finished then, free …'

'Furniture? I'm doing my house and studio. Can I see?' He brought the car to an impulsive halt on the verge and turned towards her.

Funny, she didn't feel a bit nervous in a lonely lay-by with him, just defensive about her work. 'I told you it's very traditional,' she warned. 'Nothing sophisticated, but they're solid and they work, and anyone could have them in a house beside the TV or the dishwasher. That was my brief, and I believe in it too. Okay?' she challenged.

'Okay,' he agreed absently. 'Lets see. Mm, nice drawing for a start anyway – I could never draw.' He studied her artist's impressions with lively appreciation, and then turned busily to detail.

Síle turned away, suddenly embarrassed that he had her so easily in the palm of his hand. Was he laughing at her? Unsettling too to see her work appraised with such detachment as if it were a business proposition. Until now she had traded among friends and fellow-students. This guy was intriguingly different, but she was annoyed that she had delivered herself to him for judgement. He was definitely younger than her, probably no experience of design at all.

She peered at her drawing again; not much at first to distinguish it from a traditional wooden chair of the more elaborate kind with a round, inlaid seat and a semi-circular back-support projecting forward in two sturdy arm-rests. She'd emphasised all those characteristics, and then altered the proportions for a more – well, rakish appearance. These chairs looked as if they were ready to dance and only waiting to be asked.

The motifs to be carved on the wood were semi-original ideas; they meant to imply motion, a difficult thing with something as stable as a chair. Síle felt confused. He was still studying them, as if memorising the design, or was he composing something plausible to say?

She turned to look up at Tonelagee, the sun now kindling the heather to golden warmth, and she seized on the memory of the heart-shaped lake up there, hidden except to those who made the effort to walk up the mountain.

'Ever been up to Lough Ouler?' He interrupted her solitude.

'Yes, often, I was just thinking of it. Well, do you like the chairs?'

'Definitely! Respectable without being genteel. I hate smugness, don't you? I can imagine elderly aunts being tempted to too much sherry in those. There's a sense of discreet sin about the shape.'

'Is there?' Síle was amused. 'That doesn't sound like me. When I sin I'm not a bit discreet – I get carried away.'

She stopped, embarrassed again; she didn't usually get carried away quite so soon. 'Sounds interesting!' he encouraged innocently with wide-open eyes. She noticed again their compulsive colour.

Probably no bluer than ordinary eyes really – it must be the vivid way they caught the mountain light that brightened them. She found herself laughing with him, as if they knew something between them that no one else knew.

The other thing about his eyes was the way they distracted attention from the rest of his face, as if they were compensating for a plainness, which of course he didn't suffer from at all. He was too dangerous to be left driving around picking up romantic young women and setting them down again as if they were shapes in clear plastic for displaying garments. Síle was veering towards indiscretion and steadied herself for whatever he might do next.

What he actually did was fold the drawings carefully, hand them to her, gaze up Tonelagee with narrowed eyes and murmur, 'Terrific site for a hotel up there!' Then he started the car and drove away. She was relieved, not only that he hadn't made a pass at her and put her in the difficult position of refusing the desirable, but also because she'd have been bitterly disappointed by such predictability. Particularly after he'd liked her chairs.

She was used to being pursued, but how to pursue? Did he live on his own, that was crucial.

'Do you live on –' lost her nerve '– on the main road?'

'No, up the back behind Annamoe. I can be on the hills in minutes from my door!'

'Lovely! Do you get out much?'

'Not until the studio is finished. I know the hills pretty well though – I used to belong to a mountaineering club in college.

'Hey!' An idea struck him. 'Maybe we could do some walking together!' He turned towards her, beaming with pleasure, and the car almost left the road. 'Look out!' she cried, and threw her hands up in fright.

He fell off the bike again trying to force it straight uphill. Then he got smart and began to zig-zag; a wobble at each verge and a horizontal lurch across the road and back. He might make it that way, but it would take at least a week. A sheep popped its head over the wall agog with critical alarm. He wobbled the wrong way in response and plunged back towards her.

'Let's leave the bikes here at Pier Gates,' Síle pleaded, 'you'll never get to the Sally Gap. We can walk down by the lakes here and up Knocknacloghoge instead – save Lough Ouler for another day.'

'Okay, you'd need the muscles of a postman to pedal this.'

'It belonged to a District Nurse,' Síle scoffed. 'She used to overtake motor cars. You haven't got the legs for it.'

He stretched long, fine limbs for her inspection. 'Are they up to walking do you think?'

Plunging downhill at the half-walk, half-trot the slope requires he caught her swinging hand and closed his own around it.

'In case I get lost,' he confided.

'Get lost!' she parodied, but she held on tight and gazed with absurd contentment at the quiet lake below, a fringe of forest along the near shore, then a sandy beach and the big house behind it guarded by steep slopes, a boulder field along the far side, and above it a huge, hanging mass of rock. Out of all that tranquil enclosure the lake drained south along a green valley-floor between tawny slopes of heather and fern. A second lake, Lough Dan, was partly visible a mile away surrounded by low hills that rolled lazily away on every side without any of the crowding steep-ness of a mountain-range.

'Isn't it beautiful?' she sighed, feeling sentimental and apt. 'It's got everything – trees, water, rock, heather, sand ...'

'Midges,' he slapped busily at himself. Síle was above minor irritations; only something volcanic or nuclear would disturb her now. She pointed across the valley with her free hand. A small area of hillside lay softly lined with ridges and furrows, blurred by heather, almost re-absorbed into the earth.

'Lazy-beds, the remains of old potato-drills. Look at the colour and texture! If you could knit it or weave it just as it is!' she teased longingly. 'Plastic will never mean anything rich like that.'

'Of course it will, when we've lived in a plastic world long enough – then it'll be quite normal ...

'Look,' he continued briskly, getting it straight, 'you see things in a different way to me, Síle.' For a terrible moment she thought he meant something more important than the view. 'I mean, we both love the oaks and all that, and we hate the creepy dullness of the conifers, but in a way I walk to get *above* the claustrophobia of the earth and the bog. Sorry if it sounds pretentious, it's not meant to. I don't look at my feet. Sometimes the ground hems me in with its gravity; it's full of memories and promises of – of decay.'

She was staring with profound anxiety and interest, and he laughed nervously at himself. 'Don't get me wrong! I agree the mountains are lovely, that's why I'm out, well, part of the reason.' He grinned and blushed but didn't stop. 'You like the density and the texture of the mountains Síle. You'd like to wrap them around you like tweed or a plaid rug, but when I look at the hills I like to see space, not substance. I don't think it's the way most people look. To me the landscape sort of gets in its own way sometimes. You know those photographs with huge hunks of geology and vegetation stuffing the frame? I find that boring, even if the colours and textures are ... interesting. D'you think I'm a philistine?'

He watched her worriedly and at the vigorous shaking of her head he plunged on: 'What I like is lots of shifting sky shaped by the profile of the landscape. Wicklow is very friendly that way; it's so rounded and open it lets the sky through in great curves and arcs. A tent of light. And I love the way the lakes reflect it, and make a full circle –'

He seized another strand, '– I'm the same with houses and buildings, I sort of look past them and in between. There's plenty of people concerned with the density of things. I think it's really important to appreciate the spaces – the way light is allowed to make its own designs. It doesn't happen at all in Dublin because it's flat and sort of *tight*; if I had to live in a city I'd definitely go for New York.'

'I see ...' Síle broke the flow. 'Town-planning as sculpture.'

'Well, that *is* what I try to do in my work. I know you haven't seen it yet, but that's *it*! It's always groups of objects arranged so that I can emphasise the spaces between them. The trouble is, it results in draining the objects of any meaning in themselves, otherwise they'd take over; you know, as if letters and numbers were just the limits to the space between the ink and meant nothing more than that. See what I mean?' He bounded in front of her waving his arms vigorously. 'Think of a number, take your own age, twenty-three; I bet you've never examined the shape of that space between the two figures before! Or your name; you make extra-ordinary patterns between the letters every time you write it. Why shouldn't that be important? I'm trying to liberate that space.'

Síle's hand had cooled by now, and her heart was steady with caution. Was he garrulous – or actually inspired in some hectic way? It was very important that he should not be a sham. She still hadn't seen any of his real work. His house was empty while he rebuilt the big attic as a working space. She was impressed by the enthusiasm of the project, but she needed hard evidence as to what he was. She needed to see his work.

'Maybe you can see my problem now, with the sculpture I mean? People say it's all very well, but they want to buy *objects* – they don't want to spend money on *space* which they feel they own already! Now if I could make objects that were both valid in themselves *and* definitions of space I'd be on a winner.'

'Make a chair!'

'A chair? A Chair! Why a *chair*?'

'It'll give you discipline in structure.' Síle was very firm.

'Good furniture is unobtrusive; it's sort of invisible in a way, and yet it defines a room. You can concentrate all you want on the spaces and shapes within a chair – but if it doesn't work as a seat then it's worse than useless. Burn it! There's nothing worse than a chair that doesn't work … except maybe a jug that dribbles. Oh, and that's another idea; I don't want to set you up as a craft-centre, but you could design all sorts of pots and jugs that make fantastic statements with the space between them – everybody knows the urn/faces trick – but if they don't pour properly, I'll take a hammer to them.'

'A chair!' He sneezed it quietly again, 'Could I make yours, Síle?'

'Mine? Of course! I'd love to see it made. Can you do all that stuff, wood-turning, carpentry? That's real craftsmanship. Much harder than sculpture.' She grinned.

'Just leave it to me!' He grabbed her hand again, his bright face full of restored confidence.

Mike threw the door open and she walked into his studio screwing up her eyes. She was ambushed again by the vigorous light inside the attic.

There was no sign of rafters, roofing-felt, or the underside of slate. The white room was full of long windows angled across the hilltops at the sky. Bright surfaces and mirrors intensified the daylight; like passing through a door into foreign weather.

The room was empty still; he'd been working on her chairs. She looked around for the dark, rich wood. Mike was silent for once, and then she realised – they were there. She was looking right through them.

A gasp of disbelief and she turned a withering glare on him. He quailed but managed a weak grin. She strode across the room, heels hammering the bare floor. Her chairs alright – but pale, transparent ghosts of her intention, not timber at all, but a thick see-through substance moulded smoothly onto a thin steel frame; a parody of texture – what had he done there? For she saw that the chairs were indeed the colour of some strange kind of wood; a subtle stain had been added to the plastic, and there were traces of texture too, at random; one seat had the undeniably natural grain of wood, though when she felt the surface there was nothing there. Then she saw the mandala from a child's marble embedded within the ghost of a knothole, and she understood the trick – the textures and the marble were all inside, pressed onto internal layers.

The seat of the second chair had hints of fine, old lace in it and a blurred corduroy imprint too as if someone had thought of sitting in it while it was still soft. She ran a fingernail across the furrows and ridges. 'Lazy-beds,' he reminded nervously, but there was nothing there on the surface except that infuriatingly funny blandness. And there was a sense of, well, of exposure about the glassy chair. She had a disconcerting flash of someone – herself? – sitting naked except for a see-through plastic mac, seen from behind drinking gin?

Mike was still grinning at her, his eyes held the only deep colour in the room, his expression a blend of enquiry, apology, affection and sheer cheek. She knew she was being, not ridiculed or parodied, but laughed at? No, it wasn't that either, and whatever it was she was beginning to mind less as he smiled at her. He simply couldn't resist statement, like the day at Luggala. There it was, embedded in the thick arm-rests of the chairs, that day again – strands of moss, heather, blades of grass, leaf-imprints, and somehow as well a stitch-motif from the Aran jumpers he detested.

But the joke was on him, for the whole thing was beginning to work, in detail if not quite in total. It gave character to the vacant plastic. She followed the exquisite footprints of a bird small as a wren around the rim of a seat until it took flight. It was so meticulously done that it revealed his respect for the materials he satirised as clearly as if she had found a scrapbook of pressed flowers under his bed.

And the colour too, a kind of tawny, golden transparence owed more than a nod of submission to wood. She returned again to a tiny tuft of moss, a few blades of grass, a quartz pebble and a twig or two, arranged so that between them they conjured up a whole landscape; and something warm and permanent – the rhapsody of the scene, settled into her heart.

Mike nudged her attention impatiently downwards. He tilted the chair to show how the legs had been moulded to her design, but as she bent closer she saw that he had infiltrated a joke in the form of tiny labels into the mixture, so that the carved sections of the legs now resembled slender bottles and jars stacked on top of each other. The labels were transparent of course – strings of old fashioned print just beneath the surface.

A plumply tubular section near the seat read Pure Natural Honey, and she giggled helplessly because the smooth plastic with its delicate, mellow stain did indeed look fit to spread on bread – home made brown of course. There was even an uncanny trace of something like honey-comb stirred in. Just below it, the next section was labelled Vintage Cider Vinegar; the same colour was equally apt and the taste of honey turned apple-sharp and sour in her mouth. He'd caught her lifestyle exactly, for another label announced Twelve Year Old Whiskey and without effort the rich substance glowed amber.

There was lemon tea as well, complete with rind, and a plain section of leg at the floor that contained either wine or urine – but the two words, and samples, were so remarkably similar that she didn't dwell on that, in case he was taking the p ...

'Okay,' she surrendered, stifling laughter. 'Okay, you win; though I wouldn't sit in one! I don't see why you changed the shape.' She pointed at the D-shaped seat and a missing arm, 'was the symmetry too much for you?'

He danced in front of her, beaming with relief and pride, grabbed a chair and swung it between them. He sat down solidly, braced his left arm on the single arm-rest, grabbed a sketch-pad to his knee, and with elaborate motions showed how he could sketch freely without any obstruction to his right elbow. It made devastating sense.

'That' s all very well for you!' Síle fought to the end, 'but it's selective design. One-offmanship! What about me – I'm left-handed?'

'I know! And this is the Ciotóg-model; this is *your* chair!' He pressed her into the other one, taking a delicate liberty while he did so and she found her left arm unrestricted while her right was supported. The opposite to his.

He thrust the sketch-pad at her, drew his chair across and placed it down beside her. The cutaway sides of the seats butted perfectly together, while the two interrupted back-rests now made a continuous arc. It was an intimate double-seat. Síle slapped her forehead; she had just spotted the purpose and the punch-line. As they sat pressed warmly together, he slid his arm along the joint backrest and tightened it round her shoulders, 'We're arm-chair mountaineers!'

'Wait a second, hold on –' she was still a designer, 'what about a normal couple, right-handers, how will they get on?'

'Who cares?' He shrugged her firmly against him. 'Let them make their own chairs.'

WALKER SPUR

Always a revelation, every season, that first view of the Alps, impossibly elegant, the evening spires gilded with alpenglow; or black, triangular teeth in the morning slicing a high, icy dawn. Once she saw them in moonlight, the moon itself a galleon of light sunk behind the reef of the Aiguilles so that a misty shadow, notched and crested, haunted the night sky above Chamonix.

And though she had climbed the cleanly equilateral face of the Blaitière and found it wanting in quality, the mountain still projected an image of tapered perfection. And the comb-crested facets of the Peigne, just to the right looked as solid and pure as if the scree-chutes of the hidden descent were a spillage from some limestone memory.

She looked up with perplexity at the Frendo Spur, a great climb, her first in the Aiguilles, its ethereal snow-ridge supported on a springing pillar of rock and soaring above into a high horizon of light. She remembered tottering there once, below the final rocks, hammering her trembling legs down into the deep post-holes kicked in the snow by a hundred other feet, feeling the rush of falling space sucking her down, so that she leaned forward in the footsteps and thought she saw her own wild-eyed face reflected in the blind mirror of the snow. The first cable-car to the summit swung through the air a few hundred yards away and she wept for the barred security of that cage.

Now she could approach that single memory from many points of view: perched on the exalted rib of ice, a cage-bird terrified by freedom; looking back from the swinging box of the cable-car at a minute crumb of life on the knife-edge of eternity; and standing here on the edge of town, transported through five years and five thousand feet of space by the dizzy flight of the first escape.

Climbing had not become any easier after that, but she got used to the pain. It was a matter of perspective, realising that even the harshest moment would have an aftermath of relief.

Cathy was tall and lightly built, with a sense of concentrated strength about the shoulders, a kind of muscular grace. Unruly black hair was drawn back with severe practicality in a Doris Lessing bun, but now stray wisps and curls framed an expression that was radiant with arrival. She heaved her rucksack off the pavement and trudged on after her companion towards the familiar campsite.

Her elation was rebuffed by Peter's silence and a profile that seemed more than usually tightened by lines of age and fatigue. He had said very little while contemplating the Aiguilles. It was his first time back since a serious accident put him out of alpinism for four years. His partner died in a fall on the Eckpfeiler and Peter was slow to recover from his own injuries. But he had been climbing steadily at a good standard for more than a year now, and his ambition – with a chill undertone of vindication – was to return to the Alps and make up for lost time.

'Weather must be good; there's not much snow about.' His voice carried none of the enthusiasm good conditions should induce. It might be travel-weariness, but to Cathy's disappointment it sounded more like depression. On the occasions when they climbed together she recognised that Peter's attitudes to mountains and to climbing were completely different from her own. She was a romantic, and felt as if all the imagination and fantasy of the long winter was about to be realised now among the mountains that crowned the whole horizon. Peter glumly tried to see them as three-dimensional topos to be climbed via cracks, corners and slabs with clearcut techniques and grades. But there was a dark side to his vision, which, if it predated the accident might even have caused it: sometimes mountains terrified him though he would not define the fear. Cathy visualised it as something like the brooding menace in Victorian mountain pictures.

'Remember that day on the Midi-Plan? I think it was the best day I've ever had here,' she said cheerfully, trying to revive an occasion that scintillated with laughter and light, a rebel crystal in the past. It was the last day of her first season and they raced along the snow-ridge that divides the human habitat of Chamonix, its forested slopes, alpine meadows, and granite walls from the glacial smother of the Vallée Blanche. A single day that might be the only reason she was here with Peter again

'Will I ever forget?' he said ruefully. 'I thought the Envers Glacier was going to avalanche any minute and sweep us down to Montenvers like surfers. All that fresh snow. The Grandes Jorasses was wiped out.'

He lapsed into a contemplative silence and she caught a chill reflection of what that polished day had meant to him: the Walker Spur on the Grandes Jorasses, buttressing a remote corner of the sky, clad in the white rags of its own bad weather. *That* was where Peter had wanted to be, straddling that vast rock-rib, the greatest climb in the world. Not plodding along a snow-saunter with a novice.

She was barely aware of its existence then, and the pleasure of a perfect day had remained intact until she looked inwards now and discovered with a shock of recognition the same Walker Spur standing out in sharp relief against the background of her own ambition. She tasted briefly the sour flavour of Peter's point of view, and felt diminished as the Midi-Plan, the Frendo, the Dru, the Gervasutti Pillar, Route Major, shrank in status from unique experiences to mere reconnaissance trips for one great climb. The Walker Spur was the secret they were both harbouring silently – he like a grievance or a wound, and Cathy like a hidden talent.

They trudged out along the forest-road towards the squalor of Snell's Field, heavy boots dragging through the gravel, slouching under the weight of rope-hooded sacks, and buffeted by the constant blast of passing cars. Under the grime and sweat Cathy's face flickered with suppressed excitement.

'Fancy a crack at the Walker?' she remarked breathlessly to the downcast profile.

The expression cleared slowly, a cloud drifting aside to let sunlight filter in.

'Well there's not much snow about,' he responded, nodding thoughtfully.

Two days later they were on the North Face of the Dru. It was early August, the weather had been stable for several weeks and conditions were good – very little ice in the cracks and the snow-ledges clear. Peter went into overdrive, the confidence of a man who had forgotten how brutal a mountain can be. He wanted to travel light, hammer the route in one day. Cathy refused. She was not a fast climber, she argued, disdaining to imply that he would hardly be a speed-merchant himself after four years' absence. And anyway, it was no harm to get used to carrying a bit of weight.

So they bivouacked on big ledges a few hundred feet above the start. Climbing solidly from dawn the following day they struggled out onto the Quartz Ledges below the summit well after dark. They were both exhausted, but Peter had suffered a psychological deflation as well. They swapped the lead after every pitch, except once low down, when Cathy opted out of a wet chimney with a twenty-foot icicle jammed in the back. She acknowledged immediately that blunt male arrogance was the most effective weapon to force that kind of problem, and was rewarded for her good sense by the next pitch, an exposed ramp and a fine, steep crack. Having climbed with a wide variety of partners over the years – including continentals – Cathy had no neuroses about ethics. She clipped gratefully into pegs whenever they presented themselves, and climbed free when that seemed logical. Peter was impressed by her steadiness, and embarrassed by his own lack of it. He was way out of touch with alpinism. Her experience was particularly obvious in route-finding; she seemed to know instinctively where to go, while he felt totally lost in a vertical wilderness of ribbed and seamed rock. The route was twice as long as he expected, and a good deal harder.

On the summit bivouac he devoured the extra food Cathy had insisted on carrying, and that irony was not lost on him either. She was wrapped in the light sleeping-bag she always brought, while he tried to hide his shivers in an anorak and over-trousers.

Seeing him stare silently into the darkness in the direction of the Brenva Face of Mont Blanc and the Eckpfeiler buttress where the accident had stamped its epitaph on his past, Cathy realised they didn't know each other at all. Hers was a silent alpine career; she certainly didn't publicise it herself, and not being attached to any particular scene or climbing group, no-one else knew the full scope of her achievements. She climbed mostly with men to whom she was introduced casually; occasionally they didn't even speak a common language. People who did hear of her ascents usually assumed she was a second anyway, not a leader in her own right.

Cathy enjoyed climbing with Peter at home because it was unusual to find a man who didn't want to use her for some purpose or other. Some were looking for romance or sex with their climbing, many wanted a perpetual second, some felt their own climbing contrasted impressively with a woman's. Peter seemed to want someone who didn't talk a lot, and was free, like himself, midweek. They both worked weekends and this kept them at a distance from the normal climbing scene which conducted its initiations, graduations, assassinations, and post mortems on Saturdays and Sundays.

She couldn't resist a curious question. 'What's it like to be back, Peter?'

'Not great' he admitted honestly, after a long silence. 'Not worth freezing for anyway.'

'Still,' he shivered and pulled himself together, 'we have to pretend, haven't we? I mean you have to admit the futility of it all, it's obvious – and still believe in the value of it at the same time. It's a kind of juggling, keeping two contradictions in the air at the same time. I feel if I told the truth about mountains I'd never bother to climb another one, but then the illusion of value is worth believing in for the sheer beauty of the defiance. It's a myth, but it's a mighty one.'

'Defiance?' She recoiled in bewilderment thinking of the serene aesthetics of the faces ranged around them in the night. 'I thought the great thing about climbing is that it gets you away from all that kind of thing.'

A week, two more routes, and two minor storms later, they tramped up the Leschaux Glacier towards the little hut perched like a tin drum on the moraine. The North Face of the Grandes Jorasses rose above them. More tiny pilgrims picked their way over the devastation of the glacier converging on the hut. Peter was fretting over details, the forecast, the amount of snow, bivouacs, food.

To Cathy it all seemed simply impossible. You couldn't climb that blank, overpowering pillar that thrust into the sky as if it was about to blast off into a bigger, purer universe. But she was going to climb it. She knew. Two days later she intended to stand, invisible from here, an angel on the head of that four-thousand foot pin.

Heart and head filled and reeled with awe at her own power. Peter was trying to forecast the best way up the glacier to the foot of the route. He fussed.

'There'll be footprints,' Cathy said absently. 'And head-torches.'

'If we leave the hut at two,' Peter calculated 'we should be on the route in a couple of hours. Before dawn anyway. And if we go like hell and we're lucky, we should be on top in a day.'

The hut was full; every new candidate for the Walker was greeted with a sardonic shrug by those already there. Such good conditions and a good forecast were rare – nobody would back down, even if their numbers cheapened the experience. The guardian, a young Frenchwoman, took Cathy aside and advised the Croz Spur instead. There was only one party going for the Croz while eleven parties were bound for the Walker, she said, rolling her eyes and r's dramatically. Cathy discussed it with Peter but he wouldn't hear of it. It was the Walker or nothing.

She felt the same. She gazed sadly up at the unearthly pillar glowing in the evening light and felt she would be just another acrobat in a circus troupe. And still she wanted it. Her instincts had been compromised.

They bivouacked below the hut but Cathy could not sleep. The air grew heavy and turgid, and the golden nails in the night-sky blurred and disappeared. The forecast was wrong. You could never forecast for the Walker: it made its own weather.

At about midnight it began to rain, fat heavy drops that penetrated the sleeping bags like little water-bombs. Draping their raingear over the bags they heard each other cursing and laughing in a kind of idiotic relief as rain soaked the tension into an anticlimax. They slept until dawn, when the sun shot up without the slightest trace of guilt. No one had ventured out of the hut. It was usual to start the climb either before dawn or else in the late afternoon in order to reach a bivouac on the face by nightfall.

As they ate a silent breakfast before descending to the valley a pair emerged hurriedly from the tin shack and headed up the glacier in the direction of the Spur. With surprise and interest Cathy recognised the weather-beaten rucksacks and old-fashioned gear of a central European couple who had sat solidly among the flashy crowd on the terrace the previous evening. Czechs or Yugoslavs, she thought. The square-faced, sensible looking woman spoke French and German readily to people near her.

Cathy got to her feet and began to pack, her back turned against the valley. A surge of nerves in her stomach constricted her breathing, but her face and voice were relaxed.

'We might as well go up,' she said.

They reached the frozen waves of crevassed ice at the foot of the face in two hours. Briefly the pillar appeared to Cathy like some great war-sculpture: a broad, bronze horse up-reared with hooves thundering against the sky. But that was Peter's style of paranoia she realised, and hoped that he could visualise himself as the masked rider standing up victoriously in the stirrups for the duration of the climb. Looked at coolly, she saw that the Walker Spur was like any other big rock-climb, a broken, foreshortened buttress lying back against the sky. Of course she could only see about a third of it, but that was a reassuring illusion in itself, and it certainly looked climbable: a short ice slope, a rock-step and a long stretch of easy ground below the first barrier of slabs.

Peter was striding ahead on the glacier, setting a punishing pace, obviously winding himself up to take a run at an obstacle. He was still sweating from his exertions when she caught him up at the foot of the ice.

'We'll have to move fast,' he grated. 'It's dangerous here at this time of day. There might be stone-fall.'

'Not half as dangerous as burning ourselves out. Relax, Peter, there's only one party ahead of us.'

He looked at her resentfully, feeling the criticism.

'We'll solo up until we hit something technical,' he ordered, producing his ice axe. He had opted stubbornly to carry the little Terrordactyl with its outrageously drooped pick, which had been unjustifiably popular during his last season.

Cathy would have preferred to rope up, but she didn't want to aggravate the tension, and there was a reassuring chain of steps cut up through the little ice-field. Peter moved up without gloves so that he could use the steps as handholds too. He struck at the ice above his head with the Terrordactyl, and uttered a sharp howl of pain. A little knob of ice had trapped his thumb against the handle, and the force of the impact ripped away the nail at one side. A jagged edge of nail like a broken shell stuck out at the side of the thumb, and little globes of blood dripped and dissolved on the ice. It was the kind of injury to take to a doctor if it happened at home; here there was nothing to do but swear and continue climbing.

There were flat ledges above the ice, and a rock-bulge with a short jamming-crack running through it. It was grade IV, but as Cathy dropped her sack on the ledge to take out the rope she saw Peter, to her great annoyance, attempt to solo it. She was about to express her exasperation forcefully when he stepped back down cursing his injured hand. He tied onto the rope and clipped into a peg for protection with the expression of a man going to the gallows rather than a mountaineer embarking on the route of a lifetime. She had seen that expression before on the faces of strangers who found themselves committed to something above their ability, but with Peter it was different: he simply didn't believe in what he was doing. He was here out of bravado or defiance, not desire.

Above, there was a long stretch of mixed ground, awkward scrambling on broken rock embedded in ice. They moved together, the rope between them, Peter still leading. Gradually Cathy's awe at the overwhelming situation relaxed into confidence and she began to catch up on Peter, taking in coils of rope as she went. The guttural Europeans were only a short distance ahead. They were climbing in pitches, the man leading and belaying every hundred feet until his partner reached his position, when he surged forward again.

Cathy saw that Peter's headlong momentum derived from his determination to pass the other pair. She wondered what he was going to do for route-finding when he found himself in the lead – he was certainly no Cassin – but she stifled the sour thought.

Soon Peter passed the woman as she stood on a ledge belaying her partner, and a minute later Cathy drew level with her. She was about forty with a cheerful weather-beaten face, wide-set grey eyes, and big, white teeth. She grinned amiably as Cathy saluted her in French. The woman answered in English and chuckled at Cathy's surprise.

'Where are you from?' Cathy called curiously.

'We are Romanian,' came the proud answer. 'You are English, yes? American?'

Cathy cleared her throat. There was something emotionally charged about the encounter, two remote countries meeting in this spectacular place.

'I'm Irish,' she shouted back a little more loudly than was necessary. The other woman beamed a delighted understanding. She pointed at Peter churning ahead.

'He is good, yes?' she asked. 'You will be okay with him?'

Cathy understood. The Romanian woman automatically assumed she was simply a passenger being guided up the mountain by the man in the lead. She felt a great surge of affection for the cheerful woman, below her now. She wanted to shout, 'He's not bad, but I'm a lot better than he is.' Instead she only smiled, said 'Good Luck' with a kind of despairing warmth, and swarmed on after Peter.

They arrived together at the toe of an immense buttress of bulging slabs. The scale was vaster than anything Cathy had faced before. Her courage shrank. The parallel pillar of the Croz Spur rose on the right, another column of the proscenium arch, while the snow-hushed theatre of the Vallée Blanche waited for the tiny climbers to give the performance of their lives.

Cassin had arrived here in 1938 from Italy, never having seen the area before, and had marched straight up this mighty pillar without a pause.

1938 she thought in an agony of amazement, contemplating the apparently impenetrable barrier above; this was 1983, they had every conceivable climbing tool and technique at their command now, and it still seemed impossible.

Peter was consulting the description nervously. Then he was off again, a rising traverse leftwards, searching for the key to the barrier above. Wait till we get to the real climbing, Cathy thought grimly. She was reasonably content to let Peter dash about now on this easyish terrain if it kept his mind and his nerves occupied.

An uncertain shout ahead started her moving again along a lip of ice that lay against the rock. Peter was belayed at the foot of a steep groove. He had spotted a piton higher up.

'I *think* this must be it,' he muttered doubtfully. 'I'll go up and have a look.'

'That's okay, it's my turn,' Cathy said reassuringly.

'Are you sure?' He wore a troubled expression.

'No problem. If it doesn't work out I can always lower off that peg.'

She began stepping delicately up the steep shallow groove, bridging deftly between small holds and tiny ribs. It was a technique she developed to a high degree when she didn't trust the strength in her arms, and learned to let her feet do most of the work.

Peter scrambled up, wincing silently when his thumb touched the rock. They wandered erratically up ledgy slabs until the walls closed in ominously above them, penetrated by the unmistakable Rebuffat Crack, where the hardest technical moves on the whole climb are located. Cathy took off her rucksack and sat down.

'I brought rock boots for this pitch,' she announced happily. Peter looked down at his great clumsy footwear, then up at the delicate, overhanging dièdre with its small, sloping holds. He sat down glumly and prepared to belay her.

Using the pegs in place it was not particularly difficult to swarm up the first crack, and then came the move of VI, a long step across on friction, off-balance, to a sloping hold. Peter found it desperate to follow. He blamed his thumb and his boots, justifiably enough, Cathy felt, and gave him a tight rope. With a flash of egotism Cathy wished the Romanian lady could have been on the ledge below.

They traversed on ice for several rope-lengths, and then up another section of broken rock towards the 75m dièdre. Cathy simply strapped her rigid crampons on tightly over her rock boots for the ice.

Peter looked on in appal, and when Cathy told him patiently it was a customary practise now for short sections of ice, he took on the righteous expression of one for whom alpinism would never be the same again.

When they reached the foot of the great corner Cathy whipped off her crampons and began to lead again. The crisp, golden granite gave beautiful climbing with the boot-heels constantly silhouetted against the chaotic glacier.

There was a moment of uncertainty on every belay as she silently offered Peter the option of leading through. He dragged with him a grizzled air of misery up onto the belays, which mingled with the smell of their sweat to generate a sense of depression. Cathy couldn't wait to be off again, springing elatedly up the superb rock.

Over and over again the resounding name of the climb rang in her head and once she seized a handhold, a solid flake of golden granite, and tried to shake it like a door-knocker as if she were attempting to stir the whole mountain, whispering fiercely to herself, 'This is the Walker Spur. The Walker Spur.'

She was afraid this might be a sign of delirium but suspected it was really a symptom of enormous happiness. There was the beautiful thrill of arrogance in doing all the hard work too.

At the top of the dièdre Peter decided to lead the slabs and traverse to the short abseil at the foot of the Black Slabs. He was slow but looked happier to be out in front and Cathy was content with the arrangement. The early evening sun was shining obliquely on the tilted towers above. They were looking for a suitable bivouac-ledge. A traverse led abruptly to a notch with a weathered hank of ropes hanging down diagonally towards a blocky pedestal.

With the querulous gaze of a blinkered rock-climber Peter was sizing up a traverse that avoided the well-known abseil.

'That looks okay across there. It avoids all that messing with the ropes and climbing back up again. I'll have a go at it.'

Cathy regarded him with surprise and dislike. 'Don't you think if it was a better way it would be in the guidebook,' she said pointedly. 'You're hardly the first to spot it. There must be some problem out there.'

'I'm going to give it a try,' Peter said obstinately. 'Looks okay to me, and it'll be quicker.'

He was obviously salving his ego in some private way and Cathy belayed herself with extra precaution. Peter edged out onto the slab and it was clear immediately that it was harder than it appeared. He fiddled some protection into a crack standing on his tiptoes on the bald rock and lurched across onto a sloping hold. He was committed now and could not return. His expression made it clear that he regretted his position, but he would not admit it.

Cathy's impatience gradually froze into anger as he tried ineffectually to step farther out on the slab. She concentrated on the mountains across the glacier, the rock reddening in the setting sun, and picked out the climbs she had done: the East face of the Réquin, Mer de Glace face of the Grépon, the Ryan-Lochmatter on the Plan; she had stitched her way up and down the seams of the Aiguilles without ever visualising the unity the complete ridge possessed. The real route over there, she grasped from this magnificent viewpoint, must be the complete traverse of the Aiguilles.

Her reverie was stamped out by the scrabbling of Peter's feet and a harsh cry as he skidded off the foothold and slid down the slab. The rope came tight with a jerk. There was no danger. Cursing hoarsely Peter swung back, she tossed him a loop of rope, and he dragged himself back to the ledge.

'Sorry about that,' he gasped. 'It's a lot harder than it looks.'

Cathy laughed. 'Depends on who's looking,' she told him cheerfully. There was no use getting upset, and suddenly she felt sorry for Peter, out on a limb in his climbing and out of depth in his feelings.

Above the abseil there was a small shelf carved out of an ice-ledge, large enough to seat two bodies with their feet hanging down in space. Cathy was determined to raise Peter's spirits to the level of the occasion – her own satisfaction depended on it too. She had great difficulty with her toilet arrangements in the confined space, whereas Peter could simply stand casually on the edge of the ledge.

Eventually she forced herself to abandon years of reticence and do something similar while he melted snow for the evening meal.

She remembered the absurd contortions she went through on previous mixed bivouacs, and managed to reduce Peter to a semblance of mirth describing some of the more embarrassing scenes.

Late light accented every needle-point in a sunset world. Two tiny climbers stood up like millimetre marks on a ledge on the Croz Spur; the sharp ridge of the Periades supported a row of barracuda teeth and the spire of the Aiguille du Midi pointed into the sky like an arrow poised for flight.

The second day unreeled a slow spool of tension and pain. Cathy postponed satisfaction and simply endured. This climb was too big to enjoy. It had to be fought for, and pleasure would come with success.

From midday onwards she was constantly in the lead. The weather held steady, a clear sky and dry rock. She felt her dazed thoughts emerge occasionally as staccato prayers: let the weather hold, let my strength hold out, let us get off today. Please let it get easier. But it never got easier, and sometimes it felt so hard she thought she must be off-route.

Peter staggered up the relentless rock towards every belay, his face white and strained, teeth gritted, cursing every hard move and shouting for a tight rope. Stripped of superiority, his illusions had caved in. Feeling him drag behind her like a brake, Cathy realised how easy it would be to hate someone. But when she saw the jagged pain of resentment in his eyes she realised with a shock it would be much easier for him to hate her. He was the one who had to swallow the bitterness of failure.

All through the morning and afternoon she hoisted her exhausted body upwards from hold to hold, up thin cracks, wet grooves, exposed ribs, and awkward chimneys, watching the distinctive sprawl of the pillar below her as it tumbled lazily into the blind labyrinth of the glacier, the distances so great that motion was meaningless. One particular pitch she had heard described as an icy overhang: 'Sometimes the hardest pitch on the route': It loomed askew in her imagination. Over-reacting to the ominous prose of the guidebook she dismissed all the technical problems she encountered as nothing to the doom-invoking overhang she expected above.

Of course that took some of the sting out of the lower difficulties, made the climbing more automatic, and when they finally reached the little overhang she laughed aloud in near-hysterical relief. It was easy in comparison to some of the pitches she had dismissed below. A couple of stretchy aid-moves and she reached over the bulge and thwacked the ice axe with deep satisfaction into a pocket of frozen snow. She was about to pull up strenuously on the axe handle when she realised with dizzying elation that this was the last of the major difficulties and felt an irresistible urge to celebrate. She clipped an étrier to the axe handle and, instead of the muscular lunge demanded by speed, she moved up luxuriously loop by loop enjoying the frivolity of the situation as she stepped regally over the bulge. As soon as she gained a ledge she whooped with uncontrollable delight. Nothing could stop them now.

'What was that in aid of?' Peter growled irritably. His hair was plastered to his forehead with sweat, his eyes were sunken and bloodshot over a grizzle of beard, and he looked like a stranger who had been hooked by the end of her rope as it fished in the depths.

'We're going to make it,' she yelled exuberantly, her voice cracking with strain. 'We'll be up in an hour or two.'

'Not we … you're going to make it,' he told her miserably. 'I haven't done anything.'

'Don't be ridiculous. You made all the moves too.' But the reassuring words sounded hollow in her own ears. She didn't believe them either. Climbing was about motivation, and if you didn't really want to be there then you didn't have it. But there was a thoughtful look in the stranger's eyes now, and his mouth was firm.

'He's telling himself he's done it,' Cathy told herself with a stab of amazement. On any other climb she would have dismissed the matter, believing a partner's reactions were his own business. But the Walker Spur was different. Maybe her instincts had been compromised, but she would not let this achievement be denied. Peter wouldn't need to tell actual lies to distort the truth in his favour.

'The Walker Spur … with Cathy,' she imagined him announcing quietly with his customary lack of detail which people took for honourable reticence, and they would all visualise Cathy being piloted up the mountain.

Well, not this time, she thought fiercely, as she began climbing again with renewed vigour. On the next ledge, as she waited for Peter, she began idly framing an article about the climb. And while she was at it she might set the record straight about a few other routes too. Why not begin at the beginning, as you stepped off the train, and caught the various visions of the Aiguilles; gilded with alpenglow in the evenings, raking the frozen sky in the morning, and there was that moonlit night …

THE PRIEST'S BREAKFAST

From below I'd seen him seated on top of Slievenadubber, hard and hunched as the statue of Ó Conaire in Galway's Eyre Square.

I ran steadily towards the summit, threading a path between the Holy Wells that name the mountain. Close up he bore no resemblance to that benign old storyteller; he had instead the hawkish look of a hill-farmer.

Had I scattered his ewes? Was it lambing-time? I was hill-running in Connemara, anxious not to antagonise. Gnarled hands clamping the knob of a stick, he sat astride a rock surveying time and the earth. Old eyes narrowed to focus on my arrival in running-shoes and shorts. Beneath us the sea, inland the Twelve Bens.

'Dia dhuit,' I offered nervously. He answered in the local gaelic, drawling consonants and vowels, jaws slack so the words came from further back. 'Dia's Muire dhuit. So you ran the mountain. You're not the first, a mhac. Sliabh na dTobar, the Hill of the Wells, has been raced before.'

'I suppose so. Hill-running is popular now.'

'Long before your time. Sagart is gréasaí.'

'Who won?' Sweat chilling, I was anxious to be off. Sagart is gréasaí had the slow echo of folklore, the priest and the shoemaker ...

I'd run for hours already, wild rocky ridges close to the coast, not a soul in sight – all day swooping under a dizzy sky while the smooth Atlantic shone and islands drifted on the skyline. Then Slievenadubber had drawn me on to the spiral of its well marked path. I ran past the village where I'd meant to stop, and began to climb. Only the parish calls it by name – to the rest of the world it's a spur on a Galway ridge. The path zigzagged the slope and crossed fourteen streams, or one stream fourteen times, the Stations of the Cross. The junctions were dug out and ringed with stones to serve as Holy Wells. Rough crosses stood askew beside them. On one June Sunday every year a procession prays at all the wells. I said no prayers, but the mystery of mountain pilgrims – some still barefoot on the screes of Croaghpatrick in neighbouring Mayo – stifled the running-pain.

The path was twice the length it looked, full of cunning detours to collect the wells, and the added length gave the feel of a high mountain. The people's summit was this hollow on the ridge where the old man sat and counted the rocky parish, its strip of shore, and the treacherous fishing-grounds beyond.

'Who won? There's no winning that kind of a race –'

'Dead-heat,' I offered in English. He made a literal joke of that harsh language, 'The two of them are dead anyway, and you may say they're feeling the heat too –' He pointed downhill, the stick sharp and steady as a rifle, 'It happened in the time of Father Clarke ...' Ignoring my wretched shivering, he faced into his story.

Father Clarke turned against his own people and bullied them body and soul. 'Foiréigean anama,' the old man called it, violence of the soul. He renewed the ancient march up the mountain, not from devotion, but as another form of spiritual aggression. The head of every household had to trudge behind the muscle-bound priest: men that spent all their days on the sea and the bog and the mountains, and could do with a Sunday's rest. Carrying the Blessed Sacrament Father Clarke headed his grim procession up Sliabh na dTobar and when he reached the top he would look down on his parish holding the Sacred Host on high in a show of power. No man dared cross him – until the shoemaker, that is – and indeed the priest had his own henchmen, the publican, the grocer, the teacher, the civic guard, to carry his power into the temporal sphere.

The shoemaker was a different class of man altogether, but he had his own devils too. He was reared beyond in the hills where there was no living to be had at all, but he was a great man to build anything or make a thing out of nothing and he got himself a name for work. He remained high up on the outskirts of the parish, out of the way of the village, until one night he tumbled off the mountain going after a clifted sheep and lay out for days before he crawled down, so that his injuries never mended and he was left with a twisted leg.

There was nothing for him but to move into the village and set up as a shoemaker, a trade he was known for, where he needn't stir abroad again. But he missed his free and active ways, and as he sat in his little shop chained to the boot-last he turned sour with the frustration of a spoiled life. He fell out with Father Clarke straight away on the matter of the Easter dues, but he was a great hand at the boot-making while the heavy priest was hard on footwear, so they needed one another to survive.

That's how it was until the priest got a housekeeper. She was a big, shamefaced lump of a girl with a soft look to her, and she was Father Clarke's own niece. She had been in trouble, and of course everyone knew what that meant. But it was nothing to the trouble she was in now, landed below to look after her uncle in all his ignorance and frustration. Of course there was no money for the job, no time off nor any benefits; it was a cross between a vocation and a penance. No one would talk to her either after her shame; it was a relief to the village to find someone lower than themselves. That was how bad he had them driven.

The only one who had a civil word for the woman was the shoemaker when she was in with her uncle's battered boots or passed the door where he huddled in the shadows. He'd call out to her kindly and shake his head at the bitter mystery of their predicament. The shoemaker had an eye for suffering, and he saw the wear and tear the silent girl was taking. Nor was he the only one who thought she was getting worse from her uncle than the fist.

Word went to the priest that his niece was friendly with the cripple. On the eve of the pilgrimage he brutally corrected that error in her ways, then sent her out to fetch his boots for the climb on the morrow. The shoemaker saw the bruises around her dull, tearless eyes – he smelled blood too, and he couldn't get a word or even a look out of the poor girl. He held the boots back for an hour to finish them. In the morning after Mass the congregation followed Father Clarke out of the chapel and up the hill – all but his housekeeper who was sent an hour before to reach the summit by the back side of the hill and have sustenance prepared on top. She had a little pot, a bottle of water, and a few sticks to boil a cup of tea for him after his exertion.

Father Clarke wore his vestments for the climb and he carried the Blessed Sacrament raised before him, gloved in its golden cloth like the fist of God. No one was ever allowed to pass him on the hill. He must lead his people to the summit as a sign of authority and power. The procession jostled along behind his rheumatic tread and with the terrible hysteria of oppression they jabbered rosaries at his bulging back. At the third Holy Well there was a change in the mumble, an excited buzz, and when the priest dipped the well and turned to spatter a blessing, he saw an unholy apparition lunging up the track behind.

The man was leaning on a crutch and vaulting forward with the power of his arms and shoulders while one leg swung uselessly and the other barely supported him on the ground. Veins stood out on his forehead and already his face was lathered in sweat. He caught the tail of the procession and the people fell back from him in mortal fear, but he passed them without a glance. Father Clarke held up the Host against the challenge as if it would fling him to the ground or strike him dead. The shoemaker came stumbling on. At the last moment he veered aside to pass the priest but the teacher took a cruel swing at his legs with a blackthorn stick. The cripple fell, tumbling over and over like a tripped hare. He lay still at last, face down at the side of the well, his thin ribs heaving.

The procession moved on in a hurry. As they passed the ruined creature some blessed themselves in terror, some aimed kicks, and one old widow at the very tail, with no hope at all of reaching the summit, scooped a little water from the well and shook it on his forehead. Then she dipped again and made him drink a drop from her hand.

The shoemaker heaved himself upright on the hillside. She spoke to him in soft Irish, urging him downhill to the empty village. He seized her stick, brushed her aside and lunged upwards again. A terrible grinding noise came from his teeth now, as if there was a broken engine in there driving him on. His eyes burned with a yellow rage and again the people cowered back. The shoemaker left the winding path and lurched straight up the rough hillside where he could not be stopped. At the sight of further challenge, the priest cursed, lengthened his stride and leaned into the hill.

His hob-nails rang with effort on the rocky path, and straightaway he bellowed in pain. He stumbled a few paces on his left boot, and then roared again. The shoemaker looked full across the hillside and his wild laugh rang out.

Nailing the new leather onto the boots he had planted two nails full in the centre of the soles, and with all the cunning of his trade had gauged their length and depth to penetrate under heavy pressure. That pressure was on.

To Father Clarke they were the bullets in his body, the spikes in the foot of the crucifix. They spurred him on to martyrdom. He must beat the godless shoemaker to the top and assert the force of the Church. He strode forward on the nails and began the race uphill against the devil.

They weren't running: neither man could run. The shoemaker hadn't the limbs, and the priest was bound up in vestments and pain. His feet were wrecked with varicose veins, and bad as the nails were he couldn't remove the boots and go on barefoot.

There was something so unholy in the spectacle of two mad men racing slowly that the people stood spellbound. All except the teacher. He lumbered after the shoemaker and made to fell him with a mighty blow to the head when the priest saw he was outstripped now by his own henchman and gave a strangled roar, 'Back! Get back!'

Curiosity overcoming their fear, the people pressed along the track behind the priest, keeping a distance in case he turned on them. The publican offered twenty to one on the cripple to anyone who'd take a long shot, but no one would bet against the strength of the priest who was sticking to the track and the Holy Wells, while the other man was taking all the rough ground, swinging uphill between his crutch and the widow's stick. You might have expected the people to be on his side – an unfortunate like themselves – but no. They were for the priest and every time the shoemaker toppled, or hit himself against a rock and opened up a new wound, they lifted a jeer against him.

They knew nothing of the boot-nails; they were only found later when the priest was stripped for the laying-out and the boots had to be dragged off his feet by a strong man, full as they were of blood-suction and nailed almost to the bone. Had they known in time they could have seized the publican's odds and cleaned him out.

For the shoemaker won the race.

The girl jumped to her feet as he breasted the ridge and lurched towards her in the summit hollow. She screamed once then ran to him. With one strong arm she stopped him in his final fall.

Pity turned to terror as the beaten priest, his vestments hemmed with blood, bore down upon her. At bay, here in this hollow, she sheltered the dying shoemaker, turning her blank, black eyes against her uncle. He raised the sacrament in his hands, aimed it at the pair and began to curse them from the depths of his power.

She screamed again, a different scream, dragged the crutch from the shoemaker's body, and swung it at the priest to stop the curse. It caught him full across the swollen throat, but she struck too late and the words gushed forth in blood, The curse was fully spoken.

I ... yes, yes, I – I was shivering with cold and loathing as the story stopped. Sweat lay icy on my skin, and mist swirled across the ridge to fill the hollow. The figure sat in silence looking down on the lost village.

'What happened?' Ragged hysteria in my voice, 'What happened to her?'

He made no sound but sat on, like a statue or a stone. I turned in terror, blind in the mist, and glimpsed the girl there, on her knees and burning eternally at the rock. With a bottle of water and the priest's kettle she was trying to quench her hell.

THE LUG WALK

John Paul asked Maria to marry him on the last stage of the thirty-three mile Lug Walk across the Wicklow mountains. He had just located Lough Firrib, in thick mist and rain, with some acute map and compass work. But the navigation wasn't quite as inspired as it might have appeared to Maria, since John Paul was covertly following the trough of footprints, some ten feet to the side, left by the ninety-two other participants in the walk, all of whom had already completed the course. Furthermore, the footprints were following the pipeline from Turlough Hill to Lough Firrib. Navigation wasn't necessary at all.

John Paul was thirty-three years old, so he hadn't actually been called after the travelling Pope-show. They were simply the plain names his plain parents had conferred upon a son whose brother had already used up Patrick.

As a boy, with thin hair around a furtive face, he was known simply as John, but he thought of himself secretly as JP, and sometimes as Justice of the Peace, an image that accorded vaguely with Marshall Wyatt Earp.

But when the Pope toured Ireland with such romantic success – 'Young people of Ireland, I loff you!' – John, like many of the less personable young people of Ireland who had never before been loved by anyone, and would never be again, felt identity stir in his compulsive soul. He launched his double name first on his very small circle of friends who were jealous of its fortuitous aptness since most of them were of a similar bent, and then on a cynical public, who combined it with the thinning hair and ascetic beard and recognised a failed vocation.

John Paul still lived at home with his resentful mother, a wiry wisp of womanhood, in a redbrick house in Ranelagh. He referred to the box-room he had occupied since childhood as his 'study'. His mother called it his hutch. He worked ineffectually in the Civil Service, where serving ambition is the only work done.

The Climbers' and Walkers' Club was his passion. Actually it had changed its name since the unfortunate initials led to its being known universally as the Country and Western club. It was now presented as the Walkers' Club, the WC; the earnest committee hadn't yet perceived the irony in the new title.

In the hall at home John Paul kept his rucksack and walking boots. Once, his mother added a forked stick and spotted kerchief, but he missed the point. The boots were the first items to strike his eye as he entered or left the house, and he cultivated an indulgent notion that he might step into them some day at a moment's notice and abscond into the romantic wilderness.

He kept a long-handled ice-axe in the umbrella-rack for a while to broaden the geographical range of the illusion, but his mother relegated it to the wood-shed, where she found it moderately effective for chopping kindling.

The boots were standard walking-wear, bendy and bulbous like a pair of cut-down leather wellingtons. They seemed to suck the bog-water in rather than keep it out.

The rucksack was an up-to-date model in flashy fabric with adjustable waist-belt and a plethora of straps totally incomprehensible to John Paul's mother who tried it out as a shopping-bag on her little trolley, and found the straps kept catching under the wheels.

When Maria joined the WC, John Paul sized her up as a large woman of little ambition who would not be seeking relations with men of rock and ice pretension, a companion whose plodding abilities would never outstrip his own. She seemed to be composed, not altogether unpleasantly, of circles; a round head with tight black hair that formed thousands of little key-ring curls; a rotund, round-eyed face that was further divided into circles by the superimposition of round-rimmed spectacles. Short-sighted, navigation not too hot, JP judged. The circle motif continued to develop below the neck in all sorts of obvious ways in which John Paul wasn't interested; what he wanted was companionship and solicitude.

Maria was a domestic-science teacher after all, though what science had to do with housekeeping was as much a mystery to the man as to his mother.

He courted Maria assiduously through the introductory Sunday walks; saw her through the difficult period when her new boots cut her feet like steak-knives; taught her to set a map, with limited success, since very often her view of a landscape was a confused blur. He failed utterly to teach her to refold a map with the same alarmingly practised ease she used on the restaurant menu the Sunday evening he finally asked her out after an intimate 'FHS'(WC code for a Foot-Hill Stroll).

But the poker-players's flick of the *Carte* was a false alarm. Maria was not a Good-Time Girl. She ordered a modest salad and a pot of tea, and chattered excitedly about the walk and the fine views the group had enjoyed under her patron's tutelage.

John Paul ordered a grandiose hamburger, with 'Seven Seas' sauce thrown in as a dash of romantic afterthought. The kindly waitress knew he meant 'Thousand Island' dressing, although John Paul always looked like a man who could do with a good laxative.

He spoke with a faraway look in his pale, pink-rimmed eyes of bigger and higher things, of mountains and mountaineering, of rock and ropes and more. But when he caught the frightened look in Maria's rolling orbs he shifted down a gear or two and confided that he was 'In Training', as if this were a mystic condition. He was In Training for a Big Walk, perhaps the Biggest Walk, far bigger than the Reeks Walk, demanding stamina and endurance; unknown in the Maum Turks a thirty-three-mile struggle with nature and the landscape that cuts right to the heart of the Wicklow Mountains... er, Hills, he amended immediately, when her eyes distended again.

The Lug Walk next year, he announced, was the object of all his desire and ambition, a snot of sauce slipping furtively down his beard.

Maria giggled nervously. It wasn't just the eloquent sauce, but the sound of the Lug Walk reminded her of a bold child being taken firmly by the ear between thumb and forefinger and marched out in front of the class to be chastised. But she thought of Lugnaquilla towering immensely above a wilderness of remote geography, and swallowed her giggles, and her questions.

John Paul conducted Maria to her bus-stop with some reservations in his mind. He had quite forgotten these by the following Sunday when, as a qualified member of the WC he led his charges on a Preamble (Preliminary Mountain Ramble), which was really just a detour cunningly devised to eliminate several stages of the Glendalough bus-route.

He spent much of the walk deep in monotonous conversation with a breathless Maria, while the rest of the group were left to trample flowers and be terrorised by browsing cattle without advice or instruction.

This pattern continued weekly with Maria asking questions – 'What makes it point to the North?' – and developing a ring of confidence. But as her assurance grew she became bossy too. Like a teacher who breaks down a class by boring it to death, she took over the control of the trudges, rambles, tramps, and scrambles, until the group dwindled to a tiny circle of eccentrics (she was good at circles). Eventually even these fell away, thrown off by the centrifugal force of John Paul and Maria's partnership.

John Paul did not allow the semblance of romance to disrupt his dedication to the Lug Walk. Instead he planned it like a campaign, introducing Maria whenever possible to short sections of the great monotonous marathon that seeks out the most boring sections of high bog in Wicklow and then links them by a devious route that concludes on top of the most complex lump of turf and rock in the county.

Maria walked wherever directed. Up or down, wet or dry, seemed to have no effect on her incessant questions. This in turn allowed full rein to John Paul's taste for the expression of his opinions, attitudes, and confusions on every subject under the rain clouds or the sun. Since Maria paid scant attention to answers – already chewing over her next question – there was no need for John Paul to be over-concerned with accuracy or truth.

On the slopes of Mullachcleevaun he misrepresented exhaustively the workings of combustion-engines and gas-fridges. He abused his unfortunate mother as a shackling tyrant on the track to Seefin. Once, on the bus to Enniskerry, he expounded an original technique for the use of oxygen at Himalayan altitudes. John Paul proposed that mountaineers should uncoil a long roll of thin tubing as they mounted towards the limits of the atmosphere. Oxygen, being a gas, should automatically rise within the tube from bottles kept at Base Camp, and if it didn't … well, the climber could always suck hard.

He got carried away by the theory and, in a flash of inspiration, perceived the possibility of merging the climbing rope and the air-tube into a revolutionary hollow rope.

He was quite unaware that he was the subject of a bus-full of suppressed mirth, and that he was rapidly becoming one of the many comic myths of the walking-scene. Their arguments in the hostels were being greedily collected and embellished by observers (the ultimate accolade), beginning with the evening in Glencree, over a meal of burnt toast and sausages, when John Paul himself asked a burning question; namely, what 'Science' had to do with domestic housekeeping?

Maria responded haughtily that any body of information or knowledge might constitute a Science. John Paul replied, banging his empty cup on the table, that it was certainly Science that had determined the temperature at which water boiled but he could not see why she needed a degree in chemistry to drop a tea-bag in it when it began to bubble.

Maria pouted, her mouth the round O of Outrage, and John Paul enquired provocatively whether she had required much Science to burn the bloody toast.

And yet, every Sunday throughout the long, wet winter and the long, wintry spring, they walked and talked. Sometimes it was John Paul himself in his comic-opera tweed breeches, thick plaid shirt, and the absurd balaclava cradling his monkish little head, who grew breathless. At such moments he was forced to resort to questions as a ruse to gain breathing-space.

Maria was refining her geometry, tightening some of her rotundities to mere curves and arcs; even the famous fullness of the breeches was slowly waning to a parabolic crescent, assisted in its decline by the friction of innumerable mud-slides taken in descent. A John Paul encyclical would be punctuated suddenly by a high-pitched squeal and the oily slither of over-trousers on wet grass as Maria tobogganed bluntly down a slope upon her back.

They discovered 'Sessions' in January, and took to visiting the Glendalough and Glenmalure hostels on Saturday evenings for a while. As a self-considered expert on the 'traditional' field John Paul insinuated himself into the rabble of guitar and banjo-men frequenting the local public-houses. He was content at first to clap spasmodically out of tempo, like a plainclothes Christian Brother, to the pedestrian inanities of 'Fiddlers Green' and the 'Streets of London'. But this reticence couldn't last, and on the third visit he brazenly produced the harmonica he had been torturing at home for weeks.

It was in the crowded, festive lounge of the Royal at about ten o'clock on Saturday night.

There was a brief lull in the ribaldry and jollity. The singers were preparing for the fourth assault on 'The Bunch of Thyme', when John Paul rose to his feet with all the gargling solemnity of a white turkey making a speech from the dock, and called for order. He fluttered his bony elbows, waggled his shoulders, placed his cupped hands to his mouth, and, as a hush of smothered glee fell over the congregation, announced in the reverent, rural mumble befitting the tradition:

'I don't know the name o' this tune, but I got it from the playin' o' the Gallowglass Céilí Band.'

He closed his eyes humbly, and blew a long, piercing note on the miserable wedge of saliva-soaked tin and timber.

The crowd released a shuddering sigh as if punctured, as if it had sat collectively on a long, sharp splinter while the note rose slowly in pitch gathering and rejecting cracked discordances. John Paul's rigid frame was seen to bend forward, one leg lifting like a dervish about to kick off a rain-dance; then the note swooped, broke, and slobbered into an unrecognisable semblance of a tune. It was obvious from the man's frenzied hopping and jogging that it was a dance-tune, but it seemed to centre around a very limited number of notes despite the embellishments and accidentals the crazed musician was spitting into it.

The crowd gazed at each other with that sublime and wild-eyed elation that comes upon people only in the presence of great art – or of supreme idiocy – when an individual displays absolute mastery of one or the other extreme. Someone noticed that Maria was humming stridently along with the music, her eyes closed and hands clasped, a Botticelli balloon. All ears bent upon the tune she was shaping, since John Paul's version was unidentifiable.

Dum-dum, da-daddle, da-dum-de-dumdum, Maria sang obliviously, and continued dum-dum, da-daddle-di-dum ... Understanding dawned.

As the second part of the tune broke on the audience like the opening of an abattoir door the happy voices crashed in as one; 'Ant-y Ma-ry hadda ca-nary, Up the leg of her drawers ...'

On and on they went, pounding fists and glasses on the table, stamping boots on the hollow floor, pummelling each other weakly in the hysterical enjoyment of another soul's insanity, only stopping when hilarity had exhausted them into whimpering submission, and John Paul collapsed into his seat with the beatified radiance of one who has controlled the pulse of his audience.

Elation galvanised the mirth-stupefied crowd and a rib-cracking nudge passed around the circle as John Paul jumped to his feet again, one hand raised in the air like a station-master about to send off a train.

'A slow one!' he barked fiercely. The unspeakable instrument went to his lips again, and to the lugubrious chugging and steaming of spittle-choked notes, *Danny Boy* churned out of the station.

Immediately a female voice tore into the silence of non-participation:

'... the pipes, the pipes are caw-aw-ling,' it asserted belligerently across the room, cutting like a siren into a brawl. An axe-faced local lady with an acidic reputation was not going to let any brat of a Dublin jackeen desecrate the real spiritual anthem of a great and proud people, and she had the voice to back up her intention, a fine nasal abrasion like hard chalk whining over slate!

'... from glennnnn to glennnnn annnnd downnnn the Mounnnn-tainnn side,' she continued aggressively, keeping pace and pitch with John Paul while transfixing him with an eye like an engraving tool.

The local team knew they had a winner in their corner.

'Good man, Mary!' they roared in jubilation. 'Give him stick!'

John Paul was attempting to bow courteously in mid-squawk, thinking he had the cultural pleasure of a duet on his hands, but he forgot to lower the harmonica in time with the bowing of his head and his teeth gnashed against the sharp edges of the metal. Mary stepped up the pressure, contemptuously scenting weakness, and it was only when she abolished the summer and executed all the flowers that he realised it was actually a duel he was in.

He swelled his chest with the wind of challenge and puffed his cheeks like pig-bladder footballs so that the world-famous sighing sequence of notes concluding the first half of the tune ripped out between his fingers like the phantom of the opera wrestling with a Wurlitzer.

In the small bar, just the other side of a baize-clad mahogany door, Tony Maloney, local pool-shark, leaned over the antiseptic green of the table and lined up the shot that was going to pot one ball with clinical left-hand spin and set up the remainder to win him the fifteenth game of the night, bringing his winnings to the level of a modest weekly wage. He shook his head in irritation as the confused cacophony penetrated the two inter-vening inches of hardwood.

'Bloody hell!' he thought. 'Sounds like an Orange March in there.' He had absolutely no sense of tradition.

He sized up the crucial shot and began to concentrate again.

Mary went into the high second half of the verse like a champion coming out for the final round, full of nonchalant, practised venom, showing plenty of power but keeping the best in reserve for the big punch she knew was coming up. John Paul was at full throttle alongside on '... sunshine and in soho-row, or whennnn the va-halley's hushed and white with snooooow/Tis I'll be ...

'HEEEEEEEERE' screeched Mary, launching the notorious high note in an uppercut that soared from G to high E with a vicious tone full of bare knuckles. It was no canary – more like an ambulance siren – she had up the leg of her colloquials.

John Paul reeled under the onslaught, and lost his grip. He hit, and held, high F instead of E.

Critics argued the issue later as to whether the upper end of the trashy implement was simply a half tone out of pitch, or whether John Paul panicked at the crucial moment and sucked instead of blew.

Either way, the consequences were disastrous.

Mary held and amplified her 'HEEEEEEEERE' not merely in the service of the song, but asserting her own continuity despite any combination of war, death, revolution, famine, or hikers. John Paul, hopeful that perhaps no one had noticed his slip of the tongue, decided to brazen it out.

Several things happened as the raucous duet chain-sawed through the lounge. Big Jim O'Rourke, a splinter of agony in his ear, gripped his pint-glass so hard that it burst, and deluged his new pale-grey suit in Guinness. For years after it was sworn locally that Mary's voice had shattered the glass, and Big Jim never begrudged her the glory. But for the moment he had business to attend to: he was lumbering towards John Paul, shedding beer-drips like a lawn-sprayer, with the jagged butt of the glass clenched in his fist.

Simultaneously, the manager hurtled out of that mysterious back-space hidden like a sacristy in the architecture of every pub. He skidded through the bar just as the precision-driven tip of Tony Maloney's cue approached the bottom left-hand side of the cue-ball. The manager burst through the mahogany door and dived into the scrum around John Paul.

The swinging door batted a wedge of sound into the pool-room, driving Tony's cue like a huge darning needle through the plush green cloth, nudging the cue-ball conspiratorially as it ripped. The white sidled guiltily across the table with a Judas-kiss for the black, which dropped apologetically into the pocket.

Foul shot, and game forfeited.

Before the embarrassed *Oops!* of the balls had died away Maloney was on his way to the lounge, his cue gripped overhand like a Zulu assegai.

John Paul felt himself lifted bodily out of his standing, past a gamut of barbed weapons, by the manager who didn't want blood on the new carpet. The door crashed outwards as in a Western, except that this was solid oak and normally it opened inwards. John Paul hit the road outside with great relief considering it was his turn to buy the next round for the rabble of spoon-players and tin-whistle men within.

As he lay gratefully in the gutter a hard, choking sensation in his throat roused him to panic again, and his fingers flew to his prominent adam's apple. He remembered that prior to his ejection, Tony Maloney had been attempting to push the blunt end of the cue down his throat without first removing the mouth organ.

John Paul drew an experimental breath. The wheeze in his chest sounded alarmingly like a B-chord. If he expelled the air and produced a C then he was in real trouble. Just as he ventured on the crucial test the door swung open again and the harmonica skittered viciously off the tarmac, striking John Paul in a highly sensitive area. He produced the high-C with no mechanical assistance whatsoever.

Lying in the ditch at Glendalough, like his namesake stricken down on the Road to Damascus, John Paul pondered, and abandoned the flesh-pots of culture for the hardship of the outdoors again.

There was a lot of suffering to be indulged in before the great marathon flog with which Irish walkers re-enact Napoleon's retreat from Moscow.

It was late spring now, and all the Heavy Walks must take place before the sensitive growing season ended, so that the armies of booted feet could have the maximum impact on the ecology in order to underline their domination of the mountains.

At the last moment John Paul made a major sacrifice. He bought a new pair of boots, guaranteeing himself even greater pain than the most rigorous Catholic upbringing and Christian Brother education could have required.

The morning of the Lug Walk didn't dawn at all.

It was raining so hard at the Stone Cross in Bohernabreena that light couldn't possibly filter in between the dense clouds and the flying mud. Right from the start John Paul and Maria had great difficulty clinging to the sturdy quartet of walkers he had marked down as his guides through the muck and murk. They were known popularly as Male Members of the Gents section of the WC.

Unable to secure a lift to the Stone Cross for himself and Maria, John

Paul had eavesdropped on the other group's arrangements and turned up at their rendezvous. It was proof, not of schoolboy humour, but of earnest innocence that the group met opposite the public toilets on O'Connell Bridge.

An elderly Volkswagen, grossly overloaded with five bearded gents and the mammoth Maria, lurched and squelched into the Dublin foothills, belching chagrin through its exhaust. Maria was squashed in the middle of the back seat – having refused the front on grounds of safety – between John Paul and a morose individual who would not speak but was audibly digesting his breakfast porridge.

In the thick of Tallaght Maria made an urgent request for a toilet-stop.

When the driver finally found a suitable spot she was purple with enforced continence. The entire contents of the car, including the frothing driver whose seat wouldn't tilt forward sufficiently, had to be unloaded into the rain.

At the start they registered their presence and time of departure with a snug man in a tent and were instructed to register again at every checkpoint along the thirty-three-mile route.

Their 'keepers' attempted to slip away from them on the rain-swept track across Seahan when John Paul paused to relieve a blister in an achingly new boot. But Maria foiled the escape bid by scuttling along in their wake, leaving John Paul to hop along behind as best he could.

Reluctantly daylight seeped through the dense rain clouds and illuminated the swirling wraiths of mists that clogged the bog-slopes of Kippure. The silent, bearded men were growing desperate at the slowness of the pace, and Maria's incessant questions – 'Why are they called peat-hags?' – when a suitable accident occurred.

At the reedy edge of a rift in the bog each man in turn launched a flying leap to land on the rim of a peat-hag, one of the mushrooms of turf protruding from the ooze.

Maria jumped in mid-question and failed to reach the rim. She landed six feet lower on one leg and promptly sank to the knee, driven into the sludge by the pile-driver of gravity. She waved the other leg fastidiously in the rain, but all efforts at equilibrium failed and she was forced to plunge the dry foot into the slime. It was immediately sucked into the morass in a welter of bubbles. She stumbled forward, finding no support.

The bog released its grip on the first foot, retaining the boot and sock as consolation.

Now Maria was balanced again on one boot, and waving a plump, pink foot in the air while a row of hairy faces goggled down at her.

Again she toppled forward, and the naked leg dived to the knee, transferring the strain to the anchored boot which yielded its contents with the same squidgy ease as its partner had done.

Maria fell forward, flat on her face in the mud, a pair of fat, bare feet waving in the air.

As John Paul slid reluctantly down towards her the four silent men looked at one another, shook their dewy beards and melted into the mist.

John Paul and Maria arrived at the Sally Gap checkpoint just as a hurried search-party was being assembled. John Paul offered advice with such officious authority that the group had almost departed on his instructions.

Supplies of official tea and soup had long been exhausted, so they guzzled the marshals' private supply and complained about the shortage. They ignored with haughty disdain the most strongly worded suggestions that they drop out of the running at that point, since at their present pace the walk must take at least twenty hours to finish.

John Paul removed the more excruciating boot, and studied the impatient legs round him. Under his stern scrutiny the ring of feet became increasingly nervous, and an embarrassed pair of wellingtons made a cringing attempt to curl over, one on top of the other, like a child controlling an urge to pee. So hypnotised was the wearer by John Paul's persuasive obduracy that he yielded up his rubber boot with little more than a whimpered demand for later restitution. So John Paul and Maria strode and waddled into the mist again, to the bemused shaking of heads, the single wellington adding a dry, satisfying thud to the triple-squelch of the sodden boots.

Many hours and mishaps later, John Paul stumbled into Lough Firrib, which he only recognised when the water-level wavered an inch below the mouths of the rubber boot. It was only a few miles to the conclusion now, and he felt he knew this section intimately.

He was wrong, of course, and they would be found the following day on the wrong side of the mountain, but for the time being, in a burst of thoughtless elation, John Paul proposed marriage.

There was a brief and breathless pause while the proposal quivered in the air and a ripple of icy water slopped over the rim of his boot. John Paul resonated to the appalling echoes of his suggestion.

His heart cringed with regret, a sponge wrung by ruthless fingers. And then Maria, with the wild look in her headlong orbs of a compulsive questioner who could not resist what she was going to ask, although it was as ill-timed as a period on a honeymoon, demanded querulously, 'What does Lough Firrib mean? … What did you say?'

John Paul considered briefly, not the questions nor the answer, but his own merciful deliverance. 'It's probably a derivation of Firbolg, one of the original Celtic tribes in these parts,' he offered happily, brushing aside his error of judgement like one bum note in a rhapsody.

*

WHOM THE GODS LOVE

No one will die in this story. That is a promise (as if I controlled events, pen slicing and splicing ropes at will). Good health to the unhappy child, and long life. He deserves it for a multitude of reasons, not least the coal-black wing of hair across (I swear) a green-eyed glance, or that grin of rapturous collusion with his mother when one of his many skills delighted her.

I do not control anything here. It wasn't I who chose climbing for him. She got him into that. Until then Alan held the reins; afterwards he was just his mother's son. And yet, how often does one encounter that much grace, talent, imagination, heaped upon each other without conceit or reticence, all reflected openly in a generous gaze that searches for the best thing in you, however deeply hidden. When it happens the world had better keep its distance and its balance.

I fell in love with Alan's mother, incurably, long ago before he was born. Before the story started. We all did. We walked and climbed with her like courtiers on weekends in the Wicklow hills. Her vividness intoxicated us until gusts of wordless feeling strained the dullness of our skulls and our voices barked with ecstasy running wild on windy summer days.

We were in love with fantasy, an image by Mills & Boon, daughter of the mountains, hair blowing in the breeze, one hand shading a faraway, eclectic gaze, the other fondling a long-tongued adoring dog. That is not how she ever was at all – although she had that face, the impossible cheekbones, the rich hair, green eyes, slender, striding figure lost in lyrical distance then moments later laughing, singing, shouting out energy while we yelped and bayed at her heels, feeling not like dogs but heroes, or fine horses at the least.

She betrayed us for a stranger. He came strolling in from someone else's story, assured and powerful with officerly manners and swept her away for a whole day to climb an unexplored cliff. It hangs hideously on the hillside opposite the real crag at Glendalough. Born on the wrong side of a granite rift it is illegitimate geology, sunless, uncouth and overgrown.

She left the hut again with him in withered moonlight and returned alone at dawn. Though we were all awake no one stirred or whispered, not even I who blazed with pain in the darkness. I raged against the sound of tears. What right had she to cry?

She lay between us sorrowing as if no one else existed. What window had he revealed onto a radiance that none of us would ever feel? She owed us nothing, but it was still betrayal. A soldier on holiday, who never came again; only his initials appeared on that route-description, unrepeated and long forgotten, and yet she bore Alan not like a grudge but with all the radiance of a state of grace.

I had no influence then, I have none now. Description cannot catch her for me. In truth she controls me, refusing the slow redemption that ageing memory should allow. I will not change her story! There is a tempting notion (you know it if you have been hurt enough) that existence is a thing already written, beyond revision. Too late to leap up on the page in the shadow of the fatal word and wrench the inky keys aside in a skid of asterisks and fractions; already, in some other universe, monstrous and sentimental, something turns the pages, devouring us …

I do not believe it. All of us, Alan too, create our own existences. Independent of our creators. Some die on absurd mountains having brought themselves to that. Most live bedside lives the surer to die that way. Some are dispatched like crows as warning to the rest. And a few hang themselves with the shadow of a rope.

She took Alan to the hills before he was six months old. Always alone except for him. It was she who kept her distance. Some tried friendship and were shunned as if their sympathy was suspect. Alan grew to be extraordinary, no one could deny that no matter how they wished to hurt. He had her kind of beauty, and more. And he had something else that was less definable, more dangerous – a sense of intensely temporary presence, that vulnerability of the foundling, as if he might disappear as shatteringly as he had arrived. But the ache of his presence was irresistible, signifying urgencies we could never have known, never have suffered without him.

And none of us could have fathered a magical child like that. Our creatures, those of us who tried, were dull, wooden things by comparison.

He had talent of course. He glowed with abundance. Often, as he grew older, I saw them outlined on some neglected ridge in Kerry, Connemara or Donegal, the tall mother and her skipping child singing crystal-sharp harmonies that ached against the sky and rang close, too close, to – disintegration? Bitterly I questioned the clear air around my solitude, hammering these knuckles on its empty mirror that reflected everything in my heart. I heard them on frozen Brandon once, overlooking the Atlantic when the child was ten, and then it seemed to me that a shivering fracture ran out across the sea and cold as ice I trembled there and felt the mirror shatter in the thin, high air.

I protest my innocence again in all of this. No, I do not choose climbing for the child, the way one might place a cherished thing in danger in case the urge to kill struck suddenly at midnight when the pen is drained of all compassion and only revenge will ease the pain. And death so easily written.

She could have chosen music, painting, dance: anything but this frightful leap and recoil, leap and recoil, and the dreadful lunging for the edge of the obvious, struggling to re-enter this flat, simple world, as if being born into it had not been hard enough to last a lifetime.

Of course she wished to follow him.

Alan took to it with delight at first. He thought it hilarious, it seemed so extraordinarily ordered. And yet how subtly it changed the physics of his world. As if he had found wings and discovered the buoyancy of air. In every element now he saw the hidden ways and secret corridors of fantasy manifest themselves. If he could walk up cliffs then surely he could pass through walls, thought-transfer to other planets.

His mother's slow, uncertain progress gave him his first exhilarating taste of scorn. She who always seemed so proud and purposeful grew ponderous on the rock, could not see into it at all. She fought blindly for concessions. Alan was gifted: rock seemed to flex to his hands and feet.

He played to his audience, she above or below, and I – I was always near, ornithologist with beard, tweed hat, binoculars and camera. And the third ... The soldier still appeared in all my nightmares, bright and fleet as Mercury, mocking me. My only consolation was that he could not see the dazzling iridescence he had wrought. And yet with every year he came closer to reincarnation in his child. No one could forget.

She knew it, wanted it. She pushed him fiercely towards the source. Maternal love became a hard excitement, it was her will now that drove him towards achievement. He lost his own determination. He was leading hard, skidding through the grades and often now the holds were tilted upside down and all the cracks were blind. Surface had begun to close against him.

And yet he retained enchantment, though under pressure it became a fugitive charm, wide eyes too wide, the skin transparent, hair limp with sweat, limbs trembling towards escape as he reached the final holds on an adult route.

At thirteen he stands below his first Extreme. She fusses round him, plucking, fitting, fixing, crooning. In another moment she may attempt to comb his hair and he will wrench away. But that's not it at all; he doesn't want to leave. He lingers, clinging, until she straightens, shoves him firmly towards the rock.

At the base of a granite slab that steepens at twenty feet into a wall and then at forty feet becomes an overhang so that the whole climb points to the ground like a harshly polished chute, she stops to tie him on. Drapes the new rope on the ground and kneels to the level of his harness. Above her shoulder, released from observation, his face is a mask of fear. The camera whirrs.

The sun glares into her eyes from the mica-sprinkled slab with the dazzle of another day. Blind behind its prism she binds him to the shadow of his father's rope and pays it out into the past. He is gone, stepping gravely, grievously onto the slab without a kiss or any murmur of farewell. The old rope tears at her heart, she pushes it out to spare the pain, up the slab on tiptoe, onto the wall – it overhangs a little and he swings from hold to unprotected hold towards the looming roof.

Scrabbling at the lip his feet swing free, he starts the dreadful mantelshelf, she hears the breath rattle in his throat and her heart stammers in unison. The only sound in all the world. He drops to arms-length, feet kicking for support and then begins to haul again.

In her hands the rope is loose and useless as memory. It cannot draw him back. Panic-stricken she tugs and the coils twitch unattached towards her. Slowly the child unsticks from the rim of the story and tumbles backwards into space. The camera whirrs and whirrs.

Falling on her knees against the slab she throws out archetypal, anguished arms.

He will not die, for there was a promise made, but he has reached his highest point and failed. And now, throughout their lives, he'll be forever falling towards her.

THE WHITE GRAPH

It's been snowing now for days, snow to 2,000 metres last night. I'm getting nervous. It's just like the first time twelve years ago. That summer too I came from chaos ... drink, debt, divorce, I didn't care, I was in Chamonix where the sun shone and nothing mattered but sky-high rock, ice, and dreams. Rousie, Tut, Minksy, warlords of the Alps, were on Snell's Field pulling off First British Ascents every day of the week. Seemed you only had to stroll off the campsite to bag a first ascent if you were one of their gang. They hadn't heard of me yet, but I was determined they'd never forget. I came to the mountains of my mind like a thunderbolt, mad with pain and a rage to do great things.

The Blaitière was a buzz-route then, the West Face of the 'Blat' famous for the Fissure Brown. The good weather hadn't ended and we marched uphill the day we arrived. I'd a mate from Salford in tow, so morose he hardly ever spoke. We humped our new rucksacks all the way to the Plan des Aiguilles full of paraffin, tins of stew, and no stove, broad feet tormented in narrow French boots. We bivvied badly by the Lac Bleu and ate the stew cold, grease and all. The Blat was the biggest crag I'd ever seen, but it looked easy. I couldn't make the guidebook's figure 4 of that rock-scar though: more like the aftermath of an earthquake.

We left the bivouac before dawn and got to the Fissure Brown at nine. Started in the wrong place and climbed dribbling, gravelly pitches before we found the famous crack. From far below it looked like a secure hand-and-fist job, which meant it must be stinking off-width. Close up, in the morning mist, it was a broad black cleft in cold granite. A short pillar at the foot, and after that nothing at all but the Fissure itself. The face leaned back a bit but the crack bulged to contradict it. No wedges either. I'd been promised wedges. Sometimes, they said, you could climb it like the rungs of a ladder and get on with the real climbing then. It had been stripped by some thieving purist.

I attacked at the run in rucksack and boots, that mad flourish meant to bulldoze an obstacle with a frenzy of confidence. Like a bad fighter. Foreign leather thudded on foreign rock, and rebounded.

Fists, arms, shoulders rattled within the crack. I squirmed up a few feet and stuck solid, arm-wrestling the mountain. The right edge of the crack leaned out past my shoulder. The harder I wriggled the more firmly the sack jammed and dragged my hands out of the crack. I had no sense of discretion then, no idea how to retreat gracefully and sneak back streamlined so that the Fissure wouldn't notice me any more than it had to.

Instead I pulled brutally. Trying to pass through a narrowly opened door with a rucksack on. Something had to give. And it wasn't even a French crack: I didn't have the excuse that it was some kind of Frog-stuff that a Brit wouldn't know how to stoop to. Brown did it first, Joe-bloody-Brown whose routes I was flashing in Wales with the arrogance always typical of the next generation but one.

Something gave. It sounded like muscle or bone; it should have been, but it was only the metal stiffener in the toughest sack ever made. Bending to my fury.

The left edge of the crack is composed of little overlaps, snub shapes as tightly moulded to the rock as paint-runs to a doorframe. Nothing to get the fingers behind, the rock gloss-cold and hostile. Higher up, a peg. Someone had nursed a blade into a fault. I hung on it, swung on it nearly an hour before I got the next moves figured – a hex wedged between crystals, slings to step in, slings to haul on and a sling to lasso, and the huge squashed rucksack still on my back.

My mate said nothing, but the pile of butts grew around his solid feet. He accepted that this was how it was meant to be, because I said so and there was no reason to doubt it. Above our heads a thousand feet of grooves and cracks burrowed into the low, grey clouds towards the summit – where we bivouacked exhausted and storm-tossed in the dark after twelve hours' climbing, never thinking not to finish what we'd begun, since life was hard anyway so why would climbing be any different?

So where does this wisdom, this sanity, come from at last? Is it a victory over myself, or just the peace of exhaustion? Wisdom, I know now, is a kind of dignified cunning. The same goes for sanity. Quote me on that.

What happened in those bitter years? I could describe the breakdown maybe, or the climbing, its occasional success, the relationships like feverish collisions, rebuttal and rebuff ... but what really happened overall was, hardship. Emotional hardship, as if time was a long journey in bad weather and I could seldom see clearly enough to know if I was getting anywhere at all. But sometimes the clouds parted and there was a flash of intense perspective. Lucid moments when the heart was seen to have failed again. The shape of my life linked those moments together.

A black graph. The white graph is only its shadow. An illusion.

In a cold dawn, less than a week ago, I left the Plan cable-car at a run. My partner this time was young and ambitious, a good rock-climber, if hints were facts. We met in the Bar National. First route of the season for both of us.

He was keen enough to do the Blaitière though I got the feeling he was lowering his sights. He knew a lot about the trendier lines on the face but I was set on the old British route and there was no argument. He knew I'd been on it before when he was a boy. I think he viewed the idea with as close an approach to indulgence as he could manage.

I tried rapport for a while, 'What d'you do for a crust, Andy?'

'I don't.'

Standing in the dark in Cham while the guides filled the first 'férique, 'You married yet, Andy?'

He jerked his head at the boring idea. They don't scramble to marry in their teens like we did. Not the smart ones anyway.

'You?' He had no interest.

'Yeah. Four kids.' He was totally shocked; obviously I'd sold out. No commitment to climbing. He shuddered at the prospect of dribbling snapshots, or worse still – when courage was wanted on the route would I plead fatherhood?

So I didn't tell him I hadn't seen my kids for two years. While I'd been locked away. Or about their various mothers ...

I set a scorching pace across the moraine, breakneck boulder-hopping to rattle him. I know there's no way to beat these younger lads technically: all you can do is concede their strengths and maybe gain a little on the rough ground. Andy tried to keep pace with me; once or twice he found quicker detours until we left the moraine and headed up the glacier below the Brégeault Ridge.

The remote smoothness of the Blaitière had broken into features: the Red Pillar, the slabs, the grey scar, the sceptical wrinkles of the Brown Route, all showed the versatility of a face that used to be known for one route only.

Irritated by Andy's grimness I didn't pause for crampons. I counted on the gravel embedded in the ice to get me up the glacier, guessing from his comments that he might be less cocky on ice. Last year his first season finished in a crevasse in the Argentière Basin. Could happen to anyone, sure; those holes are so crowded it can be hard to get in.

'Ice is basically boring,' he'd lectured me, 'Same move over and over. Now, Rock makes you Think.'

A dead give away; never done any mixed!

No, I wasn't putting him down competitively – just storing up space for myself in what I feared could be an unbalanced day at my expense. It worked so well I was almost ashamed when he crawled onto the rock white-faced after resorting to crampons on the lip of a crevasse for the last snow-bank. A fall there would have corpsed him. He admitted to feeling shaky but he put it down to a bad stomach, 'Dodgy bottle of wine last night...'

Pathetic! Obviously it was altitude, acclimatisation, arrogance, but he had to learn all that himself. He was in the right company. Efficiently sorting rock-gear and ropes, I offered without actually pausing, to sit around for a while till he recovered.

'Nah, I'm alright.' Curt, as if to say, Rock? I won't have any problems. It's you I'm worried about, mate!

The grey stubble and the belly can have that effect. But it never fails to disappoint me how fucking military the young alpinists are now, as if – under a veneer of anarchy – survival is a strict Commando-code forbidding any weakness or self-doubt.

Well, if he fancied discipline – 'You start,' I gave him his orders. 'There's the Fissure Brown. It's off-width and it overhangs, but it's not too bad otherwise.'

He looked as shattered as his stiff lip allowed. 'Don't think I feel up to it yet...' Nausea churned audibly in his stomach like an undigested fry. He looked around for a hole to crawl into.

Not broken enough yet to drop his salopettes on the windswept terrace.

'Okay, I'll start,' I offered. Kindly, exultantly. I was prepared for this: one of those victorious moments brought about by willpower and pure need. It was going to be my day after all.

'I'll do the variation-start. No sense repeating myself.'

To the left of the Fissure Brown and climbing to the same belay, there is an alternative pitch, a hand-crack! Visually stunning. The first section is littered with easy flakes, and then the clean crack rises, sinuous and soaring as if it had sloughed all its features without quite extricating its tail from the clutter.

And up at the top there is a thin, sharp snake-bite.

Beside this elegant pitch the Fissure Brown is a boa constrictor. How had I missed it a dozen years ago when I needed it most?

And Brown and Whillans? Had they ploughed their muscular furrow by choice, or had the hand-crack been cleaned into view since?

I like jamming-cracks. Don't ever go by grade: there are cracks designed to encourage you up a wall, and cracks that try to throw you off – no matter how hard or easy. The two starts to this route are perfect examples of that.

After the flakes the pitch came clean and then it was perfect hand-width, no holds, and so deep it must go right to the core of the Mont Blanc range. I swear a distant breath of lava warmed my fingertips as I reached inside. I might fail here for want of strength or will, but I could not fall off. The grey rock clamped me to it, clenched me hand and foot, owned me.

I was gripped like a fossil, a lichen, a micro-insect whose wildest scuttlings down a hundred generations could not take it off the mountain. This crack absorbed everything. It was no random fault like the Fissure Brown but one of those points where the perfect geometry of rock forces the imperfect nature of the climber to submit: no, not to its difficulty, but to its relentless form and meaning. I'd been thinking a lot about climbing while I was ill, and it was as if I'd created this pitch for my return. But already, on the first move, I was afraid. Afraid of myself. Afraid I would be climbing this ruthless crack forever, jamming on past the belay, past the Fontaine Ledges, past the summit, climbing on into personal space, permanently locked away in its cold, burning grip.

I climbed it to preserve my identity, my freedom – flailing forward the way a swimmer among sharks lifts himself whole out of the water; I climbed without a pause for protection, lifting myself whole from the rock with every stroke …

Yeah, I know that's complex – schizoid maybe, but I take climbing seriously. I'd a lot of time to work it out. Sometimes, at bare and powerful moments it stood for all the things I've never done or felt.

At the top it squeezed, demanded more, a finger-jam with the toes twisted and chewed, exposed ankles trembling a rope-length from the terrace, too fast and late for protection now. A huge handhold … Like too much dope too soon, heart and brain ejaculating through the skull. I doubled over on the belay to control the dizziness, the fear of pitching head-first down the crack – and found I was staring down the cold slot of the Fissure Brown, listening as I groaned and cursed towards the light in that tunnel of years.

Andy came up grey-faced, technically perfect, mentally stunned. No aesthetic spark. Looking at the thin mouth and inward eyes I knew he never recognised, never trusted, anything outside himself. And that he was ideal for me; I could do him no harm. 'You mad bastard!' he grunted, and then in case any admiration had shown through, 'Didn't have gear in your day, did they?'
   'You still sick?' I didn't wait for an answer, 'I'll go ahead for a while.'
   I felt great, perilously liberated from myself and yet complete, as if a thin gap – the width of that crack and no more – had opened up between me and the past. I'd have to cross over again on the way down, but things might be different, or I might have changed by then.
   You can't change reality, I know, but you can see it differently.
   For a while.

A groove hung above us, steep, tight, V-shaped, heading into overhangs. I had worked it grimly before, a miner in a sullen seam. Now I could bridge, chimney, shimmy, lean out or in, use the groove or refuse it. Clip a peg and skip the next three. I whooped past belays to run out a full rope every time, forcing Andy to climb with me till I reached the stance I fancied.
   The overhang on good holds. Strenuous, not hard. Belayed above I scanned the routes I knew; the North Face of the Plan had lost its simple trick, the séracs a shambles, the ice-corridor gone and no safe way through. Over on the Peigne the North Ridge was deserted too, a grovelling grooveline totally out of vogue. But the routes on the slabs would be alive with dancers dressed for the crag, a cluster of bolts the only summit they sought. I could hear them yodelling on the Blaitière too.
   'Wheeeeeeeee-Hah!' I responded. Good luck to them!
   Andy was on the overhang. He'd solo it at home if he stooped to the standard, barely 5a, but he grappled with gritted teeth, body trembling with the effort of altitude. Yet he unclipped a sling from a peg and looped it neatly around his neck while clinging to the rock with failing fingers; just because I was watching him. Pride!

'Pull on 'em, Andy,' I goaded, 'That's what they're for!'

A ferocious glare, and I tried to think how to say I hadn't pulled on them either – because I hadn't *needed* to.

The route unravelled at a manic pace; grooves, cracks, a delicate slab, all free and sound. Heart and breath raced like rock and roll towards a climax, yet I consumed every move with the greed of the half-starved, the long locked-away. What else is there, apart from good sex, to equal it? Big game hunting? Bull-fighting? War? Hemingway missed out on the best.

Andy was losing his grip. I had to be impressed with his staying-power though; he'd a hell of a last gasp in him. He'd suit me alright. Badly dehydrated too, and I'd left the water bottle at the foot of the route. Yeah, sorry.

We were on target for a three-hour ascent; not bad for a first route. He was too burnt-out to argue, too proud to plead, but his whole manner was a violent complaint against the route.

He wanted to go down. I could feel it in the drag of the rope, hear it in his strangled curses. He couldn't handle the climbing on the day, so he didn't care about the mountain. It was not a thing in itself apart from his capacity for it.

I may come across as a hard bastard here, but I do have standards. I have respect. Even at my worst a dozen years ago I only wanted to match up to the magnificence of the Alps, to find some reflection of them in me. Andy wanted to use them to exhibit his own talent, and when it didn't work out he blamed everything but himself. Especially the mountain.

The last pitches to the Fontaine Ledges were sustained cracks, sweet and cunning as anything on a Yosemite wall. People abseil off there, the best climbing over, the summit irrelevant. I'd been to the top so I felt no need to go again, but I owed Andy a little further education. No, I didn't want to make a better man of him – I wouldn't presume – I was just trying to stop him getting worse.

'We're going to the top, Andy.' He was slumped on the last belay, destination and descent on his face. 'It'll take another couple of hours.'

He had breath to spare for a snarl; 'I'm not going to any bloody top! There's just rubbish left.'

'Is that so? You'd better traverse off the Brégeault Ridge on your own then, because I'm going up. I'll nip down the Spencer Couloir on the other side, so I won't be back this way.' That was a bluff; I wouldn't touch the Spencer at dawn, never mind midday.

He almost came. The soldier in him struggled to submit to discipline. Then the human being, the failed mountaineer, conquered him for the best. 'I don't want to go any further,' he whimpered, 'I want to go down … now!'

'Want to?' I echoed with interest, 'Want to! Why?'

He scraped together the shreds of his ego, and threw them away: 'I'm not able to go on. I'm done for. Burned out.' If there had been enough liquid in him he would have cried.

'Why didn't you tell me, Andy?' Full of shocked sympathy and surprise I fixed an abseil.

Maybe I did rub his nose in it; but believe me he needed it – just as I need the elation, the power, the control that I know – I *know* – are only an illusion. The fact I can race up a small mountain won't make me any better at the other things I do and don't do.

Still, it will calm me if I make it endure; it will dissolve the poison in my blood, the anger that builds up and up till it threatens the heart and must be purged.

If there is any such thing as wisdom for me it means knowing when to cut loose. And choosing a victim, to spare the ones I love.

If I do half a dozen routes with Andy now, get the Walker and the Frêney done, maybe shoot over to Zermatt, I just might … pull things into shape this winter. If she's crazy enough to let me try.

DARK MOURNE

Steve was disappointed already. Green hedges and fields, green leafy trees, green sky; he had expected the Republic to start thinning out by now. Where was the red and blue of Northern Ireland? Standing up on his pedals, he scanned the wide, green landscape.

The three boys had left the train at Dundalk and cycled north towards the Border. Jim rode in front, as he had all the way. Fair haired, serious, stocky, he set the pace with muscular monotony. The trip had been his idea; a week in the Mournes, cycling and hillwalking, a little rock-climbing too, an exercise in self-reliance and observation. But he had failed to enlist ideal companions, friends who shared his own solid outlook and physique. The North was off-limits to most parents.

'Hurry up!' he shouted back importantly. 'We're near the *Border!*'

'What's the matter?' Steve grinned, 'does it shut, or what?'

Paddy, the youngest, had persuaded his family that the trip would broaden his horizons. He half-suspected his mother would let him go to a brothel if he could prove it was educational – and easy on his asthma. He was proud of her tolerance. To Paddy, everything in his life so far was an opportunity for the intellect.

His glasses were steamed up with the effort. The saddle was too high for his small body and he lunged at the pedals.

Formal education – he thought excitedly, sweat flying from his face – distorts reality. It does! It was obvious outside the classroom cage. Take geography. Take history! Look how this landscape had absorbed its past like fertilizer and become ordinary, neutral farmland. He had been led to expect the topography of violent division. School history gave an impression of endless ancient conspiracy tearing the country. But this modern Ireland was not an extension of the past at all. It was an extension of the EU! Bland as butter. And there's another thing, he thought severely: television! That doesn't do much for reality, either.

'Why don't you shorten the pedals?' Steve interrupted cheerfully.

Paddy's brain seldom stooped to mechanics. 'I couldn't,' he flustered. 'It's my brother's bike.'

'Oh well in that case – we'll drop the saddle instead.'

Jim cycled back, 'What's wrong now for God's sake?'

'Looking for a spanner,' Paddy explained.

'To drop the saddle.' Steve added. 'The nut is rusty.' He eyed his friend thoughtfully. 'Maybe we could build up your feet.'

The small intellectual poked a lurid packet back into his saddle-bag. 'What's that?' Jim demanded, 'let me see.'

Paddy coloured miserably.

'*Snake-bite Kit*,' Jim read in strangled tones. '*Antidote to all poisonous snake-bites including Rattlers, Cobras, and Black*... Black Mambas. Black Mambas? In the Mournes?' He goggled at Paddy

'It was a mistake,' Paddy mumbled.

'That's right,' Steve defended breezily. 'Could happen to anyone. He meant to get spider-stuff instead. Tarantulas, Black Widows ...'

Paddy lifted a look of hurt betrayal but Steve was launched. 'You missed it, Jim. We were in the Mountain Shop last week. You know your woman there?'

'Martina?' The story threatened to dissolve into enjoyment already.

'Poor Paddy didn't know Martina's form at all. He had her on the gallop for half an hour, trying things on, changing his mind, asking questions. All in the interests of science, of course, and free exchange of information, nothing commercial involved. And she waiting to go to her lunch! In the end ...' He giggled affectionately at Paddy's downcast face. 'In the end he bought a pair of bootlaces and when she slapped them up in front of him only asked if she had them in a different colour!'

Jim hooted incredulously, 'Martina!'

'Well they *were* bright yellow!' Paddy muttered.

'Just as she was about to break him in two, Paddy spotted all this junk on a shelf. Commando Packs! There was a bit of sharp wire in one, a Survival Saw: that's for firewood, amputations, useful stuff like that ... never know when you might want to whip off a leg, but Paddy zoomed in on the Snake-Bite Kit. You should have heard his voice! Pure rapture: "How much are *they*?"

'Martina ripped one off the shelf – nearly took the wall with it and into the bag it went along with the yellow laces.

"Snake-Bite Kit," she said, "Two Pound Fifty." Steve choked on her husky snarl.

'Two Pound Fifty?'

'Well he couldn't turn it down. He'd have been bitten sooner than he expected if he had!'

'And you know what the worst thing was?' Paddy let out a snort of reluctant laughter. 'When she yelled the magic words "Snake-Bite", everybody in the whole shop turned round to gawp. They thought I was off to the Amazon or somewhere. I couldn't let them down!'

He grinned and replaced the packet. 'Anyway it might come in handy some day.'

'If we meet Ian Paisley!' Steve giggled.

'Oh no!' Jim shook his head emphatically. 'That fellow doesn't bite you. He swallows you whole!'

The Border was an anti-climax: an ugly building by the roadside, shrouded trailers in a lay-by, Ireland stretching meagrely ahead. They obeyed the battered STOP sign. Two cars flashed past, one in each direction, without a pause. Jim held his breath for the high-speed pursuit, the sound of sirens. Nothing stirred – officially. A crow settled on a verge and began unofficially picking seed.

A hand waved behind a window. Jim waved back, almost a salute. He was conscious of cultural identity clothing him like a uniform. Steve and Paddy were already careering into the North. Jim was forced to follow, unrecorded. His passport rankled in his pocket. He was fond of correct procedure.

'My God!' he exploded when they were clear. 'We could be smugglers or terrorists, or –' He glared at his two companions, their pink legs protruding from wrinkled football shorts, innocent surprise in their eyes, ' – or schoolboys,' he finished sheepishly.

Round the first bend Jim pulled in. 'Map time!'

Next to his passport Jim loved his map. Paddy took his glasses off. An impressive spray of sweat sprinkled the dust. 'Don't bother,' he chirped. 'It's the A1 to Newry four miles, turn right B8 to Hilltown nine miles, B27 towards Kilkeel. Four miles to the Spelga Dam, four more – turn left towards Newcastle, mile and a half to the Silent Valley.'

He gasped for breath. 'Uphill all the way!'

Steve took Paddy's brain for granted, 'How far's all that?'

'Nearly twenty-five miles.'

'Are you sure you didn't add in the road-numbers?' The two friends rattled together with enjoyment. Thwarted, Jim fondled his map. 'I thought you said you were never here before.'

'I wasn't! I checked the map on the train,' Paddy beamed. 'Measured it with a thread. While you were chatting up schoolgirls. Or trying to!'

Before they moved away, Steve nudged Jim. Gleefully he indicated their small companion wobbling at the roadside. The bike was absent-mindedly stuck in top gear and the loaded panniers clamped the back wheel to the tarmac. Paddy's pert features were concentrated with effort and his baggy shorts gave the impression of creeping up towards his armpits. Affectionately Steve tapped a hollow-sounding forehead. 'He's got it up here, though,' he said. 'Where it counts.'

'This *must* be it!'

Twenty-five miles later a dark laneway, overhung with hawthorns, tunnelled into the night.

'Bloody dynamos!' Jim cursed wretchedly. 'Why did no one bring a torch?' He felt their disapproval glow in the dark. Wasn't he supposed to be the expert?

'Shine a light!' he snapped. Sighing, Steve heaved his rear wheel in the air and kicked the pedal. The dynamo lit up wanly. Wheel ruts, a tufted ridge of grass … Jim slapped the map in front of the light and ducked towards it. Paddy ducked too. Their skulls met with a dull crack. The panniers dragged the wheel back to earth and the light went out.

A hopeless silence settled. Abruptly Jim shunted into the lane. 'This'll do me for tonight.' Darkness swallowed him instantly. The alien night tightened around Steve and Paddy. They were in the black heart of a Unionist landscape, clad only in shorts and sweat-soaked football shirts. Their scalps prickled with apprehension.

'This is the third lane in a mile,' Paddy breathed. 'We've only a one-in-three chance of being right!'

'Yeah, but there's three of us!' Steve strode forward, his dynamo brightening with confidence.

'I found it. I found it!' Jim's squawk rent the darkness. Lunging towards the sound, Paddy caught his bare shin on the steel pedal.

A large farmhouse loomed at the end of the lane. White-washed, two-storeyed, deserted. Jim cavorted in front of it, arms raised in the air as if he had just conjured it from the ground. Skeletal conifers leaned like dead sentries around the walls. On the gatepost a faint blotch of paint. Jim translated confidently, MMC, Mourne Mountaineering Club. I found it! I found it!

'Are … are you sure we're allowed to stay?' Paddy quavered. 'There's no one here.'

'Great!' Steve was in no doubt. 'Let's break in. I'm freezing.'

'I'm told they hide the key over the outhouse door,' Jim deliberated importantly. 'But which outhouse?'

He and Paddy darted off in opposite directions to search. Steve pushed open the front door and entered the house, where the others joined him a minute later, painfully rubbing bare legs.

'You might have told us, idiot! I barged into nettles looking for the bloody key!'

'Me too,' wailed Paddy, 'I got stung right where I scraped my shin!'

'That'll take your mind off the scrape,' Steve offered reasonably. His thin shoulders rose towards his ears bewildered by accusation. 'I thought you were gone exploring.'

'Put on the light! Idiot!' Jim snapped. 'Why are you standing in the dark?'

'There isn't any ...'

'What the hell do you mean, there isn't any?'

Steve made himself absolutely clear. 'I mean there isn't any.'

Jim raked the wall for a switch.

'There's no poles ... no poles in the laneway,' Steve said.

'And no wires on the chimney,' Paddy added.

Jim's fingers faltered among the cobwebs. Something fat and squidgy jumped onto his wrist and galloped up his sleeve. 'There must be some kind of light,' he spluttered, scraping himself in disgust. 'They swore there was electricity.'

'Here's a candle!' Steve offered brightly.

'Well light it, man, for God's sake.

'Give us a match, then.'

Jim cleared his throat and turned to Paddy in polite despair. 'Have you got a match? Please?'

'Sorry Jim. 'Fraid I don't smoke.'

Silence fell again. The house smelled of damp decay. A rustle came from upstairs, a hollow rattle.

'Mice ...'

'Rats ...'

'Loose plaster behind the wallpaper, that's all!' Jim scoffed nervously. 'Old houses make a lot of noise. They rattle like packing-crates. Everyone knows that.'

A stealthy creak from behind a door seemed to reinforce his words; it was as if a listener had shifted its weight. Jim snatched the door open. A stairway mounted into pitch blackness. He slammed it shut and lay against it.

'I don't want to scare anyone,' his voice quavered to a higher pitch, 'but I heard this place is haunted. Course I don't believe it ...' The hidden stairs creaked again as if the listener had taken a sudden interest. 'Some of our club stayed here last year. They heard all sorts of stories ... a lot of nonsense.'

'Like what?' Paddy demanded faintly. Steve slung a reassuring arm around his shoulders and cleared his throat at Jim. Too late.

'Oh noises and ... things. Footsteps, screams, you know, the usual stuff. Someone got the chop here ages ago.

'Murdered you mean. Who?'

'We-ell, a family actually,' Jim said with uneasy relish. 'Butchered in their beds. Some of the fellows from our club said they heard it was, you know, people who didn't leave when they were ordered out. But it was a long time ago ...' He pulled himself together. 'Of course the lads were only making up the story to frighten us when they got home. They didn't actually see anything themselves.'

'You mean they didn't have a torch either?'

'Lay off, Steve! They said there was electricity here. I thought of everything else. There must be matches somewhere. Where's the kitchen for a start? We'll poke around till we find something!'

In the yard the wind sighed. They heard a hasty brushing overhead, as if someone were sweeping a bedroom for their stay.

Paddy fluttered under Steve's arm, his voice high as a bat-squeak, 'We ... we can't stay here!'

'Only a branch against the slates,' Jim growled uncertainly.

'Everyone stays here. It's a club hut for God's sake! Anyway ... where else can we go?' He felt for the kitchen door, hands paddling cautiously in the dark. A loud ticking came from behind him and every hair on his head tingled.

'Just bringing the bike in!' Steve barged his handlebars through the front door, took off the panniers, lifted the back wheel and pushed on a pedal. The room trembled into cavernous existence.

Paddy cheered, his glasses gleaming gratitude. Giddy with relief, Jim dangled his arms like a broken scarecrow and howled ghoulishly. Steve responded with the wail of a skittish banshee. As the brief light faded Jim was almost certain that Paddy had wet himself. 'Light up again!' he ordered inquisitively. The wheel whirred. No, just a wrinkle of shadow in the baggy shorts.

A doorway. As the light died Jim darted forward.

'Follow me – oooohhh!!' A low lintel! Steve rushed to the rescue. The bike stalled against the sofa. He tumbled across it and Paddy pitched headfirst into a tangle of arms, wheels, pedals, legs and handlebars. Jim drew a shuddering breath, postponed his headache and assumed control.

'On your feet Steve! You too, Paddy. Pull yourselves together now!'

The last command renewed the convulsion. Jim dragged them upright and straightened out the bike. 'You steer Paddy! I'll lift the back wheel. You're on pedals, Steve. Now when I count three, start!'

He lifted the back wheel by the carrier, 'One two ...' Steve leapt into the air.

'Owww! Get off, Eejit! Turn it with your hand.' The room sprang to quivering life again, monstrous shadows swinging around the walls. 'And God said "Let there be Light!" ' Steve chanted, lurching towards the kitchen, 'and Jasus you could see for miles!'

He was shorn off by the doorframe. The bike slewed and Paddy lost his grip. Jim's fingers entered the spokes. Steve thought the howl was aimed at him – for letting go. He grabbed the pedal again and churned mightily. The howl rose in pitch as if powered by the dynamo.

The kitchen was cold and stark; stone-floored, with a heavy wooden table. A shelf bore a litter of broken Primus stoves, cracked cups and a Cow & Gate tin. There was a stone sink, chipped and stained, two broken chairs, an empty dresser. The one small window was curtained with cobwebs, the back door secured by rusted bolts. No-one had ever been happy here.

Jim felt tentatively along the shelves.

'Mind the rat-traps,' Steve grinned. The hand retracted instantly.

'Doesn't s-seem to get much use,' Paddy whispered, shrinking from a mound of bullet-shaped droppings on a shelf.

'Sure it does!' Jim was dismissing his own fear too. 'Most people bring their own gear. Like us. I've got a gas-stove, right!'

'I suppose it's got a pilot-light,' Paddy complained aggressively.

Jim glared at him. Bad enough taking that kind of guff from Steve without Paddy getting cheeky too.

'You know, I've been thinking,' Steve interrupted at knee-level. 'We've got three bikes here, right? And three rooms we want to use, right?' He beamed up at Jim. 'Why don't we hang a bike in each room, from the centre of the ceiling. We can take turns to pedal, and we'll save all this humping around.'

Overwhelmed by his own brilliance he paused. Darkness closed on the idea but Paddy saw potential: 'Good thinking Stevie!' He brightened, 'I bet there's a stream outside. We can rig up a hydroelectric scheme! All we'll need is a little waterfall, a paddle-wheel, and a belt-system to the back wheels.'

He was jigging with excitement. Jim gave the bike an impatient jerk, 'Get moving, Einstein!' he growled. 'Upstairs ...'

The long, narrow stairway was panelled off from the living room. Jim and Paddy gnashed the bike up the bare steps. Steve squirmed to reach the pedals. He halted in mid-ascent: 'Did you hear about the fella that was sick in bed at the top of the house?'

Baffled, they glared at him. 'The doctor came up to see him. Your man was expecting a cure. The ould doc was puffin' and pantin' – "Begod Mick," he says, "they'll have a quare job getting the coffin down them stairs."'

The light revealed extensive desolation. A gaunt room had been adapted roughly as a dormitory. No bunks, but half the floor consisted of a raised platform scattered with mildewed mattresses. Another platform overhead was similarly equipped.

'A *Matratzenlager!*' Jim was proud of the technical information. 'This is what they use in alpine huts.' Paddy saw what he meant; the mattresses looked as if they had come down in a glacier. 'I don't want to complain but this won't do my asthma any good,' he warned dismally. Jim ordered him in to search for matches. As he scrambled reluctantly on to the top platform a sudden icy breeze whirled through the room. The door slammed.

'Draughty dump!' Jim shivered uneasily. He caught a look of frozen terror on Paddy's face and flung the light around.

'A man ...' Paddy gasped. 'There was a man.' His trembling arm pointed.

'*Where?*'

'There! In the door. On the landing.'

'Paddy, the door's closed!'

'I know ... but I *saw* him ... he passed through it.'

'Through the ... *timber!*'

'Oh Paddy, for God's sake.'

Paddy's terror was real. His teeth rattled and his eyes, magnified already behind his lenses, were huge with evidence. The wheel slowed to an appalled whisper of light.

Paddy's arm still pointed. Its dancing shadow faded across the wall.

'A shadow! A bloody shadow!' Jim exploded with relief and disgust. 'That's all you saw, you EEjit. A bloody shadow!'

Steve released his breath in a long, whistling puncture. There were tears in Paddy's voice. 'Not a shadow,' he insisted weakly. 'It was a m-man … in a tartan shirt with sort of … yellowish hair and …' He coughed defensively before adding in a small voice, '… and short trousers!'

Jim and Steve exploded in high-pitched laughter. 'Short trousers!' they echoed in hysterical relief, 'Ha-Ha HAAAH!' Jim sobered abruptly, 'Clean your glasses or you'll frighten yourself to death. Short bloody trousers indeed! Look what I'm wearing!' He plucked at his shorts. 'You saw *my* shadow, you gobdaw!'

'Not … shorts,' Paddy whispered, ashen with fear and abuse, 'breeches.'

Jim ignored him. 'Wind up that light', he ordered.

Steve bent obediently to the pedal, and paused. 'D'you think', he wondered quietly, 'are we in the wrong place or something?'

The hall door crashed open. A scraping rumble resounded through the house. The noise increased until it came to a halt against a wall below. There was choked silence for a moment, the house catching its breath, then the intrusion rattled dreadfully. Steve pumped the pedal till the wheel hissed: 'Imagination …' he droned hoarsely, 'Imagination …' The radiant spotlight jerked across the walls and settled on the frail wooden door. Sharp blows below were echoed in grunts of effort. The bedroom door unlatched and silently swung ajar.

Paddy shrieked. Jim's fingers lost their nerveless grip and the bicycle crashed to the floor.

'What's goin' on up there? Is that you, Billy?'

Steve stumbled out to the landing. 'No,' he shouted in a ragged voice. 'It's us! What's happening?'

'That's what I was wonderin' meself!' A cone of torchlight exposed Steve's gaunt form. 'Well, well! A footballer! That explains the noise. Ye're playin' a match up there!'

'Noise!' Steve gasped in outrage, 'What about the racket downstairs? Was that you?'

'Oh that?' the voice chuckled pleasantly. 'Did I frighten ye? I'm sorry. I didn't know there was anybody up there.'

Steve scrambled downstairs followed cautiously by Jim. Paddy lowered himself weakly from step to step, clinging to the banister. The torchlight flashed across the floor to the fireplace.

'I was just bringin' in some firewood. See? Found it in the lane.' The voice was a chatty drawl. It went up and down the northern scale. 'Hey, welcome to the Hut! Ye should have lit the fire. It's cold.' He rubbed his hands briskly. 'Did ye not find the candles either?'

Paddy's teeth chattered audibly. The stranger bent towards him in concern and Paddy shrank away, 'Hey, this wee fella's perished.' He hurried into the kitchen and pulled out a drawer in the table. A lighter flared with an old-fashioned whiff of petrol and a candle flickered alight. He handed it to Jim. A heavy scent trailed the flame. 'Now,' he urged, 'there's whiskey-bottles out there for candlesticks. Set them round the room, one in each window, two on the mantelpiece, and mind you put a couple by the door. Hurry up now and we'll get this place ready yet.'

Steve examined him in the light of the second candle. He wore a heavy greatcoat with the collar turned up, and the peaked cap of a country farmer. His features were fleshy, a soft face with pale skin and uneven stubble. A good bit older than themselves, Steve thought. Impossible to tell though – the difference between age and experience. Loose, mobile eyes unnerved him as the man handed him his candle with a ceremonial nod. Large and liquid they squirmed uneasily in red-rimmed sockets. They belonged in a finer face. But the friendly concern was reassuring. They marched one by one through the draughts, sheltering their candles with transparent hands. Paddy looked just like an altar-boy, Steve thought affectionately. Exorcism flickered through his mind, but the domestic ritual eased his imagination.

The stranger followed them into the room and fell on his knees before the fireplace. He began to chop kindling with the spike-end of a peculiar hammer. Steve peered at the implement, puzzled.

'It's a piton-hammer,' Jim opened his mouth for the first time.

'That's right,' the stranger displayed it, the head narrow and heavy, the spike viciously stubby. 'A climber's hammer. That spike is for pullin' out pitons. Pegs we call 'em. That was my job! Billy knocked 'em in and I pulled 'em out!' He smacked his lips in satisfaction.

'I thought pegs were out of fashion now,' Jim commented loftily, 'modern climbers don't use them any more.' Steve suffered a twinge of embarrassment for the friendly stranger.

'Aye, maybe so, maybe so,' the man smiled at Jim's presumption, 'but we're very traditional here.' He laughed benevolently. 'You lads must be rock-climbers then?'

'I've done a fair bit,' Jim boasted outrageously, 'they haven't.'

'Great! We'll have some fun on the rocks tomorrow so. If we can get round Billy, that is. Used to be a damn good climber, Billy. More of a walker meself, hadn't the guts for the rock' He whacked away with the spike, 'Billy was the boy for the climbin".

'Oh,' he interrupted himself. 'Nearly forgot me manners.' He threw the hammer into a meaty left fist and thrust out the right in a clammy handshake. 'I'm Robert Grey ... I use this old place a lot. Me and Billy. There's not many comes nowadays. They go to the new hut up the road. But me and Billy, we're too old-fashioned to change.' He winked at Jim.

Steve completed the introductions.

'First time up from Dublin, eh?' Robert grinned with pleasure.

'We'll give ye a good introduction tomorrow so. Three wee Fenians from the Free State, eh?' His eyes danced at them. 'Don't mind my big mouth. Nothin' to me where a man comes from. Long as he buys his round, eh? Only jokin' boys, only jokin'.'

A shadow crossed his face, 'Ye'll maybe find Billy a bit rough at first, understan',' he warned, 'but he's a good lad behind it. Used to be an army man. He misses it y'know. Excitement an' all – damn good climber too, till the hand seized up. War wound ... made him bitter y'know. We might get him goin' again.' He sat back on his heels and the fire lit his flickering features. 'Let me think now ...' He scratched his head with the piton-hammer. 'We'll maybe start on Lower Cove and work up to Slieve Beg. Or round to Annalong an' maybe Hare's Castle, how's that sound?' He beamed at their puzzled faces. 'Aye, I'll take care of Billy, don't worry about that. That's my job!'

Snatching up an iron kettle he headed for the door. 'Just goin' down for water. Only be a wee minute.'

'Quick!' Jim hissed as soon as he was gone, 'get that bike downstairs or we'll look like right eejits!' Steve stuck his head outside. A shadow moved among the dead trees.

'An illusion I tell you Paddy, that's all you saw. A trick of the light. Imagination!' Jim was arguing.

'But I *saw* it! I saw it ... through the door ...'

Jim turned to Steve as if to an unimpeachable witness. 'Did you see anything upstairs, Steve?' he asked in a weary, long suffering tone.

Steve hesitated, grappling with temptation, then grinned apology at his exhausted friend. 'Not a thing I'm afraid.' He shook his head in sympathy. 'Eyestrain, Paddy old son. Eyestrain and over work. Soon as you get home take a holiday.' He launched up the stairs. Mechanical struggle erupted on the landing. The front door flew open and Robert hurried in with a slopping kettle.

'Soon have a brew,' he promised. 'Where's your mate?' He cocked an interested ear at the stairs, 'kickin' football again?'

The stalemate in the stairwell broke and came crashing towards them. A tangle of metal and flesh burst through the door and sprawled at Robert's feet. He peered up into the dark in case of further traffic, then he helped Steve gently to his feet.

'Son, don't take it personal,' he shook his head sadly, 'but you look like you could use a big mug of hot tea!'

Robert produced a bottle wrapped in brown paper and laced his own cup. He tried to treat theirs too but Jim refused severely.

'Why not? Warm ye up, help ye sleep. No harm in it.'

Steve waggled his eyebrows in favour but Jim's refusal held. Lolling drowsily on the sofa it was obvious they'd have no trouble sleeping anyway. Robert occupied a bursting armchair. He pushed his cap back on his head and it left a thin red line across his glistening forehead. Irrationally Steve found himself looking for stitch-marks.

Robert regaled them with mock-heroic tales of cowardice and cunning on the local crags. Frequent sips from the bottle underlined the satisfaction of events: 'I could see he was in trouble for all his big talk – not used to soloin' y'know – so I dropped him the end of a rope. Right in front of his big policeman's nose but he couldn't take a hand off to scratch himself, never mind tie on, he was that frightened, so he grabbed it in his teeth! An' hung on like a wee tarrier right to the top. I had to wring the spit out of it after. Only time he ever stopped braggin' – when his jaws were clamped around that rope.'

He interrupted himself at last when they yawned in unison.

'Ye'd best be off to bed,' he allowed reluctantly. 'I'll wait up a wee while for Billy. I'm afraid he's fell by the wayside again!' He clucked his tongue and the sad, dry ticking went on and on till he took another sip. Steve caught a look in the rolling eyes for which he had no words, but it startled him with an unexpected sense of pain.

Jim took a candle and they wobbled unsteadily upstairs, sleeping-bags bundled in their arms. The damp air in the bedroom roused them again. The candle stood on the windowsill. The reflection revealed wooden storm-shutters outside the glass.

'We're locked in!' Paddy shivered. 'I didn't notice that before.'

'How could you?' Jim rebuked him sharply. 'Wasn't it dark when we came? That's only to protect the glass from vandals. All the huts use them. Still I'm glad Robert is here; even if he is a bit thick!' He smiled sheepishly and yawned, 'Old-fashioned is right. That's an army coat he's wearing. Did you see the state of the buttons? They haven't been polished in years. He should try that stuff he's drinking on them!'

Steve could not sleep. Urgency shrilled in his head. He couldn't reach its source. His brain rang and rang like a distant telephone. Sparks of perception flared and faded, left a sense of dread at the failure to understand. No idea what he was meant to know; he felt tiny voices scratching at the dark side of language. The candle shivered on the windowsill. Jim snored and Paddy's breath wheezed and rasped in his airways. Steve dozed at last ...

He jerked awake to the sound of footsteps. Creaking heavily up the stairs. The long, steep stairs to a child's ear. The nearer they came, the more his terror sharpened. He wanted to scream, to waken someone strong beside him, but already he was conscious of an extra presence in the room. And still the footsteps mounted the endless stairs. Steve peered through trembling eyelashes.

A heavy figure leaned towards the candle. The flame had dwindled to a midnight flicker. Thin straw-coloured hair, plaid shirt, knee-breeches. The man cocked his head suddenly and looked straight at the sleeping boys as if he detected an error in their breathing. Blood ran jagged and fiery in Steve's veins. Ugly shadows blackened the mouth, the eye sockets, the nose. But the candle flared again and he was smiling over them, a strange tenderness dissolving the bloated face from within.

The light died. For a moment the sad, smiling stare lingered in the burnt darkness. Then Steve heard shuffling feet fade into the constant footsteps on the stairs.

He lay absolutely rigid in his sleeping-bag, every nerve stretched tight. Afraid to turn. Movement might snap his spine. His whisper clawed at Jim's sleep. 'Wake up! Ssh! For God's sake, Sssh!' Paddy sat up instantly. Jim shook his head, groaning.

'We've got to get out of here,' Steve hissed. 'There's something terrible ... Listen to the footsteps.'

Jim listened, his head lolling in the dark. Not a sound, except Steve's heart stammering in his chest and Paddy's wheezing breath.

'For God's sake Steve.'

'No. No! It's true! I saw the same as Paddy. It was Robert ...'

'So what? Go back to sleep.'

'No! I tell you – We've got to get away.' His voice was a whispered wail – 'We're in the wrong place ...'

'OPEN UP!' Fists battered the front door. 'OPEN UP!' A raucous roar. They froze together. 'OPEN UP!'

Steve felt his senses dissolve with shock. Sick, slow thoughts drifted into his skull like the shadows of stunned fish. It was starting again, and again, over and over. 'OPEN UP!' so frail Paddy's wrist in his frantic grip. 'OPEN UP!' Frail and forever the bones of a ten-year old ...

Robert's feet running across the floor. His anxious voice as he struggled with the door, 'Oh my God, are you full again Billy? Keep quiet for God's sake you'll wake everyone ...'

'There's on'y us,' Billy laughed loud and coarse, 'out in the middle of nowhere. I'll shout as loud as I like! And you won't stop me.'

'Aye that's right Billy, that's right, there's no one'll interfere with ye,' Robert soothed nervously. 'Come over here to the fire. I was sittin' up for ye.'

'Who owns all the fancy stuff?' Billy snarled suddenly.

'Ach, a couple o' youngsters Billy, that's all. Couple o' youngsters!' His voice rushed to reassure, 'But they're gone! Up the road Billy. They're gone! They'll be back tomorrow maybe ... Sit down here now,' he wheedled, 'like a decent man, an' I'll make us a sup o' tea.'

'Tea! Tea is it? Are you mockin' me with tea? Is that all ye have?' His voice cracked into curses.

'Och Billy! Billy! What's come over ye? It's a while since ye were this bad. I thought ye were gettin' better. What happened at all?'

A brief, charged silence. The boys strained towards the floor.

'Jesus Christ, Billy, don't take it all in one go! It'll kill ye. Give it here ...' An enraged roar, a sharp blow. A bottle smashed to the floor. Everything stopped dead. Stunned by the explosion.

Paddy shuddered. His skull jolted against Steve's shoulder. The room filled with a choking rasp. Steve threw an arm around him fiercely. 'Not now Paddy! Not now! Not now ...' he pleaded over and over again. 'Where's your inhaler? Where is it Paddy? Where is it?' He was shaking his friend desperately as if he could stifle the attack. In the relentless circle of his arm Paddy writhed and choked, his response a voiceless gasp but Steve heard him clear as a shout. Frail wet fingers clawed at his wrist as he broke away.

The voice began again below, snarling fury. 'You broke it on purpose, you – I'll KILL Ye ...' The darkness seethed with struggle.

No impact. The disembodied violence of nightmare. Like the roar of a radio – sound without substance. Steve swam towards it. The shell of the house hung lifeless, deserted, around him. An old house should rattle like a packing-crate. He felt his nerves strain in a wave of unreason till he was barely holding on, wading through dark water.

He pulled the door open onto the landing. Paddy's crisis pitched him through. Struggle raged beyond the panelled stairs, bone on bone, snarl of vicious breath, boots kicking and skidding. But an icy stillness enclosed the turmoil; furniture skidded without vibration, bodies rebounded from mute walls.

Steve shivered from step to step, wading deeper into the dark. He realised he was almost naked. Vulnerability froze his will.

No farther. The door at the bottom was closed. He could never open that ... that ... lid. He tangled his arms across his chest, crouched on his heels paralysed. Struggle reeled through the room inches from his head. He resisted the bloodless vacancy of a swoon.

There was no one in there; he knew it by the dead drift of the air, the stillness in the flimsy walls. The house echoed emptiness. Echoes and shadows. Reflections. Brutal memories trapped in place. Images, not his own, burned in his brain, things he had never seen; bleak faces staring into the ground. The corner of a soft mouth bleeding; hysterical shreds of battle; black trains thundering. Blood trickling from the mouth, her body naked and vague; cold-eyed men with marching banners. Then – shockingly clear as a portrait – a child's face at the window and through the boy's eyes he saw a soldier running, running and screaming...

The trees! Those trees, leaning at the house like dead sentries! Blood from the soldier's sleeve, running and screaming, the wrist slashed. Behind the eyes the woman lay, Steve could not turn his head, could not ... blood from the soldier's sleeve, wrist slashed to the bone ... could not turn his head.

It was old, old and still burning somewhere. His brain tightened fiercely against the invading flames. Threads of candlelight pierced the panel beside him, knitting and breaking in the dark. Slowly, with infinite abhorrence he leaned towards the crack. His cheekbone trembled on cold paint, eyelashes bending against the light. Thin neck, and brittle bones in his bare back ...

Flailing shadows resolved to one transparent shape, Robert dancing through the room, his face swollen, sweating, hair in tangled locks. In one hand, the glittering neck of a bottle, in the other, the spiked hammer. No one else in the whole room. Thick lips strained across his teeth, a tormented whisper broke from his throat,

'Billy ... Billy ... don't. They're only children ... No!'

He shook his head hopelessly. A jagged wound in his cheek and the hammer bled softly.

Nausea closed Steve's eyes. He slumped against the stairs. Billy's voice grated through the panel, strangled with rage. 'I'll – KILL ...' Steve lifted his head to look for Billy. It took a long, long time. He saw Robert's bloated face again, eyes blazing through the flimsy panel, long teeth grinding curses, 'I'll KILL ...'

Fingers gripped Steve's shoulder. Ice round his heart. 'Come quick! Paddy's choking ...' Jim was shaking him.

He seized Jim's hair, dragged his head towards the crack. Overhead a terrible, tearing rasp. Tissues screaming terminal distress. Steve sweated terror. Knew what he must do – No. No! Impossible. That door –

In the dark pit of the stairwell the brown door pulsed. Paddy's inhaler the other side. He panicked, crawled upstairs. Jim caught him on the landing, 'Murder ...' he mouthed frantically in Steve's ear, 'He'll kill Robert ...'

'Who – ?'

'Billy! He'll kill him ... and then us ...'

'Billy? Did you see ... Billy?'

'Yes, yes! With that hammer ... We've got to escape. Now!'

'No! We can't leave Paddy!'

A strangled shriek rose from downstairs and dwindled to a bubbling moan.

'Oh God. He's done it.'

Steve faltered into the bedroom. Paddy's efforts came at long intervals. He was drowning under the air, his lungs sealed, brain starved. The fire in his chest lit the darkness for Steve. He crouched where Paddy lay sprawled on the platform, his head hanging over the edge. Steve saw him utterly clearly: the veins in his forehead, glazed eyes, blue lips, and the rigid arch of the throat. His inhaler downstairs. Too late. Minutes without oxygen and the brain decayed. He reached for Paddy's hand, found a cold, contorted claw. Tried a kiss of life – breathing into unresponsive bone. He turned from the platform, brushed Jim aside and stumbled to the stairs.

On the first step he pounded the panel with his fist. The whole house drummed. As he descended he began to scream, still drumming. It started as a wail of fear and grief trembling in his throat and rose to a wiry howl of outrage. In his bursting lungs he held all the air Paddy was denied. A scream to scar the ear. And the relentless rattle of the drum. He hurled the door open, entered an icy stillness. Candles guttered in their bottles. A circle of light sucked towards the centre of the room. The air shivered, swirling with invisible shape.

Steve crouched by the panniers. Cold force flogged his body and his skin crawled. The scream moaned in his mouth. His senses narrowed to a single point as he ripped through the pockets.

The inhaler ... Where? Dragged out clothes and shoes. *Where?* Pulled out a lurid packet. Forked tongues squirming ... How much are *they* ... Hurled it away in anguish. Skidded under the sofa. No inhaler. Yellow laces ... Steve wept savagely. Grief and guilt. He found it in the last pocket. Intimate. Essential. Plastic. Useless. How could everything depend ... Too late. He saw Paddy's face again, glasses shattered, cold eyes staring through the rims. In the room candlelight swarmed among the shadows. Steve felt the skin flayed from his back when he rose, took a candle, dragged towards the door.

The house strained against a terrifying suction. Footsteps raged behind him on the stairs. Steve entered the bedroom, locked the door. He pressed the inhaler to Paddy's cold lips and nostrils. The head rolled limply aside, all strain gone. Jim huddled on the platform, his eyes fixed on the door. A string of spittle hung unheeded from his chin. Heavy steps on the long, slow stairs. Steve faced the door. Robert was in the room again – and the steps still rising. A pulse! He felt a pulse in Paddy's wrist. It beat with every ... No ... Every step on the stairs shook the floor and echoed in Paddy's bones. That was all. He dropped the lifeless arm. The door rattled and shook. Vibration shuddered through the room.

'No, Billy ... No ...'

A rending crash. The spiked hammer pierced the door above the lock, withdrew and smashed again. Wood burst inwards, splinters stabbing the air. A fist punched through the hole and groped towards the key.

Steve rose, remembering. He drew the candle from the bottle and broke away the neck. As he approached the hand it turned and offered him its urgent veins and tendons.

THE CLIMBER WHO COURTED DEATH

He left sheaves of scribbled description strewn in friends' houses where he stayed between trips. And wrote bundles of letters; everybody had them. No detail of his wandering was undescribed. In an effort to clear up his effects I collected all the known material, though I am sure there are folders and barely legible journals exiled in England and elsewhere that may never surface. The season in Africa, for example, which began with the Shipton-Tilman traverse of Mount Kenya in honour of two of his heroes, is missing though undoubtedly recorded.

But, finally what was to be done with all these wads of words when I had them stacked in order: notebooks, foolscap, writing pads and six piles of airmail? He was a very ordinary climber by modern standards, so a book of exploits would be unjustified. Neither was he literary in a creative sense – he favoured quantity of description rather than quality of evocation – so no original gem of mountain literature is about to surface. I read and re-read responsively in the hope that a significant form might arrange itself, an obituary or an epitaph emerge of its own accord. He used to be incensed by the media when they made a sensation of climbing accidents. And yet, when he died there was not a single word in any paper. He would have resented that too in his contradictory way.

That was my fault: I could have informed them, I suppose. But I didn't.

The earliest writing is a diary kept when he was twenty-three, before any of us knew him and before climbing became the motive force of his existence. The Alps appear marginally in these obsessed notes; he passed them by, a tumult on the horizon. Love had let him down, literature had failed him, mountains were not yet a distraction. The most recent record is a letter I received two weeks before his death at the age of thirty-four. He was killed in the Alps, below the Flammes de Pierre at the foot of the Dru. Killed by stonefall.

After this letter like a full stop comes Henri's telegram from Chamonix: 'Accident. Jack mort. Quoi faire?'

The first and last writings are the most affecting of all. They reflect the contrasts of the life between with a stark clarity. The final letter bubbles with self-assured opinions and exploits from Yosemite and the climbing-resorts of the American West.

Yosemite is a dream of El Dorado and Disneyland, valley of invincible legend and tasteless tourism. Escape via paradisal rock from the trash of expensive leisure ... Camp 4 is a Who's Who of international competition. Every exchange of greetings is a discreet clash of swords. I'm relieved by my own mediocrity ... Went up to do the Chouinard/ Herbert on Sentinel with a bowery bum but he chickened out on the walk-in. Raged on alone and did the Steck-Salathé instead. Took me the whole damn day. Not quite your respectable free 5.9. either. Got my skull stuck in the Narrows. The scene is burnt into my brain like a colour-slide, 1000 feet up, 15 feet inside the face, headjammed in a rock bottleneck, staring out between granite blinkers through a chink in the cliff at a vertical slice of sky, a strip of Sunnyside Wall, a green stripe of Valley. Picturesque, but I had to push on ...

Of course he was rubbing in (with his light allusion) the two days I spent on the same route last year. He never missed a chance to compare and excel.

When Jack said he soloed a route it could mean a lot of things. The only definite interpretation was that he climbed it without a partner. But he seldom ventured onto hard rock without a backrope and the possibility of protection. He picked routes which should be well within his capacity and so a good deal of his soloing was authentic with the backrope trailing in case he needed to throw in a nut and rope off. For longer, less predictable routes he developed self-belay techniques to a high degree of speed, and claimed he could abseil a pitch to clean it and jumar back to his high point faster than the average second could have climbed it. Or so he liked to think.

Not that he was particularly concerned with ethics anyway. He climbed to get up the route, and enjoyed it best on his own. Lack of technique was never allowed to interfere if a sling could pull him over a problem. He didn't give a damn about great climbers either. Except for Walter Bonatti. Bonatti was his hero. 'It would take ten of your average great climbers to do what Bonatti did alone. And they'd all die young,' he wrote back to me in a kind of postal yell when I expressed reservations about one of Bonatti's books. But that was another time, another needle. That last American letter continued:

Those slab routes on Glacier Apron and the Tuolumne domes are the most enjoyable climbing I've ever done. Getting used to friction is like being a novice again, you have to learn techniques, tricks, tolerances. We get jaded by habit and experience, and lose the fun of novelty; but I think I've rediscovered enjoymen – especially this sunny honey-coloured stuff, if you can imagine that in the drenched deprivation of an Irish summer!

I could imagine him alright, front-pointing up golden acres of slabs, invisible crampons on his rock boots, and the rope tied off to a skimpy bolt. It was the sourness of my envy that turned the sun to ice.

There isn't a trace of shadow in that last summer; it's all sun and jubilation. He enclosed a slide: unroped on a slabby arête, his wiry figure bunched in concentration, black hair tied back in a pony-tail and his dark skin smeared with chalk in elaborate patterns of war-paint. That was meant to provoke, some of us didn't agree with chalk at that time. But the overall effect was electric: I looked for the tomahawk.

But that was the summer chapter. The previous winter had been a different story, the winter of his thirty-fourth year. He came into the States deviously from Canada. He had been to Alaska, to climb McKinley of course, and to work, to do whatever occurred, but some kind of muscle injury in his leg began to gnaw at his nerves and he moved south instead. Not far enough though. He spent an appalling winter working in Connecticut, an even worse fate than spending it in Scotland he reckoned. The leg kept him out of good jobs, the heavy work, and he had to double-shift to earn enough, working in a hotel kitchen and then bartending at night. He felt he aged unbearably that winter, while all his claims were on youth and being young.

Hartford is a fatal city, a precast mausoleum. The Insurance capital of the world reeks of security and death. I'm staying in the YMCA for the sake of the gym. I play endless games of handball in streamlined alleys with elderly fitness-freaks who accept me as one of their own. We're a sorry crew, Budweiser and small cigars, our knees strapped up in pink elastic, stinking of wintergreen ...

Whenever people asked me for news of Jack, in the ironic tone of voice that expresses the envy of the bound for the free, I heard myself reciting landmarks on an exotic itinerary: Peru, Nepal, Africa, Norway. All the places I wanted to go myself. Sometimes it was hard to resist using him as an *alter ego* and pretending it was me out there gallivanting around the mountain-ranges of the world, impervious to paternity, impecunity, mortgages, the various conditions that shackled the rest. Not to mention motivation. Jack maintained we married and bred to excuse our lack of motivation.

But on the other hand, it wasn't really difficult to understand how much his freedom cost. After a while it became obvious that Jack's mobility was not by choice. He always grew irritable and irritating after a long lay-off, pettily argumentative; and then just on the margin of dislike he disappeared. He abandoned people and places not because he wanted to – in fact he never stopped talking about involvement – but because he grew bored with himself and his own restrictions. He couldn't bear that sense of futility that most of us have to put up with and learn to ignore.

'The claustrophobia of the quotidian,' he growled in an English diary with that tedious taste of his for genitive phrasemaking. 'This must be how a battery-hen would feel if it could think.'

It seems a bit melodramatic because he liked a lot of people genuinely and kept in close touch with them. In fact those letters are usually cheerful celebrations of some exotic environment and there is little if any pressure or resentment apparent.

But the diaries are the shadow-side of the story. It seems as if the private writing is a kind of one-man dialogue to talk away isolation. It is ironic that, in spite of all his efforts at communication, his best writing occurs in passages that were never meant to be read. He unleashes real feelings there, even if it is a kind of despair.

1st of May, feast day of the sun, national day of distress, Mayday! Mayday! Outside the window it is snowing vehemently, all the apple-blossom in every suburb of the world stripped violently from the boughs and whirled before the wind. A naked shrub in the garden disposes snowflakes among its branches like bleak petals, but lower, on the slushy grass, daffodils thrash in panic. How bitter that yellow. There is nothing redeeming in it.

Staring through the window into the ironic snow on Mayday, rubbing the fogged-up glass of April and March, peering through the February pane, breathing on the January ice, I am struck by the sense of winter as a taste, a taste remembered like a clot of glass in the miserable mouth, and I cannot spit it out, and I cannot swallow it, it is there until ... until it dissolves.

Something grievous that happened long ago is settling into a groove of years. Something else is jagged as ever – like an accident hidden beneath the skin. We are wrapped around our secret accidents. Continuity freezes in the blood; it scrapes against the bone.

When I was twenty I regarded myself as about sixteen. It wasn't a matter of numbers, just a feeling. And the decade that wound up to the thirty mark passed as if I was just slowly, thoroughly, turning seventeen. Then suddenly Time couldn't take the strain any more; like stretched and stretched elastic it shot back into shape this winter and I was catapulted viciously into the fact of my consolidated years. For a fraction of time things continued out of focus like the final, brief vibrations of rubber in its regained shape, but the images quickly overlapped, and now I am what I am, and there is a slackness where elasticity has been lost.

Loneliness is a tangible aspect of things, the sour rind of existence.

It seems after his break-up with Margaret there were none of those alliances of the heart, or even of the head, that contain assurances of a future. In fact I think the failure of all his attachments – to romance, creativity, or work – must have wiped out *any* future. He was dedicated to climbing; a terminal devotion in more ways than one, for when the body and the nerves begin to go down hill at an unreasonably early age, what is there left for the mountaineer? Is there any future in gradually climbing down the grades at lower and lower altitudes, watching unrequited aspirations vanish behind impossible clouds?

So he was desperately impatient to get things done. Especially when he began to suffer what he described variously as rheumatism, lumbago, arthritis, sciatica, and fibrositis, sometimes all at once. He wrote to me with a savage snap when I turned down an expedition he was trying to organise. He never understood the mundane problems and responsibilities of normal people. When I told him something would turn up to salvage his plans he wrote back, 'What's the use of saying "something will turn up."'? Half the world is waiting for something to turn up. They die of waiting and that's the only thing that ever happens to them.'

He had been climbing, it seems, on and off for a while before he really discovered it as a lifestyle; that is to say, he might struggle up three or four climbs a year if he happened to find them in his vicinity, but it wasn't a passion. Water was his element then. He lived in Kerry, Clare, Galway, Donegal, along the Atlantic as much as he could, working on trawlers, diving for illegal lobsters, selling black sea-urchins to the exporters.

Margaret lived with him through most of that time: about five years, she says. We wrote to her after the accident to tell her what happened. It seemed the right thing to do, although I have only met her once. She teaches in Mayo and never comes to Dublin. She confirmed a few hints he dropped about that period, his urge to write, copious drinking, irritating restlessness. But she refused to let me see any letters. They were private, she said. Of course I shouldn't have asked; it's just that I was collecting them from others and forgot that hers would be different.

I knew his original ambitions had been literary. Margaret says he slaved over it hopelessly. When he gave up there was nothing left, not even a manuscript. He told me once on our way through Germany how he left his entire opus in a luggage-locker in Frankfurt. When he returned to empty the locker he didn't have the money to pay the extra charges, so he abandoned the lot. It was a gesture. He accepted there was no loss to posterity. And I accepted the story as a metaphor.

And that brings me to the notebook, the first one. It is a brief diary of that brief trip to the continent during which he lost touch with everything, including Margaret and his epic novel. ('Epic novel' is a guess, but it feels right.) He was a shattered twenty-three year old, a depressed romantic, wandering around in a bad winter with a cheap sleeping-bag and a Gibson guitar. The disjointed entries show him busking in freezing subways, sleeping under bridges, drinking malevolently in bars where he refused to tip the waiters. He gets beaten up twice in two months. The writing shows lingering traces of the literary urge in its tone of the studied throwaway.

Slept in a tennis-court in Liege last night. It froze viciously but it's another luminous day. At daybreak I heard a leaf fall from a tree at a distance of at least thirty yards, a staccato measure of the sharp frost. The leaf snapped decisively from its twig and rattled down a lattice of bare branches hitting the concrete below with a final crackling report.

He moved across to Paris in a shower of unquotable references to Joyce, Beckett, and Ezra Pound. 'The sturdy, unkillable infants of the poor' he called them mysteriously, without any justification that I can think of. Awoke shattered this morning, in ribbons, in a doorway near the Gare de Lyon. Cambodian Airways, I think. The usual fragmented memories of an excessive evening. Luckily I had the instinct to encase myself in cardboard, because it froze poisonously last night.

Hounded by a sequence of hangovers and venomous frosts he explored the city, 'I walk, and walk, and somehow waste the city. I walk until my legs ache from hip to ankle. Scenes impinge upon my retina, slide off, are lost, without awe, indifferently. My mind will not connect. I cannot experience enthusiasm.'

Arrested by the police for persistently busking in the subway under the Etoile – it was the warmest one – he spent a miserable week in jail, the rhymed entry reading:

> All dreams are sad dreams;
> Sad in their failure to come true,
> Sad in their consequences if they do.

But that week in the cells seems to have given him the necessary perspective on his drinking, because he moved to Germany, distractedly noting the Alps *en route*, intent on saving some money and establishing a 'sense of purpose'. Weeks later, after a harrowing excursion northwards involving a blizzard and tattered tennis-shoes, he is on the ferry out of Ostend where he landed a few months earlier:

The circle curves into its final arc.

As we leave Ostend the continental coast is visible only as a carious ridge of apartment blocks trailing their disjointed geometry along the shore. The sky is in virtuoso mood, a full range of variations from inviolate blue to hammersnouted thunder clouds down the edge of which the sun streams in yellow strains onto a turbulent sea, sullen with shadow and the hue of churned sand.

It must have been soon after that morbid interlude that he arrived in Dublin and I met him for the first time. I was looking for a climbing partner and he was enthusiastic. We met in Dalkey Quarry in the evenings and went to Wicklow or Clare on occasional weekends. He let me lead a lot at first, though I suspected he was a better climber than I. Afterwards I understood that this was because his interest had not yet focused into the passion it later became.

Fascinated even then by the idea of soloing he was certainly not an ideal partner. The classic route on a crag which anyone else would have wanted to lead he aspired to solo on sight, so he was constantly avoiding those plum routes that I particularly craved. If there was no one else to do the necessary, he would reluctantly concede and second me on a classic, although he did refuse point-blank to follow Pis Fliuch one weekend when we were alone. He held my rope of course, with a suitable blend of regret and determination and I only had to abseil to retrieve my gear. But I missed the fellowship of shared climbing while he shakily soloed the pitch afterwards, and I could not make up my mind whether I should wait below to scrape him off the rocks, or above in case he needed a top-rope.

It was the same in Wales: he had to solo Cemetery Gates, though he followed my lead on it then. I tried not to feel upstaged, but sometimes I felt it was becoming a bit of an act with him. Afterwards he seconded Cenotaph Corner – he expressed no desire to solo that one – and pulled heartily on the upper peg. When I ridiculed him for this breach of ethics he showed no interest in the issue.

When leading, he climbed rapidly, using strength just as much as technique, placing competent protection if it was available. Soloing was a different matter; he rested a good deal and moved in short, sharp bursts between stances. He was not averse to pulling up on a sling for prior inspection of a move, though afterwards he might climb it free.

He lashed across Dream of White Horses one sunny afternoon as if it were the cliff-path walk, which I suppose it is, and I got the best sequence of pictures I've ever taken.

Perhaps that's not a bad image for our lopsided partnership: the leader way out in front on a top quality route, unfortunately without a rope, while the second consoles himself with a camera. But that doesn't mean he took advantage of me either! I was no more a natural second than he was. Climbing, to me, means leading. I had no hesitation about finding another partner whenever a route rankled between us.

Vector, for example, was a glint in his eye and a taste in my mouth at the same time. I argued that it would be a clear suicide verdict if he attempted a free-solo of that poisonously polished route and that anything less than an ethical ascent would be cheap. The glint remained however and I did the route with a Yorkshire climber who found the whole episode a great Irish joke. I've searched his notes for any later mention of Vector but it doesn't feature and I somehow doubt that he ever ventured onto it.

Still, despite its imbalance, the partnership had its rewards. He was intense company and would go anywhere, anytime with or without money. We spent several seasons in the Alps, shivering in wet tents, while the routes snuggled deeper into the eternal snow. But we met everyone through his celebrated Gibson. We became acquainted with a whole generation of musical mountaineers over Bob Dylan, Woody Guthrie, the Dubliners, and the bit of Bach that was obligatory then in the late sixties and early seventies.

To pay our boat-fares home we busked in Geneva and Paris, and here his infuriating obstinacy revealed itself again. Though an exceptional guitarist, he was only an average singer. His voice was pleasant enough, but it didn't have the power for cinemas and subways. But he always insisted on singing when he busked, though he could have made a fortune as an instrumentalist, playing blues, ragtime, classical. When he sang, usually Dylan, he let the guitar lapse into simple background rhythms, and it was only between verses that he impressed passers-by. But he insisted that singing was what he preferred. It took a week to raise the money we could have made in a day.

After two or three of these sodden seasons he began to travel further, managing trips that were off limits to me with a career to look after. But I upstaged him on America by combining a seminar in Los Angeles with a month in Yosemite. I'm still paying for it in credibility to the job, but I'll get over that.

Jack resented me getting there first. It took him completely by surprise, like a mutiny. I was supposed to be his shadow, his photographer, following behind. He was building up for a long time to Yosemite: he wanted to be good enough to solo the Nose! But when I broke away and asserted my independence and *my* values he had to get there quick and set the record straight. People tell me I'm being paranoid about things like that, but I can't see why else he would have soloed all my routes, and made such a point of telling me about it. There is no further mention of the Nose either. The nearest he got to that was the East Buttress of El Capitan.

I certainly have happier memories of the Alps. Competition doesn't seem to have soured our climbing there, but maybe that's only because we never got a great deal done anyway. Despite endless misfortune with the weather Jack never relented in his alpine ambitions, and he headed back there this summer as soon as California overheated. That last letter from Yosemite ends:

> Henri has invited me to stay with them in their chalet, but I rather think not.
>
> I suspect I don't get on too well with Julie; she thinks I'm a bad influence on her cher Henri. Personally I think *she's* a bad influence on cher Henri, but anyway I shall probably be on Snell's Field if you make it.

There was no chance of me making it. I was due to become a parent in August, and still placating the firm over that embezzled month. But I enviously anticipated the next letter. Was I wishing him success, or hoping he would fail without me? His prime ambition in the Alps was to solo one of the routes on the Dru. Not the famed Bonatti Pillar, nor the excessive American Direct, but the beautiful and original North Face route, the Allain-Leininger. Of course it is the most visually arresting aspect of that improbable monolith, with its snowy niche like an eye of paradise blind to the inferior world. He felt that a man alone, frontpointing across that olympian névé would have transcended the flat laws of destiny. And though he had climbed harder and more technical lines, that one was always 'the great route in the sky' since the first day we stood in Les Praz and stared up in awe like savages confronted with the Statue of Liberty.

People will want to know what he was doing in the couloir under the Flammes de Pierre if it was the North Face of the Dru he was interested in. That couloir leads to the Bonatti Pillar. The North Face is around the other side. I would say it was just typical Jack. He was gratifying a fantasy, taking a look at the Pillar – that sheer monument to his deathless hero Bonatti who soloed the first ascent over six days of total immersion in self. Jack would have looked, and then gone round to the North Face. The weather would turn bad as it always did, and he would go down. If that sounds sour it is only because it's sad. With people like Jack all truths, like dreams, are sad truths.

So, I suppose, here too at thirty-four, a fuller circle curved into its final arc. But I owe one particular last debt.

It is a memory of a sombre June morning a year or so after our partnership began. We were attending the funeral of a friend. Jack and I had found the broken body at the foot of a crag and gone through the grim recovery process without flinching. But in the church he suffered an attack of nausea. Pale candles guttered beside the polished coffin, the brown benches creaked with mourners, he saw the old priests genuflecting, gliding, dipping, like birds of prey he thought, and he turned visibly green before stumbling out into the world of sky and air. Afterwards, in the gloomy fellowship of grief, he said defiantly:

'If it happens to me I don't want any of those mealy mouthed bastards near me. Chuck me out to sea or something instead.'

I saw what he meant alright – though I tried to make a joke of it.

'I won't have it either. Over my dead body,' I said.

And that is the final reason for this valedictory memoir; that no one was there to see the dealers in death didn't get him first. My daughter was born in early August, two days before Henri's message arrived. We were expecting congratulatory telegrams and it took some time for the truth to penetrate. Under the circumstances I could only reply: 'Enterrez.'

THE GIFT OF TONGUES

'Brake!' Jacko yelled. 'Now!'

The silver car dug into the road. Invisible impact. Rubber howling, the back end skated.

'Handbrake. NOW!' Light and noise streaked the dark. Was it a roll? Jem's skull shrank. Long, shuddering skid, hurled round the handle in his fist. Still upright. Police lights scorched his eyes, veered at him.

'Now! Ram! Now!' Powerful blast in first, lift-off in second. The blue flash jerked aside. Space-invader. White-hot glimpse of faces, gaping mouths, bonnet vaulting the grass.

'Chicken! You shoulda creamed him –'

'Too fast Jacko! Too fast! We woulda been wiped –'

The car was loose in Jem's hands. Sweat and street lights blinded him. The needle at eighty and creeping up. It controlled the car: Jem only clung to the wheel. Too much road all of a sudden, a whole runway. Headlights flashed panic at him.

'You're on the wrong side!' Jacko whooped. Wrong side of the carriage-way. Weaving through a chaos of traffic lights, pinball reds and greens.

'Where are we, Jacko? Where –'

'Cabinteely bypass. Headin' into town. You're gettin' the feel of her, Jem. The handbrake turn was ace.'

Rush of pride along strained nerves. Cars scattering, horns blaring. The dashboard winked and glowed below eye-level. Jem saw the bony fingers fiddle through the static on the radio. 'Want to hear what they're saying?' Jacko's left arm was folded in a sling inside his jacket. Smashed in a head-on a month before. Then, he drove twenty miles in a wrecked Orion, two cars on his tail and shook them off. Jem envied the cool nerve. Nerve pulled Jacko's face tight as an axe-head, sharp forehead, beaked nose, pointed chin, the cheekbones flattened back to wiry hair.

... BMW. Silver. British reg. Foxrock 9.50 towards city-centre. Aggressive. Stand clear ...

Jacko bared his teeth in pleasure. Jem felt the net closing.

He slipped out of it, into the TV thrill. Waiting for the silver car to punch across the screen, chrome flaring, hunched stuntman, squad cars closing like jackals. He'd turn up the sound, light a smoke, drink tea, scratch an armpit, sit back – but he was into a bend, wrestling the wheel, real walls rushing. The car went down on one knee and wailed around, tyres shrill as sirens.

'Can't take it Jacko. Too much.' Too much for Jem, the real thing.

'Get a grip, man!' Contempt. 'Get off the main drag. They're waitin' in Donnybrook. Get a grip.'

A trail of shock, Foster's Avenue to Dundrum, outraged lights and horns. Denim stuck to Jem's short legs. Sweat slid into his shoes. The seat held his plump body like a catapult, skull aimed through the windscreen. He peered out onto the flying bonnet, jet-wing touching down, taking off. Another mistake and Jacko would take her one-armed. Pull over! You short-arsed spa!

Swooping from the Bottle Tower down to Terenure. The fancy arch. Trees on the pavements. Houses hiding. Toy cars behind tin gates. A park by a river. No caravans, no horses.

Red lights. Jem put the boot down. To show Jacko. Through the junction, blind jolt of terminal fear – like the electric chair.

Jacko didn't blink. Colour-blind and speed-crazy. The best.

'Coppers!' Jacko pointed. In the park, running figures. 'Stop!'

Jem went through it again. Brakes, handbrake, car writhing all over the road. He saw them coming. Two cops, one shadow. Jacko threw the rear door open.

'In!' he yelled. 'Take her away, Buttsy!'

'Taxi' the passenger gasped, 'Taxi, I –' Foreign. A fit of coughing. Jem spun around. A featureless silhouette.

'Jacko!' he hissed, 'he's fuckin' Black!'

Jacko was clicking fingers, impatiently. 'Got smack, man?'

'Taxi, I –'

'Don't come the tourist, Sambo! Them coppers weren't running for a bus. What is it; H? Coke?' Full of harsh threat.

'Friend. Friend, I have nothing.' The voice had leaned forward, spoke behind Jem's ear. Never heard anything like it before. Like water feeling its way in dry ground. Words poured between pebbles, polishing edges.

Jem pursued the voice. It seemed to come from somewhere remote, over distance and effort. There was an echo in it too, a strange sense of chorus. It was more than accent. His ear had to work to recognise language trickling in the complex sound.

A siren slashed. Close. Jem panicked. 'They're coming. In front! What'll I do?'

'Put the boot down, and Keep it down. Don't stop for nothing!'

The squad-car swung off the road. Word of the ramming had got through. Jem saw the strength of Jacko's tactic. Lash out loud and early. Violence had right of way. Confrontation wasn't Jem's style.

Cunning. But he was learning. The lesson continued; 'Don't bullshit me, blackie! You're dealin'. Cut us in or you'll have to be scraped off that road.'

'I have nothing to give but gratitude.' Deep resignation saddened the voice. Jacko lunged one-handed. Jem stalled him. Honesty stuck out a mile here.

'What were they after?' His voice sounded like broken glass in his mouth. 'The police. Why were they chasin' you?'

'They were not police. Not your *police*.' The words rippled in Jem's head, like water insistent among stones. Not your police. Whose vigilantes were they so, these men with the brutal look of assassins? 'An oil ship. Many days ...'

'Drug Squad,' Jacko snorted, 'I smelled them a mile off.'

'No I am alien!' Jacko spun again. 'Refugee. Illegal immigrant in Ireland.'

'Where you from, George?'

'I come from B –' Consonants buzzed in Jem's ear, 'near to Ethiopia and Sudan.'

'Africa?'

'Af-ri-kah –' The syllables sighed, breath of the burnt continent, land of safari and starvation.

'What brought you here?' Jem was interested.

'Dope, man! Dealin' dope,' Jacko was still certain.

The voice cut him off with passionate insistence, 'I did not come to buy or sell. I have nothing that you need. My people are lost and broken. I come for help ... to Mister Geldof.'

Dun Laoghaire 2, Jem read, dislocated. Picture of a carferry on the sign.

'Kick him out!' Jacko raged. 'He's takin' the piss. Geldof!'

'Sir Geldof!' Jem sniggered. 'How did you get into the country?' He was always interested in the angles. A planner.

'On a ship to your city.' A shudder of disgust. 'An oil-ship.
'Many days and nights from Suez. I was sick, hidden in a sm-a-a-al place.'

'What do you want Geldof for anyway?'

The silhouette in the mirror trembled. 'Our mountains have turned to dust. Soon they will blow away. Four years without crops – !'

Jacko exploded: 'Are yez bleedin' hungry *again*? Turn around,' he ordered Jem, 'He's not getting a lift home!'

The African resumed, his words booming gravely and for a moment Jem imagined the single voice came from many mouths. 'Our people were proud. We lived among high mountains. In dry seasons we held the soil with the weight of our existence. Now we are scattered below and our blood sickens. There is nothing for us there. I am sent to seek help.'

'All the way to Ireland!' Jacko yelped. 'We can't even help ourselves!'

'We know your country is an enemy of hunger. A priest was with us many years. He spoke often of your own famine. We could not accept his teaching. We do not change our ways. But he taught us anyway.'

The interior of the car was drenched in familiar, ghastly amber. Jem recognised the bypass once again. Perhaps it was another one. Round in circles. The law was gone to ground and the car seemed to float above the road drifting in and out of light traffic, the occasional air-pocket rippling the wheels. Jem dreamed of a jet-wing swooping across continents and oceans.

Day and night, dark and light around the spinning globe. Palm trees, blue seas, brown bodies on golden beaches. Broken bodies in ditches. Hunger and health, rags and wealth, life and death, day and night, dark and light, hour after hour after hour; boats, trains, cars, bikes crawling below him.

He saw a tall, black figure race across a blazing desert, slipping over the surface like the shadow of another plane. Disturbing images. Not the way he was accustomed to dream. He pulled backwards on the steering-wheel with a sudden longing.

The car lifted smoothly and soared away from the earth. A hostess brought tea to the flight-deck. Nice take-off, Captain. Barrels and a bumpy junction and he broke blind lights at the church for Jacko.

'What do they call you, George?' he enquired over his shoulder.

For the duration of the impossible syllables the confusion surrounding the voice was resolved. Then it returned, a weave of echoes.

'Will you take me to Mister Geldof, please?'

Jem felt a frightened chill at the back of his neck. It shivered down his spine and he accepted it. The power in the voice! Not asking a favour. Just stating a right, politely. His leg flexed in a decision and the brake bit slowly. Halted on the crown of the road he switched on the interior light and turned around. Silence – except for Jacko hissing *Don't like Mondays* through his teeth, rapping the rhythm on the dash.

Jem stared at the man behind him. His own body was squat with a short thick neck and to look around he almost had to flop on to his belly.

In contrast, the African almost touched the roof of the car with his astonishing head. He did not look hungry; indeed, like sculpture he seemed self-sufficient as if capable of maintaining the same polished shape forever. The skin was absolutely black, so black that streetlights, reflections, the pearly radiance of the interior lamp, drowned in it without a glimmer. With its delicate features exquisitely drawn, the face at first looked small and childlike and it was only when he realised again the height of the man and the size of his extraordinary head that Jem understood the nature of the person gazing quietly down at him. A child grown old without the loss of innocence.

Pain had spared the dignified, dark eyes under arched eyebrows and there was no bitterness around the mouth. But as he gaped in fascination Jem slowly penetrated the illusion. Something had worn away the flesh beneath the skin and brought the bones agonisingly close to the smooth surface, and soon the skull would be exposed without any camouflage at all.

The cropped hair shaped to the head was dusted with silver and Jem's sacrilegious fingers itched to feel where the texture lay between black lamb and steel-wool.

He sat in the back of the huge car with his knees heaped in front of him and his arms draped around them as if those were his only belongings, although a small, incongruous suitcase rested on the seat beside him. He wore a loose boiler suit, probably – Jem reckoned – the property of the distressful oil tanker.

He seemed relaxed now, as if he had placed himself with total confidence in the hands in which he found himself. Jem and Jacko and their silver taxi.

Jem broke the hard news.

'Geldof's not here,' he said. 'He lives in England. Sorry.'

'He is here.' The answer was not contradiction. A guttural sigh of assurance.

'He's not bleedin' *here*!!' Jacko exploded. 'Wrong country. Tough shit!' Yet he stopped short of eviction. Was he afraid, Jem wondered? Jacko was afraid of nothing. It was the compulsion in the voice, the madness of belief.

'It was a long, hard way. For a long time I ran. Without food or water. Then the sea. I was guided on my journey. We know many secrets.' And again he said it, infinitely confident, 'He is here.'

He sat behind Jem solid as a hump on his back. Jacko scratched his narrow jaw and scowled. 'Leave him. We'll find another jammer –'

He prepared to walk away. Fast lights in the distance raced towards them. He leapt in again. 'Go!'

Newpark Avenue down to Blackrock, out the seafront to the Punch Bowl, the shore of the world black beside them. They lost the tail in Booterstown. Jem handled the car as if he was born to it. All the time the impassive face stared over his shoulder hardly rocking with the motion of the chase. The great dark eyes were open, but they glanced neither right nor left, nor did they blink at the strobe-lights of frantic cars. They simply stared straight ahead to a final destination.

'Any ideas?'

'Try the Pink,' Jacko growled.

Jem stared at him, amazed at the concession, then he covered it smoothly. 'Time we had a pint in anyway. And a change of wheels.'

He turned to his passenger with the self-importance of a guide, 'We'll ask in The Pink Elephant. They'll know if he's around.'

'Don't count on it, but. Far as I know he hasn't got the boat fare home. He gave it all away an' now he's skint. The Rats haven't had a hit in years.'

'Like hell he's skint!' Jacko jeered.

'Yes,' the voice interrupted, 'we must find him soon.'

It sounded faint and faraway and when Jem glanced in the mirror the statuesque head was no longer directly behind him but slumped sideways against the seat. He recognised the symptoms, screeched to a halt outside a chip shop and threw Jacko a fiver.

'Burger and chips. Quick!'

'Bloody hell, do they never feed themselves?'

'Smoked cod for me and whatever you're havin' yourself.'

Jem waited nervously, engine racing. A thought struck him – 'D'you eat meat?' The head shook weakly, but the eyes remained closed. He hopped out and roared after Jacko, 'Get fish! He's a bleedin' vegetarian.'

Jacko streaked through the door, loaded with food and pursued by a fat man in an apron. The car sped away and Jacko stuffed the fiver in his own pocket. He dumped a steaming package in the African's lap. 'Meals on bleedin' wheels!' he grumbled.

'Get that down ya,' Jem advised generously. 'You can't go drinkin' on an empty stomach.'

Jem spilled his own chips into the space behind the gear stick, apparently designed for that purpose, and angled the greasy mirror to watch the performance behind.

The passenger sat up weakly and held the food in his two hands. His eyes were open again in a visionary gaze, and his lips moved in clear, poignant silence.

Jem was staggered by the sight of prayer. The chips in his own gullet turned to wet ash and he gobbled fiercely at the smoked cod to overcome an extraordinary distress.

The African was still praying. Or else he'd forgotten where his mouth was. Jem could stand it no longer.

'When did you eat last?'

The man bowed his head and thought. He selected a chip between long slender fingers. 'I cannot say. A long time. Before the ship – I do not know,' he admitted simply. And ate. A little. Some chips. The shrivelled fish he ignored.

Jem was suddenly terrified. He felt himself on the verge of the unthinkable. Alien. Far worse than foreign. Foreigners ate four or five meals a day like himself. They were human. Now the idea of starvation as a way of life struck him with the force of blind terror. Again he saw the shape racing across the broad, burnt earth. It was thin and tall, hard as a needle. A bone needle.

The city centre was quiet. Jem drove decently now. No coat-trailing.

'Dump it!' Jacko ordered impatiently as he sought a parking-space. 'We'll get something else after. Turbo maybe.'

Jem stopped in a loading-bay. No Parking Day or Night.

'Right George,' he invited the African, 'let's go find Geldof.'

He was amazed at the gentleness of his own voice. Never sounded like that before. He spat on the pavement to compensate.

The stranger grew suddenly agitated at the conclusion of his mission.

There were tears in his eyes and his hands fluttered up and down his person. He seized the small case and drew out a long, coloured garment, fold after fold of radiant material. Handling it reverently he slipped it over his head. As it unfolded down his body he shed the boiler suit, rolling it neatly and placing it in the suitcase. Jem and Jacko prowled uneasily, trying to seem a thousand miles from the stolen car.

He lifted each bare foot in turn, dusted it carefully and inserted it into a sandal of soft leather laced with thongs. Then he handed the suitcase to Jem who received it without question.

Stepping out onto the pavement the African stood up slowly to his full, uninterrupted height. Even Jacko stared, helpless.

The man was ridiculously impressive, a head and neck taller than Jacko but slender as a sapling and somehow leaning gently backwards all the way from his waist to the tapered crown of his head as if he possessed, instead of normal balance, some defiant sense of grace designed for looking upwards rather than down.

Jem was totally convinced and knew this was his weakest moment.

He could go along with a joke or a whim or any mad dash in the night, but this dark truth was too demanding.

He was about to point the way and disappear, but Jacko was already striding towards The Pink, and Tzammeniya Maseratu Harathanazu followed in his wake.

'Who?'

'Geldof! I said Geldof ' Jacko rapped. 'Is he here?'

'You mean *Bob* Geldof?'

'You mean *Mick* Jagger!' Jacko mimicked the barman.

Typical, Jem reflected. Hadn't the brains to get the pints before he started a row.

He nudged the African who stood aloof from the crowd, arms folded within his sleeves. The serene face and huge, unfocused eyes burned with a clean, ebony flame through the clamour, the colour and the smoke. In the long, loose robe, standing perfectly detached, he looked like a supreme magician who had just materialised on the spot and was about to do something simultaneously simple and stunning. Every voice hushed in expectation.

Jem was overawed but manners prevailed. 'What'll you have, George?'

No answer. A cup of water he thought obscurely and called three pints.

He saw a rock-star on a velvet bar-stool between two blonde companions. The girls stared at his African. The rock-singer stared at his drink.

Jem thrust his low, fat grin into the group. 'Hey,' he enquired, leaning on one of the velvet girls, 'is Geldof around? My friend wants to know,' he indicated the African for support. 'Matter of life or death.'

The rock-star shrugged. The pupils of his eyes were saturated.

His companions giggled. Jem felt he was not being taken seriously. None of his guest's charisma had rubbed off on him

'Who is he, your friend?' the rock-star mumbled.

'You mean you don't know who he is?' Jem's lip curled in contempt.

'Well he's not Joan Armatrading! So who the fuck is he?'

'Nelson Mandela.' The first name in Jem's head.

'Yeah. Heard of him. You his roadie? Tell him Geldof's not here.'

He turned away, and one of his attendants cradled his petulant face in her thin hands.

Farther down the bar Jacko was engaged in a row of his own. In a revised mental aside Jem wondered was it a reflection on the upper classes that he and Jacko could never enter their pubs without trouble.

The impassive stance of the African was unnerving Jem. If he was left there much longer this crowd would hang coats on him.

Time was running out. Voices raised – chiefly Jacko's.

'Hey Roadie!' Jem was tapped on the shoulder. A tough, handsome young man with the muscle-vest, worn jeans, battered boots, and the cynical face of a road-show driver.

'Geldof's in Wicklow,' he drawled. 'At a party. They flew him over.' He nodded at his disgruntled boss, the rock-star, 'He wasn't invited.'

'They flew him over? For a party?'

'Yeah, man. This evening. In a private jet. Just to be there –'

'Where's the party?'

'Near Ashford. The Viscount's place. They won't let *you* in though. He should be alright. Some kinda witch-doctor is he?'

'Yeah.' Jem whistled between two fingers. 'Let's go Jacko!' One on each elbow they hustled the African like a hijacked statue out of The Pink.

While Jacko slipped back to hurl bricks Jem stole another car. Something dignified. He had a stylish sense of mission now. A limousine with tinted windows? CD plates?

He found a silver Mercedes, beautifully sleek, so sleek it was hardly a

Merc at all. He had to check the badge. He stumbled heavily against the car. No alarm.

Smiling apologetically at his black friend – again the feeling was new – he reached inside his jacket and drew out his personal persuader. It was a metal bar shaped like a small starting-handle. There was a slender key-shape of hardened steel mounted on the end of the bar.

Jem stabbed it into the keyhole and with a sudden wrench burst the door lock.

'Belongs to a friend. He won't mind,' he assured the African.

As the long, black legs disappeared into the cream interior Jem saw that the bones were entirely without flesh or muscle. He reckoned they must work on will-power.

The steering-lock went the same way as the door. Jem hoped it belonged to the rock-star. He stared at the knot of wires behind the steering-column. Might as well be looking into a bush.

Jacko arrived at a run, hostilities concluded. In one second he had ignition, two seconds, power.

'*Nice* car!' He exhaled rare approval.

'Hope it doesn't rain.' Jem pointed at the naked windscreen. No wipers. Like an eye without eyelashes. 'Some hoor musta broke them off. Jasus you can't leave anything.'

Jacko stabbed a button and from below the lip of the bonnet long arms silently climbed the wind-screen. 'Retractable. Helps the air flow. No rifle-sight on the bonnet either. Aerodynamics. *Nice* car!'

Jem wondered about retractable wings and wheels.

'Over the mountains or down by the sea?' He offered the choice to his passengers.

'Take the high road. Sally's Gap. Your man'll feel more at home.'

Jacko was on the crusade, too. 'No law up there,' he explained defensively.

Out of the decayed city through the redbrick suburbs the silver car slid smooth as water on the broken streets. Dublin looked and felt like a film before the action starts. Not a whisper on the surface but the tension rasping like a chainsaw underneath. 'While the city sleeps danger stalks the streets.'

Guided by Jacko, who knew it like a taxi-driver, he struck the road to the Hellfire Club and the noble bonnet of the car lifted to the angle of the Dublin mountains.

The hostile darkness that surrounds a city closed in on the winding road, until they broke out suddenly above the trees at Killakee and saw below them a broken branch of stars blazing in the bay.

'Jasus,' Jem breathed reverently. 'Great place to bring a bird!'

Behind him the African sat silently seeing something different. He stared down upon a jungle, and Jem following his eyes caught a glimpse of the black holes between the lights and the sinister blocks of darkness that had almost swallowed the stranger. For a second Jem felt the rotten undergrowth stir within the phosphorescence of the city. Heartbeats raced in the distance like naked feet chased by the whip of a siren. For reassurance he looked to the home-lights of Ballymun, brave rampart against the northern night, and pride restored itself.

On a whim he joined the row of parked cars and lay back luxuriously in his seat. Flying must be like this; swooping at night out of the Milky Way, across the burning city, the velvet streets and the neon river, houses streaming like candle flames, the sci-fi airport lifting up to meet him, concrete tilting to the wheels.

He couldn't admit his fantasy to Jacko. 'Nick a plane. What's stoppin' you?' It used to be horses – now it was all one to Jacko as long as there was an engine in it. A race, a chase, wreckage, a fire ...

But flight was Jem's private dream, too pure for crime. He saw himself – not on the run flapping in panic – but seated coolly in a cockpit, the uniform sharp as only respect could make it, a model of authority and skill, adored by tall, blonde stewardesses.

He was a street-pigeon with the dreams of a hawk. A patriot too. He'd fly for Aer Lingus only, he was adamant on that. He imagined a laser-gun in the cockpit for sorting out the foreign airlines.

Ah well – he sighed for the moment – great place to bring a bird!

A savage poke in the ribs –

Beyond Jacko's warning hiss and the hand that hid his face, beyond the electric window and not two feet from the side of the silver Mercedes – both vehicles facing the city like seats in a cinema – a huge, black car was parked, bonnet bulging with a V8 engine and bristling with aerials. Two big, red faces on top of jackets, shirts and ties snarled at Jacko, Jem, and the thin African as if they had found the ultimate subversion.

'Pigs. Hit it!'

The Merc lunged for the road, stalled, shook itself in a spray of gravel. Deep in his throat the African growled. The first hairpin doubled back above the car park and Jem saw the city lights reel below as if something monstrous had smashed into the night.

Real driving now. Not brute power. Control was everything. Jacko rapped commands. Skill and nerve. No street lights. No guiding kerbs. No walls to throw him back on the tarmac. As if he had driven over the edge of order the white line stopped. The road humped, tilted, swerved. Bog sprawled on both sides. A blur of black trenches, steel flash of water. Nightmare beyond the wheels. Rip the skin off the country and this flesh was bared. Only concrete kept it down. Jem prayed for concrete – for the erased city. If he lost the road the silver bubble would submerge in cold, black slime. He searched in panic for pursuit. Craters and ridges threw the flying car into the air. The road behind never appeared in the mirror. He was too far above it or travelling broadside. Above the bog the sky was soft with summer night and the higher hills ran smoothly alongside, devoid of detail, dark curves closing the horizon. Silent space sucked his blood. The dam burst; the African was speaking. Speaking ...

The sound filled the car, drowned the engine. No ordinary speech. Hardly speech at all in the way that chant and exhortation are not speech. There were no words that he could seize. Solid, sibilant sound pitched high and strong against the rumble of the road. It issued like the roar of falling water and its meaning should have plunged down the valleys below the ridge but the car contained it, threw it back upon itself in waves of resonant repetition.

Jem felt potent emotion washing through him, dissolving his greasy skin, surging in his blood. He glanced in elated terror at Jacko and he too was in the grip of fervour, eyes bulging, mouth wide open, passion corrugating his forehead. Then Jem went careering through the bends above Glencree, swatting ditches, walls clubbing at him, frenzied sheep leaping into holes in the dark. Jacko's face was in his hands, head down, as Jem pulled miraculously out of the turmoil and began the long burn up beyond Lough Bray.

The voice in the back still poured forth. Jem slowed. No tail could have held that pace; there was no light in the sky behind and he had recognised something else. On the underside of the voice there was a flash, a quick-silver gleam of language.

Cruising uphill, his ear strained; he seized a loose thread of English. Overlapping it there was a guttural tongue, German, was it, or Russian,

African? – while the English also shaded away into a gabble of French, Italian, Spanish ... Jem could not identify anything but it was like listening to random radio after midnight. Except that this was not electronics. This was one man, beyond himself, speaking passionately in tongues. To anyone, anywhere, who might hear.

Not about his own people, or the hunger they inhabited, or Af-ri-kah, but everyman – as if he had experienced everything possible on his journey and now he spilled its meaning over Jem and Jacko, the only witnesses to a doomed truth.

... like blown leaves and feathers loose in air enter the earth only to begin again and again ...

... do not drift in corners and multiply. Sand that settles chokes the soil ...

... in the high branches of the world the air is sweet and sudden. Hide in the uplands above the poisoned world ...

... travel only on escaping wings, alighting to hide, not to plunder or to build ...

... put away machines. Until the spirit learns to float, go on foot. In silence ...

... slip like shadows over the surface under the sun but let your substance be elsewhere, in memory and dream ...

... do not take root. Earth is the one root and it is poisoned ...

... now. That time is over ...

... I have seen the agents of the new world. They are everywhere. They are here ...

From a childhood pulpit Jem caught the echo of persecution. Biblical. Feathers weren't his idea of flight. He latched on to one thing only. Put away machines ... Get out and walk? Jem cringed like a slug. The car was a shell against the bog. The black breath of night swamped his eyes and headlights. He wouldn't last a minute out there. Clinging to the steering wheel for survival he wept for the livid tunnels of the city.

Why? Why? Hurtling through midnight mountains for a stranger. Why?

The moment they picked him up power and direction had changed utterly. Now the prophet was commanding them to live like crows. He must deflect these harsh orders before they got a grip.

He yelled desperately into the flow; 'Hey! George! What's your place like, George? Home? Is it like this kip?'

Tzammeniya Maseratu Harathanazu fell completely silent. It was a vacant, eerie silence, a gap in the air, as if Jem had tuned to a source that was no longer even there.

When he spoke again his voice had ceased to boom. It thinned to a single strand, a dusty thread trying to spin delicate images in the air, to fix bright colours on the flying night. There was a faint rhythm of sun and rain, seasons and moons that meant nothing at all to Jem wrestling the car through tangled bends.

He heard of sand and snow, of mountains that were more than elevations of the lowlands, they were separate elements in themselves, homelands above the setting sun. Sometimes in the mid-afternoon the mountains barely existed, they were painted dimly on the sky and called for faith; at night they were their own shadow against the stars; in winter they cut the surface of the earth like broken bones. In the growing season green buds sprouted in secret hollows. Sometimes they came to leaf.

Near Ethiopia and Sudan, yes, but not of either, remains of an ancient, uneroded Af-ri-kah above the borders. On one side now, in Ethiopia, there were Russians, on the other, Americans in Sudan. The people on both sides starved.

The crops withered, the animals died, then the children and the old. The high ground turned to dust, the dust blew away from the rock, blew away between their fingers. The sun had turned and burned them out of the mountains. The survivors were led down to the famished valleys and herded into destitution-camps, the strongest loaded in army lorries and taken a thousand miles to the south to be resettled.

In Jem's hands the car slowed to a crawl as the dusty voice whispered of travelling day and night for a week in wheel-ruts and dry river-beds through the famine lowlands, crushed together on the hot steel under a canvas sheet. The weakest died and were buried in passing. The mountains dissolved in shimmering air and the sky burned down to the ground on every side. There was nothing ahead but cracked, black earth and withered bush. Once they saw a line of people who envied the awful lorries and the unknown destination. Some held their children up to be taken.

When the journey ended, the earth offered no welcome. They were released without resources in an alien place.

A few turned their faces at once and began the long march home. There were dead voices calling and they could not be deserted. They walked a thousand miles through the hot season to reach the mountains before the rains came. They trudged the borders for three months living on memory and when they reached home – two men of the score who started – the rains failed them again ...

A faint glow silhouetted the speaker in the mirror. It came from behind and was increasing every second. A crossroads, the Sally Gap, caught the silver Mercedes in its net. Jem swung left. The car knew instinctively where to go.

... But a crop was impossible anyway, for there was a road now, a ragged new road cut into the mountain, and high up a fence surrounded the harvest-plateau; squat, grey buildings stood where the maize-fields used to be, and helicopters, jeeps, uniforms – Yanks or Reds, it didn't matter. There was a hole in the mountain near the ruined village, an enormous mine ...

'What were they after?' Jacko's voice had diamonds in it. The African had not heard him right, 'Hunger,' he said, 'they had found Hunger.'

And after he had left his mark in blood the second man turned to travel south again. But Tzammeniya Maseratu Harathanazu faced north this time – and started running.

The light behind was relentless now, burning like a laser. The tapered head caught in the mirror seemed transparent.

'Hit it!' Jacko roared. Jem thought he wanted a handbrake turn and ramming-session, but he was doing eighty, downhill, the road no wider than the car. His eyes blurred. The road wriggled faster than the lights could find it. At the bottom a twisted bridge! He skidded bluntly, sickening slam against the side, stonework shearing past his shoulder. Through and into another bend. The engine note was higher, harsh with injury. The lights behind clawed the darkness. No ordinary chase. Not your police. Jem expected bullets.

A second bridge. He slammed the other door. Screech of steel, silver sparks. Jacko clutched his wounded arm. He was ready for the third bridge, took it like a slalom-gate.

Uphill again, clean sweep along a slope, kick through a hairpin and then the steep road narrowed, pinned to the mountain by a fragile wall, vacant space below it. Sheep on the verges luminous with terror.

And then the long descent urgent as gravity through forest thick with spiky shadow, and out below into sleeping fields and farmland, Roundwood, reservoirs, and everywhere the random roads of Wicklow. The car found its own way, always trailing the lights behind, sometimes a glow above the trees, sometimes a ravenous glare until Jem stamped on the throttle and broke away.

Jacko was awed, disbelieving. 'They can't be this good.'

'They are not what you think –' the African warned. He was ignored. They had their own skins to save.

Whether the car found it or he did Jem could not say, but the huge gates gaped open, black and gold, between ornate pillars in a high stone wall and he swung on burning wheels. Shouts from the gatehouse, running shadows. Up the avenue, lawns and woodland, torn fence trailing like ivy-strands. Between tall trees the floodlit castle stood. Fairytale towers and terraces, a forecourt packed with cars. Jacko jerked reflexively. Limousines, sports cars, huge saloons, two helicopters with rotors discreetly folded.

On a low terrace under blue and silver lamps guests danced in imitation moonlight. Jem skidded against a CD Jaguar. The familiar cruelty of steel. Gravel strafed the granite steps. The music broke. A squad of burly men bore down. Jem struggled with the welded doors. Jacko stabbed a button and the sun-roof opened. He slithered out on the shadow side, disappeared in the bushes. Jem tried to follow as the tuxedos tightened, but the exit was too small.

'Please?' The African tugged him down and climbed out onto the roof where he rose thin and splendid in his radiant robe, hands folded, head high and tilted back.

Jem decided to see it through. He poked up head and shoulders and addressed the heavies in a well-bred croak. 'Is Geldof – Mister Geldof about?'

'No Reporters! Get Out!'

Jem gestured at the figure on the roof. 'Does he look like a newshound? Geldof!' he bellowed, 'GELDOF!'

The terrace stirred. A shiny blue dress suit detached itself and slouched towards the steps.

Entirely unnoticed a black car with a bulging bonnet and dimmed headlights slid towards them along the drive. Without any lights at all another passed it, escaping sleek and low across the shadowed lawn towards the gates. Only Jem felt Jacko go.

The man in the blue dress suit scuffed onto the gravel. He wore sneakers. He came with the casual assurance of one used to spotlights.

Some distance from the car he halted, shook lank hair from his forehead to examine the supplicant with shrewd eyes. Slowly, affirmatively, he lifted both hands in welcome. In the lazy gesture of those arms was the power of mass approval.

Jem felt the stranger tremble with conclusion. His eyes closed, he bowed from the waist. Tiny splashes hit the silver steel.

In the midst of his own panic Jem felt enormous pride and pity. The African moved down invisible stairs towards the outstretched hands. In slow motion, gliding through sea-level air, in the dim reflection of the spotlights. Savage engine-roar, full headlights. The bulging bonnet with the V8 engine hurtled across the gravel, struck the stranger behind the knees, hurled him in the air. He crumpled back across the roof and drifted to the ground as light as a fall of leaves. The car vanished into the avenue.

On the terrace, hysteria, screaming chaos –

Jem and Geldof remained motionless, staring, leaning slightly away from each other, as if the tightrope had not yet broken and the figure was still in mid-air.

Voices announced police.

'That *was* them,' Jem whispered, 'they followed us –' Not your police. And he knew them then for what they were: the hunger-police.

Jem slipped through the sunroof to kneel by the dead stranger.

Skin and bone, no blood. The face was serene and final. He fumbled with the eyelids as if his fingertips could hurt. The garment drooped between the hipbones across the stomach as if the body had already melted in the ground.

Sirens screamed along the avenue. He jumped for the Mercedes.

Squeezed through the sunroof, headfirst. His hips jammed. Rough hands hauled on his ankles. Suspended in the car he clung to the inert steering wheel and rattled it in a fury of injustice. A gap opened in the uniforms and Geldof's head appeared. It seemed upside-down to Jem but the eyes were full of questions and unmistakable importance.

AT THE
RISING OF
THE MOON

First published in 1994 by Bâton Wicks, London
and The Collins Press, Cork

LIGHTNING IN THE DARK

'Oh where's that place called Lonely street', Tony howled, flinging it
accurately at the melody. Helen picked up the line on the flute, flicked it
round, played it back. The Sherpa whooped, whistles from the porters,
the omelette beamed up at Tony. But the tea-kettle spilled sulkily into the
flames and no one but himself had noticed. He hadn't the energy to rescue
it. He looked at Helen with marital affection and despair. She had blown
the dinner again.

The sun slumped among the Annapurnas like a shot balloon. Sweat
cooled, night-shadows gathered. Helen strained after the devious tune
heard on the cook-boy's radio along the path below. She snatched harsh
breaths between staccato phrases. At 14,000 feet music thins out. Rhythm
falters like the heart. She sat cross-legged against a boulder. Eyes closed,
her face was tired, smudged with the grime of a day's march. Rucksacks,
porter-loads, tents, kitchen-gear littered the hillside hollow. Sleeping bags
absorbed the evening sun. Sheltered by stones the big Primuses hummed
and flared.

Helen's tall figure was bulked out with a heavy duvet. At thirty she
looked twenty-five in spite of fatigue. Striking, Tony judged her curls, eyes
and broad mouth; there was a different image of beauty in his mind now.
He closed his eyes and thought of Alice. It wasn't difficult; the moment
his lids shut she shot into clear vision so abruptly he felt his face bulge
with the impact.

She was naked, apart from incidentals: an open blouse, something
clinging to her left ankle. His heart winced with desire. He began to sweat;
opened his eyes. The cold omelette sneered up at him. Above Helen's
head multiple Annapurnas gleamed against the sky.

A young porter beamed, bare foot hammering the ground. With a
curved bow he scraped the Nepali tune from a homemade fiddle. Flute
and dissonant strings charged the air with the raw gaiety of a crossroads
dance. The music made a hedge against barren space. Ragged phrases
flicked and teased like thorntendrils in a breeze. The cookboy crouched
over his narrow drum, the sirdar stamped and swayed.

Before they left London for the Himalayas Tony had an affair. As sexual
encounters go it was of the briefest duration, and the maximum impact.
Its consequences increased with distance and altitude. Although she

sensed the fall in temperature Helen knew nothing about it. Alice, the naked woman, was her closest friend.

'How could you be in love with TWO people? It's ridiculous.

'Alice, Alice,' crooning her name, 'It's perfectly simple, you're irresistible, and I have lots of spare emotion. It's the way I am. When I was a child I was in love with the girl next door on both sides, *and* the entire Senior Infants class: ten of them were boys.'

'That's not love. That's a virus.'

'Alice! I've been in love with you since – I first met you. You ignored me completely. You talked to Helen all night, drinking white wine the way you do. You hold it in your mouth and laugh bubbles through it. You were funny, you were clever, you were sexy. So was Helen. I loved both of you.'

'THAT party!' Derision. 'I was drunk and depressed. That wasn't wine; it was turpentine. You bought it. I wanted to spit. I was having a period and I hated London. You're looking for an easy substitute for Helen. She's miles too good for you. If you think I'd betray –'

'Alice, we've had all this before. I love her; you know that. I happen to love you too.'

They couldn't help grinning; the recurrent absurdity, his intensity, the carefully tuned ho-hum expression on her otherwise interested face. They'd been having this conversation for weeks, in pubs, coffee-shops, parks, flats. The conversation was a relationship in itself. All that was missing was sex.

'... called Lo-onely Street?' he bellowed his line again, to general delight. Dorje threw an arm over his shoulder, echoed the phrase. Tony had been on trips where the staff and climbers were worlds apart. But Helen changed all that. Being Irish helped; she didn't feel superior. She was one of those seriously happy women who dressed in long skirts because of Bezruchka's remark that female shorts were an affront to the Nepali culture. The skirts stopped three inches above no-nonsense trekking-boots. Stripped of this frightful uniform, which included head-scarves worn in the most unbecoming manner and foully tasselled Peruvian caps, his wife was a striking, strong, fit woman. Talented. Compassionate.

She knew the staff, the names of their wives, how many children they had. She worried if someone unpronounceable was unwell, had a word with the sirdar and saw that loads were changed around for awhile.

Among these openly familial people Tony was embarrassed to be child-
less. It felt decadent. A lot of his climbing-friends had no children either.
Independence, or selfishness? Musicians too; he glanced at Helen again.

Something was irritating her. He knew the signs, tension stated in the
music, not just revision of the tunes heard during the day. The porters
thought it was the usual party starting early. Tony was relieved the storm
wasn't for him, though he knew he was the unacknowledged cause. As
soon as the sirdar began to dance, arms swarming sinuously above his
head, Helen stopped. Dorje was the problem. The fiddle faltered but the
drum tapped on in deference to the foreman. Dorje stopped as soon as
he could without losing face and called Shiba from his drum to tend the
kettle. Across the valley the sun hit a notch on the Annapurna Ridge.

'What's the matter?'

'It's bloody Dorje. He's not paying them properly.'

'How d'you know? He says he is.'

'I asked them. They're not happy.'

Tony understood his own fatigue; he was used to mountains. A long,
hard day above Ongre and the altitude had begun to bite. Nerves flared
easily. He didn't want a row with Helen or a trade-dispute when things
were going smoothly.

'They're happier than any porters I've ever had. He must be doing
something right. It's his job to pay them. I don't think we've any right to
interfere.'

He was equally disturbed by Helen's anger and the greasiness of his
own response.

'That's insufferable Tony! You don't think we ought to interfere? Well
I do. I'll have it out with him tonight if you won't!'

'But Helen –'

'They haven't even got shoes. We're meant to provide shoes. We've
given him enough money. How are they supposed to get over the high
pass in bare feet?' She was inexplicably in tears.

'Helen, this is Nepal, not England. They have their own system. Shoes
will appear if they're needed. No use getting yourself worked up!' The
sting slipped out against his will; he resented her missionary attitude – as
if no one ever understood porters before.

Her head snapped back; 'Worked up! You just don't care, do you?
About anyone! He could be charging them, as well as us, for the food. I'm
going to find out ...'

She struggled to her feet with a suppressed groan and marched towards the fire.

Dorje, fashionably clad, straddled the flames supervising the porters' rice. The young Sherpa, at home on the mountain, joked raucously with the lowland porters seated around him under coarse pixie-hooded cloaks. At Helen's approach the group fell silent, studying their toes. Rebuffed, oddly helpless, she veered into the darkness. Tony stamped angrily to his feet. Dorje left the fire at once, wiping his hands, smiling amiably. 'Some problem, Tony? Dinner Ok?'

'Dinner was good, thank you.' Conscious of the listening porters, as yet unfed, Tony considered tactful English, but Dorje could evade that, misinterpret it.

'We need to know how much you pay the porters?'

'I pay one hundred fifty rupees, Tony.'

'But they say they get one hundred and twenty, maybe less, so we wanted to know for sure what ...' straying into minor clauses, conscious of Helen listening in the shadows.

'Porters not speak English. Porters my job. If I pay everything now, maybe no porters for high pass. I pay full money in Jomosom, other side, Ok?'

Tony smiled in relief. They had till Jomosom.

Helen interrupted. 'That's good Dorje. We understand that part. Now, about shoes. We gave you money to buy these shoes. Did you give this money to the porters?' No doubt about meaning there. Tony saw Dorje squirm. But the friendly smile remained. 'In Chame I gave money, but they didn't buy ...' He shrugged with a broader smile.

'But Dorje, this money you paid, was this wages – money for work – or was it extra money for shoes?'

Dorje was an accomplished dealer; he pretended not to understand, while yielding graciously to Helen's logic.

'They didn't buy.' What could one do with such porters? 'In Manang I will buy the shoes myself and give the porters. Ok?'

'Ok, Dorje. Manang.'

'Ok, Ok! No more problems? Porters eat dinner now? Ok?'

Tony giggled. 'You caught him there, Helen.'

'I don't trust him.' She was not entirely appeased. 'I like him, but I don't trust him.'

'They have to make a few bob, Helen.'

'I don't mind him trying to make it on us. Up to a point. But if he's exploiting the porters ...'

He steered her into the cold tent, saw her into her sleeping bag, fussing over her with affection. He lit a candle, wrapped her duvet around her feet and tied the sleeves, rooted out a bar of chocolate intended for the mountain. Helen pushed it away. Her face was grey in the candlelight.

'Tony, I felt dreadful today. Depressed, worried about everything, inadequate. I don't think I'll get to Base-Camp, never mind climb Chulu. I don't know what's wrong. I've never felt so helpless.'

'It's just altitude, Helen. You'll soon get over that!' Deeply anxious he hurried on. 'You're pushing yourself too hard. You don't have to prove anything. We can't go any faster than the porters. For eighty rupees a day I wouldn't like to push them.'

Helen's eyes were shut, her forehead the helmet-shape of a headache. Her lips tightened against the joke. He saw how she might look when she was older.

Helen had waited a long time for this trip, but as she waited its terms had changed. She had left Dublin at twenty-one with a music degree. London was to be the start of a world tour. But it had quickly become home, exciting at first, happy later, and then, comfortable.

It was during that comfortable stage that uneasiness had surfaced, roused by the very lack of disturbance. The comfort was dull. It collapsed quickly under its own weight. It was like a kind of sleep, the drowsiness from which people rouse when it is too late to live. She almost decided, at twenty-five, that it was time to have children, to renew her life at secondhand, but she remembered she hadn't travelled yet.

Tony would have had children straightaway and been a loving if inconsistent parent, inventing it as they went along. He grew up in a passionately irregular family, always on the move, coming apart to come intensely together again. Helen admired his odd tribe, and Tony was proud of them; they ran their relationships as theatre, disciplined by the principle that the show went on. He believed in opposites, contingency and the heart, and he was far from insecure.

Helen though, was sensibly afraid of two extremes; the traditional conservatism she had emigrated from, and the footloose disasters that passed as marriage in the two areas she knew in England – music and mountaineering.

She resisted children. She had sound, practical reasons, and many of her friends felt the same. Career, creativity, child-rearing in London, she wasn't ready. Tony accepted this with an ease that first relieved, and then unnerved her, considering his urge towards parenthood.

If she had loved him with a little more distance she would have admitted that he was even less ready. With the best will in the world responsibility would always devolve on her. Whenever Tony announced another major change at short notice, she looked at him with a quizzical silence that unsettled him till he put it down to a culture-gap.

Sometimes she thought children might solve this; at other times she knew they would aggravate it. In moments of strength she trusted her instincts but she always felt guilty at the inability to make up her mind about her motives.

Other people who actually got on with things seemed equally indecisive when she listened behind their language; they groped confidently in the dark. Many of her friends, who had made big decisions early, confessed that they hadn't reasoned at all and saw Helen as the decisive one. She realised she couldn't trust anyone's opinion then; they were all confused – the practical ones who were too materialistic, and the idealists who were often dreamers. Was this uncertainty all that had been achieved? Having conquered the old structures there was very little evidence of a new order; in fact, it was obvious people were rapidly reverting to roles they could trust for continuity.

Even Alice, who had always had a lucid scepticism, had turned broody now that she was in London. It must be the city. It was essential to get away to a fresh perspective. Tony injured his back in a climbing accident, nothing too serious but it lingered. He dropped out of an expedition. Why not go out anyway, together?

It was one of those fictional moments like a marriage-proposal, when she could have been stunned, or victorious, or angry: a queen cheaply manoeuvred on a chess-board. Stand-in for a two-month expedition? It wasn't how she had imagined travel. And yet she jumped at it.

'Three months.' Bargaining for a little more.

'Six! And we mightn't come back.'

Tony folded his jacket into an expert pillow, sleeves packed either side to stop his head from rolling. Helen breathed unevenly beside him in the tent. He pressed appreciatively against her, closed his eyes and was invaded.

'You're not my type ...' Alice argued, with the faint hint of desperation that provided his excuse. They would go on talking; it wasn't the words or the logic that mattered, but the emotion aroused.

'You're MY type, I'd be satisfied with that!' He played at teenage conversation with rapt absorption.

'I used to wonder about you,' she mused, 'before we met. Helen told me a lot, but she only saw the good side.' She frowned, clearly seeing the rest. Tony had a maddening itch to hear himself discussed.

'Not particularly handsome, but she found you attractive. She was right about the looks, but I can't see what the attraction was.' A grin twitched the corner of her mouth.

'You haven't seen everything, Alice.' She raised a wry, eyebrow. It brushed the quick of his existence. Every move she made generated this erotic charge. Beneath his skin nerve-ends flicked in shoals. He was trapped. It was sexual hypnosis. Granted, one had to be willing at first, but after that there was no choice.

When he thought of Helen it wasn't guilt he felt, or sadness. He loved her. He rejected the accusation of betrayal. It was as if he had been invaded; colonised by sex. And yet – it wasn't happening.

Tony was a teacher who never taught.

He had started with a degree in English and a Master's thesis – the Influence of Celtic Poets on the English Tradition. It left him out of work; people didn't care about crossbreeding in literature.

Helen did. Alice didn't, but that was later. Meanwhile, he concentrated on climbing and took an Outdoor Education Diploma in Wales to be near the action.

He was surprised that the course was inspiring in itself, even more surprised to find himself a P.E. teacher in a progressive school in London. The other staff ran football courses, Tony started an Outdoor Pursuits programme to loosen things up and provide an excuse for his own climbing. Trips away with canoes and climbing-ropes were so popular that he became an entire department, which undermined his own priorities.

He ran courses for his colleagues to show the value of the outdoors. They crept around cautiously, referring to themselves as being "in Snowdonia", as if it was an exotic safari-park instead of old, worn North Wales.

But Helen was different. He met her at a time when all the London women he knew – maybe it was his fault – were either overwrought or sedated. Helen had talent and no neuroses; she taught music for a manageable number of hours, London animated her, and she loved North Wales.

Tony seemed quite accomplished himself; too many minor talents, as it happened, to develop a single one. Romance was inevitable. Alice didn't appear for six years.

She mightn't have appeared at all, except that Helen got homesick in the fifth year of marriage. She didn't want a lover, the usual solution, but she encouraged Alice to move to London, away from a crisis – got her a job in the Phonetics Department at the BBC. Tony had never heard of it; he had assumed whatever pronunciation the BBC broadcast became local usage immediately.

He hadn't met Alice; they bypassed so often it seemed almost deliberate. He knew her colourful career. She worked in Brussels to escape a relationship at home. She left Brussels to end an entanglement with her boss; returned to Dublin to another drama and was on her way to London now.

He was disappointed by her; quiet, reserved, almost ordinary. He had looked forward to excitement, but at the same time he'd been afraid she might distract Helen from him. They had a history of shared experience which might exclude him like a hostile culture. In a reverse of the married itch Tony feared he was about to lose Helen a little, and he resented it.

Alice conversed intelligently, dressed calmly, was conservative. Most of the new Irish were. She didn't harp on the past, and he and Helen didn't exclude her from the present.

Friends of theirs, disengaged males, queued to take Alice out, looking for someone like Helen. Everyone got on well; the social circuit hummed – a flurry of small dinner-parties, called anything but that, in little houses temporarily worth a fortune. All the things that could be done with brown rice.

Helen played in a jazz-quartet on Saturday nights. Alice liked walking. Tony took her to the Lake District on a weekend with a couple of climbing friends. She went up over Scafell, down into Wasdale and they picked her up in the evening, pleased with herself. They found the remains of a wedding in a hotel-lounge and took it in turns to dance with her. It was the first time he'd seen her animated.

The little stoop was gone, shoulders swinging, classic body in motion, slender waist, breasts tangibly imaginable through the blouse, narrow hips, legs that gave eloquent rhythm to the beat. When she whirled on her toes the hood of black hair lifted, her eyes opened wide, full lips blew invisible bubbles at the ceiling.

Gazing intensely he was startled by the exquisite lines of cheekbone, jawline, elegant neck – every few seconds he saw a lightning sketch of pure grace. He kept peering to catch it again, couldn't tell was it imagined or real. Twice she caught him staring, his own jaw hanging stupidly. She tossed her head. There it was again, that fleeting grace – his eyes went off like a flash-bulb, missed it.

There were ways of making it happen, triggering the sudden dazzle. He experimented with animation. Talk could never do it. Surprised laughter could. Anger made her look unpleasant; her eyes got mean. A car-horn behind her, a slammed door, elbow grabbed in a shop, all could induce the exquisite flash, or not – even retain it if he handled the follow-up right. Soon, he didn't need the secret stimulus anymore. Even when she looked bland and shallow the vision was fixed in his mind's eye. He was in love.

Thursday nights Tony went down to the leisure-centre. Helen had a rehearsal later.

'Alice, why don't you try the pool? You used to love swimming. Tony will give you a lift.' In pursuit there are no coincidences.

When he skidded in after pumping his muscles solid on the climbing wall, she stood on the tip of the diving-board in a marginal bathing-suit, springing rhythmically, arms raised. Her dive cut the water, barely a splash. It hit Tony's pumped blood so hard he thought he would haemorrhage through the ears. To his horror the result was a massive, adolescent response. He tumbled into the water to drown it. He floundered, swallowing water. Alice sliced through the blue pool, polished, pure, impersonal. Under a tight, white cap her face was naked and austere.

Embarrassment convulsed him; to think he had chased in to show off the choppy stroke that drove him through the water, blunt as a tug-boat.

She got a flat near the pool. Helen said; 'Maybe you'd give her a hand to sort that place out. It must be depressing to move into.'

He was a bona fide social worker then. Years of happy marriage had left him without any skill in seduction. He hadn't fooled Alice at all. He tried brushing warmly against her, but she moved coolly away. He embarrassed himself dreadfully with double-entendres.

Lying on his back in the kitchen, fighting a pipe-joint, and thinking of nothing else, he heard her say; 'Okay, let's sort this thing out. Now!' He sat up – whacked his forehead off the sink. Alice, in a mercurial change thought it hilarious. Instead of having to slink out the door he clutched his head and moaned comically. 'Look how I suffer for you!'.

With that change of tone came open acknowledgement.

'What do you expect, Tony? That I'll betray Helen?'

'Betray? I wouldn't betray Helen; I'm her husband. I love her. Betray means hand over to the enemy. You're not the enemy, for God's sake!'

'That's why I can't betray her.'

'Alice, listen to me. We're going away. For a long time. Six months, maybe a year. Helen's been looking forward to it for ever. It's got to be special. For her! I mean it! For her.

'Alice, something has to happen or it'll be a disaster. I can't leave like this. I don't mean … Something has to happen. It'll be over when I come back. Maybe I won't come back. It won't be over. It couldn't. It's too strong.'

'This is ridiculous, Tony. You're ridiculous! How can you do this to Helen?'

'I'm not doing anything to Helen. I love her! She knows it. Damn it, I sleep beside her every night. I miss her if she's not there. I'm not going to tire of Helen. That isn't it! You must understand, for God's sake? This is something completely different. It's between me and you. Damn it, Alice, can't you see something has to happen. You're not indifferent to me. I know you're not. You needn't pretend. I can feel it.'

She didn't look at him, stared straight ahead, eyes wide and blank. He felt the moment shift, as if he'd found the secret button. He leaned on it. His voice wasn't his own now. Desire spoke hoarsely …

'If it wasn't for Helen, you and I … It's not presumptuous. I know we would. So do you. And I know we can't. We can't! I want to go away with Helen, and be what she needs me to be – which isn't much, because she's everything in herself. But Alice, I can't leave this. I'm not fit for anything. Anything! I'm out in empty space, completely seized up. I can't think of anything but you. I can't do anything, go anywhere. I can't work properly. I'll be the same when we go away. What good is that going to do Helen, for Christ's sake?'

The moment moved again, rocked on its base, a panel shifted. 'What am I supposed to do?' Alice's tone was shaken, troubled. Tony felt his chest swell and constrict. Hard to breathe. The new air flared in his lungs, his heart beat so hard his body hung onto it for fear of being shaken off.

'Alice! Alice – it's simple. For me it's simple. I need you. I've got to ...
how can I get out of this? It's not just sex ... it *is* sex, but it's everything
else as well. I love everything about you. My mind, body, emotions,
everything is trapped. I've got to get past it. For everyone's sake! I need
you now, Alice – I need what you are. Otherwise, I'm stuck in this.'

'But that wouldn't fix anything, Tony. You'd be the same afterwards.'

'NO! No, I wouldn't! I'd be gone away. Time to heal, to get over it.
You'll have someone when I come back. That'll be that! But I wouldn't
have this terrible ... feeling. Not just a feeling, it's a paralysis, incomplete-
ness, a curse! This thing has to be finished, Alice; certain things have
to finish properly, or else they haunt everybody.'

It didn't matter what he said anymore. He had arrived. The welter of
sexual emotion spoke for itself. Desire and impending consent. He could
wring consent out of the air like juice. Whether he had seduced it into
being, or whether its prior existence had lent the sexual tension to his
babbling was irrelevant. He rose abruptly to his feet, reached, but didn't
touch her. Every word, every move was explosively spontaneous, yet he
knew he was directing it.

She sat still, elbows on her knees, face hidden in her hands. 'Alice!' She
didn't move. 'Alice ...'

She turned nasty. Sentimental fierceness sharpened the rejection. 'If
you ever hurt Helen you'll suffer for it, Tony.'

Back to the starting-line, but not disqualified. He had won ground. Her
anger was not for him; the harsh look on Alice's face was directed against
herself.

Jomosom, November ?

Dear Alice,
We've climbed two (2!) mountains now; both 20,000 feet. The
first one was a mini-expedition. I couldn't believe the work involved
just to get to the foot of it. And then the climbing! We had a base-
camp, a high camp, a gear-stash, a midnight start, crampons, axes,
rope, an ice-col, snow slopes, steep bumps and humps, a '*mauvais
pas*', an '*a cheval*' ridge, a summit, a Himalayan sunrise, a tumbling
descent. A week later we took the second peak like an afterthought.

We should have done this years ago. Maybe we left it a bit late –
that teenage thrill is gone. Tony knows the place so well that we

waste no time. But it takes some of the discovery out of it. This must be the most beautiful place on earth but I'm still shocked by the poverty. He gets a lot of mileage out of my innocence. The contrast between the country and the city seems acute, although there is poverty everywhere, but the slums show it up more clearly than the hillsides.

The staff are astounding. Dorje, the Sherpa, does everything. I didn't trust him at first, which shows how far you can be wrong. He works twenty hours a day if he's let. Even though his job is foreman and guide he does most of the cooking and seems to work for the porters as well.

We crossed a high pass a few days ago, 17,000 feet. Dorje accompanied us over it, starting at 3 a.m., carrying a huge load himself. He saw us to the foot of the mountain we were climbing, produced our lunch – chapatis and cheese – out of his rucksack before we left. Then he went back over the pass to pick up a load left by one of the porters who got sick a long way back. He crossed over again and descended to Muktinath, with a double-load which took all day while we were climbing. He arranged accommodation for us down there, and then came back up to meet us so he could carry my rucksack down. And all with the kind of cheeky grin that cheers you up no matter how ruined you are.

Oh yes – the chapatis; he'd cooked them himself that morning, along with the porridge. He's twenty-five and he owns a small herd of yaks. Alice, I think I've found the man for you ...

I don't know where Tony is at the moment but he sends his love.

Tony woke to the sound of Kathmandu rasping like a glass-cutter at the hotel window. The last traces of darkness were being scraped from the city, releasing the exact cacophony sleep had drowned the night before, as if day were a nonstop affair in the street which never actually ceased, but was subdued by bouts of darkness. He had formed this impression on his first night in the city years before. His jaw had swollen twice its size and a brutal abscess throbbed all through that September night. It was the tail-end of the monsoon, before the city dried out, and tiny stukas strafed the room. The torn window-mesh was designed to let mosquitoes in and sieve sanity out. He thrashed on a hard bed for hours hallucinating on pain and pain-killers. The sheets clung to his skin in a suffocating poultice. Traffic, voices, music maintained an insane crescendo in his skull.

He had longed for Helen, the only assurance in a demented world. Next day he sent her a shaky postcard; 'Abscess makes the heart grow fond.' Since then, never quite fooled by the charm of the city, he tested morning gingerly before trusting its strident undertow. But there was nothing at all unpleasant out there, apart from the slick currents of the trekker-trade, and if any of those were abroad at 7 a.m. they were on the way to take flight to Thai beaches, where they would drawl stories of great heights gained, and icy dangers undergone in search of a braver beauty than sand and sea.

Tony yawned and decently wished them well. In most cases – he stressed the exceptions – their form of wandering is a fashion. When the time comes that affluent youth, whether hippies, yuppies, or some new breed of pup, discover that the great caves of Guinea are the current place to go they will flock there in droves and engender the local version of a tea-house culture, with chocolate-cake and potato-chips. Tony yawned again with the contentment of superiority; there was nothing to that form of travel but the pursuit of indolence in the guise of curiosity. By comparison, mountaineering was a semi-respectable excuse. Helen was still asleep. He resisted the urge to wake her. She might not be pleased. He found her overwhelmingly desirable, a long, languid shape stretched out under thin bedclothes, nothing showing but dark curls.

For distraction he separated the noise outside into strands of raw sound, listened to them individually as she had taught him to do with music, and then let them merge again in raucous ensemble. He heard the voice of the city and understood it. No longer foreign or frightening, it was universal. Horns blared incessantly as taxis threaded the streets in short bursts of speed. A violent rumbling, directly below their first-floor room stirred Helen but didn't wake her – the steel shutter rising on a souvenir-shop. Cycle-rickshaws massed outside with loose chains and rattling wheels. A solid chugging approached; no need for a horn – the third world tractor; tough, simple engine on two wheels. After it a brief vacuum, then the calls of bike-renters, rickshaw-men, and Tiger Balm boys, 'Hallaw! Hallaw!' assailed unseen passersby, and Tony caught their curt refusals.

The flute-seller arrived. He was in expressive form – long, graceful cadenzas, every note perfectly pitched, a flute he would certainly never sell, probably the only one ever made without a bum note of any kind. He kept it in an inside pocket, while the rest – nearly a hundred of varying lengths and thicknesses – grew on a flute-tree, a long pole butted on the ground. Thin, wooden spokes sprouted from the tree, each branch inserted in the core of a flute.

Later he would tire of virtuosity and play with one hand only, three fingers on the top notes squirting endless triplets like variations on Three Blind Mice. Must be more effective, Tony reasoned; supermarkets don't play Mozart before announcing a bargain; they use electronic chimes with the repertoire of a doorbell.

Helen was awake. Tony knew that slight change in her breathing. He couldn't check without turning his head but he thought she hadn't opened her eyes yet; the rhythm of her breath would change again.

Twin single-beds, ridiculous arrangement. Of course not everyone was married, or even intimate if they were. They made their own arrangements. Stretching, Tony considered the advantages; no disturbance on restless nights, no contagion during illness. Hardly convincing arguments. But lots of marriages lived apart and only came together for convenience; separate beds, separate rooms – a development of affluence. You had to be able to afford the space. If you could move that far apart it must be easy to move further.

He knew that Helen and himself – no matter how intimately their skin touched, how searchingly their eyes met – were separated by his dreams. She didn't recognise it yet, but Helen was locked out of his imagination and he had moved another woman in. The fact that Alice would resent a further role in which she yielded anything she had wanted to withhold, made him deeply uneasy. To what extent was her image her own property? His imagination was using her, he was helplessly aware of that. But he had lost control. It was as if every move bred further infidelity. Had he any choice at this stage, he wondered? He fled the consequences in panic.

'You awake, Helen?'

'Mmmmmmmm ...'

'Nice to be back, eh?'

'mmmmmmmMMMM!'

'Sleep well?'

'z-z-z-z-z-z-'

'Helen?'

'Sh-sh-shhhhh ...'

'What next, Helen?'

An exhalation, unlettered, 'Breakfast ...?'

'I mean, what next in a general sense. Breakfast isn't a choice. Breakfast is a function – like getting up, or going to the loo. It's important to get them in the right order, that's all. Although, breakfast and going to the loo can be simultaneous if you eat in the wrong place here.'

'Damn it, Tony –' she spat the fringe of rug out of her mouth, 'you've woken me up now.'

'That's the idea. So what next, Helen? Want to go to Thailand with the nouveau-hippies? Lie on the beaches, take in a hill-tribe or two, a tan? I see you've already got one. Lovely ...'

Helen was on her feet, stretching. 'We'll price a flight to Bangkok. If it's cheap we'll go, if not we won't.' She settled it without much interest. 'Are you getting up for breakfast or not, after all your talk?'

'Not. Let's have a closer look at that tan!'

As his arms closed tenderly around her his eyes closed too. At once he felt the familiar impact as the other body cannoned out of his imagination onto his retina.

After a breakfast of coffee and croissants, delicious in Kathmandu though it would have been third-rate in Europe, they strolled fondly downtown.

The city was still new to Helen. It had been a blur of heat, noise and colour a month before when she dropped from the sky and bounced off the tarmac onto the mountains. On the edge of Thamel, the tourist-enclave, a beige heifer lay chewing the cud in the middle of the street, undisturbed, too bony to look placid. In a closed garden there were tall, dusty trees festooned with bats as big as pigeons.

The street became a wide boulevard with a pavement so high you could break a leg if you fell off. There were traffic-police on duty at the junctions directing the chaotic taxis, cyclists, rickshaws. Neat young men from a standard mould, their well-pressed trousers were tucked into white gaiters over small boots; they wore a blouson-style jacket with a little fur collar, a flat peaked cap white on top, and a belt to accentuate the typically slender Nepali waist. The taxi-drivers, no angels, accused the police of corruption, but their pleasant faces and toyshop uniforms looked remarkably innocent to Helen.

They turned onto sophisticated Durbar Marg in front of the palace gates.

'A bit like a moon-shot,' Tony dismissed the King's modern residence, 'a concrete rocket.'

'Meaning if it doesn't look like Buckingham P. then it's not a proper palace?'

'It's a palace alright. Could be the Palace Cinema, somewhere like Brighton.'

Helen ignored him. Even when it was a deliberate tease she resented the tendency to dismiss anything that was not British. Tony knew he wasn't like that, but her reaction could provoke it in him.

A man whose arms and legs were boneless stalks, a head and torso with rubber tentacles, lay belly-down on a trolley and propelled himself along the pavement, chin close to the concrete, singing.

Helen stopped aghast but he seemed reasonably jolly, going about the business of charity as if he had just rolled in after a late breakfast and had work to catch up on.

'I remember him!' Tony said, 'I gave him ten rupees three years ago in the exact same spot.'

'I'd say he has it spent. Give him another instalment.'

'But he'll expect it then.' Tony rooted in his pocket, 'It's like foreign aid. He'll be dependent. You wouldn't want that?' He dropped a handful of notes in the tin.

By contrast with the homemade trolley, Durbar Marg, a wide, fashionable street with some of the city's top hotels, was lined with airline offices, established trekking-firms and jewellery stores. The standards of each airline, Tony pointed out, were showcased in its office. One or two of the smaller ones were like dressed-up Portacabins, suggesting one boiled sweet and two lumps of cotton-wool, while the office of Thai Airlines, its uniformed staff seated like pilots behind computer-consoles, seemed just short of take-off to an exotic location. That it stopped short of this, that it gave no twist of orchids in silver-foil and served no gourmet dinner in reclining seats, that it could turn down human need without apology and land it flightless on the pavement was proof of the hard magic of the dollar and the power of market-share.

Kathmandu to Bangkok was booked solid, months ahead, they learned. An Australian in the queue broke down at the news. As if it was an in-flight movie Tony sat back to watch.

'But I hev a tickit! I pide for et!'

'Madam, you may have ticket, but it is not possible you fly without Confirmed Reservations.'

English jargon spoken by a Nepali has a satisfying ring of finality, pronunciation polished, head thrown back as the phrase is efficiently fired.

Arguments broke out in the queue.

'There's a frightful sense of escape about' Helen breathed, 'as if the glaciers might engulf Kathmandu? I'm tempted to stay!'

Wide-eyed, in wordless agreement, they slipped outside.

'That settles it' – Helen was determined. 'I didn't want to leave.'

'You didn't? I thought you ...'

'I thought *you* ...'

'Why didn't you tell me?'

'You never asked!'

'It's your holiday, Helen,' he affirmed with an emotional rush, 'we've had my bit.'

'Your bit!? That's what I came for – snow and ice and altitude and scenery and culture –'

'Headaches and diarrhoea.'

'– and I'd like more of the same. I've been reading about Solu Khumbu. Island Peak, Everest in winter –'

Next door, the Annapurna coffee-shop had the feel of a coffee-lounge in any solidly unoriginal western hotel; a lot of decor and service, ornate uniforms, busy little managers in tight suits, and not much on the menu. They poured Helen's coffee with a plate under the pot so that it didn't dribble into the saucer from the universally useless spout, but the coffee tasted much the same as anywhere else. Tony was exultant. 'TWO mountains! The most successful trip I've ever had – the only successful trip I've ever had. It's thanks to you, Helen.'

'I don't think I can take the credit. Except for keeping them easy. If I wasn't here you'd be swinging from an overhanging sérac.'

'See what I mean? Thank Christ you're here.' He clasped her hands unconditionally across the table. Life was so simple. The cups rattled and a busy little manager flourished a waiter forward again.

Immediately, as if he could no longer sustain simplicity, Tony's brain surged with caffeine and doubt. Could he justify her expectations? Could he endure a familiar mountain area with his hands in his pockets? Would it be a relief? And if it was how would he live with a failure of motivation and nerve? Weighting those concerns was a heavy sense of time to be bought hour by hour until he emerged after a lifetime and found Alice again. Four weeks apart and no relief; he wouldn't get over her now. He wouldn't break down either, go into a mourning decline or openly distress Helen, but the pain and desire would increase with the monotony of minor addiction. Through the mask of a relaxed grin he looked miserably at his wife, drinking her coffee with innocent satisfaction, smiling back as she stole crumbs of chocolate from his plate with her finger.

Helen, not Alice, was the real problem; she had never caused anyone anything but happiness and deserved the same. He could live with loss and absorb it, but he knew he couldn't endure Helen's pain if he hurt her. Was that concern for himself, or her? He knew he was guilty, and that the fault would continue. And yet, he was certain that he loved his wife in a predictably continuous kind of way that had temporarily – he hoped it was temporary – lost its joy.

'How'd you like to go home now?'

Her eyes widened. 'I'd hate it! I was about to get more coffee. '

She leaned forward with sudden concern, alerted by his stricken eyes. 'What's wrong, Tony?'

He pulled himself back, terrified by the brink he trod.

'Let's get up there quick, Helen, and make the most of it. We've got the acclimatization so we can fly into Lukla and save four or five days' walk. We could be well up into the mountains two or three days after leaving here.' Briskness would become enthusiasm if he maintained it. He whipped out a pen and notebook: 'Let's see; a rest-day at Namche, a short day to Tengboche, another to Dingboche, four days, we could be at Island Peak base-camp a week from now; give us four or five days – a week if we like – to climb the mountain and recover. That's about two weeks, right? We've all the time in the world, then back down to Dingboche, easy day, round to Lobuche, that's another short one, three lodges there, you're right up under Everest then, just a couple of easy hours to Gorak Shep, lodges there at the foot of Kala Pattar, everyone climbs that for sunset shots of Everest', no pause for interruption or consultation '– then back to Namche whatever route we like. You'll be interested in the monastery at Tengboche – home of Sherpa Buddhism ...'

'It burned down, Tony. Don't you remember?'

'What! When? I stayed there three years ago ...'

'No one is blaming you, don't worry. I showed you the headline at the time, WORLD FAMOUS MONASTERY UP IN SMOKE. An American foundation installed electricity as a gift. It burned to the ground. No one died, but they lost priceless relics. They're rebuilding. I'd love to see it anyway.'

'Electricity! Is nothing sacred? MacDonalds at Base Camp? So that's two or three weeks to climb Island Peak and get back to Kathmandu. A bit colder, not so many tourists, what do you think?' He sat back, flushed with recovery.

Oblivious to the spate of detail Helen watched excitement wipe the tension from his face. His blue eyes focused fully on her for seconds at a time, sparkling brightly against bleached eyebrows and golden skin before darting forward to the next detail. His eyes had seemed dulled for days as if sunglasses and constant squinting against sun and snow had given them an inward cast.

Since leaving the high mountains his face had become unusually drawn and tense but now it reflected the lively thrill of a new plan. Still barely listening she looked at his mouth as he spoke; the lips were full, undiminished by sun and wind, but somehow the tenderness had toughened – perceptible not by feeling but by a subtly painful comparison of memory. The light fell sideways on his handsome head and she examined next the eloquent lines that curved around the sides of his mouth giving his grin its rakish edge. Now that he smiled less, perhaps from unacknowledged disappointment, those elegant lines often held a thin trace of shadow and defined a lean, new face where the boy had lost the struggle with the man. Helen had fallen originally for his determined sense of youth, smooth and tough. When at last she marked the future making stealthy raids, first on his face, then on his hair, she was relieved to find she loved that too, in a realistic, unromantic way. This new affection was sharpened by something approaching pity for the shocks his resistance must absorb. And there was a premonition of fear, probably for herself, that he would not accept the demands of time and would involve her in his struggle. She knew that his injury had undermined him more than he admitted, and suspected that he was suffering now from the lack of a serious objective to test himself. There might be an unclimbed ridge they could try together? It was tempting to fantasize in a coffee-shop but she knew they would never make an expedition partnership. She liked summits rather than the climbing itself and would choose the simplest route. She had no intention of regretting this.

'When you say Island Peak is easy, do you mean easy as in E-A-S-Y, or just not horrific?'

'Easy as in A-B-C. A bit of steepish ice near the top, grade 2 perhaps, and the rest is scrambling. The views should be sensational – right under Lhotse, looking across at Makalu. We can skip the peak-fee and save $300 ...'

'That's illegal, Tony, and immoral.'

'Illegal, yes, but a lot of people do it. I'm thinking of bringing a school group out here soon. Put this down to research. What would you like to do now, Helen?'

'We'll come back to the permit later. I want to drop these cards in the Post Office. Let me finish this letter to Alice first. Have another bun or something.'

'Alice! Can I see?'

'There's nothing about you in it at all. Your secret is safe.' Teasing, she rejected his grab, but her smile was puzzled. He grinned awkwardly, flexed his arms behind his head, threw them nonchalantly on the table, leaned forward to arrive six inches from her face.

'I might ... send a few cards from Namche,' he yawned. 'I never write letters – except to you. That's why I brought you out – to save on postage.' He had slammed so fast through conflicting emotions before hitting subterfuge that the process had scorched him like electric shock. He was eye to eye with Helen in a moment of outstanding clarity, lightning in the dark. It had flashed on her side too because she was no longer smiling, her eyes were darkly vulnerable and he saw her exactly as a stranger, a doctor at an accident, might:

"... victim; early thirties, soft flesh hardening on the facial contours, skin wrinkling, hints of grey above her ears, no external wounds."

For the first time he realised people had to have ways of loving when desire failed. Trust and friendship had to be built, romance did not last. In that startled mirror he recognised his future, and pulled away. Not ready yet. He would have said it like that if the soldiers came with handcuffs: 'I'm not ready!'

But the strain of late-night music was gone from under her eyes and her skin was a rich, healthy brown. She would never be ruined by decay; her fine flesh would tighten and grow spare with a gentle austerity that would look wonderful at a piano. Perhaps there was an interchange where the spirit overtook the importance of the body? It must be rough for lovers who didn't coincide.

A warm, protective feeling diluted the remorse in him. He took her hand; 'I love you, Helen. I haven't regretted one second of this trip. You've been wonderful. If you weren't here I'd be wishing on falling stars and writing every second day. I'll never be able to go near a mountain again without missing you.'

So what do I want Alice for: he almost asked it aloud?

The answer was simple. It had nothing to do with Nepal, nothing to do with mountains, or marriage. It was the exact opposite; a month with Alice in a bamboo-hut on a moonlit beach in Thailand, exotic cocktails and meals, languidly chasing coloured fish underwater during the day. Not a trace of rigour in sight, except the pacing of sexual energy.

Alice at sea-level, in her element, golden sand between her toes, wet hair flicking jewels of water. She stood laughing in the foam at the edge of the waves, face tilted to the sun, wreathed in a haze of summer, and the light that belonged in an azure gloss upon the water danced in lazy, blue gleams in her sheaf of sloe-black hair. Whatever vantage-point Tony held – he seemed to lie flat on his back in soft sand – he could see nothing on the horizon, no hills, no mountains whatsoever, nothing but sweet, monotonous sea; nothing distracted his vision of long, dancerly legs in sand, utterly remote from snow and mountain-boots, and the spiked rat-traps for climbing ice.

'I think I've missed a period, Tony.'

'Oh? That's not unusual when you're travelling, Helen? You're often … well, you're not exactly regular?'

'I suppose not. It's not that unusual. But I am sure I have missed one.'

'I'm sure it's just a delay, sweetheart.' He beckoned the waiter abruptly with a scribbling motion for the bill.

Tony led the way, drawing Helen in his wake with a brusqueness that startled her, ducking among pedestrians and diving across wide streets thronged with traffic. She registered occasional landmarks for the future; the Bir Hospital announcing a full body-scan, an ornamental lake opposite the teeming market-streets, the military parade-ground, scorched grass and review-stand in curving concrete.

Royal Nepal Airlines occupied a large building facing the parade-ground. From a distance the main tower was richly decorated in the traditional style, with Newari wood-motifs, but on closer inspection it was shoddy, painted concrete. Helen reminded herself guiltily that cost must be a massive factor in third world design, and as for wood-carving –

timber was a precious resource in Nepal. 'They must think it grows on trees!' Tony remarked when they saw it burning lavishly in the hills.

Inside, under an enormous and ghastly mural not even Helen could excuse, they queued for tickets to Lukla. The line, mostly patient Sherpas, was static. Behind the counter a severe Hindu lady examined her nails and picked invisible threads off her cardigan and sari. A boy brought her tea. Tony fidgeted, looking at his watch. He leaned across the counter and enquired in a manner that always amused Helen – the tone of a Briton who thinks he is eminently reasonable, 'Is it possible to buy tickets to Lukla, please?'

She regarded him with cold patience, the power-failure obvious, tapped a teacherly nail on the extinguished screen beside her; 'The computer is down.' The clipped precision implied – any idiot can see that. Though sorry for Tony, Helen smiled inwardly; she knew the feeling.

'Wonder if there's anything in *Poste Restante?*'

'I doubt it. They haven't missed us yet. Still waving in the street and spotting us in the pub – "Saw ol' Tone 'n Helen down the King's 'ead last night; never go anywhere. Course she 'as 'er music. Gawd knows what keeps 'im goin'."'

'So where's *Poste Restante?*'

'Are you expecting something?'

'Alice might have written.'

He steered her numbly out of the main cavern of the Post Office into a separate area. Tourists crouched over trays of mail laid out on a big table. Helen headed for her own initial – greeting familiar faces from the trek. Perhaps the slowness of the post had held it back; but if Alice's conscience had got the better of her it would have come on wings. He shuffled through his own tray, hoping she might have used their joint surname, a forlorn hope thinking back over her slapdash, occasional post. He speeded up in case Helen finished first and came to look. He had to find it. But the pettiness appalled him – he couldn't accept what he was doing. His attention balked, snagged on postcards, torn envelopes. "Interfering with the post." He wouldn't steal the damn thing if it was there. If a crisis was forced he would face it now. He looked down the line at her intent head to confirm the decision; love might have wavered but respect stood firm. She straightened up gaily and waved a blue envelope.

She went on riffling, rapidly, carelessly, in case there was more. Tony sweated, fingers slipping; he thought he saw, shuffling back ... his own name, familiar writing; he fumbled, Nepali postmark, local stamps ...

Ripped it open, single notebook-page. 'Beloved Tony,' ... a heartfelt message, and her signature, 'with love, Helen.'

He gaped in her direction; her face ducked out of sight. Three weeks before, from the first post office they reached, at Chame, after a few days trekking, to record her joy at being there together. That was all – an affirmation. He looked again. She had opened her letter and was avidly reading. He pushed down to the end of the table and, bending, kissed the back of her neck intensely. She shivered with pleasure, and through her hair he saw Alice's vigorous scrawl slide back into its envelope. Pushing through the crowd he could not catch her eye; at the door he took her elbow; outside he searched her face for pain or anger. None, but an anxious crease between her eyes.

'Helen! Thanks for that. Thanks for ... everything.'

She took his hand, squeezed it. Helen always remembered; flowers, presents, birthdays, anniversaries, no fuss, sincerely celebrated.

'How's Alice?'

'I don't know. She doesn't say. It's a strange letter, hello/goodbye. Doesn't ask for you at all. Did we fall out or something?' She glanced at him strangely, almost in sorrow.

'Probably scribbled in a hurry to get something in the post. She'll write again.'

'I'm relieved she wrote at all. She resented us leaving while she was in London. Alice could take that as desertion. She won't let us off easily.'

'Sort of a grudge, you mean ...?'

'She ignored me once for a whole year, her best friend, something she thought I'd done.'

'You never told me. What did you do?'

'Nothing. Not what she thought anyway.'

'What did she think?'

'Nothing, Tony, nothing –' About to get angry she thought better of it; 'We were very young, sixteen, a lot more innocent than we knew. She fell in love with someone. A medical student. She was always falling in love but I suppose – well, he was pretty special. Unfortunately, he fancied me for some reason, and I was flattered enough to go out with him until I ... had to slap his face. Alice wouldn't have done that. He'd made the wrong choice. He was her first big disappointment; I think he set a trend. She didn't forgive me for a long time; I don't think she ever believed I turned him down.'

'I'm not sure I believe it myself. Tell me more about this old flame.'

Tony had his own unsettling memories of their last hours in London. He had woken to ideal conditions for departure. At 7 a.m. heavy rain streamed down the bedroom window as if the leaden sky over Islington had collapsed with the weight of winter. The curtains shivered, and the scraping that had woken him was a tendril of unleaved creeper clawing at the glass. Alice! Yesterday –

He sat up in a flux of excitement and dread. A streetlight beyond the garden swam into view, a cold, drowned moon. Lights were on in all the West Indian homes across the road. England was sinking fast beneath wet waves; what sunny shores had those warm people abandoned to sail the world in this storm-tossed ship. Nearer, my God, to Thee?

In a single day he and Helen could turn the seasons round and touch down in exotic, hot Nepal. He could smell it already in the sodden London dawn; the aromas of Kathmandu, fruit, spice, sackcloth? Poverty and plenty; the fragrance of pine-resin and dust along the trails; the thin air of altitude, its very purity a scent in itself just as snow is a colour.

'Alice!' She had detached herself from his embrace on the couch, straightened her clothes and turned away. 'Alice!' In despair he groaned it. Striding to her bedroom door, he had flung it open; she stood up like a sleepwalker, moved towards him smiling vaguely, still not looking. She tried to pass him in the doorway, walked into his blocking arm at breast-height. He brought the other arm behind her.

'My heart ... Feel my heart, Alice!'

It thudded violently against her arm. Her head drooped to listen. The smooth, black hair and pale neck were under his lips, but he held his head back as if making room for a stranger in a narrow space.

'We're off!' Helen absorbed him in blissful celebration, 'We're off today!' The rain streamed down.

Within her passionate embrace Tony found himself helplessly making love to a memory. He surged in its intimate rhythm.

Alice saw them off at Gatwick. She wore a yellow raincoat of shiny plastic, a grown-up version of the garb worn by children with fair skin whose mothers carry transparent umbrellas.

Tony, already in clashing cotton for the sunshine, found it deliberately antagonistic. He remembered she hadn't been at their wedding. Now, in the departure-lounge, it was as if she were participating in the ceremony she had missed. After hugging Helen she held her at unsmiling armslength and then handed her formally towards Tony. As she moved abruptly away he put out a drowning hand to detain her. She took it in her own, shook it like a final decision, then handed his shocked arm towards Helen, who failed to take it as if she hadn't been rehearsed. Tony was left swaying between them, a misplaced prop. In a new kind of silence they moved to the departure-gate on the very last call.

The Pakistan Airline jet, alcohol-free but for the private supplies of passengers, left England drowning; smooth and sedate as a submarine it swam towards the surface over northern France and broke out of the European waters on the edge of Asia.

Throughout the journey, behind the strained chatter, Tony pursued that silence. It was like unwinding a long bandage to arrive at a hidden wound; it uncoiled right to the heart of their union where secrecy had cut between them. All he could do was change the dressing; try to make up in manner for the loss of meaning, and hope Helen wouldn't notice.

In thoughtful silence they walked back a short distance from the Post Office, took a turn or two, left the traffic behind and dived into a swarming alley – ancient houses patched with crumbling plaster, wooden balconies nodding together across the street. Small shops wide open to the world were crammed with goods for local shoppers, racks of trousers, dresses, jeans and jackets, cheap shoes and sandals; food of every kind, groceries, cigarettes, acres of fruit in baskets and trays spilling lavishly onto the street; magnificent vegetables – big, fresh, clean, colourful – spreading down lanes and alleys, in and out of stalls and doorways, draped on bicycles, heaped in shoulder-baskets. Everywhere, clamouring crowds sifted and sniffed, selling, weighing, buying, hawking, shouting, spitting; old women mummified in wraparound shawls; beautiful, fine-boned girls; slim, vivid boys in jeans; dark-skinned fruit-sellers with doleful eyes; chubby, runny-nosed children; no space anywhere, every inch occupied by a product or a service; ten-geared bikes racked tight as teeth in a comb, shining pots and saucepans stacked ten-feet high in dwindling sizes; in primus-shops huge, multi-burner stoves were stripped, brazed, refitted in a space where one man could hardly move but several worked; another stall fixed motorbikes, spare parts heaped in greasy corners, a Honda 175 spanning the entire space, handlebars locked sideways to decrease the length.

The lanes narrowed, grew tight and squalid, dwellings sagged with age, still no easing of the crowds. In open-fronted rooms too low for head-height Helen saw craftsmen squatting in shadow, hammering meticulous rhythms into metal. At intervals these sub-floor hovels were abattoirs; cheerful women hunkered on a square yard of floor in a bleeding mass of offal chopping sinewy flesh with cleavers. From outside it looked as if they must hack away their own limbs in the spreading, sprawling gore.

Tiny cafes were tucked in there too, stoves flaring under cauldrons of rice and curry, disposable leaves for plates, table-tops gruesome as butcher-blocks. After the magnificence of their vegetables it distressed Helen deeply to see these peaceful people wallowing in slaughter, much of it gruesomely graphic – skin delicately stripped from skulls and carcases, the choicest flesh folded pinkly back to seduce the buyer. Tony, despite taking casual pictures and revelling in his own composure, was equally relieved to steer back towards the sanity of pottery and fabrics, vegetables and fruit.

'Let's have dinner in K.C's Helen!'

'But you hate that place. Tourist-imperialism was what you –'

'You're right. I know! But I'm not going –' Tony argued shamelessly – 'because I like it; I'm going to see who's in town. It's a practical visit!' After all the years it amazed and gratified him that he could still trigger Helen so predictably.

'Sounds more like hypocrisy!' she humphed. 'You can despise the expatriate club but you still have a good reason for eating there. What's the difference between you and the ones who worship it? I'm sick listening to them, up and down the trails, drooling over K.C's, all the fat trekkers whose only other topic is Thailand.'

'The difference' Tony teased, 'is that I know what it means: Romans in the vomitorium. But it's no good ignoring all the people we know just because they're not as enlightened as us. Don't worry, Helen; I won't have a drooling steak; something suitably penitential instead. Salad? On the other hand,' he mused, 'maybe I will have a steak. No point in a principle if you don't break it now and then to remind yourself; otherwise there's no sacrifice. That's why you have the odd cigarette. You suffer even more after it. Yes, let's go to K.C.'s and eat steak and chocolate-cake! It will be a truly moral experience, afterwards. And a drink in the dreaded Rum Doodle too, to wash down the remorse.'

'You've certainly knocked the good out of it for me.' Helen was indignant until she caught the quiver of a grin in his voice so she focused on his teasing instead. 'Englishmen think they're being moral when they're only uncomfortable,' she attacked with obscure accuracy.

K.C.'s was crowded. Its grey decor reminded Helen of a set for a Behan jail-play. To Tony's chagrin they were forced upstairs to find a table. The ground-floor was packed with all the people he had hoped never to see again after the Annapurna trail, and others who would probably inspire the same response in Solu Khumbu. The Frenchmen from Manang, who had scattered an old woman's goats to get a photo, were there guzzling steaks and beer. Grease glistened on their plump cheeks and the sweat of gastronomic dedication dewed their balding foreheads, but they smiled and waved at Tony in friendly fellowship. Waiting for his tomato-soup Tony shuddered with enjoyment. He was a fiercely social being. Meeting old friends was what he liked best in the world: meeting enemies ranked only slightly lower. The soup was magnificent, hot in taste and temper. Garlic stung the lips and tongue and black pepper seized the back of the throat. Hiccupping, he took Helen's hand in the candle-light to toast their success in soup.

"Allo, 'Allo!' A clamour of British voices, thunder on the stairs like double-boots on a bridge –

'Steve!'

'What're you doin' here?'

'What're *you* doing here?'

'I asked first –'

'I was here first!'

'Oh, you know – been on a little trip, Tony, spot of climbing with the boys. You've met Stevie haven't you?'

'Course I have. Hello Stevie.'

'Hi Tony. Hiya Helen –'

'... and Stephen here, this is Stephen, he's American.'

'Hi guys –'

'Well –' Tony was expansive but Helen detected anxiety, 'two's company but Steve's a crowd, eh? Going or coming, lads?'

'On our way back.' Steve admitted casually. A flat pause told Tony everything. Helen watched him brighten. They hadn't done it.

'Ama Dablam, was it?' He could afford to remember, 'Be-bop-alamma-bamma-Ama Dablam!'

'Yeah, new route, West Face, did it in three days –' Steve's evenness was almost plausible, but Stephen's Mormon-jaw dropped.

'Bad luck, lads,' Tony sympathised. 'Weather, was it? Too much snow about. Séracs and all that?'

Steve sat down, grinned, 'Yeah that's it, the usual. So what're you two doin' here? Thought you'd more sense Helen. Nobody gets up anything with old Tony.'

'Seems you can't get up without me either!' They grinned amiably, biffed each others' shoulders. 'We're meeting the Kusum Kanguru lot here', Steve explained, 'Dave North and his mates, seen 'em yet?'

Tony shook his head.

'No. No luck either,' Steve responded to Tony's quizzical look, 'they all got the shits in Lukla. Didn't even get up the ordinary-route in the end. Fancy a go at the Curtis-Ball next year, Tony?'

Helen waved a hand for her husband's attention. 'It seems we're the only ones to get up anything, Tony.'

'You mean you're not trekking? You've been climbing?' Steve was startled.

Tony began a deprecatory gesture.

'Two. Two peaks!' Helen interrupted firmly. 'We've climbed two peaks. So far. And done the Annapurna Circuit. In a month!'

Stephen was impressed. 'Two peaks. Gee! Guess I been with the wrong team –'

'Nothing technical,' she assured him, smiling with a luminous pride that Tony cherished, 'nothing like Ama Dablam; just good 6,000 metre mountains, snow and ice and Himalayan views and all that.'

'Wow, that's what I'll do next time I guess; move around and climb, and get a feel for the country.'

'He just spent three weeks dodging avalanches and squatting in Base Camp with the shits,' Steve explained.

'Sounds pretty bad,' Tony nodded in self-satisfied sympathy. 'Get anything done at all?'

'Oh, yeah, sure –' quick to reclaim ground, 'we did some rock-routes, new lines. There's like an apron on the North-West Buttress where it comes out to the left of the west face at about half-height. It's just like the West Face of the Blat, big sheets of slabby rock, first-class except for the top. We did some great new-routes, man, good as anything in Cham.'

Tony looked impressed – you had to give concessions – as if he might rush off tomorrow for a second ascent. 'Sounds great! Any problems with the L.O.?'

''Ello, 'ello! None at all. Best Liaison Officer I've had. Followed us up the first route. He reckoned it was a bit harder than anything on the army-crag in Jomosom. There was a 6a slab in the middle. I gave him a tight rope; brought it down to Severe.' Sensing disapproval he dropped the bragging; 'How'd you find the climbing, Helen?'

'Hard going, but –'

'Helen was brilliant,' Tony boasted, 'carrying like a horse and looking like a beauty-queen!'

'Better than this lot,' Steve responded. 'Looked like horses and carried like beauty-queens.'

The stairs thundered again. 'That'll be the Daves.'

They tumbled in, a medley of small moustaches and once-shorn temples; one carrot-haired, another dark, one brownish with a blonde splash, and one with a wrinkled, hardy face, hair grizzled, not with dye but age.

'Heroes of Kusum Kanguru,' Steve trumpeted, '– the Four Daves!' They skidded into a curtsy, three of them, the grizzled fourth was already at the drinks-list.

'You're not a Dave!' Tony accused. 'You're Tim Brown as ever was.'

'I bloody know, Tony. They insist on calling me Dave. They say it avoids confusion.'

The new arrivals were still fumbling at the furniture, squinting for chairs through greasy hair and glasses.

'I reckon it's a great idea!' Steve addressed Helen again, as a jury. 'It's going to rationalise sport. I propose we drop the geographical club-structure; it's outmoded and inefficient, too many small clubs and splinter groups. In future there'll be a Steve-Club, a Dave-Club, a Nige-Club for the Oxbridge lot, one for the Tonys, and that's about it, I reckon; a few Micks and Johns maybe, no one else really, is there? Same for expeditions; simple really!'

'What about the women?'

'Good question, Helen! I can see you're thinking "What about the women, eh?" Good question. Simple answer! Deed poll: Marriage.

'Take yourself, associate card-carrying member of the Tony-Club, special rate for family-membership. Fact is women do very well out of this scheme. If you want to join the Steve-Club you've only got to divorce Tony here and marry one of us! Or, you could 'ave one of that lot –' He sniggered; the three Daves, engineer, physicist, computerist, were still bumping into each other in the centre of the floor while two burly Australian girls, wearing shorts as loose as army-tents, had taken their table.

Steve had a squint downstairs. 'Come on, team! Cushions!'

Tony winked apologetically at Helen who had finally caught a waiter's eye, and joined the stampede.

Downstairs, deep cushions in an alcove around long, low tables created an area of spacious intimacy. A group could spread itself out here with a sense of privilege and set its own standards, anywhere between indulgence and decadence. Platters of sizzling food flew around like frisbees. Clumps of beer-bottles, ice cold, rose and fell like automatic skittles. In the cosmopolitan buzz the Daves and Steves felt securely British, solidarity augmented by their status as climbers rather than trekkers or 'touroids'. Their volume increased and they stared around for approval with the excited pride of children on a birthday-outing, as if paper hats and flushed cheeks were a true sign of distinction.

Other races were equally festive though not so enviably seated. Australian women – there were so many about that there could be none at home – barged in and out, wearing 3-man tents, kissing each other goodbye with loud lipsmacks, making assignations in Delhi and Bangkok.

'America!' a voice yearned in the distance, 'Gawd, America – where you can shower with your mouth open!'

'Americans!' Dave North snorted through a headcold, 'They do everything with their mouths open.' He caught Tony's warning eye, seated beside Stephen who went on serenely eating.

'And the Dutch,' Steve veered hastily.

'Oh my God!'

'And the Danes!'

'And the Swedes!'

'They all speak that disc-jockey English you can hear miles away.'

'Yeah, but it's good,' Steve reconsidered, 'I wish I could speak a foreign language that good.'

'I wish you could speak English that well,' Tony jibed, 'And it's not good! It's slick, pop-culture idiom.'

'What about the climbers?' Helen was a little cross. 'They're a funny lot too.'

'Different kinds of climbers –' Dave North began.

'Them as keeps their mouths shut, and you lot.' Tim spoke irritably, hinting at suppressed tensions post-Kanguru. Dave North, expedition-leader leaned over, a concerned sneer on his face, put his mouth close to Tim's ear and bellowed, 'Are y'alright, Grandad? Is yer hearin' aid switched on?'

Tim's rancour couldn't quell them; they were on a tribal spree.

Tony had a catalogue of types in his head; he launched into mimicry.

'There's a lot of these about –' his face turned square, '– the Hemingway types with heavy bones and mahogany faces. The skull is a traditional mansion and the brain lives solidly in the right wing. Life is a safari, they're looking for something to shoot. The nouveau-hippy might do –' His cheeks thinned dramatically, '– he wants to make it to Tibet, man. His, like, spiritual destiny lies in the high, wide, empty plains, not here in Kathmandu with us touroids. He's eating a plate of chips and tomato-sauce, none of that expensive tourist-shit you're eating. It's a rip-off, man! He's got a female counterpart; keep your fingers crossed they don't breed.

'And the Americans! "Dirt-cheap labour in China," sorry Stephen, we met a guy today, six feet wide across the shoulders, his skull was so narrow one eye overlapped the other. He wants to get into China for the business-breaks, exports to Texas, "Dirt-cheap labour in China!" He'll make millions.

'And the Brits – not us – public school army-types, think they own the country; "Damn it man, I asked for tea! This tea isn't coffee, it's cocoa! We taught you everything you know and look at the mess. What? Never in the empire? you are now, mate. Who d'you think we are? Foreign-aid? Good God, man, we're the Tourist-Empire"'

Helen's head was in her hands. She knew self-righteousness would only provoke them. And Tony piled in with such relish, no detachment whatsoever, quivering to the slightest whim of his peers. If anything, he was growing less mature.

'What's next?' Steve asked her quietly, undercover, 'What're you two doing next?'

She sighed. 'We're going up to Solu Khumbu.'

'Oh yeah!? To do what?'

Tony fielded the question. 'Oh, this and that; we'll have a look round, see what looks good.'

'We'll climb Island Peak,' she interrupted wearily, 'that's what we decided.' Why did he take the good out of it?

'Island Peak!?' Steve was mock-pensive, 'what's this you used to say Tony?'

'Island Peak,' Tony defended with heated dignity, 'is a mountain of great distinction. It may not be a test-piece, but the term "trekking-peak" has nothing to do with trekkers. It applies equally to Island Peak and Kusum Kanguru ...'

'Not paying a peak-fee surely, are you? Not for Island Peak!'

'Maybe, maybe not –'

'Oh yes we are!' Helen was resolute.

Steve's jaw dropped, 'Three hundred dollars! For Island Peak?'

'So?' Helen grew belligerent, 'a hundred and fifty each. We won't have to duck around, hiding and pretending, and maybe get barred from Nepal for years.'

'I think they've a bloody cheek,' Dave North was bitter, 'three hundred bloody dollars to climb a hill! And the extras!'

'You don't know what you're talking about –' Helen's patience snapped.

Tony cheered, 'You tell him, Helen!'

'First – it's not a hill; it's twenty thousand feet, high as Kusum Kanguru, but you didn't get that high, did you? Second, and much more important, Nepal is a third-world country. Nepal needs –'

'Helen knows about the Third World,' Steve explained kindly, 'she's Irish.'

'Nepal needs foreign currency to raise living standards. Lucky they've got the best mountains in the world. That means tourism. Tourism should mean foreign exchange: dollars, marks, francs, pounds. But tourism also means damage, destruction, change of lifestyle in remote areas, decrease in farming, lots of ugly little lodges, massive deforestation for firewood to feed and warm the tourists. Deforestation erodes the slopes. That means landslides, floods, loss of good soil in the mountains, rivers clogged up all the way down to India and Bangladesh, and you know what happens there. On top of that, and this is the real irony, the bulk of the money we spend doesn't benefit the average Nepali at all; it goes straight out of the country, either as black-market money when you do a deal with some grubby little tout and his boss salts the dollars away in Hong Kong –' they were listening now; they relished anything shady, '– or, it gets spent outside Nepal on foreign imports to service the tourist. Imports! Imports don't generate any wealth in a weak economy. They bleed it! Work out for yourself how much of the stuff tourists use and eat in Nepal is actually made here. A lot less than you think. I'm not talking about dal bhat and rugs. Furniture, taxis – start thinking!

'On top of all that, a lot of tourists are like us, back-packers of one sort or another, whether we call ourselves climbers or trekkers, living cheap, trying to spend as little money as we can, as much as possible of it on the black-market. But we're the ones going into remote, obscure, vulnerable places, carving out trails, wrecking the ecology, turning farmers into innkeepers and Coca-Cola porters – and we don't pay our way; not that it can be paid for!

'I think it's perfectly obvious what the government should do: in their interest, not ours. I suspect they've started already. Cut down the number of tourists to minimise the damage. And keep the revenue up by taking more from that smaller number. You don't get in unless you spend X number of dollars, and spend it on worthwhile projects. And keep that income out of the pockets of middlemen. Plough every cent of it back into the country as a whole. It means increased peak fees and trekking fees, shutting down areas like Annapurna to let them recover: the Indians did it with Nanda Devi, it'll have to happen here too. Otherwise we'll ruin the country.'

There was an uneasy silence, as if a teacher had called a halt. Frustration too, because Helen was ... protected from counter-attack. Her anger had reached other tables, drawing sidelong glances, covert grins. Tony cleared his throat as she simmered beside him, 'Remember that porter we had in '86,' he reminded Steve. 'Same thing. Helen is absolutely right! I forget his name,' he told the rest of the table. 'We always forget their names. He was much older than the others. He wanted nothing to do with them, or us. This guy was barefoot, tough. He worked in silence. Okay, it was voluntary, he was reasonably well-paid, he didn't have to work but, thinking about it now ... he was more like a prisoner on forced labour than a porter.

'The second night out of Dumre we stopped outside a village, some of us went in to look for beer. This chap was there before us, in the pub. We could see right off he resented us, and the local lads didn't welcome us either, sort of contagious, but we weren't leaving. They made us feel like invaders. I'd never felt that before: like a member of a garrison. The local lads in the shack were farm-workers; they didn't have much to gain from the expedition-trade.

'Our old boy was knocking back rakshi in a serious way. We sent him over a bottle of beer and he didn't touch it, wouldn't look at it – though it's a real luxury to the old chaps compared to the home-brews, chang and rakshi. Still, maybe it's like wine in a navvies' pub.

'He always wore the traditional kit, big loose loincloth and a rough sort of smock, no concession to the trousers and track suits most of the others wear. I have to say he looked uncouth, sort of neanderthal, not twentieth century anyway, but part of that was the anger coiled up inside him. I don't know whether I thought it then or later, but I reckon the ferocity was a sense of dignity betrayed. I know we talked a lot at the time, didn't we, Steve, about Eskimos and American Indians?

'Anyway, the old boy got worse and worse that night. He was mumbling away into his rakshi, clenching his fists and giving out these angry barks. Some of the other porters came in. They were all bunched together in a corner fascinated by this monologue while we were down the other end pretending there was nothing on. I felt like an officer in the wrong place; the squaddies are off-duty and they're getting out of hand. Time to melt away. The others wouldn't leave – I don't know about you, Steve – they were a bit miffed at their evening being ruined by a rowdy porter. You know how Mick is! The old man got really passionate, and just when he was steaming up to boiling-point, Alan laughed out loud. Some laugh he has! It was just nerves really, but the porter choked on it. His fist went up in the air like a cudgel and smashed down on this table loaded with drink. The others were all putting up rakshi for him, though they weren't having it themselves; he meant something to them alright.

'He smashed the table in two, a solid plank it looked like. You could lay his fist beside a lump-hammer and never tell the difference. There was broken glass and spilt drink everywhere, people jumping for cover, but he just crouched there staring straight ahead with a frozen look on his face like he was turned to stone. He was never going to do anything: one of those cigar-store Indians.

'We took off sharpish – Mick was first out. There was a lot of talk about being murdered in our beds, some people wanted him sacked on the spot. He was a threat, not a physical threat, more like a cultural discomfort in the folk-paradise of Nepal. Like being spat at by a child-beggar in Kathmandu when you're on holiday, that kind of thing.

'Me and Steve were against sacking him. It didn't seem fair. He wanted to work, he hadn't done anything to us, he was drinking on his time off and it was none of our business; we should have left him to it.'

'He was a really strong bugger,' Steve interrupted, 'always out in front. The others were a lazy lot. He set a standard.'

'Not lazy!' Tony argued irritably, 'that's the whole point. Anyway, I asked Nima, the sirdar, to find out about him for me. Nima is a modern Sherpa from Namche, he's young and sophisticated; I bet he's working for the big expeditions now. Those guys are detached by their background from lowland Nepal. In that sense Nima is part of an elite caste; he could comfortably look down on the Dumre porter and laugh at the hopeless fatalism of it all.

'At the same time they're all part of the same culture-crisis; Sherpas Tamangs, Newaris, Gurungs, highlanders and valleymen, they speak completely different local languages, but they can all communicate in Nepali. In the long run they're all subject to the same political and economic squeezes too, like Helen said. Nima got the story bit by bit; in the long run he was just as interested as I was.

'The porter came from a small, remote community in the agricultural Terai, far enough off the main road from Kathmandu to Dumre to be aware of it, but unaffected. They had a language, traditions, architectural style, crop-system, irrigation-terraces that could have been there forever as far as they were concerned – and a future that would be absolutely the same as the present and the past. Untouched by the outside world. Nima made a big point of the fact that they'd never worked for anyone but themselves – never had to.

'Meanwhile – the twentieth century was revving up outside. To provide electricity for the villages sprouting along the highway a valley had to be dammed and flooded. Seemed like a brilliant wheeze: hydropower, grants from China, India, the West? It wasn't meant to touch these local people at all – they probably wouldn't even get work on it – but they were promised compensation if it did any damage, and of course they'd get power on a spur-line. It was sort of their area after all. Seemed a good deal all round.

'Two years after the dam the electric glow of the towns could be seen on the rim of the night-sky. Our people still had no power. That didn't surprise them very much. Then their water dried up. Streams stopped running, wells disappeared. They lost one season's crops entirely before anyone official came near them. Obviously the drainage had been miscalculated and the scheme had sucked in all the local water. There was probably a subtle balance and it didn't take much to shift.

'There was no compensation. The community collapsed overnight; whole families moved out to live in poverty in town. Young people disappeared off to Kathmandu.

'Our porter lost his farm, his house, his animals, his future. The following year, in Kathmandu, one of his daughters died in childbirth and a son went to prison. Soon after, his wife died where they were living in the slums of Pokhara. She didn't know how to adjust. You could probably call it a broken heart.

'That's how he came to work for us.'

As the mountain-plane scooted up and over the foothills towards Solu Khumbu Helen felt gravity shear away from her senses with a lurch alarming as an air pocket. Tony revolved in his seat, camera squinting through the scratched perspex. She shrugged as he identified peaks in all directions, routes, ridges, first ascents. 'You're like a boy on a date naming galaxies, Tony. I don't want a lesson in astronomy.'

The girl on the date already knew they wouldn't be gazing hand-in-hand at faraway stars for long – he wouldn't be content to observe and share – he would lose himself in the distance of everything he saw. She could cope with that, if he came back to earth at intervals. She had distances to travel herself, inwards, towards the centre perhaps; a more important journey, though she wouldn't have said so.

She wouldn't have said it either, but she was increasingly aware that her journey had broken down, was going nowhere. The small motor of the heart was quiet, and in its place was the muffled roar of engines climbing the sky. The plane banked and she tugged his elbow to show a tiny village perched on a spur in the dizzy depths, houses studding the terraces, wisps of cloud in the valley below as if the village belonged halfway between earth and heaven. A few green trees and a golden crop against the planetary brown, the most beautiful colours in the world. Tony jigged, impatient for the plane to level and bring Gauri Sankar back to view. When he turned and kissed her absently, as if to shut her up, it was the excitement of his own dreams she tasted. She wouldn't follow him into that space and she would not be asked.

The small plane zipped through the rugged airspace as if it had been fired briskly aloft. Helen felt the uneasiness of this new beginning; it flushed through her in spasms of doubt. Gaining height, changing direction, the plane swerved and gambolled as if it might kick its heels, clap its wings in the freedom of flight. Helen strove for the same feeling; she would be in control this time; no longer a novice she knew the ropes. She looked at distant snow-slopes, gauged their angles and knew they could all be climbed – if necessary. It was a lonely feeling, no thrill of aspiration; there was nothing up there apart from challenge, and too many people of the kind they'd met in K.C.'s. Others too of course, like Tony.

But her eye was constantly drawn down from the empty sky into the folded valleys and ridges in the blue-brown haze where people lived, conscious of mountains on the rim of their lives in the same way they were aware of stars.

Children down there, after dark, held hands and pointed out the planes that slipped between their constellations, inspiring dreams of Hong Kong and Kathmandu. Did they wish for love, and fame and fortune, with no idea of the cold, bare slopes where any dream can lead – on a mountain or a city street? A bitter taste, cold as disappointment, rose up in her throat. Appalling ground lunged up to meet her. The plane throttled back, braced itself, shuddering – not a level inch in sight. The view was a physical impact in itself; hostile slopes scraping by on either side, glaciation above, a river-gorge below.

Over the rim of the ravine, engines howling, Lukla slammed into sight; dilapidated sprawl, brash tin roofs, tilted airstrip strewn with stones, one end tipping into the gorge, the other climbing towards the town. The small plane lifted its beak, flexed its wings, stuck out its feet and landed, running steeply uphill to a halt.

On the scuffed clay runway Helen struggled with her pack, felt the familiar weakness of altitude. The air had a thin, sharp taste, hard to swallow, unexpectedly depressing. Fresh snow whitened the slopes above the tree line, and an edgy crowd pressed against the barriers in the passenger-shed. 'No flights the last few days,' Tony guessed, '– bad weather. There's been a back-up.'

Lukla itself was more like a stagecoach stop than an airport town, an unplanned huddle dragged into being by the accident of a patch of ground on the edge of a ravine where planes could fall away into flight. On a good day regular flights reach Kathmandu in less than an hour. People depend on this. It saves four days walking, out to Jiri, against the grain of the land. But tickets are confirmed, in advance, for one flight only. On bad days, fog blinding Lukla, or snow on the runway – or smog in Kathmandu grounding the planes – a trap springs shut. All flights are cancelled, and today's passengers huddle disgruntled in Lukla's lodges. That night, tomorrow's passengers arrive, cold, miserable, fed up with mountains, and they have priority now, while the others retire to the waiting-list. And if tomorrow's and the next day's weather is bad, which it may well be – weather being a matter of unpredictable patterns, but patterns nonetheless – then the waiting-list grows and grows, disconsolate trekkers pile up in the lodges jerrybuilt round the airstrip for just these chances; they congregate every morning in the passenger-shed and grow hourly more querulous, bitterly resentful of Nepal's bureaucracy and weather, as if one is responsible for the other, and the innocent trekker is the victim of both.

Tony had seen fights break out between tourists and staff, more often between travellers themselves who had international connections to catch. A notice warned: *Please keep all knives, khukris and other arms in checked-in baggage.*

They lingered to watch as a crowd vied for seats on the plane going out. A big Japanese group, confirmed to the minute, mopped up all the places. The haggard waiting-list spilled round the counters issuing sardonic bulletins to keep their spirits up. They had whatever news there was even before the staff; strike in Kathmandu, smog, ten planes today, no planes today. Although she was being shoved and jostled by the crowd, Helen was glad of the distraction. She found herself watching avidly, yet coldly detached from what she saw. She observed every human detail with an almost shocking clarity, her own reactions numbed as if she was directing her intense attention away, feverishly away, from herself and her own feelings.

They spent the night in Lukla. Helen wanted to move on but Tony was keen to stay. He had been trapped there twice before on the way out from the mountains and he wanted to luxuriate in his freedom this time. Lukla, he said, was one of the great bottlenecks of human behaviour and it should not be missed.

'Have it your own way!' she snapped with such unexpected aggression that he was forced to defend himself with logic rather than yield.

'We wouldn't get anywhere useful this evening. If we leave early tomorrow we'll make Namche in a day. But if you'd rather –'

Helen had already stamped into the nearest lodge. Standing outside in shock Tony felt a confusion of shame and the inability to express it. This new silence of hers was a kind of general denial, unspecific, like being ignored. Once identified, he recognised it as something he already knew intimately.

All evening, as they wandered round the village arranging porters, drifting in and out of lodges, he was full of humour and direct concern. He persistently linked her unresponsive arm and kissed her cold cheek on the principle that enthusiasm is contagious. Helen was unwarmed, untouched, still observing others with a cold fascination from which she drew no comfort.

She kept bumping, as if by design, into a tall, solitary girl from Leeds in a capacious denim skirt, an ethnic cardigan on top. Her hair was probably blonde, but nobody would ever call it that. There was something decently sexlessly British about the pleasant face and jolly manner. Her grey eyes were intelligent, but although she was alone she was not self-sufficient. Her manner was a brave attempt to make the best of things.

'You're lucky to have someone close to travel with.'

Tony had dashed gallantly off for further supplies of tea.

'Not that one needs ... independence has its own rewards.' She tried to look wickedly gay, too honest not to blush at the effort. Helen thought sourly that Tony was at his very best impressing strangers.

Then there was a bony young Scot with an inflated ego. No opinions, but a stream of anecdotes to show how cleverly he'd extricated himself from difficult situations. He had irritatingly innocent skin with raw, red-tipped ears that barely protected him from Helen's exasperation. His friend had no defences; an overweight American with bristly jowls, sentimental eyes and an unctuous sincerity that was doubly annoying for being real. He dropped his voice towards the end of every sentence into that crusty tone bad actors use for both weariness and awe, and made Helen scream silently. Tony mocked him openly and he focused on her instead, telling tales of Dublin bars where he'd had mystical experiences listening to old men talk – and then, a minute later he was flying helicopters with total awe in Alaska.

'Me an' my old camera here' he patted it, just barely not calling it Ole

Betsy, 'we're gonna stay out tonight, mebbe take a moon-shot ...'

'Like the Apollo moon-shot?' Tony was in quick.

Helen sensed the bleak loneliness of the outsiders haunting the tourist-world in search of fulfilment. This evening they seemed to latch onto her, all these strays, as if they knew her. It was obscurely terrifying and brought out sparks of cruelty in repudiation.

Doug locked his Labrador-eyes on hers and in an attempt at a creative image patted Ole Betsy again, 'Good ol' camera. Had her twenty years now and served me well. Gotta couple screws loose in there now; airplane vibration, I guess.'

'Maybe it's you has a couple of screws loose!' Even Tony was shocked by her sharpness. The victim's jaw dropped and he slouched away.

Ignoring Sandra from Leeds she entered into passive conversation with a plump Nepali, in a Michelin duvet, who worked at the airstrip. From Kathmandu, he missed his family. He realised the mountains were beautiful, but beauty wore thin with long acquaintance; '– and here there are no facilities, no transport, no nudes –' it was "news", but it sounded better the other way in his precise, lipsmacking English with little runs of idiom sliding smoothly into the monologue to be derailed every now and then by grandiose eloquence, as when he remarked that the government could not afford to provide another airport in Kathmandu, 'surrounded as it is by hills and –', his lips smacked on the juicy word – 'hillocks!'

They slept in a crowded dormitory on separated bunks. Sandra lay nearby, her feet pointing at Helen's. Unused to altitude she panted and moaned fitfully. At dawn Helen found two shivering boys outside; the porters Tony ordered. One, at sixteen, was lean, seasoned, tough; the other, a year older, had the moonfaced roundness of a child. Helen decided to remain detached – these boys needed work. She gave them a silent breakfast of chocolate and woke Tony with a curt order to lighten the loads. Across the valley, Nup La, black rock gleaming with ice, hardened her heart.

A Norwegian family, Christian missionaries, set off with them. They nodded at Tony's cheerful salute. Helen had watched them the previous evening keeping coolly to themselves. They were on holiday – proselytising is not allowed in Nepal – but their very appearance was a lesson in dutiful Protestantism. Again, this morning, they managed a virtuous sense of family, shepherding their offspring as if nothing existed except for its impact on their principles and their children.

Helen was fascinated and repelled by the parents; the father tall and thin, with a distinctly bony skull, see-through hair plastered to its strong contours, pale eyebrows jutting over light-blue eyes which held an expression of slightly humorous scepticism that might have been a conscious lightening of his Christian severity. He had sunken cheeks and a thin-lipped, preacher's mouth. His wife, attracted to his principles rather than his presence, Helen thought, had a clear, youthful face excessively exposed by the plain scarf that bound her hair back tightly. A teenage daughter walked beside her mother with a pale prettiness that made her almost invisible.

Then the younger children tumbled onto the trail. Helen felt an unaccountable stab of pain. The twelve year old daughter was young enough to be shy but not at all self-conscious; with her big eyes, her mother's wide mouth spread in a smile, transparent skin and long flaxen hair – a blue ribbon at the back of her neck – she had the devastating charm of innocence. A younger brother hurtled past, singing with excitement, sending his parents into a flurry of protective concern. The father's thinness reached its limit in his son's features, bone-thin with a razor-blade profile, dazzling eyes, a shock of loose hair tumbling down the left side of his forehead which would surely have been shorn off by its own weight if it sliced across the meridian of his lively face.

Helen walked alone. Occasionally she caught up with the children and chatted stiffly to them but they deserted her. An odd, unhappy weariness weighed on her senses, not quite a headache, not quite nausea. The trail meandered above the glacial torrent of the Dudh Khosi, crossing and recrossing it on flimsy bridges. She concentrated on the solid houses under a rash of shiny, tin roofs, the sturdy, fresh-painted chortens, the straggling farm-terraces where women in long, grey skirts toiled, bent double, feet and fingers rooted in the rich soil.

More and more this gruelling work was giving way to lodges and tea-shops. It seemed a precarious transition, thriving at the moment with the Everest Trail, and this might increase eventually to the wealth of a European alpine economy or it might collapse back into desolation further undermined by the abandonment of farming and the loss of delicate irrigation and terracing systems built up over generations of labour and maintenance. Tony was bursting to relate previous adventures on this track, to point out Kusum Kanguru, Kwangde, and other landmarks rich for him in expedition-lore. She refused to reassure him. It was hardly even a conscious silence; it simply didn't occur to her to talk. She was cut off by an instinctive pressure as if he were an irrelevant acquaintance. And yet they were entering what should be the most satisfying phase of their lives. When she thought of it like that she felt like an old wife at a wedding, confronted with her own unhappiness by the transparent apparatus of the dream.

Encounters confirmed her isolation. The Everest Trail was sufficiently busy that trekkers were embarrassed and bored by each other's presence – in some cases angry that they didn't have it to themselves. They often ignored each other, like tourists on a city street, who hadn't come all that way to see their own kind.

On the other hand some were completely oblivious to the locals and were relieved only by each other. Sometimes – Helen had excused it before – this was simply a feature of youth, the need to feel experience collectively; but now, sick of Goa, Thai beaches, and bus-roof marathons, she recognised it as superficial character, the arrogant sense that culture was only a performance, relevant for as long as these people were passing it by. Instead of challenging their presumptions it reinforced their superiority.

'If ya wanna enjoy this country ya gotta block the people right outta your mind, man; they're rippin' ya off!'

She found it increasingly hard to concentrate. The sense of uplifting detail – smiles, flashes of colour, casual songs seemed to have deserted her, and the outside world had a closed, cold feel to it like the faces of the locals hurrying by on their invaded trails, indifferent to the visiting hordes.

Just beyond Ghat she found a small European girl, ten or twelve years old, with reddish hair and scrubbed, pink skin, sitting desolately on a rock surrounded by Sherpa women and children. The distress on both sides was palpable but there was no resolution; the child was frightened, the big, greyskirted, head-scarved women discussing what they might do, the wide-eyed toddlers who cry so little themselves, silent in the presence of tears.

They stepped back on Helen's arrival; here was the mother, no doubt. The child shrank away from Helen's flushed face.

'Are you alright? What's your name? Do you speak English?' The Sherpini giggled loudly – 'do you speak English?'

The girl faltered, still avoiding Helen's eyes; yes she spoke English, she was lost, separated from her parents on the way down from Namche. She thought her father might be ahead already and perhaps her mother behind. More tears. Helen soothed awkwardly, patted her shoulder, she was too curled up to hug – there was no problem if she stayed here, her father would come back or her mother would arrive –

Freckles, red eyes, sandy lashes, smudged tears, she couldn't be comforted; her parents were on a different trail altogether, fresh tears, and the women were upset again, crowding closer. Not the right mother – do you speak English!

Helen persuaded reasonably that there was still nothing to worry about; they would obviously return to the right trail and find her. But the child had thought it all through and she knew the worst; 'No. My father will think I'm with my mother and my mother will think I'm with my father.'

Helen's heart dissolved at the fear that could express itself so clearly in a foreign language. Tears flooded her own eyes. She changed the subject for want of a solution. 'What's your name?'

The little girl didn't really think it was relevant and had to be asked again.

'Louise,' she admitted bleakly.

'French?'

'No.'

'Swiss?'

'No. Danish ...' and that low, flat field of a peninsula far, far away at sea-level emphasised even more her predicament, lost, among the highest mountains on earth. Just then her parents burst through the crowd, together, in a flood of recrimination and concern. Helen, feeling inexplicably guilty, slipped away.

Further on, at Chumoa, a narrow wooden bridge spanned a stream in the permanent shadow of trees. The water below was frozen at the edges, and a small, intent boy in a frayed tracksuit held a plate-shaped chunk of ice in his fingers sliding it along the handrail of the bridge.

Helen paused, but instead of rumpling his hair as she meant, she reached further in abstraction, touched the frozen dish, and recoiled in shock as if her fingers had been burnt.

The child paused, stared up at her, his grimy face expressionless.

Beyond the bridge a water-driven corn-mill squatted over a stream, compact, stone-built, roofed with weatherbeaten boards. At a second mill upstream, a wizened old lady squatted on the floor feeding handfuls of corn into the wheel. The mills at Chumoa; as natural as if the landscape had thrown them up long ago to conspire with the people in the simplest possible existence. The old woman turned abruptly away, for fear of being photographed.

When, at last, beyond the ravine entrance to the Sagarmatha National Park the trail took off viciously uphill in tight switchbacks Helen's spirits lifted a little with the effort.

Sweating porters carried up bundles of planks and rested at every turn. The planks were lashed together into solid loads and carried upright, jutting over the head, slung from a headband. The powerful neck and shoulders took the carrying strain while the legs grappled with the climb. A cord, attached to the top of the load pulled it forward into balance when they bent over. These were long-distance, heavy-duty hauliers carrying double-loads and paid to match. To Helen's horrified eyes they looked as if they were playing an enormous, punishing instrument strapped to the back with the string in front of their noses.

Bushy, black yaks loaded for market, laboured up the zigzags, panting in short gasps, jaws open, pink tongues hanging.

'They're burning oil.' Tony passed her at a constriction where a convoy of yaks and porters were blocked by fallen boulders. They exchanged reluctant smiles before irrepressible energy took him up a steep bank overhanging a ravine. Helen knew she would find him at the next tea-shop. That had been his style all day, vaulting from lodge to lodge, greeting her with a quizzical grin as she plodded past.

Tin roofs. High houses with tin roofs –

Her first startled impression of Namche Bazaar, the Sherpa capital, was a horseshoe of high houses perched on a slope overlooking the abyss from which she had emerged. It stared straight out above the plunging forests at the shattered teeth of Kwangde Ri.

Namche bustled with prosperity, a medieval market-town in the twentieth century; hotels, shops, stalls, bank, post office. Sherpas and Tibetan traders strode about its lanes with the heightened excitement of cowboys in a frontier-town. Tourist, grain sack, plank – every incoming item was grist to the mill.

In the Lodge, still avoiding each other, they glanced into the dormitories and the dining room full of youth-travellers huddled round the pot-bellied stove as if it was theirs alone. Sharing a married grimace they rejected the dormitory and took a double room. Chunks of thawing silence kept them apart, although years of experience made the outcome inevitable. Casually Tony wedged her in the doorway and her withering glance had more to do with dignity than anger. Warmth stirred secretly within her. Soon, it would be difficult to remember what…

They ate silent soup, meditative pizza, conciliatory dessert, ignoring the group – English, Australian, American, Dutch – who passed a guitar around the stove like a joint, performing for the girls who gave nothing at all, except advice about going to Thailand, having been in Thailand, and parts of Thailand being destroyed by tourists but if you got there before the rush – 'there will be', Tony giggled, 'still plenty to destroy'.

'Remember *Animal House*' he reminisced with unnecessary volume, 'when Belushi took the guitar at the party, smashed it politely across his knee and handed back the two halves?'

'Hardly a valid form of criticism.'

'You're missing the point. Sometimes decisive action is the only possible course. Why don't you take over, Helen? Play. Sing. You could turn this place upside down in ten seconds, blindfolded.'

'Because I don't feel like it!' Somewhere within was the echo of a snarl she would never express in words.

'What's the matter, Helen?' He was good at self-righteous crossness. 'This is what you always wanted. What's wrong? I can't get a word out of you. Is it altitude? A period? Maybe we shouldn't have come up so quick.'

'Not now, Tony. Don't bully me now!' The snarl was closer to the surface, and she added with a fierceness that chilled him: 'and it's not just me, so don't pretend it is.' Furiously aware that she had no argument, couldn't put her finger on any event. Like accusing him of absence when he was always there.

Their room was a square cubicle of stout planks, privacy undermined by knotholes and warped joints.

Helen sat, unyielding, on the edge of the plank bed. He fussed pleasantly around her, humming his innocence, brushed out her tangled hair, kneaded her shoulders, fed her chocolate – as if she could be bribed!

Hm! – she thought dismissively, keeping it to herself, as he hooked his arm around her finally and drew her down to stretch out fully-dressed.

Boots clumped past in the corridor, the room shook, ill-fitting doors thudded upstairs and down. Music filtered through the building. Helen hadn't heard a note for days; her ear had switched off. A light came on somewhere. There was electricity in the evenings; it leaked under the door and through the chinks in the walls. Low voices came from both sides, and muffled laughter. Tony hugged her tighter, burrowed an arm around her waist to lock her to him.

Warm, wordless breath stirred her hair. His jaw settled against her cheek with practised assurance. At intervals, as if a specially fond thought occurred, he kissed her dry lips, being particularly careful not to scrape her with his bristle. Once, when she glanced up, he seemed to be gazing over her head, his eyes lost in shadow.

Now that she could almost answer, he wouldn't ask what was wrong.

Awkwardness was excluded from the circle of his embrace. Her mind floated; how to know you loved someone? More urgent; how to know she was loved?

No answer except instinct, and to take his word.

She came to depend on it, and when it was most important there was silence instead, or distraction.

Impossible to imagine anyone else in her arms, beginning all over again. Resenting the tight cage of his limbs she tried, defiantly. Images flickered, detached as calendar-leaves. Nothing. She lingered experimentally on a face downstairs: cleancut features, polished skin, beach-boy hair. Typically, he had a whining voice and a sawn-off, squat body. She kept him seated in her imagination, his mouth shut, until Tony stirred and shouldered him into oblivion.

Part two – she grinned cynically within. Tony knew her weaknesses and his strengths; she had never disguised her feelings. Perhaps she should.

'You'll rue the day,' Alice had said once, with almost elderly bitterness, 'when you let them see you care.'

Too late now – he had already prised her shoes off with his toes. His arms were inside her duvet, she was slipping out of the sleeves, as if he had received a definite signal and gone to work with several pairs of hands; zips were open, and her legs were arching busily into view. Complying, she alternated between pleasure and anger as the tension seeped away and flooded back in sharp spasms. To be so reduced, so easily handled, switched on and off at a touch!

Capitulation so outraged her at the critical moment that she almost jerked her limbs away in stiff resistance, and yet she yielded. It was choice, not submission, knowing that whatever shadows melted briefly, they would return. Intimacy was essential; it wasn't any less addictive being used to it, although she knew the ordinary was there behind it all the time, as plain as old wallpaper, or the street outside.

But there was no street outside; this was Namche – crooked alleys and melodious lanes. A dream-world where nothing signified? She allowed reluctant sweetness to melt her limbs as if her blood were honeyed.

It was dark, a velvet blackness threaded with mysterious light, and there was an intensely preliminary silence, not only in their room but in the cubicles on both sides. Gradually her breath began to issue in short, involuntary gasps, audible to the others, just as she could hear their inhibitions fade.

There was nothing delicate about Tony's presence. He worked, she thought, like an outboard motor; head down, muscles clenched, inexhaustible.

Later, her breath seemed to come from outside her, in deeper, harsher gasps; she heard it from a distance, as if the night were breathing through her body. Eyelids twitched beyond control, eyes rolling, desperate to see where she would plunge within herself. Her spine locked in an arch that remembered every contraction it had ever launched. She could hang endlessly, humming like a bird in this starved pre-ecstasy when the suspension was right. A dream of flying – until at last she would float and swoop, pleasure building like speed and she vanished through some condition she could never remember after.

This time she would not yield and leave him churning smoothly wherever it was he went, towing her body with him, netted in seaweed and streaming hair. They would go down together. The rising arch of her spine prepared to break him.

But there was a relentless vigour there, as if he felt the challenge – no kisses, no whispers or caresses; powerful hands forced her hips back against the arch; not quite breathing now, but exhaling, in deliberate grunts, both, timed to the blunt impact, flesh on flesh.

A lonely flare of passion threatened to betray her; she cast around for cold bearings, thought of the butter-haired dwarf next door, and the rush subsided. Silence in the other rooms now, quiet river-banks, while Tony powered on, and Helen held him deep as a drowning breath.

All the while she knew. The body, the heartbeat, the hands were his – but Tony was somewhere else. If she shouted he might hear the voice – but not the question.

She knew; of course she knew, and was used to knowing – and would forget when she had to; and now he was urging her firmly towards the edge, and she had forgotten already – her head and shoulders out in unsupported space, limbs clinging to some root deep in the current. She would not go ... until that came too; and then – in a tearing, throttled rush everything tumbled with her and was swept away in a flood of vacant sensation, frantic fingers grappling the foreign body spinning past her in the dark.

They came to rest drifting in the shallows and found each other again by touch. They rolled into an old, comfortable embrace, and purged of memory Helen fell instantly asleep.

Tony lay wide awake, his body humming bitterly. Alice had been there in the dark. Just as he grasped her she vanished to the far side of the world. Helen stirred in the tender hollow of his arm murmuring sleepily. It might indeed be possible to love two people, he understood – but he could only be faithful to one.

Solu Khumbu, December 5

Dear Alice,

We climbed another one yesterday, 20,000 feet. Today is a rest-day. Don't let this letter worry you – I just need to talk to someone ... The trip is terrific, but I haven't been all that well lately. Probably nothing much, altitude and so on, but if I tell Tony he'll take it too seriously and we'll get nothing done. You know what he's like.

Between you and me ...

I've crossed that out, but I'm sure you'll manage to read it any-way. It seems unlikely because we take no chances; it would be madness for me in these conditions.

All the same – oh, never mind, I'm addled with fatigue and altitude – I just need to say it to someone.

I won't bore you with the mountain, but it definitely deserves a mention. It's surrounded by enormous monsters, the biggest on earth, so it looks fairly handy. I barely made it to the top. The last bit was quite hard – hundreds of feet of ice, not my style at all, but it brought me close to an awareness of what the whole thing must be about. There's a thrill to climbing something steep and high which has nothing to do with the summit or the view or any of the obvious virtues. When you have to fight I can see the fight becomes a worthwhile end in itself. Maybe I'm becoming a climber at last, in a reluctant sort of way.

It's a lot to do with Tony, of course, though not entirely. I'd hate to be here and be a wandering distraction. We need to do things together – that's why we came – but it's just as important that he should come down to my level as it is for me to move up. I'm not sure how often that'll happen. Maybe it's just the way I'm feeling at the moment, but aren't most of the fanciable ones like that – into achievement before sharing? Is it only the mediocrities that want to be equal?

Okay, I wasn't great on the bloody mountain; I was slow and sick, and I even cried at one stage, but I put everything I had into it, and won't have it ignored or dismissed. How can I get better without encouragement?

My performance yesterday reminded me of music, Alice – long afternoons in the practise-room when you were all out at games and I plodded away on that bloody piano. When I think of it; inkstained fingers, cheap nail varnish, ivory keys the colour of nicotine! You thought I had talent because I could rattle out dance-tunes blind-folded, but that stuff is programmed; once you know the pattern it plays itself. What I really wanted, and you thought a complete bore, was to play the likes of Chopin – from the heart, not from the page. I didn't have the expression. Too much rhythm, insufficient feeling. That's why I work in entertainment. You thought I'd found my vocation; I hadn't – I'd lost it.

Even now, thinking about it, my fingers ache to poke holes in a sonata, even thought I'd crawl out the far end with frostbite. Maybe it's a personality-problem, not a creative urge, because I think – I think I could feel the same way about mountains now. I hope not, but I'm afraid so. I'm hooked on the grand scale again. It'll be a lot to ask of Tony, to come down to my level. He's already looking for someone else to try something frightful called Taweche. Much too hard for me ...

In the lodge at Lobuje, the last settlement before Everest, a young Korean held forth to an amused company of Sherpas, trekkers, a Nepali army-officer, and Helen and Tony who were not amused at all.

The youth had nothing to do with the winter-expedition on Everest. Attracted by its glamour he had come to climb in the same area, and he boasted feverishly of what he might do. His broad, flat face was inflamed with adventure, a young warrior in the final village vowing to slay dragons on the morrow. In ringing tones he told the villagers exactly what kind of hero he was, and the dragons he had already slain.

The Sherpas sniggered into their chang and the army-man mused on his role as liaison-officer, responsible for permits and climbing-fees. The Korean's new boots and gleaming equipment stood outside the door, ready to go.

It had threatened to snow for the last two days since Helen and Tony had returned from Everest Base Camp, where they walked up Kala Pattar, a pleasant little mountain without snow or ice.

Helen had seemed unnecessarily slow on the ascent. Tony allowed himself to grumble and she hardened into a familiar silence. At the top she stood on the highest boulders, and then – scrambling down, she slipped and fell.

There were no tears, no injuries, and although something collapsed inside Tony whenever Helen was hurt, this time concern was over-whelmed by irritation; it was almost as if she'd fallen on purpose, let herself go out of ... because she didn't understand this climbing thing and wouldn't try harder while they were here – and wouldn't under-stand either the effort he was making to help, to choose things they could do together.

'Don't –' he warned the Korean grimly '– don't tell the Liaison Officer we're going to climb. We haven't PAID.'

Helen slipped silently past. Tony put a hand out but she was gone.

The Korean hadn't quite understood, but he put a shh-finger to his lips like a drunk. Tony sighed and drew him round the back. The North Face of Taweche hung like a gable against the grey sky. Kyoung Bae Kim made martial gestures at the direct line up the face. Tony, recalling all the idiots he had roped up with, checked the two snow-ramps escaping to the right.

'Tomorrow morning. 4 a.m!' He punched four fingers at the grinning face and went to pack his gear.

On the mountain the Korean was fast and fearless. Conditions meant nothing to him; old snow on rotten ice. Tony would have turned back from the bergschrund. Instead, he laboured onto the slope and scraped upwards. Before he had climbed twenty feet the youth was level with him, grinning with glee. The rope hung down between them, unattended, already snagging below.

Tony swallowed his anger and humiliation; they would get up the route, that was the main thing. A significant achievement, maybe even a new one. He began to phrase the description, but after a few judiciously heroic words he concentrated on the gruelling task in hand.

Throughout the morning he used every trick he knew to save energy. It was steep ground, unstable rock jutting through the ice. Kyoung Bae Kim was prodigal with strength; by afternoon he was tiring – twice his feet slipped and he hung on his axes laughing at the joke. They were only half way up. Like a dog on a lead with only one direction, the Korean strained towards the distant summit. A couple of hours before dark, Tony took the escape-ramp. The youth clipped into his axes, untied without a word, threw him the rope and went on alone.

The escape and descent were perilous; a freezing bivouac on the ramp, his back injury returned, locked him in a rigid stoop inching downwards all next day in a snow choked gully, to a second bivouac. In the morning the valley looked desolate, as if everyone had fled under cover of darkness. When, at last a plume of smoke rose from a distant cluster of cairns he felt a flare of relief; the first sign of life below.

Back at Lobuje Lodge he looked wearily for Helen. Her sleeping bag lay spread out in the dormitory. At the sight of its solitary limpness he was deeply upset. Gone for a walk, maybe, or to another lodge – He returned to the smoky kitchen. Excitement congealed within him, turned to irritable hunger. He ordered dinner, ate it, looked outside again, finally asked the lodge-owner.

Yes, she remembered – black hair, she was here yesterday, not today.

Sick, she recalled, patting her stomach vigorously, very sick, maybe gone down?

Tony reeled. Impossible; her gear was still there, her sleeping bag. She couldn't be without a sleeping bag.

The woman opened the order-book, found Helen's entry; 10 Black-Tea-No-Sugar, nothing else. She pointed to it meaningfully.

'Oh yes, I'll pay. My dinner too. How much?'

'No pay. No problem. When you come back, pay.'

She tapped the ten teas again. 'She no eat. No food. Very sick. Maybe gone down.'

'But her sleeping bag ... she must have left word! A message?'

She shrugged, unable to help, turned to the fire.

He stumbled to the other lodges, uncomprehending faces, back to the kitchen again. A girl hurried in behind him, handed a note to the cook who glanced casually at it. Tony saw his name.

12 December. 2p.m.

Mr Tony Waters,
    Please come to the Clinic at Pheriche as soon as this finds you.

(Dr) Alan Lutrell.

Helen had woken to a numb sense of daylight, feet frozen in the bag. A persistent crackling – breath in her blocked airways. She sat up shakily. Nausea squeezed her stomach.

A silhouette at the far end of the room leaned into a pool of torchlight. Static spattered from a radio clamped to his head. A peaked cap jutted. Tony? No – gone. As if struck in the chest the figure snapped to attention, stared at the radio then slumped. Seconds later he jerked to his feet and flung out through the door. Morning lit the room before the door swung to – boots on icy gravel, yak-bells.

Smoke from the kitchen seeped through the wall. Loud voices, rattling. Helen tested her throat. Ravaged. She needed tea.

Vigorous figures in the kitchen. Excitement palpable. Mingma stacked yak-dung in the stove. Tall, broad-shouldered, with even features and a generous mouth, a handsome Sherpa face. She smiled in welcome. Her sister, cheerful, plain, in full-length corduroy skirt, poured out black tea unasked.

Thermos-flasks held milk-tea, black-tea-no-sugar, coffee, milk-coffee. Expedition leftovers on the shelves; tins of meat, fish, fruit, cheese; packs of soups and noodles; bales of biscuits, bars, chocolate; labels, logos in every language; EVEREST in every shape, size, nationality. In an alcove, Mingma's bed, photos of the King and Queen.

There was something in the air; five Sherpas hunched by the stove. Stirring porridge, pouring tea, Mingma held forth, fine chin jutting, lower lip sagging sometimes in a vulgar lapse. Heedless of the smoke the men gave back long salvoes, thawing some ordeal into speech. Now and then a belly-laugh, the women too, showing big, white teeth.

Can't be too serious, Helen thought and felt better; held her mug out. The door opened, closed before any smoke escaped. Silence fell. An oriental in down-jacket and pants sat into a space that melted for him. Helen knew the overhang of the cap from the dormitory. She saw a fine-boned, sallow face aristocratic in its superior expression. The chin receded, nose and mouth jutted, the moustache of fine hair gave a delicate, marsupial air. Not Japanese; narrow cheekbones, too tall.

Mingma presented milk-tea in a special cup. Silence continued, all eyes on the floor. Tension gathered in Helen's stomach, nausea renewed. Mingma brought more tea. She whispered, 'Sherpa dead on Everest.'

The mug lurched in Helen's hand. The moment of death on the radio. The winter-expedition. She'd seen the base-camp from Kala Pattar. Pan-Asian, various countries involved.

'How did it –'

A man leaned helpfully; 'High-altitude Sherpa. My friend. Coming down from high camp to base. Avalanche. Ice fell on him. Killed.' He smiled at Helen, pleased with his clarity.

Helen felt a fascinated revulsion for the sport she had adopted. Heads turned towards her, nodding, smiling. She dropped her eyes. Within an hour all the climbing-Sherpas clattered into Lobuche to fill up Mingma's kitchen; a dozen men, in their twenties and thirties, in duvets, canvas jackets, ski pants, breeches, boots, sneakers. Rucksacks heaped outside they tumbled in, as if to a party.

Steam rose off them, talk and laughter bubbled. Mugs and mugs of tea, Mingma scolding, listening, ministering like a fond sister, while her own sister, bare-armed, flushed with important exertion, laboured at the chang, squeezing heaps of wet, sour rice, sieving the rich, white liquid into a plastic bucket. She churned it over with a ladle, not a lump or a grain, filled a kettle, dumped it on the fire to take the bitter chill off the beer. She shoved the men aside, no one seeing her except Helen because of her absolute lack of looks, and bustled out the door to return a moment later with an armful of logs, then out again with a five-gallon drum, brought it back full, slung by a rope on her back – she swung it round and filled a barrel near the fire, then out again for more – or maybe just a reflex ricochet out the door, nothing needed.

In the press of bodies and the swirling smoke Helen could hardly breathe. There was internal pressure too – she was ill; not altitude, she knew, but something worse by far. She couldn't return to the bleak dormitory, sleeping-bags scattered like loose skins. She wouldn't sleep, she would suffocate in the cold loneliness that lay around the corner, minutes, hours, a lifetime ahead. Whether it waited outside or inside her body she wasn't sure, but it was there, a miasma of sickness and misery.

Once, she pushed outside to vomit. She stumbled round behind the lodge, thought of climbing up the slope to see the north face of Taweche, but uphill was impossible and she pushed back into the choking warmth. More tea. She had to fight dehydration.

Seated between two Sherpas she was jerked to and fro in the vigour of the argument, jokes, laughter, loud denials. The one on the right, wiry and short in winter-clothes and boots, grinned apologetically with lively eyes, a crooked nose, a merry mouth full of broken teeth; 'Sorry, sorry ...'

He was first on the chang, gulping gratefully from a brimming glass, bouncing up and down, commandeering the kettle, sloshing out glassfuls for the others, insisting, expostulating, overriding refusals, slapping flat palms aside from the rims of tumblers, carrying on two or three arguments at once, while Mingma stood, arms folded, the lower lip dropped between raucous exchanges, surveying them all – Ang Nima in particular – with affectionate irony.

He gave Helen a dig in the ribs, a cheeky grin – 'Where you go today? Kala Pattar? Base Camp?'

'I've been there. Yesterday ... no, the day before. Did you come down from Base Camp now?'

'Yes, all here come down this morning. Everest expedition. My friend –' his own eyes beamed with life '– he died last night. Is coming now. Down.'

'Was it an accident, or was he sick?'

'Sick. Altitude! Many times to Camp four, above South Col, many times, quickly up and down. Then yesterday, Camp four, very sick, slowly coming down, no good, Camp one he died last night.'

He looked at her merrily, '– Chang, you like chang? I pay!' leaning forward for the kettle.

'No. God, no – Your friend, where was he from?'

'Kumjung. Near Namche. Me also. High-altitude Sherpa, many expeditions. Also this man here, my friend, our Sirdar –' He poured chang onto the tall man's fingers so that it splashed onto the floor; everyone laughed and the grinning foreman was forced to remove his hand and accept a refill.

'Sherpa-style,' he said ruefully to Helen, 'Say, "No, no, don't want," then take. You like some?'

'Just like at home.' For a while Helen had forgotten her illness. Another cup of tea. This was a wake.

'Was he married? Children?' She couldn't resist.

'Yes, yes, married. Two doctors – one eleven, one eight.' Helen translated the daughters. She felt sick again.

'You married?' he asked with genuine social interest.

'Yes, yes I am.' She even showed the ring. 'My husband was here yesterday. Back soon. Gone trekking with a friend,' she extemporised.

She needn't have worried; no opportunism in his manner, just curiosity and chat.

'And you? Married?'

'Yes married!' He grinned proudly, hoarse with amusement and self-mockery; 'I have three children, all doctors, one twelve, one six, one ten months old. Now I need a son.'

In another corner a sudden argument broke out, voices raised, between a Sherpa in tweed breeches and another with angry eyes and a curling lip. The liquid in their glasses looked sour and dangerous.

Mingma glared in mock-exasperation. Helen thought she might box their ears, and yet, when the angry man drained his glass and demanded more she poured it out at once.

The tone all round became aggressive then. Helen was ignored. A youth, face slack from drink, stood up, confused tears in his eyes. He was jerked down sharply by the jacket. Mingma's sister, bare-armed still, shuttled in and out with water.

A small, distraught woman edged in through the door. The raised voices continued – then, as she stood uncertainly, fingers picking at her apron, the noise dropped and a nervous shuffling began. Helen felt a nameless, hot ache pass over her as the woman tried to melt into a corner. She offered her seat, insisting gently. Ang Nima had the matter in hand, on his feet shoving, shooing, exhorting, until everyone moved up and a space was made. The small woman in the standard grey, back-pleated skirt with striped apron and grey jacket, her face lined and desperate beneath a scarf, sat on the edge of the seat and rocked back and forth in silence.

Mingma pressed a cup of tea into her kneading hands. The men were silent, heads hanging, staring into their drink. She began a bitter weeping as she rocked, and when she spoke, head bowed, her quivering voice rose slowly as in a ritual, keening words that were half-spoken, half-wailed and went on unbroken except for sobs of breath in a stream of grief. The untouched tea, was spilling on her lap.

Listening, understanding, no one moved except Helen who only understood the appearance and gently prised the cup from the knotted fingers before the stain could spread. Then the others, Mingma, Ang Nima, the sirdar, leaned in with words of comfort, disclaimers, promises, but to no avail; the widow's rocking and wailing continued. Helen heard an unbearable echo of children's voices, clear and sharp.

Someone pressed a glass of clear liquor, rakshi, between her hands; everyone and everything concentrated on making her sip for comfort and control, as if they had to prove to themselves that there was some cure for such distress. They even raised her hands with the glass between them dripping on her apron, but she turned her anguished face aside.

This was love, Helen knew; fierce attachment without romance or sentiment; the instinctive love that is always perched on the edge of pain.

Whenever the door opened as Mingma's sister hurried in and out, the widow's yearning eyes swung to the opening as if someone else must surely enter.

The third time it happened she darted to her feet, pushing away the untouched glass, and stumbled out.

Then grief, as well as chang, went to the heads of all the mourners. All of a sudden they were drunk. Horrified, Helen understood. They worked under pressure, in a strange cause, in a bleak and deadly place. It was a gamble with death – someone would usually die; sometimes more. This season's victim was coming down now. There was a release of tension and a deep awareness of its cause.

The Liaison Officer became the butt of their anger. A small man in jeans and a huge down-jacket his feet tapped the floor in a non-stop, nervous rhythm. The sirdar led the attack, drunk but eloquent, waving an arm too slack to be a threat while the mild L.O. stared at the floor, shook his head slightly at moments of particular vehemence.

There were other trekkers in the room now, avid eyes recording details. The sirdar switched to broken English to make his accusations public.

'That is one way, but is not my way! Men sick on the mountain and the Lazy Officer laying down in Namche. Supposed to be in Base Camp to help our problems, not laying down in Namche. Lazy Officer and sirdar supposed to sign report of expedition – I will not sign. That is not my way. Men sick!' And then, in a burst of increased emotion as if blows were coming –

'One day I come down the mountain, and my head is swelled ... like a Pumpkin!'

Noise outside. Ang Nima whirled to Helen; 'He is coming. He is coming down.'

Draining their drinks they rushed out. Already, a big green tent had been erected beyond the river. Three men, one burdened, came hurrying towards it. Yaks grazed, the Norwegian children slithered on the ice, and Helen – through the silence and blinding light – heard the fat American from Lukla; 'Is it at all conceivable that he is being carried down in a foetal position on another man's back? Is that conceivable?'

Down by the tent the widow's slight figure stood apart, facing his arrival, and the mountain behind.

The Sherpas returned briefly to the kitchen. More than a team of workers they were a community. Mountains were their work. No one seemed to resent or blame the expedition. Mingma joked with the tall man in the peaked cap; all the climbers were tired – she would go to the top herself.

Before dispersing, aggression broke out again, on the verge of a fight. Mingma barged in to break it up. She turned away in a fine show of anger – and winked roguishly at Helen.

The day sank slowly, hour by hour. In the late afternoon Helen crept to the dormitory and lay shivering on her bunk. Her stomach cramped over and over again, staccato lines of pain stabbing the abdomen; giardia, she thought, infected food – this must be giardia ... But she felt a deeper signal in the pain, barbarous, incoherent, shocking.

Later, she wandered outside – moonlight and frost – and saw the glowing funeral-tent afloat, like a medieval barge upon the night. As if in a dream she waded slowly through the fluorescent dark, not towards the boat, but at a tangent of her own. Shadows shivered on the luminous walls, bells tinkled within and tiny drums thocked.

All night the lamas were busy in the tent of the dead.

Helen thought of the other solitary men suspended in that darkness at the end of the world; Christophe Profit on a pinnacle of Lhotse, Tony on Taweche. She dreamed of blood, and felt it, out of control within her. There, in the cold moonlight she knew what was wrong: she had been alone for months.

Behind his very presence he had left her quietly, and she knew now where he'd been. Scored by bells, and drums, and the violin-whine of pain, the thread of circumstance was clear.

Later, wisdom settled on her like cold ash. It was over. She knew it was over, if only because she had discovered it. They would wander on together, upright in their lives, but damaged beyond repair. The walking wounded.

Pain knifed her again. Deeper, sharp as a scalpel; she understood its message: what it was taking from her. Anger would follow the blood, an anguish of rage. She knew she had to let the anger come, at its own cruel pace, like a birth.

In the morning she recalled it first as a dream, but the blood was there again as proof.

She followed the funeral downhill towards the chortens, walking behind the widow in the dawn. High above her, on Taweche, a single speck, motionless, directly below the summit. She left the funeral at the cairns near Dhugla and walked steadily towards Pheriche. Behind her, in a sudden plume the grey smoke of cremation rose into the air.

A TALE OF SPENDTHRIFT INNOCENCE

I'll begin with a bang and save the whympering for later.
We cowered near the violent summit of the Dru, Tom Curtis and I,
trying to bury ourselves alive on a high mountain ledge. The midnight
wind was acrid with the sulphur of a storm. Hail pelleted against the
anoraks wrapped around our sleeping bags. Lightning flailed and the
slender mountain jolted like a whipping-post.

Shall I introduce Tom first, or the Dru? Tom, I think. The Dru has been
there forty million years and knows how to wait. Tom was twenty-one
then and not expecting to get much older. After five alpine seasons,
including climbs like the Walker Spur, the Frêney Pillar and the North Face
of the Eiger, he was probably the best of the young British alpinists.

Stocky and bespectacled, with a tangle of fine, fair curls, he had plenty of
other ambitions. He wanted to find and liberate the joke trapped in everything; he wanted to expose the exploitation of the Third World; and he
wanted a permanent sun-tan for his social image. Earlier in the week, relaxing
in Grindelwald, Tom surveyed himself with a happy gush of satisfaction:
'Brown legs, North Face of the Eiger ... I've had a bloody good holiday!'

The ledge was agonizingly inadequate. Two bodies in a single grave.
Before the storm struck we spread the sodden ropes under us. We slid our
feet into the rucksacks and pulled them up – up to the knees in my case.
I insulted Tom's stature, insinuating he could pull his up as far as the
shoulders. Our axes hummed like Chinese fiddles in the electric air. Wet
hail built up on our huddled forms, sliding down between us and melting
into our bags. Cold encroached with the insidious certitude of disease.
The intense wait for incineration was a slow death in itself. We couldn't
challenge the lightning, but we must defeat the horror.

'It's not enough, you know,' Tom pronounced, hiccups of effort in his
voice, 'to boycott Nestlé because they supply baby-formula to Third World
maternity wards. Do you know how much tea-pickers earn so that you
can drink tea for next to nothing in Ireland?'

The wind stalled. A sense of violent revelation. The air chilled and
tightened. The axes hummed their unearthly requiem. 'It's coming again!'
I warned. 'Keep talking, Tom. How much do they earn?'

'The tin industry is even worse.' Tom's voice vibrated with conviction
and electricity. 'In Bolivia –' A roaring hiss. A flash hit the summit. The

explosion blocked our ears with pain. Electricity seared down the cracks. A hundred and fifty feet below the summit the charge hit our niche, the gap in the sparkplug. It picked us up like puppets, heads, legs, arms jerking and twitching. Fuses buzzed in the nerve-circuit. 'Next time,' I thought, dazed with survival, 'it must be next time. We can't get away with this.'

Tom was on the outside of the ledge and getting the worst of everything. He was still kicking and twitching well after my strings had been dropped. I thought he was overdoing it to get more space.

'Jesus Christ,' I swore and prayed simultaneously. My voice wobbled, as if worked by elastic bands, 'Are you okay, Tom?'

'I think so,' he quavered. 'Do people survive this kind of thing?'

'Electric shocks are good for you,' I assured him bracingly. 'They tone up the nervous system.'

The Executioner peered down into the death chamber at his two victims strapped to the electric chair of the Dru. He ground his teeth with chagrin, looked surreptitiously around. There were no lawyers at 10,000 feet to demand a technical reprieve.

'Go again!' he thundered. The air was a cold, dead skin. Nerves stretched in the body, like barbed wire, the scurrying mind caged in the skull, trying to bail out through the window slits. As the tension tightened again toward crescendo, my hair stood entirely on end.

Tom was cursing out of a mixture of hysteria and hilarity, blaming the statue for the inferno. Some of the Alpine peaks have a little storm-scarred Virgin on the summit to aggravate the pagan elements. He swore the thing was attracting the lightning and conducting it onto us. His language had the crackle of blasphemy in the tense air. I felt the primitive pull of old superstitions in my blood.

'Not now, Tom! Not now. Don't talk like that just now,' I advised.

Long years of indoctrination had left scars on me that reappeared when extremity pinched the skin. Nothing too embarrassing, no rosaries or anything like that, just ... a Catholic sense of voodoo.

I cast around for an explanation of my unease for Tom, who was actually brought up in the same sorcery, though nothing in England approaches the claustrophobia of the Irish version.

'It's – it's Bad Magic,' I offered lamely.

The Dru itself is a gigantic lightning rod anyway, and a massive statue in its own right. The rock is granite, but the colour and texture vary with the aspect. The North Face is cold and austere, riffed, cracked and grooved. The rock contrasts darkly with the eye of the Niche, a hooded icefield in the centre of the face. The West Face, with its southerly pillar named for Walter Bonatti, who spent six days and nights, solo, on its first ascent, is a sheer, smooth wall from base to summit, made all the more elegant by the rougher rock on both sides. Overlooking Chamonix, it is the archetypal column: a monolith, an obelisk, a round-tower, a cathedral spire, depending on the angle of view, comprising all the symbols of human aspiration. Difficult to say whether it is phallicism or a sense of architecture that attracts, but the great column of the Dru has been a seminal source of mountaineering progress.

The first time I saw the Dru, from the squalor of a climbers' campsite, I thought it achieved an impossible perfection of form, and something like the magic of myth. The Sword in the Stone. Only a king could rip the sabre out of the rock. Hadn't Bonatti done it? He proved that like every jutting handle in history it was not a sword at all, but a challenge to the imagination.

I was impressionable that year and determined to be impressed. An hour earlier, alighting from the train at dawn, I had been transfixed by the serration of granite peaks sawing the sky above the town. That high horizon, I learned gradually, could act like the jawbone of some insatiable carnivore, but for the time being I was all elation and spendthrift innocence. I watched the Aiguille du Midi engrave its precision on the sky with the point of a needle. Later that day I discovered from a cheap postcard that the exquisite needle of the Midi is a concrete pillar built on top as part of the téléphérique station. I felt embarrassed, caught out in a Three-Card-Trick on the first visit to town.

But the Dru didn't deal in illusions. If an imaginary architect had to design the ideal mountain, the result would be some kind of Dru: inspiring in appearance, accessible, though not without effort, with classic climbs on a number of faces and the potential to challenge new generations. Finally, it should be possible to escape from the mountain in bad weather, though not so easily as to diminish the commitment required.

Few mountains qualify under all these conditions, though they may be none the worse for that. Some boast an excess of one quality, which can be a virtue in itself. The Eiger, for example, offers a poor exchange-rate between life and death, but it pays a higher dividend on success. The Matterhorn – to stick with the public mountains – is all aesthetics from afar, and whoever makes the mistake of probing its instability will only succeed in kicking holes in that perfection. Mont Blanc, I suspect, is more than one mountain. The great faces of its Frêney, Brouillard, and Brenva aspects simply happen to share a broad summit. I calculate with a little geometry that if Mont Blanc were twenty thousand feet high instead of fifteen, all the good routes could finish directly on a pinpoint. There'd be problems of course: those easy routes via the Grands Mulets and the Dôme du Gouter might overhang in their upper sections.

It must be obvious by now that I'm reluctant to rescue those twitching wretches from the summit of the Dru. Curtis will be all right, of course: he was born to survive. But shouldn't I do the decent thing by my alter ego, zoom in on the Dru, typewriter clattering like a chopper, and pluck that lanky insomniac off the ledge?

But this is an irresistible chance to conduct an experiment, an advance on those infamous cruelty tests when people were instructed to give massive electric shocks to others, with medical assurance that it was for their own good. The torturers were the subject of the real experiment, since the patients were only miming pain: there was no current. The object was to see how much pain people would inflict, under instruction, against all the evidence of agony. Can I bring myself to extend the storm, step up the voltage, intensify the whip-flash, and make a true hell of that bivouac halfway between earth and heaven?

Back at the experiment the wires are heating up nicely, sparks spitting, and I must admit there is a strange temptation to step up the pressure on the ledge. An obscure desire to *make something happen*. It is of course a futile urge to shock one of them into some glorious statement, a timeless speech from the dock, a fist brandished in the face of fate. Something, in short, I didn't have the courage to shout when I had my chance up there to challenge death. But after all, survival is more important than heroics and, finally after two hours of torture, I had yielded up no secrets other than a feeble sense of irreligion and the politics of the left. The storm had appointments with other souls. It packed its black bag of truncheons, wires, and batteries and moved on to the next cell.

They will sleep till dawn, exhausted by trauma and the second bivouac. And there is time to abseil down the dangling puppet-strings, back to the real beginning.

The weather was perfect for the North Face. A cynic would have smelled an ambush. The mountain sweated under the strident cosmetics of the sun. Long days of heat treatment caressed the rock, massaging the ice out of the deep wrinkles. Scores of people came courting. Half Belfast was up there. They found the face in a carefree mood, autographing guidebooks, having its grapes peeled.

A clean translucent dawn greeted us – that suggestion of a polished glass sky – when we left Snell's Field, stumbling heavy-loaded toward Argentière. The sulky statue brooding on the skyline didn't look in the least like a mountain anyone was about to climb. Along the road I fought that trudging lethargy, as if trapped on a milk train passing sleeping villas, dewy orchards, and shuttered bars. The real morning streamed past me in its urgent air – light, colour, excitement speeding by on another track. I felt the illusion of sliding into reverse. Tom was leaving me behind too, with the reproachful air of one who has never quite learned to be angry. I tilted forward on my toes and kicked a gaping hole in my lassitude.

The climb began at the base of a broad gully, three hundred feet high. A long stripe of fresh snow bedded the groove, rockribs showing through. A lip of ice barred entry. It faded out on a brief bulge. Tom hacked a few moves upward, dispensed with the axe, and pulled up on rock, crampons scraping and hooking. Water flowed as the fresh snow melted. The moves were unexpectedly hard. I locked my hand between ice and rock and groped uneasily for a hold.

A flurry of small stones introduced company. Three bedraggled climbers had bivouacked overnight on a ledge system to make an early start and were outraged by nocturnal snow. They were going down, they informed us in shivering French, and formed a low opinion of our judgment when we continued. But we, after all, had spent both a dry night and a cable-car fare. As other groups of refugees plunged down past us, it was obvious that a general exodus was underway. We were pleased with the thinning out of the queue.

There was no longer any impression of the inaccessible magnificence of the Dru. It was simply another mountain-shaped cliff. After partnership on the Walker Spur, the Frêney Pillar, and the Eiger, our procedures were automatic: brief immersion in a lead, and then while Tom climbed I contemplated savagery and civilization as proposed by the wild aiguilles and the teeming valley below.

The roofs of Chamonix glowed with miniaturized perfection in the depths of the daily world. The sinuous river and the gleaming motorway flowed together through the long, tight valley. I swung a size eleven boot out over the void and casually obscured a vast area of civilization. I experimented thoughtfully, stamping out the town of Chamonix, and then, with a quick jab of the heel, I stubbed out Snell's Field.

Paying out the rope to Tom, who was involved with a steep and intimate crack, I wished I was down there, sitting in a warm bar in front of *un grand cafe au lait*, dunking the flaky subtlety of a croissant, with the climb wrapped up in a neat cassette of memory, playing away quietly behind the eyes and ears.

Half-an-hour later, I was balanced in a steep, wet groove, the minutes leaping off the face like rats, wishing I had an extension ladder. I was supported by one boot braced with an air of strained credibility against a rib of wet rock. The flared groove contained a malevolent core of old ice. It left just enough space for a fist and a boot. I scrounged and grudged painfully up the groove, my back lodged against one gurgling wall and a sodden knee genuflecting piously against the other. At the top I hauled onto a flooded ledge, soaked, scraped, and enraged.

Ladders were on my mind because the situation recalled a filthy day spent painting gutters on a Dublin school. Water and dirt had turned the paint to greasy sludge. You can save time on a long ladder by bouncing it at the top so that it jerks along the wall and gives a wider reach, while the bottom remains in the same position. Tilt too far and the ladder will slip, of course, but if there is a gutter or a window sill to hang on to, you can lean to a ridiculous extent. I had reached the angle of absurdity, clinging to the gutter and painting away, when the wind whipped the ladder out from under me. As it went, I grabbed the lip of the gutter and hand-traversed along it until I got my knees on a windowsill. Water poured down my sleeves and trickled inquisitively into my armpits, while the window was opened out against me from within by an entertained audience.

I stood dripping on the stance above the icicle and the wind skinned me like a knife-thrower's target. The weather was going downhill. Chamonix exuded a desperate nostalgia as mist erased it like a lapse of fond memory.

I shouldn't shift focus again, since mountain and story are already littered with stranded Doppelgängers, spitting images awaiting deliverance from ledges, windowsills, and waterfalls. As I write this in an old cottage in County Wicklow, I'm no better off than any of them. It's pouring rain outside, and the roof is sieving it mournfully into buckets in the kitchen.

The vast, cranky fireplace has its priorities obstinately reversed: the heat goes up the chimney and the smoke comes into the living-room. At intervals I have to stand at the back door for air and relief, sprayed by rain and wreathed in smoke. There is no comfort here at all for the man on the mountain, shrouded in mist and spat upon by the elements.

There was an airlock in the plumbing too and earwigs living in the taps. I coupled an aqualung to the sink and gave the system a blast at two thousand pounds per square inch. It cleared the blockage, and the earwigs, but now there's an inch of rusty water on the bathroom floor. Yes, and the rent is due. I wish I were back on the mountain. It might take my mind off things. Meanwhile, the fellow shivering on the ledge wishes he were back here! People are never satisfied.

Mont Blanc and the higher aiguilles were still clear of the weather and Tom was fully in favour of going on. That, I pointed out severely, was a suitable sentiment for an effervescent youth who had climbed the icicle with a rope from above. But I was less optimistic. The effects of last night's storm would be worse the higher we climbed. And how could we trust a forecast that had already betrayed us once? With all the hard climbing still above there was no guarantee of the summit that day. Still, I wanted to go on too: Tom's great ability and enthusiasm, and the deviousness I had developed with age, fitted us for this route in almost any condition.

Onward then! We turned heroic eyes once more upon the heights and blinked blindly into the mist.

We were not alone.

A pair of voices, one faint, the other frantic, had been yodelling above us for some time. Burrowing between fog and rock, I arrived below a blocky wall just as a large rump and rucksack disappeared overhead. French climbers dress to a high standard of elegance, but this rump was clad in a rough boiler suit. The rucksack bulged prodigiously and was saddled like a hiker's backpack with a roll of yellow Karrimat. The scene had the mock-serious quality of a cartoon: hapless hitchhiker takes a wrong turn in the fog, the road gets steeper and steeper, until he is hanging by a finger from an overhang, still thumbing hopefully. I pursued him and he lurched upward, blunt boots scrabbling, voice hissing desperately for a tight rope.

'*Avale! Avale! Merde! AVAAALE!*'

The slack rope jerked suddenly – a lasso coming tight on a bullock – and he was hauled bucking and kicking over the horizon. I was intrigued, as by a circus act when a bucket-footed clown wobbles on a tight rope, but the pitch ahead demanded full concentration. Its massive ice-bedded flakes stuck out at eccentric angles. Some of the bigger blocks made minor overhangs. A hundred feet higher I reached a flat ledge, hooked my fingers over the rim of the cartoon frame, and squeezed into the picture beside the portly boiler suit. I saw his slimline partner silhouetted above us, entirely unburdened by any sack at all. The mystery cleared The dungaree-man was carrying the lot: two sets of bivvy-gear, double raingear, all the food. And since the leader was wearing a light pair of rock shoes, his heavy boots, crampons, and ice axe must also be in the bag.

The man in the boiler suit welcomed us with a broad, red-faced beam.

'*Est-ce que vous avez fait bivouac sur les terrasses la-bas?*' I enquired amiably.

A flash of teeth. 'We haf bifouack on ze terrass las' night.'

My sympathy hardened instantly to resentment. If there is one linguistic conceit I cannot stand, it is that continental habit of speaking English to foreigners no matter what the foreigner wants to speak. In resorts like Chamonix and Zermatt the shops employ staff who can speak Anglo-American, and they are so anxious to prove their competence in threadbare slang that they will speak nothing else no matter how earnest your French or German may be. The hitchhiker was one of these.

'Where you are from?' he articulated proudly.

'Irlande,' I gritted. '*Je suis Irlandais!*' with a pronounced accent on the 'Irl' since nine people out of ten hear Hollande instead. If they grasp the Irish angle they differentiate between North and South, Catholic or Protestant, often accompanied by gunfire mime. We are characterized internationally by the twin terrors of violence and religion.

'Ah! I haf been many time in Amstairdame.'

'*Est-ce qu'il y avait beaucoup de neige pendant la nuit?*' I interrupted the autobiography.

'Zere was much snow,' he assured me with satisfaction, as if that was in order and the place wouldn't have been the same without it. I busied myself bringing Tom up, and soon the Anglo-garrulous Jacques was winched creaking and panting off the ledge like a fat pantomime-fairy.

'We'll have to pass them,' I warned Tom as he prepared to lead through. 'I'll be damned if I'm going to listen to pidgin English from here to the top.' A lot of British climbers would have taken this as a reflection on their own conversation, but Tom let it go.

The rock was continuously sheer and difficult now, a grainy grey-green granite with clean corners and cracks, and there was no chance of passing the pair ahead. Jacques and I worked out a stubborn compromise: he practised his foul English, and I responded in what I hope was slightly less atrocious French. Tom led our rope with panache up the severely exposed Lambert Crack, a thin slit in a solid wall, hounding Jacques' heels, and I stepped up the pressure on the next pitch. Unfortunately, Jacques' partner wasn't always responsive to his panted needs - '*Avale*, imbecile! *AVALE!*' – and at times a dribble of slack rope gathered on his paunch while he hung by his fingertips and hissed for tension.

Finally, we seized our chance to pass when the route branched in the uncertain mist. I jumped into one of those evil grooves that appear to have been built upside down, and emerged somewhere along the lower edge of the Niche. Visibility was down to twenty feet and the thick snow cover blended with the mist to rob the eye of focus. Progress in the haunted half-light was arrested by huge warts and carbuncles of rock, rheumy with ice. We were lost. A voice mewed piteously out in the mist. He wasn't talking English now, I thought spitefully.

Tom was brilliant on this kind of terrain. Being lost suited him: he could pick the hardest way ahead and pretend it was the only way to go. The guidebook had nothing to offer. I shoved it down my jumper and sent Tom out into the unknown with the air of Columbus throwing pigeons at the New World. He ducked beneath an overhanging bulge and was gone. I was left with the frail rope, the sling that bound me to a flake, and the shapes that came and went in the pale fog. The mountain was no more substantial than a pillar of cloud and snow scoured by the wind. Hunched within myself, I brooded. The human body has reflexes common to all creatures, and a mountaineer on a windswept stance bears a marked resemblance to a hen on a windy day: clucking disconsolately, the head withdrawn, elbows clamped against the ribs like scrawny wings, alternate legs doubled up under the body. Every now and then the querulous head extends a squawking inquiry into the outside world.

Eventually Tom called and I thawed into movement. I'd love to have left an egg on the foothold in a salute to the surreal. Instead, I lost the guidebook. Ducking under the bulge, I saw it swoop into obscurity, covers spread like wings. It was lucky we had maintained diplomatic relations with the French! Guidebooks, I realized, were above language barriers. I listened ardently for Jacques' voice in the mist. Beyond the ice, at the base of the pillar, lay a sloping terrace, broad enough for a few uncomfortable bodies. The wind screeched into a higher register and a spatter of hail raked the ledge. The weather was hardening, breaking up into pellets of its own solidity. The day's climbing was over, and we settled into an amicable ambush for the French.

'Allo! Can you 'elp me, please?'

Thus, we had been warned in Catholic myth, the voices of damned souls cry for release from Hell, and must be kicked in the teeth by the righteous.

'*Ici,*' we yelled, '*Ici! A droite!*'

Jacques stumped out of the mist like a refugee from purgatory and cramponed across the ice.

'*Ou est le sac, Jacques?*' I quipped, wondering if the pack had joined our guidebook at the foot of the Dru, and if it had, was their book in it?

"Enri 'as ze sac now.' Jacques beamed with the satisfaction of justice done. He squatted on the tiny portion of ledge we had allowed for their occupation and anchored himself with extraordinary thoroughness. No danger of him being pulled off his perch.

"Enri 'as no –' He pointed at his feet in explanation.

'No crampons?' We were surprised at such an oversight.

'No boots,' Jacques corrected calmly.

'No boots!' We gaped at each other in amazement. No boots on the North Face of the Dru, on a second bivouac, before a second storm?

"E 'ave only 'ees –'

'Rock-boots,' we filled in automatically, still stunned. No crampons, no boots. How was he going to tackle the icy cracks and chimneys above? Worse still, how would he descend the crevasse-ridden Charpoua Glacier on the other side? Were we being cast as guardian angels when we were looking for guides ourselves? The blind leading the blind – we were going to need a description in Braille.

As Jacques began to take in the rope, bawling instructions at Henri, an impossible suspicion struck me. Jacques was advising Henri to climb down first and traverse lower across the rock. That could only mean …

'*Est-ce qu'il a un piolet?*' I asked faintly.

"E 'ave no axe,' Jacques sighed, as if he too was beginning to find Henri's nakedness a little trying. Invisible offstage, Henri swore that he'd be damned if he would descend any of the frightful rubbish he had just climbed. He insisted he could traverse the ice in his rock boots. Jacques was adamant that he couldn't do anything of the sort without ice tools. He promised Henri that when he fell off his body would swoop in a great bruising arc across the Niche and smash at high speed into the side of the pillar a hundred feet below us.

I knew this scene from somewhere else. The dialogue and the characters were absurdly familiar: any moment the mist would sweep aside like a cinema curtain and something wildly incongruous would come trundling up the ice – not a hen or a hitchhiker but … a grand piano!

That was it, Laurel and Hardy mullocking the piano up the thousand steps all over again. There was something simultaneously disastrous and invincible about this pair – the rubber-bones of roughhouse comedy. I felt that if Henri took his hundred-foot swing and pancaked onto a rock he would simply raise his little bowler hat of a helmet, measure the lump on his head, stalk up the rope, and punch Jacques on the nose, who would promptly somersault a hundred feet down the North Face only to spring back like a Jacques-in-the-box, and …

I settled down to enjoy myself, and then Tom spoiled it all. He put on his crampons, took both our axes, and disappeared into the mist to rescue Henri.

Henri and Jacques, it transpired, had embarked on the North Face of the Dru under the impression that it was a straightforward rock climb. They knew nothing of the complex descent. Henri was a good rockclimber and Jacques wasn't bad on ice, so here they were. They had light sleeping bags, already soaked from the previous night. They had no stove and little food, but they gave off a fine sense of tolerance for their shortcomings. The final touch of distinction came with a pair of old fashioned cycling capes that buttoned around the neck and covered the sleeping bags in condensation. We gave them tea and studied their route description. It was a French pamphlet notable for the number of synonyms it offered for the word fissure. Everyone knows the North Face of the Dru is composed of slits, slots, fissures, cracks, grooves, chimneys and off-widths, but this pamphlet was a full page from a thesaurus.

It snowed intermittently through the long night, but the weather cleared before dawn. Shining snow amplified the lucid brilliance of the light. The Vallot Hut, a gleaming trinket, winked on the shoulder of Mont Blanc. Chamonix had sunk to an immeasurable depth below the huge headland of the mountain. Lightly hazed in blue mist, the tiny, clustered town – pale pebbles and mica-flashes of light – was no more than stony shingle at the bottom of a deep pool. It had sunk beneath us while we tunnelled up into the cloud, and now it was submerged in a slow, fluid light. The current of the hours flowed into the high end of the valley, meandered through towns and tents, and washed wasted time and silted light down and out into the lowlands.

The first téléphérique cabin spidered down from the Midi: alpinists descending from the Vallée Blanche. If they considered the iced confection of the Dru, they quietly congratulated themselves on gliding down to hot coffees, warm tents, and dry clothes.

I felt the resentment of the bound against the free. There was an ice pitch ahead to avoid a snow-plastered pillar. We must bring Laurel and Hardy with us, not only for humanitarian reasons, but to share their guidebook. I chopped and kicked up the ice, warming the blood with a flurry of action, and suddenly, in that vast purity of shining altitude, the resentment burst into a flare of exultation. Breakfast sugar in the bloodstream, of course, but it had a spiritual thrust far above biochemistry. I could have rung hosannas and echoes from the great belfry of the Niche. Belayed, I hauled in the innocent climbing rope, summoning the faithful to a celebration. As a small altar-boy, it was my job to ring an old church bell with a rope that hung down the gable into the Gothic porch. A few brazen clangs were sufficient, but one splendid morning I got carried away by the mighty clamour I was arousing and the way the rope hauled me high into the echoing air with every ring and then hurled me back to earth again. I could no more stop than I could resist the temptation to pull a fairground swing-boat high enough to flip it full circle, human contents stuck to the upended seats like that mystery of upside-down water in a whirling, arms-length bucket. The valve for a fit of jubilation is a song at full volume, and I cracked the crystal air with Ewan McColl's great anthem of hard labour, *Kilroy Was Here.*

Who was here when they handed out the heavy jobs?
Jobs with the hammer, the pick and shovel.

I substituted crampons for the shovel under the circumstances. Tom came groping up the rough, easy-angled ice.

Who was here in the furrowed field stooped over?
Pain shapes a question in bone and muscle.

He had the French rope in tow, and I brought them up while Tom jumped into the golden cracks overhead. Crafty Jacques held onto the route description for an exercise in translation. Every time I asked, he translated laboriously with the hangdog hesitancy of a pupil who hasn't learned his vocabulary but is determined to bluff it out.

'Take ze fissure ... ze craque? on ze right ... no, ze left, I tink ...'

'*Donnez moi!*' I snarled at last, and grabbed the page.

Snow, ice, and error slowed progress to a crawl. There was a tedium to the terrain now, best left undescribed, or catalogued in weary syllables: long, dull, slow, wet, cold, steep.

A hole, often exaggerated as a tunnel, led through a thin ridge a couple of hundred feet below the summit. Crawling through the little hatch, I emerged on the Quartz Ledges, on the other side of the mountain. Tom's shoulders and rucksack jammed. For a moment his curly, grinning head protruded, outlined in the northern light, and he seemed to wear the rim of the hole like the frame of a baroque portrait.

In a little niche on the Quartz Ledges lay a couple of characters, sound asleep, smouldering with sulphurous dreams. We kicked them back to the start of the story and settled down in their places under a sky pregnant with apocalypse.

'*LES HAUTES ALPES: spectacle en Son et Lumière.*' The performance began at dark, with muted pyrotechnics in the distance, spotlights warming up, flickering across the walls and ramparts of this Acropolis among mountain ranges. Tympanic voices rumbled the ritual responses among the ruined temples of the aiguilles. Lightning outlined quivering horizons. The storm drew in its acolytes toward the great central altar, and the focus concentrated on Mont Blanc, the very Parthenon itself, the ice-marbled temple of the Alps. A subtle crown of lightning glowed behind the peak.

The scene was prepared for some unearthly set-piece now, a tableau vivant to generate the temple goddess, Athena, who sprang by partheno-genesis from the cleft skull of Zeus. But within the burning chamber of the storm an infernal metamorphosis occurred. The spotlights, arc-lights, footlights, and floodlights forked around the laboratory, and, instead of Athena, the mountain gave birth to a fire-and-ice Medusa, with lightning snake-locks to turn observers, if not to stone, at least to ash.

'By the way, congratulations!' interrupted Tom.

'Congratulations? For what?'

He broke into an excited sports commentary: 'Mr. Dermot O'Murphy, first "Oirishman" to climb the six north faces!'

Ah, yes, I thought, shivering in my bag: *This is Your Life!* And isn't it wonderful?

The magnificent menace of the *Son et Lumière* spilled over the edge of the stage; the occupying Turks stored ammunition on the Acropolis, and in 1645 lightning struck the powder. Then they placed their guns in the shattered walls. Massive eruptions ripped through the orchestra pit, drums and cellos burst like balloons. Flash-fires raged in the front seats. The audience fled up the aisles, out the exits, into the téléphériques. Modern theatre is okay, but who wants audience participation in a Greek tragedy? Who wants to go home with his eyes poked out? The flames were racing through the balconies now and licking up into the Gods.

The sports commentator came on again: 'The award was conferred posthumously on O'Murphy.'

At daylight we began the descent. Jacques and Henri, further along the ledges, were having a lie-in, so we left them there in their cycling capes and bowler helmets. Another fine mess. The abseils went smoothly, stitches of rope unravelling, and soon we were on the knife-edge of the Flammes de Pierre. The blazing sun stripped the sheets of snow off the rocks like an angry host whisks off the bed-linen of an unwelcome guest. We left the hungry ice behind, shuffled down weary paths, and then scrabbled across the endless gravel to the Mer de Glace. I loathed the mountains and every atom in them. After every hundred yards of jarring descent I collapsed on a rock, cursing the gratuitous idiocy of mountaineering and the pangs of hunger, thirst, and pain.

Tom pinned down a mirage and filled a mug. Life held nothing more exquisite than the icy treble of water in the throat against the pounding bass of the blood.

And still the Mer de Glace to ford, threading a path across the ice in a maddening labyrinth of crevasses. Then up and up, up the far side to Montenvers, boots dragging, sweat dripping, and the last train missed.

Hunger drove us at a run toward the empty station. On the platform, above the sweeping ice, in spite of the disapproving Dru and the outraged Jorasses, we plunged headfirst into the garbage bins. Buried to the waist, Tom rooted out six tins of pâte, four cartons of yogurt, and a hardboiled egg. The egg was unshelled and delicately dusted with Gauloise ash.

Thoughtfully picking orange peel out of a salvaged cheese roll, I gazed around me at the savage splendour.

Satisfaction resurged as pain subsided. I savoured again the old pieties: on top of the world ... purity and peace ... at one with nature ... bird's-eye view ... lords of creation ... because it is there ... trackless wastes ... untrodden summits.

I wiped the cigarette ash off the finest egg that was ever laid and bit into it pensively. That humpy hulk of a mountain over there behind the Dru, the huge Aiguille Verte, we hadn't climbed that yet. What about the Nant Blanc Face, then over the top, and down that huge snow-gully – see it there raking down from the summit: the Whymper Couloir – to finish the season with a bang?

THE SINGER

A moment of simple magic. 7.01 on a winter's evening, the News over, fifty thousand, maybe a hundred thousand hands reached to switch the kitchen radio off. On a common impulse they turned the volume up instead. Such a simple thing –

All over Ireland they stood transfixed: newspaper, breadknife, dish-cloth in hand. Rich and hard, a song. A woman's voice, unaccompanied. No harpstrings plucked in the heart.

> *Do bhainis gealach is do bhainis grian díom,*
> *'S is ró-mhór m'eagla gur bhainis Dia dhíom.*

Ancient precisions shaped the lament. There was also the shiver of a new animation. Words that had grieved for centuries received an independent strength. The old anguish was still there, but this voice would not die of rejection. The song rose towards conclusion, improvised the crest, then tumbled in defiant spray. It did not spill easily into silence. The aftermath was rich with echoes, as if the voice had moved away and was singing powerfully through the chink of another wavelength into another hundred thousand homes. '*Dónal Óg*, sung there by Síle Connery ...' A quiver in the presenter's voice, the pride of a minor programme aware for once of a massive audience. Normally silenced at the signature-tune, tonight they ambushed the public with that voice.

'... recorded almost twelve years ago. Tonight Síle Connery is in the studio again.'

For many people the mention of that beginning was a private shock, a spring without a summer; twelve years since they first heard that promise, and the scramble for songbooks, sleeve-notes, dictionaries, anything to unlock the voice, began.

Her face on the first record-sleeve was nobly serious with square-cut, even features. Calm, confident strength. Massed hair constrained behind her head. Dark eyes outstared the presumption of the camera. A stern, old-fashioned image. In Mary Keating's *Irishwomen in History* the expression is there in turn-of-the-century pictures; resolute women in drawing-room attire who raised families, commanded garrisons, played revolutionary roles, stepping in and out of convention at will.

When Síle began a series of major concerts the response overflowed. She wore outrageous cloaks and robes and she commanded the stage, captained it with an air of piracy that drew allusions to Queen Maeve and Granuaile. The dignified critic of a great newspaper experienced an *aisling*. He wrote of his vision, in which he had seen a young woman in the concert hall, 'and she had the walk of ... etc.'

Caitleenism shimmered between the lines, a twilight phosphorescence. But Síle had no *spéirbhean* pretensions. Her roots were deep in the solid past where an unspoiled music was preserved, music – she insisted – that was closer to potatoes and turf than to harps, chalices or swords.

She took the old songs and projected them vigorously up to date. Her voice was far tougher than celtic romance, and too incisive for a folksy evasion of the present. She sang *Curachai na Trá Báine* and *Liam Ó Raghallaigh* with a force that made them speak not only for the old riders to the sea but the modern tragedies as well – the trawlers, the fires, the bomb victims, all the small lives mangled in small print. She took *Anach Cuan*, Raftery's obituary for youth, and made it clear that it challenged God, then and now, for the desolation of untimely death. She had the instinct for meaning that is akin to prophecy, and the audiences understood: as they always understand the sense of poetry, even if the words are obscure. A second reviewer of that original concert borrowed his opinion from another poet, without the compliment of quotation-marks. He said ... she sang beyond the genius of the sea. In all her phrases stirred the grinding water and the gasping wind; but it was she, and not the sea, he heard.

'... Tonight Síle Connery is in the studio again, after an absence of many years, to speak perhaps of *filíocht agus tost*, poetry and silence. She is here to introduce a collection of work, *Thar Cuimse*, by Seán MacGabhann, to be published this week by Single File Press. It was compiled and edited by Síle herself in memory of the poet. She has also written an introduction describing his life and work and sources of inspiration.'

He began to question her with awkward intensity. She was not there for culture alone. He would have that story told.

Her stripped voice was a further shock; as if an actress had broken down on-stage and become an ordinary woman, trying to explain her presence there. 'I ... I wanted to show how much Seán had achieved in a short life, how much promise was wiped out. None of this work was ever published before. He seldom had time for a final version. There was always another poem or a song pressing for attention.'

There was a tightness in the disused voice, a sense of strained control that might be more a perception of the listener than an actual quality of her speech. But it threatened imminent exposure – the pain of interview, her need to accuse. Too late now to switch off. 'And then ... he was so busy with my career. And looking after Cormac too. Seán practically reared him, you know, because I was away a lot in those early years. He came with me as often as he could, but that wasn't possible abroad. But I always felt he was in the background somewhere, looking after me, you know, managing things. He used to write to promoters over and over, laying down the conditions – transport, accommodation – all the little details that made touring bearable ...'

Vulnerability was making her garrulous; listening, it seemed best not to move for fear of dislodging something.

'He tried to arrange for flowers to be sent wherever I was staying. Roses always arrived after an important concert; you can imagine that wasn't easily arranged – three red roses every time. He phoned a man in England once, not even a close friend, and got him to drive twenty miles with flowers from his own garden in the middle of the night. Tulips that time. The poor man couldn't tell the difference in the dark –'

The story faltered; the memories were rehearsed, but they didn't match her emotions at the microphone.

'I suppose – I don't know if I was mortified or exalted; it's impossible to live up to someone else's ideal.'

'Did you find it difficult to approach this book, Síle? It comes across as a labour of love; how much labour was in it?'

'You know, for ages I couldn't approach the poems at all. If I touched them they were like sand in my fingers. Prayers to an unbeliever ... But they survived that. There's a passion in them that speaks through the darkness; despair couldn't quench it –

> *Romhatsa rachfad*
> *Ag marcaíocht im' chroí*
> *Thar machairi na h-oíche ...'*

She trailed off, saying the rest silently.

'Let's remind ourselves of Seán MacGabhann's unmistakable style now. This is Síle's original recording of his *Scáil na Gréine*.' And again that voice, old as tradition, pure as lieder, vibrant as jazz, eclipsed the kitchen radios and drowned the listeners in the mysterious distance between the singer and the song.

Early in her career her repertoire had begun to include this startling material. Someone was writing new songs in Irish for her. Most were love songs, others dealt with poverty and power. She sang them unaccompanied. The art was in the intricacy, as if she was singing a strand of illumination from *The Book of Kells*. The same melody-line in the next verse would stand stark – the notes single as stars, or perhaps the ghost of a constellation irrepressibly hinted behind a pair of syllables.

A controversial song put new lyrics to *Amhrán na bhFiann*, the National Anthem, and subverted the militant tune. After the celtic robes there was an attempt to give her a sepia image and sound. She recorded with a rockband instead. RTE posed a currach behind her; she wouldn't go on the set till it was removed. There was speculation about her roots; she must be more ethnic than the teacher from the midlands she claimed to be. The midlands – Country & Western territory – rankled with the experts. Her style was officially defined by culture-lines on a Gaeltacht-map connecting her influences. Where the song-lines crossed was a kind of musical grid-reference. Somewhere near Carna, with an echo of Helvic Head. It might as well have marked a record-shop because her sources had emigrated or died long before. She spent years studying old recordings, singing note for micro-note over and over with *Darach Ó Catháin, Seósamh Ó hÉanai, Caitlín Maude, Seán 'ac Dhonncha*, while her voice was classically expanded as well.

At first she had relished the romance of rumour. But as soon as she was established she dissolved the myths stiffening around her. She wouldn't sing the songs of aggressive history certain audiences wanted. Rejecting that tradition she hit nationalism in its softest part – where it kept its hostile identity for breeding. It did her no immediate harm. But an undercurrent swelled, unseen.

The effect was more dramatic, less enduring, when she clashed with another institution on a TV chat-show. She was asked about the new songs.

'Seán writes them for me. Seán MacGabhann!' Her face was full of humour and youth. 'That's what makes them genuine. He knows what he's talking about. And so do I!'

She was forever laughing then, a brilliant sparkle, white teeth, shining eyes.

'It's the poetry of shared emotion. Very satisfying for us, working together –'

'I'm sure it must be, Síle! Not many husbands and wives –'

She needn't have said anything, needn't have campaigned. 'Oh no, he's not my husband! He's my partner. We live in sin!' Seán was a lot of other things as well, she explained brightly; manager, poet, songwriter, father of their child. But he wasn't actually anybody's husband. He'd been married when he was a student and it had broken up, but of course he couldn't get a divorce and remarry in Ireland. She shrugged her shoulders, not quite laughing now. Anyway, she continued, they were absolutely devoted to each other but they weren't interested in marriage; well and good for those who were, but she hoped love could be its own guarantee.

'Ask me again in twenty years' time!' The romantic innocence of it made her laugh with delight.

On the radio *Scáil na Gréine* faded like a sunset. Again there was an after-glow, echo of a force-field.

'Síle, what are your particular memories of Seán MacGabhann – as a poet? I mean, are there ... are there things that distinguish the poet from the ordinary man perhaps, qualities that might ... elevate us all?'

The answer was slow in coming, the silence a bitter confrontation with memory.

'It's dreadful, I know – but it's the falling away that stays in my mind most. When sensitivity lapsed and the poet crashed to the human level. It's not really a flaw in the man, no one is perfect; it's the curse of poisoned memory. At the worst of times, in nightmares, that's the meaning of his death – becoming an ordinary man. But I'm beginning to hope again ... these poems, and the songs – and Cormac too, especially Cormac, he's getting to be a miniature of his father now – they'll salvage some kind of grace from under that shadow.'

'Síle, you've said repeatedly that you won't, that you can't, sing again. Are you saying now that there may come a time when ... grief must give way to the future?'

Was he edging closer, or had he balked at his script?

A long pause. In the background a producer nervously prepared a record.

'People keep asking me. I'm grateful for their interest, but I wonder if any of the survivors ever sang *Anach Cuan*; wasn't it always someone else who sang? Isn't that why they had poets and keening-women?'

Time was running out, nothing had been said ...

'How did it happen, Síle? That night –'

The silence trembled. A different resonance. She was in the grip of an audience, an audience that was stronger than her. She must perform. Description fell like rain on stone. But it was everyone's history; and everyone must suffer it.

Afterwards, the silence was full of shadows. A silence drifting from the radios like darkness. Everyone saw them; the child's face at the window, the woman alone on the wet road, kneeling by the body. Trying to make him speak. It was here. Not Chile or El Salvador. It was here.

'You know – I believe I could forgive the most terrible things ... people can't help what they do sometimes. But they showed me something in Seán at the last moment ... something I had never seen in him before. He threw himself away for nothing, threw everything away for the right to go where he wanted that night. As if it mattered. We could have turned around and gone home. He'd be alive today. He thought he was defending us, but we didn't count at all. They made him behave like one of themselves. He shared the madness, the rage for violence. It was like a mask they made him wear. And I have to remember him through that. Everytime I think of his eyes I have to look through that ... that death-mask, and try to find him behind it. And sometimes he isn't there. How can I sing?'

Five more years passed before Síle Connery sang again. She remained alive on record. Her reputation held because she had no successor. Imitators, yes, but their inadequacy underlined her strength. Her voice alone was self-supporting, orchestrated by its own diversity; from the earthiness of a tinker's tone to the excess of operatic timbre. She had become a recluse. It was reported widely that she drank too much, that she could no longer afford silence.

There was no publicity for her first performance. She wanted to come back quietly. Rumour ran riot. She was expected to appear in a celebrity-concert to open a new theatre. Tickets vanished overnight, confirming the rumour. On the evening of the concert there was still no hint of her name.

Disappointed fans sieged the foyer. Ticket-holders had the dated look of people near their source again. They gave a string of entertainers faint attention, peering around them into the wings. The genial compère betrayed nothing, except perhaps his awareness that the occasion had its own momentum and needed nothing from him.

The intermission came. Contradictions buzzed from the bar. No unfilled spot in the programme. Hard enough to cram in all the hackneyed names, unless they came on in groups ... reports of a black car at the stage-door, a tall woman in black lace and silk mantilla.

When the curtains opened an old comedian was sacrificed. He endured the brick-wall echo for five minutes, then stalked off. The compère salvaged some applause. He stepped forward to the footlights then and made a quiet announcement. So quiet that many missed her name ... A clamour of confusion, instantly hushed. She was already moving out of the wings as the lights went down. A pale presence in the shadow of her dress. The audience held its breath against the cold shock of the meeting, each person alone in a crowd face to face with loss. At the dull border of the footlights the collision of past and future occurred with silent cruelty, the crushing of visions, splinters of memory driven into the heart. She seemed to see nothing, her eyes empty, staring at the curtain of darkness beyond the lights, the audience behind it drifting past her. Would it hurt less to pass by in silence? Impossible to know who was more unnerved by the encounter. Her face was hollow under the high cheekbones, her eyes sunk in shadows, the skull claiming the skin. She might indeed keep going, leave them a second time staring after her, this time with no hope of return.

The compère intervened. He carried out a plain chair held in mild parody of a harp, stroking the wooden strings of the back-rest. He placed it centre-stage and dusted the seat with a flourish. A relaxed, charming man. Síle smiled in response. A stiff smile, expanding slowly with its own relief. The angles of her shoulders and elbows eased; the audience was slowly released from tension – forgiven.

Applause grew in the dark theatre. It began everywhere simultaneously, not the formality of welcome but the hard sound of emotion hammered out. It swelled to the volume where applause can only be amplified by cheering and stamping, but it passed that pitch and continued to grow without any utterance, a tumult of respect. Seated on the chair she lowered her head to weather the storm. The loose, black silk seemed to stream backwards in the crescendo.

When she looked up again she was ready to sing. Bone-thin hands settled on her knees, shoulders straightened, dark hair fell back. The curve of her throat drew all the light on the stage as the first familiar words emerged;

Dhá mbeinn trí léig ar an bhfarraige …

Verse by verse the ghosts of memory came alive to gather an old friend back to their island, a homecoming and a wake. Loneliness, not in death, but in distance. *'Amhrán Muighinnise.'*

Síle's voice had grown simple, functional like the kitchen chair she sat on. The song itself was everything, the singing no more than its projection. There was a hard edge to the sound, unclouded by flesh or emotion. It came ringing from the bones of the head.

She sang in her chair on the empty stage under a spire of pale light that narrowed in the darkness overhead. Shadows bruised her face. Her voice rose and fell. Slowly the song transformed the stage. She was an old singer by a dying fire. Embers glowed in the ashes as the lamplight waned. The walls and the low roof closed in. She wore a shawl of shadows. The old song filled the air around her and rose through the warped rafters into the thatch. It could not be contained. It was a prayer going on a journey through the night.

The song built up above the ancient singer; slowly the darkness arched and then it yielded to become the inside of a vast spire, a bell-tower high and hollow built tier upon tier of bulwarks and beams, the wood of Cill Chais and the dark centuries, masts and spars of sunken ships, shaft of pike and sleán, battering-ram and gallows-pole, and the smoke-black rafters of ruin. And the song kept singing itself until that darkness yielded and a spire of words and notes rose up and up into a free space beyond, where it shimmered and gleamed like a branch of stars, and drifted slowly back to earth.

KUMARI'S HOUSE

Terry Macken saw the world below him break into Himalayan waves. It had taken him most of his adult life to realise that the earth is truly flat, but he understood now with a nervous sense of homecoming that he had held onto a secret hope for Nepal. Here, at last was his promised land where life might be lived in improbable directions: curves, echoes, ricochets. It was Monday morning and the early flight from Delhi was approaching Kathmandu.

He didn't know if he expected to find Carla, or if the excitement he felt was just a blaze in his memory. Down there, between the highest mountains and deepest valleys in the world, in Kathmandu or by the lake in Pokhara, lay the answers to questions he had never quite abandoned: love, euphoria, freedom. Could the dream still live? Was there a haven where hope survived on organic dope and Hermann Hesse, while its outriders explored the wilderness of the mind? Airborne, out of time and gravity, Terry weighed his existence. He was a journalist, sent out to observe an expedition – rope and muscle, boots and steel but, in a corner of his heart made poignant by increasing age, he was dreaming of a wandering tribe and its lost queen.

Monday afternoon he sat on the temple steps and focused through a film of sweat on Hanuman Palace. Old roofs and galleries, carved timber. The wood was cracked with age, but the peacocks, gods, devils, she-devils, human figures coupling and tripling in a maze of exotic geometry retained the energy of a passionate craft. Nearby, the modern heart of Kathmandu beat with a frantic rhythm in the pop-electronic shops and the pulse of traffic in the surrounding streets. In the whole mêlée of vulgarity and art, in the roar of traffic and the slap of sandals on stone, he chased the logic of his arrival here twenty years too late.

The movement had burned out of course, as hectic spirit does. He knew that, but the knowledge clashed with the revived romance in his heart, a powerful ache composed, at its best, from the adolescent dream of a better world, and at it's weakest, from adult desire and loss. All that loss was embodied in Carla. She was twenty-two years distant. Twenty-two years. How could that huge span coincide with a twelve-hour trajectory from London? There was some hope of meeting the love of a life once in a lifetime; it had happened already. That it should happen twice was beyond the unlikely. That it could be the same person the second time seemed to be on the far side of the impossible and yet, in a circular world, veered back towards the possible? When he imagined her in his arms again, corn hair bleached by a sixties summer, the skin of her sea-limbs sun-smooth, grains of sand like gold-dust on her cheek, his breath seized, his heart hammered in the silence. Returning to the past was like diving through blue water down to where shadows quivered and patches of icy light rippled on vacant sand. When he let go it was hard to surface and breathe again, the tide had run in so deep.

His affair with Carla represented, not experience, but something missed. If he had loved her when he should but didn't know how, he would have a different imagination now, with adult dreams and mature emotions. It reminded him of something compelling, and obscure: art films on sunny afternoons, full of powerful images, confused narrative. And simplicity missed: beaches, grassy riverbanks, green hillsides where the mind goes quiet in its shelter and life speaks mouth to mouth.

In the confusion he had missed the passion of his life – skimming its surface, always on the wrong shore, seeing it only in the flesh when it was emotional, not grasping it in the flesh when it was physical. Carla had been sudden, different, overwhelming; the same age, but only in years. He had kept one eye open, ready to back away into ordinary air, as if he could come and go when he pleased, confident of his effect. It seemed incredible afterwards not to have known how much he was in love, how little independence he had. In those heady days he simply thought that was the way life felt at twenty, the intoxicating taste of existence.

It took a while to realise he was in actual pain – and not long to anaesthetise it. That period was a blur of temporary attachments. Then, as life settled into the seventies and he found his niche writing lazily for Sunday supplements he hardly thought of her at all for days on end. But there was a way of waking, sadly puzzled, in the middle of the night, the wrong body by his side, a mistake that never left him.

In the heavy heat he patrolled Durbar Square, round and around the palace, as if he had an appointment there and dared not leave in case someone turned up hours late and breathlessly important. Urchins selling trinkets bobbed about him. Tourists cast a second curious glance. Even in his rumpled, distracted state Terry reminded them of someone from public life. His fine, sculptured head had a sense of intelligent weight without physical heaviness. He was tall, unstooped, and his clear skin was ageing kindly. The nose was strong and tilted to an angle of humour and curiosity. Recently he found a tendency towards nasal hair, and he was inclined to peer into mirrors. He laughed at himself, knowing he shared this uneasy vanity with forty-year-olds whose hair was thinning, making them reluctant to walk downstairs in front of younger women. Terry didn't have that problem. His black hair was still dense and glossy over an unstressed forehead. At an earlier age the blue of his wide eyes startled and charmed. The colour was still there, but it burned transiently in deepened sockets beset by drifts of inattention – the gaze of a tired romantic.

A week before Terry left his London home James Boland rang from Dublin.

'I hear you're off to Nepal, Terry – Kathmandu?'

'I'll have a few days there. Mostly the mountains.'

'Everest?' Jimmy's interest quickened.

'Not Everest. I can't remember what it's called.'

With old friends Terry made a virtue of vagueness, to show he was still easy. Boland had sold out; gone from Jimmy to James, advertising to insurance, jeans to suits.

A pause. 'Did you know Carla might be out there Terry?'

'I can't talk now Jimmy, there's someone here and I'm away the rest of the week on a story. Send me the details. I'll talk to you when I get back from Nepal. Maybe before I go.'

Afterwards he stared in shock at the one piece of work-in-progress on his idle desk, and was further shocked by the force of his evasion.

And now he was at the mouth of Freak Street. It was there, waiting, in the middle of his forty-second year, an address to be approached obliquely, to minimise disappointment. On the other hand ... perhaps he'd be relieved not to find her? Maybe he wouldn't care? That could be the worst discovery; that a vacant memory had sabotaged his life.

He wasn't ready yet ...

The story of Kumari, in his guidebook, drew him into her shady, inner courtyard, to escape the pressure and the heat. Kumari, the "Living Goddess", deferred to by all, even the King. A group of young girls endure a ritual of fear by men in animal-masks; the girl who is least frightened becomes Kumari, enclosed in the old house in Durbar

Square. She may be glimpsed occasionally at a window. At puberty she returns to normal life and a successor is chosen.

Stories like this were the meat and metaphor of the magazine-trade. Giving himself a job, Terry ducked into the house through a low wooden doorway. The three-storey building enclosed its miniature courtyard on all four sides. Ornate windows, unglazed, looked in on the sunlit space. Voices drifted down into the deserted courtyard. He saw no one. Terry felt himself an intruder in a private house – male, Western, a tourist. He heard a light shuffle and turned to see a Nepali woman behind him. She wore a clean, faded sari and carried a baby in a sling-cloth on her back. It slept, its tiny head covered in the lightest of hair, faint as pencil-shading.

'Kumari?' She pointed at a high, gallery window. You wish to see Kumari. Her smile was tired and pleasant. In sign language and a few necessary words she outlined a simple procedure. Place ten rupees on that plinth in the centre of this courtyard and Kumari, the Living Goddess, will appear at that ceremonial window above. 'Kumari will come.' Ten rupees, a few pence. Beguiled by her delicate face, Terry placed his money.

'No pitcher!' She shook a warning finger at the camera, then called with unexpected authority to the latticed window. As if the money had triggered a mechanism, a little girl stepped from a doorway, took the note briskly and disappeared. 'Not Kumari –'

She called again.

Terry was intrigued. There was no reason to think she was anything more than a passer-by who had followed him in from the street.

A girl's face appeared in the shadow of a room, exquisite features, soft, brown skin. Interrupted in a phone-call she held a white, plastic receiver in her hand. 'Not Kumari –'

Kumari was at her lunch, and would oblige a little later if Terry cared to remain or to return. This information from his guide came in the same smiling sign language. On impulse Terry gave her a small clump of rupees. She accepted, neither as a tip nor as alms but as a simple transfer of owner-ship. He had not expected to see Kumari; he might even have been disappointed to have seen her, the extraordinary made ordinary for ten rupees.

He crossed towards the pagoda-temples again, agonising over Carla. She walked beside him as she often did. In contrast to the Nepali women gliding by, Carla's style had been vigorous. Energy enlivened the space around her and dramatised everything within range.

Her cropped hair glowed with the cool, blonde light of a Scandinavian sunrise. Dubliners on their grey streets were jolted by the contrast between that colour and the brown Mediterranean skin drawn tight on delicate bones. Her wide-set grey eyes observed life with intense expectation. When she entered a room, or a conversation, light came on, the volume turned up, as if she trailed a party behind her. Anything absurd seemed doubly, entertainingly so. The dowdy veneers used by Irish life to bluff the twentieth century were exposed in their comic pathos.

She saw education and politics as quaintly repressive. Carla was looking for inner revolution, expansion of the imagination into some intense universe far beyond routine. No one, not even herself, suspected that she was an envoy of a worldwide movement trying to achieve meaning through excess.

Terry didn't need meaning; for him, the present was perfect – a summer without end. He didn't have to work at anything; charm, intelligence, style, came easy. He took imagination for granted, the ability to conjure images and fire them with colour. But, to create himself, to be the things he dreamed, to live the ideas he strewed around like confetti – he differed from Carla on the need for that. Perhaps he was right, and Carla unconsciously knew it; there was a temporary perfection in the achievement of such ease, and she had no choice but to absorb him, as he was, for as long as his idyll lasted.

Still unprepared for Freak Street – just a hundred metres away, beyond the pavement market – Terry circled the palace again, puzzled when the Nepali design gave way to a British facade in a country that was never colonised. Hanuman, the Monkey-god, a statue draped in red, its shapeless bulk comfortably grotesque, disturbed him with its image from a deep dream. Beside it, a guarded door led into the palace. He peered inside, so involved with the past that he could have seen her coming lightly towards him, oriental sandals slapping the wooden cobbles under Trinity College arch, acknowledging with a grin the pique of student-protest.

No older than the placard-bearers, Jimmy Boland amongst them with a teenage beard, Carla had grown up in Europe, lived in several capitals, daughter of an Irish embassy official and an Italian mother. This was exquisitely cosmopolitan to students in Ireland, where the morality of a summer in London was still in question, and a bishop's dispensation had been needed for Terry to attend Protestant Trinity College. Carla had been everywhere; Morocco, Greek islands, Istanbul, Afghanistan.

October 1965; a week late for second-year lectures, she hadn't returned from a summer in Nepal. At the Front Gate Terry loitered in undergraduate ease watching placards prepare to free the world. All week he had been erasing her sadly from his mind. It was obvious that Carla, with all her options would not spend a second year in a back-alley of Europe. Through the old, ornate railings, he saw a busy, blonde head approach from Nassau Street. Like an astronomer watching a comet blaze into a familiar sky, his heart turned over; the world would never be the same again.

The shock of an embrace promoted him from student-acquaintance to a dizzy status. He was illuminated for the first time by an adult sense of grace, and he might have caught a flash of the real meaning of university then, but there was nothing else in that laughing, third-level schoolyard to fix it in his mind. The year before, Carla had been too remote to approach directly. Her mature-culture style was austere and challenging. Taking Philosophy and Languages, she had a crisp approach to tutorial debate, an impatient reach beyond meaning. She wrote challenging articles for college-magazines. Terry, still inventing his intellect, gleefully pursued argument. But her cool, appraising eyes melted now in affection, revealing a pressure of normality behind the foreign confidence.

Receiving it all his life, on school buses, at parties, on the street, Terry was used to that melting look. He wasn't proud; he assumed it happened to everyone. He returned it in proportion to interest, and went on from there. A coy, adolescent sameness had prevailed. Carla was obviously different – adult, individual. Apart from appearance and manner, he didn't understand exactly how. There was a promise of adventure there. He imagined sex, love, travel, knowledge, excitement, but he couldn't anticipate the daring, darker romance of her mind. Instinctively, he ignored it, and responded to what he understood – the sexual tension between them.

He was led upstairs to Carla's rooms to hear exotic stories and to sample contraband. Nineteen years old, in Dublin, 1965, he smoked dope for the first time, and he smoked it in a hand-carved, ceremonial chillum. Because he'd never had to work at seduction Terry was unaware of anything unusual happening – he couldn't have described an event – but as Carla sat opposite him in a sweet flood of light and music, her eyes, lips, skin, her fluent body became the shape of his desire. Her presence melted and flowed towards him – bringing only what he wanted, leaving behind that foreign character, that inconvenient self-awareness seated invisibly apart, rueful eyes balancing his charm against his determined innocence. For a year and a half unknown to him and never understood when she explained, Carla struggled to re-unite herself. Throughout that time, Terry's ideas and language dazzled on the brink of fulfilment, requiring some simple, undiscoverable mode to lift them into passion.

In sex, after the wild preliminary rushes, he sensed dissatisfaction, never his own. He understood it as a command to try harder to project himself. Himself? He tried harder, and sometimes his body felt like a projectile that was difficult to reclaim. They made love dramatically. It was something to be seized on the run and reeled away from in a delirium of sensation – during lunch-break, a skipped lecture, after a party, instead of sleep. They were forever racing out of intimate rooms, late for some other encounter Terry had arranged in a hectic attempt to match what he felt to be the pace of Carla's life.

At first she was intricately inventive, contriving experiences he recognised within himself but would never have achieved without prompting. Later, he was shocked to feel her cling silently, frowning at his worried questions. He couldn't acknowledge youthful hurt in an adult. Although she was only twenty he didn't see the girl in her; from the start he responded to an older woman, invulnerable, complete. She could vanish into languages and foreign memories and leave him stranded in confusion. He concentrated on her sensory presence, and he never caught her own image of herself at all.

Drugs were sacramental then; promises of supercharged awareness. Terry knew he didn't need it. He was already wild with sensation. When he tried LSD with Carla he experienced a brief pirouette of ecstasy, then the thin shell of the world cracked. Terror sliced in through a brittle sky and scraped at his skull. He heard a thin scream, a fear of death sharp as a blade, operating from within his brain on fault-lines in the bone. Just before he shattered, Carla floated in and tranquillised the nightmare. He saw white pebbles in her palm, light in her hair and skin, a merciful light, warm and distant, like sun on high snow. Afterwards, he knew that the skull, with its quivering cargo of self, is like an egg bumping through a glacier. Later still, he traced his caution to that brief exposure to terror.

Drugs were different for Carla. Mescalin and LSD almost proved her questing intuitions. Scheduled one weekend a month, she treated them as serious experiments. Terry was nervously on hand, smoking dope as a gesture, primed to tranquillise if necessary, but it never was. Hallucinogens projected her towards an expanding universe where all that was needed to survive was the courage to go further, until the ego burned away like a shadow.

When she came down, exhausted, she spent a day or two gasping at the grimy surface of the city, its interiors excavated from river mud. She protested against this life on the dark side of colour, on the shadow side of light, on the numb side of feeling, in the gaps between the rhythm, on the inside looking in. She couldn't define the alternative; all she received was enigma, metaphors in sound and light, film without visual codes. She struggled to explain ... but she knew above all that it had nothing to do with definition, nothing to do with meaning; it, whatever it was, could only be reached when the intellect dissolved and the self was erased. Something held her powerfully back – the chemicals maybe, trailing their formulae in sinister subtitles across her vision, or, maybe it was emotion.

The cooling fever of her gaze settled on Terry; she smiled a sad, captive smile, a trapped angel sinking back down into Dublin.

Terry understood she was searching for "enlightenment", not yet trivialised. He argued for self-discovery through relationship. He liked the humane sound of the idea, but there was self-preservation in it too. At some urgent level of awareness he knew he could lose Carla. She was training for total detachment.

Increasingly she expressed herself in self-absorbed images. She was walking into her life as if it were a wide mirror that showed exactly what she already knew in minutely familiar detail. The mirror was always just ahead; blocking the view, insisting on repetition. The vital life lay beyond the monotonous reflection. How to find a way through, without shattering it?

For reasons he was never sure of apart from what he saw as her unpredictability, they suffered several brief sunderings, then came forcibly together again. There was a different need in her afterwards, and he was almost afraid she might have considered other partners. Not knowing how to deal with humiliation, he dismissed it as paranoia, and went on using the relationship not as a window into her existence, but as a smug mirror of himself.

Carla began to trip occasionally with a small group of older, ascetic hippies, most of them foreign, stranded in the shadows of Dublin, a city that they mistook for an island in time. The men wore long, scattered hair and prophetic beards. Their emaciated women had the raptness of medieval mystics. They lived on brown rice and hashish in muffled rooms where sitar music and incense hung in the stale, insidious air. With long, unfocused pauses they murmured abstract banalities. Carla's voice rang like an impatient bell among them. Terry felt they were no threat. They looked after her during her strides into the unknown; they knew the poisonous from the pure, and some of the antidotes to terror. His own glittering scepticism they treated with surprising tolerance, and he could never decide how much of their wrinkled eccentricity was wisdom.

Very little of this outside life was apparent in college. There, Terry and Carla were treated as models of radical romance, a showcase for the new, international culture coming to Ireland at last – liberation and style exquisitely sharpened with sexual tension. They weren't part of student upheaval either, because it was as predicable as anything on the syllabus; but as a principal in the style-faction Terry of course knew the political activists. Jimmy Boland was hardly an agitator: he was an organiser and tactician. He could make things move, get people to meetings, much as he might have run a debating-society in a conventional time.

Jimmy was fascinated by Carla. As her direct opposite he was probably closer to understanding her than Terry was. Entirely practical himself he admired the hungry, spiritual energy that gave tone to her physical existence. He approved her mature aloofness from the student issues he was involved in. He claimed detachment himself from the adolescent mêlée, except as an exercise in practical politics. Yet, despite Terry's taunts, cynicism could not be proven against Jimmy; he argued that it was honesty instead. Curly-headed, square-faced, blue-eyed in a wholesome way, he had the blunt fitness of a football-player and he cheerfully envied Terry the grace that made Carla possible. Coming from the same school they were necessarily friends, but Jimmy had managed to assert superiority over Terry that began in boyhood and would continue into adult life. It took the form of a humorously firm dismissal of style in favour of value and effect. He goaded Terry into absurd flights of fantasy, while Jimmy argued material substance. They enjoyed these extremes and the mutual tolerance that permitted them.

Lounging on a bean-bag in Carla's rooms as solidly as he would occupy a bourgeois sofa or a seat in a church, Jimmy in broadly filled denim flares, took his toke on a joint and continued, unruffled, to reason. When he went too far Carla might puncture his logic from some mystical eminence, but she never belittled him. Sometimes, when their exchanges as opposites seemed almost scripted, Terry thought Jimmy was as necessary to them as an avuncular spy to a revolutionary clique.

But Jimmy's business with Carla was more complex than that. He never gave up the effort to win her, to possess in some personal way her attention and interest. He did it openly, even as part of his friendship with Terry. In a way he was successful, because, at some level, Carla was always enmeshed in Jimmy's complex strategies, arguing, altering, conceding, as if Jimmy was the model of a plausible society against which she had to prove her resistance. Terry never resented Jimmy's persistent presence; in a sense he collaborated, as if – unaware of rivalry – he needed a witness to this extraordinary romance.

But they had a deeper bond, perceived by Carla. Her foreign background – the difference in her which refused to be over-ridden provoked a provincial sameness in them, directed against her. Faced with this European independence, which was the first wave of feminism they had met, they united in Irish masculinity and resistance. Carla worked patiently to expose it. It involved things as basic as teaching Terry to make love as an equal. In the style of the time she had an innocent concept of Civilised Man, as if he had already been excavated in the rich layers of the future, brilliant, benign and beautiful, and sent back by archaeologists-in-reverse to recreate the present.

She had another displacement too; a romance with a country that didn't exist – the primitive land of early Yeats. Brought up in Rome and London, with an Irish parent, she had a strong sense of her Celtic origins. She saw Ireland in a mythical light, made of mountains, rebels, rhetorical excess. That vision gave way painfully to the dereliction of Dublin, the rotting river, chemical sunsets, the churches full of old women.

Years later, at bitter moments, Terry understood how innocent Carla had been. The need for heroes and mysticism was part of the blind quest of a whole generation for a spirituality to counter the decay of its time.

As part of that innocence Terry had been cast in an impossible role – to become a hero, Renaissance Man reborn. He couldn't possibly rise to it. Afterwards, there were layers of pain in his understanding. He had neither been loved for himself, nor could he alter himself to her expectations. He was doubly trapped. At those exposed moments a threadbare sense of self would stretch unbearably between these contradictions, rendered the more transparent by the way he had believed in himself through her.

He had had the attributes, but not the sharpness to put them all together and convince. He was attractive, expressive, athletic, creative, good-humoured, linguistic – in the Irish time-warp he knew two dead languages – he lived on a once enchanted isle in a post-romantic culture; despite all that, Carla was a victim of a fantasy which no one could fulfil. His ultimate fault was the failure to overpower her fantasy, kill the dragon, and win her back down to earth, to know her and himself as they really were.

She was trapped in the unreal, born into it abroad; he wasn't – he chose his image from vanity. And yet, in the heat of his life, in that inflamed time, how could he have known what was superficial? He learned to avoid these lucid moments. But the buoyancy had left him, and he sank slowly into his situation. Carla moved on.

Six months later she returned without warning for someone's wedding. In the same casual way she had often disappeared into Europe for a weekend; now Dublin was the periphery of her attention. Terry knew she was there to see if she had made a mistake. Carla was thorough and would always check her conclusions. He had had no warning and the day was a disaster. He was with another girl, who made that very clear to Carla.

Fired by a mixture of hurt and anger, he was perversely protective of his girlfriend. It was as if he owed some noble duty to an emotional child, and the insufferable folly of this pose froze him into its trap. In desperation, feeling life slip away again, he tried to break through, but twitches of hysteria behind forced him to withdraw. Carla observed coolly.

On this fraught occasion her manner was a flawless blend of intelligence and humour, without a hint of stress. She was the focus of the event, and yet, lending it her presence she didn't attempt to upstage it in any way. She wouldn't let the past intrude on someone else's party. He had to leave. He caught a sardonic gleam in her eye, and knew what she thought: if you want them beautiful and stupid, take the consequences.

Nevertheless, he understood he would see her alone the next day, that she would at least wait for that. She had given no explanation when she left the first time, although he had known vaguely that her waning presence was a constant warning. He understood how much he was in love now because he didn't want an apology – all he wanted was a second chance. He would never know if he'd been given one; when he phoned in the morning she was already gone. He took a taxi, too late, to the airport and ran to the departure-gate. A first, self-conscious thought was that he had arrived in a graveyard after the funeral. Then it struck him, staring in panic around the deserted lobby, that the funeral was indeed over and he was the one left behind.

There was a parting gift – wrapped in brown paper, marked with his full name, as if she had to distinguish between various Terrys. It was a bottle of pale liqueur containing flakes of pure gold. Geltwasser. It could have meant anything. But for the first time in his life, he was frightened by someone. He had a nightmare in which a gold ring dissolved slowly in acid. He broke the seal on the bottle, almost expecting that sharp, corrosive smell. The liqueur was richly, profoundly healthy and alcoholic. He could hardly bring himself to taste it. He savoured its existence sadly, a message from a different life.

He found himself obsessively looking back, reading her essays – there were no letters – recalling conversations, listening to her friends. Carla had been their catalyst, a messenger from outside. She had opened their eyes to a different way of being, a determined freedom that had to be its own reward. She challenged everything and made no concessions. She was recalled, with the exaggerated relish of the time, as mould breaker, seeker and iconoclast. But in an age of postures, none of the others had the courage to sustain that style. They had imitated it, warming their hands at her dangerous glow. He was the one who had been brought close enough to see how much it burned. He hadn't helped or understood. He'd had a kind of observer-status in an emergency zone where his neutrality was eventually found to be a lack of passion.

One night at a party, when Terry was too drunk to notice, someone passed the liqueur around like cheap gin, in teacups.

'The gold,' Terry raged, 'didn't you see the gold?' They thought it was sediment, and rinsed it down the sink. He found a dull speck in the muck in the U-trap, but it wasn't worth keeping.

Jimmy Boland had been involved in that drunken riot, Terry remembered bitterly. That would have been his style; break the bank while you were at it, but keep a separate account of your own for tomorrow. He remembered that bottle of gold-water as a kind of inspiration he had lost. He could have savoured it slowly for years, and it had all been spilled in one night.

Jimmy Boland followed Carla. After a year in advertising he set off on a world-tour: London, Spain, Morocco, Istanbul, Afghanistan, Kathmandu, Pakistan. While others stretched themselves beyond their limits to slouch in longhaired sloth to the Greek islands, where they fried in the sun wondering nervously where all the sex and dope were, Jimmy marched around the world, too energetic to be a hippy. He sent back intensely observed letters, written like notes towards a travel-book. Terry sensed a sub-plot. He tested the language obsessively, tapping its surfaces, sounding its hollow spots, a censor hunting subversion. Everywhere, between the lines, in place-names and itineraries, he found echoes of Carla.

Jimmy didn't find her, and Terry was never sure afterwards whether he was actually searching, or simply imitating her travels with the very typical intention of surpassing her image.

In the gathering years, when she was only heard of in those faint echoes that have lost their origin in sound but travel on in time, Carla had become a myth to her contemporaries. She was living in the Orient, and dealing in illegal substances; she was living in the Orient, had given up illegal substances, and was a Buddhist nun; she had lived in the Orient and was dead. The myth put her at a safe distance. Times had changed, they had grown away from style and ideals; they did not want a measure of themselves now.

Terry noticed certain signs. As a group of graduates, they seemed to stay in touch, and intermarry, as if they had a special kind of loyalty. Was it to each other – to their shared capitulation – or was it to a symbol of distinction they remembered? None of the women ever disparaged Carla's memory, no matter how much their security was undermined. Their men had all idealised her in some way – from the sexual to the philosophical, with obvious overlaps – and the women liked to borrow some of her dangerous quality, like a perfume to wear when it suited them.

Jimmy Boland, when he came home, compressed his adventures into a thoroughly useful guidebook for students. He went back to work in advertising and quickly became successful. He was able to fuse contrasting styles, linking rock-music and banking, for example; if it did nothing for music, Jimmy said, that was a small minus compared to the way it sexualised saving.

He enjoyed business. It was like a safari, travelling light through the boardrooms of capital, the last wilderness. More than anyone, he kept up the social connections of the past and he cherished collective memories in a clubbish way that seemed to substitute sentiment for reality and set Terry's teeth on edge at the implications that they had all been one, big family sowing wild oats.

Even when he was successfully married, with two substantial children, Jimmy still reminisced fondly. Terry thought the more deeply compromised Jimmy became, the more he needed that bare foot in the sixties. He retained his careful, not unpleasant cunning, by which he balanced all his options, moral and practical. He was proud to have emerged whole, having enjoyed the excesses of the sixties, and to be capable now of enjoying the harsh, profitable world of the eighties. Could Carla have managed that, he teased?

She wasn't on the same planet, Terry thought angrily. Now that the pretension had died down, he remembered her with a poignant understanding. She had experimented systematically with experience. Pursuing consciousness she had coolly tested the resilience of the imagination. She had maintained direction and control. She had absorbed trauma and shock, and kept her bearings in a nightmare. The Irish couldn't do this, she reasoned, because of their burden of neurosis and repression.

He tried once to explain this to Jimmy who had always brushed drugs uneasily aside. In a rare burst of anger, Jimmy put another view. Carla had said she wanted a partner who could kick back beyond the blind alleys of the present to her Celtic roots, and beyond that again to the origins and the future of the psyche. It was just a silly notion, like Karma and all the rest. But a coincidence had occurred. Those undergraduate poems Terry wrote with their pagan echoes? None of that stuff came from Terry's comfortable, Catholic soul, but how was Carla to know that? She didn't realise he was part of a fashion, clearly visible in the illustration of record-sleeves and concert-posters. Carla believed in Terry for a while because she needed something different, to believe in. Anything at all …

Terry jumped to his feet. He glowered into Jimmy's plump face from which the anger had receded; 'Carla was a maker and a seeker of magic with her mind and senses, at any cost. She would give you all the magic you wanted, if you knew what you really wanted, but she would give nothing short of that.'

It was a confused obituary for both of them. Terry had formalised his grief, as tales of deaths in Istanbul and Kathmandu came travelling back.

Passing Kumari's House for the third time he knew he couldn't delay any longer. Time was melting away in the greasy afternoon heat. He suffered a dizzying burst of panic; twenty years seemed to have drifted by as disconnectedly as the last two hours. He had to seize the moment, before it was gone in a sluice of years. He drew out Jimmy's last-minute message with sweating fingers, and checked the Freak Street address again.

The fax had arrived in London three hours before he was due to leave. He had waited all week for Jimmy to phone the information through, determined not to embarrass himself further by asking. On the final night he cracked and began to ring. There was a persistent, somehow deliberate absence, and Terry finally left a tense message on the answering machine – 'Jimmy! Ring immediately. Leaving tomorrow afternoon.' He resented that 'immediately', as if an admission had been dragged out of him. Jimmy was wielding the power of his superior knowledge. At that level of self-interest he was not a pleasant man. Perhaps that was part of his success. Still no call next morning, none by midday, and no answer at Jimmy's home number. At his office, a secretarial voice said Mr. Boland was out, and promised to pass a message when he returned.

Hurling together the toothbrush arrangements he should have made the previous day Terry foamed with fury. Without Carla's address the trip had no purpose. He had researched the mountain, and done some inter-views. He found them predictable; climbers obsessed with the meaning of their event, as only they would see it. He was committed to writing about the nobility of senseless, self-inflicted suffering.

He stared into the shaving-mirror and saw what he was doing. Decay crouched in his shadowed eyes and in the dark cavern of his mouth. Behind the pale skin and hollow eyes hovered the ghost of a boy who had not survived the sixties. Consciously, he conjured Carla, with Eden-eyes and silken skin. The glass warned him she would have aged, but he jerked away from shadows. Sunshine, the past, reprieve, were a flight away. Time stalled, heartbeats piled against it, waves against a wall, building to a damburst. He was breathless, a fever in his eyes. The ghost within him came alive.

He ran downstairs to ring again. Just then, Jimmy's fax came in – the scrawl of a disturbed decision.

Nilgiri Hotel, Freak Street, Kathmandu. Good luck!

There was no Nilgiri Hotel. He had prowled up and down the dismal street several times in a jostling crowd of tourists, locals, porters. Freak Street had none of the illicit glamour it must have had in the decades that made it famous. It was tired and seedy, reclaimed by its own people, and the anti-climax in the faces of visitors betrayed their resentment of the ordinary.

'Change money? I give good rate.' The dealers were convinced he wanted business. 'You buy, good dope?'

He tried the nameless extension of the street, and all the mouldering alleys to the sides. Sounds and smells of cramped existence struck his senses, and yet he found no trace of aggression, and little real dirt. Nilgiri meant nothing at the transient stalls selling cotton trousers to the passing trade. In tiny craftshops silversmiths hunched over brooches, bangles, rings and pendants of wearying intricacy. It would be unforgivable to squeeze his affluent bulk into those workshops, to trigger hope, and then simply ask directions.

Part of him was relieved not to find the hotel. There could be no happiness in this drab street – the magic he remembered could not live here. On another level, foreboding gnawed his heart. He was afraid of what he might find if he did not escape quickly to the western hotels in Thamel. Freak Street was one of those impersonal zones, cracks in the surface of a city, where the edges of different worlds grind carelessly together. An ancient porter, barefoot, with a crumpled, leathery face shuffled by, bent under a stack of cardboard cartons. Slung from his traditional headband, it was a cargo of European cheeseballs. Toyota taxis skidded past, horns blaring, raising dust, full of tourists, businessmen, serenely pretty women in bright saris. The porter weaved from side to side without lifting his glance.

Terry collapsed wearily at a street-cafe. Umbrella-shaded tables stood on a terrace overhung by scorched bushes and old brick walls. A grinning waiter brought muddy milk-coffee. He wanted to talk, to improve his international idiom. He'd never heard of the Nilgiri but he knew plenty of hotels in Kathmandu that Terry might be looking for instead. His smile and patter were too insistent.

Terry examined the patrons. There was something dispirited about them all. They didn't have the well-fed blandness of the tourists in Thamel. He had seen this same look on refugees. Some of these sallow wanderers would argue that this was the real Kathmandu, man – but he thought they'd rather stay upmarket if they could, and visit the real thing from time to time like everyone else. Two Englishmen in their early thirties argued some obscure event in slurred accents. They had pale, bony faces, greasy hair, and their eyes glistened vacantly. With an anxious shiver Terry turned away.

At another table a sad scene unfolded. A tall, stoop-shouldered woman of about forty sat and smoked, playing idly with her spoon. In her listless eyes and sun-bleached, greying hair was the drifted look of the involuntarily rootless. She knew Amsterdam, Delhi, New York, London, but she had nothing at all to say. A much younger man, with receding hair, ponytail, waistcoat and cloth satchel, worked on her in a self-pitying tone. His letters, his cheque, hadn't arrived. In her sad, nodding solitude she invited his opportunist whine. Eventually, she would pay a little for the tedious flattery of his presence.

'Excuse, sir.' The waiter was at his elbow. 'Nilgiri, sir, we know it, sir.'

An old man approached from within, and bowed with the traditional salute, palms lightly joined in front of his face. He had the established air of an owner, in a culture where property is part of the personality. He spoke courteous English.

'That name is finished, sir. Nilgiri has no name now.'

Terry's heart thumped with foreboding. 'The hotel – is it still there? I'm looking for someone at that address.'

Calm eyes examined him shrewdly. The gaze lasted seconds only, but Terry felt his motives acutely sifted. Distress, he knew, was foremost on his face. Beckoning sombrely, the old man limped into the street. Bumping and floundering, Terry followed.

'The Nilgiri? It doesn't look like a hotel.' The dilapidated house was dark and shuttered, weeds growing out of the rotting brickwork.

'I wouldn't recommend it, sir.' Again Terry was subjected to that measured gaze, the old man raised an arm lightly, and with the other made a half-formed hypodermic gesture towards the elbow. He bowed again, and turned away. Terry swayed like a broken statue in the traffic, taxis swerving angrily around him.

There was no front door. A brick-lined hallway with a pitted dirt floor tunnelled into darkness. At the end, Terry found two closed doors. Low voices murmured to the left. As his knuckles hit the heavy timber he knew he had turned irreversibly aside.

Sudden silence within, shuffling feet, the door opened a wary inch. In the gloom Terry saw a withered child surveying him. He stumbled back, then realised it was a wrinkled old woman bent at waist-height.

'Nilgiri Hotel?' Already the door was closing on his question. Anger flared. His fist thudded on the door. He barked again, then shouted Carla's name. A bolt rattled, the door was solid. Feet scuttled, alarm spread throughout the house.

Blunt as a police-raid, Terry threw his shoulder at the other door. He pitched through into a yard. A straggle of balconies reared overhead. Gaunt faces stared down. In a ghastly, sun-blurred glimpse he saw her, high among the latticed slats; photo of a crime, scream on a rooftop.

Thudding footsteps in the hall and into the yard. Thick-set, muscled menace. Terry ducked aside, skidded in the dirt, a fist caught him in the ribs and he slammed against a wall. Bone hammered on brick, eyes reeled up the balconies. Empty. He slid down the wall, skull rattling on rough edges. A bare leg braced itself to kick. Terry rolled, seized a brick, slammed it on the other foot. Grunt and stumble, the kick glanced cruelly off his shoulder. His voice baying, he rolled to his feet and reached the door. The jamb caught his shoulder and he spun around. His attacker lunged on broken toes –

In the tunnel Terry saw her, outlined against the street. It could be anyone, it would be her. She flickered onto Freak Street in a long, light robe. Her unmistakable stride. He grabbed her shoulder, spun her roughly. Frail as a Nepali girl, eyes and mouth unknown, dark with fear. Photo of a crime. Grey skin clenched drum-tight on bone.

She spat Nepali between gasps for air, fluttering in his grip.

'Carla! Carla – it's me. Terry!' The struggle increased. Determined to exist he named himself in full – 'Terry Macken. Dublin. Remember me!' He shook her against the blaring traffic.

'I don't care – let me GO!' He almost released her, then fiercely clenched again. 'What do you want?'

'Nothing. I want nothing. To talk to you! Carla, look at me! You know me. I want to help.' He freed his grip.

'Help!' She rubbed her shoulder with spider-fingers. 'Ok, talk then, damn you. Talk!' Inexplicably, something redeeming struck her. Tendons slackened in her face, her wild stare calmed, expression jerked her thin-lipped mouth. Shock-waves coursed through her body, but she had control.

'Where do you want to talk? In the middle of the fucking street?'

They sat in the far corner of the cafe. The terrace was deserted. No sign of the old man; doubtless observing from somewhere. The waiter was slow to approach, his smile erased. She called him sharply. 'Must be a special occasion.' She lit a trembling cigarette. 'I'm not allowed in here.'

'Why?'

She shrugged. 'They don't like junkies.'

It hammered into his heart, the pain of the syringe, but it drew no blood; he already knew. Her eyes tracked restlessly around like damaged sensors, flicked across him without interest, dirty fingers rapped the table in obsessive rhythm.

Questions ticked behind his lips; what happened; how long have you been ... how much longer? Pared to the bone, nerves twitching in transparent skin, she was grotesquely beautiful.

'You do remember, Carla –'

'Remember what? You nearly broke my shoulder.' She bared her arm to look for bruises. 'Of course I remember. I'm not senile. Dublin, Trinity College. You and Jimmy Boland.' Coexistent in her memory.

Desolate anger shook him, a single, sour gust as memory collapsed upon itself. Simultaneously, a strategy formed in his brain. There was nothing to reclaim here. This stripped, haggard face was impossibly remote from anything he had ever cherished. He experienced the cold clarity that appears in the presence of death and carves a path through emotional loss, while the mourner weeps at his own hardness. He had to help her; he had to deal decently with this death – and come out of it whole himself. Appalled, he felt his own body flare with vulgar strength. At the same time, he wept bewildered tears.

'How is Jimmy?' She could have been sipping coffee in Bewleys of Grafton Street, except for the poverty and decay. He could not add to the horror of her life. That was his strategy; to protect her dignity, spare her the comparison with comfort and success. He knew he could not tell Jimmy what had happened either; Jimmy would grieve, but he would manage to make Carla's fate an affirmation of his own lifestyle.

'He's okay. Getting old –' But she had forgotten the question. 'Why are you here, Terry?' Irritable suspicion edged her voice.

'I'm a –' He was going to say 'writer', but remembered you couldn't bluff Carla. 'I'm going to Annapurna to cover a mountaineering expedition for a newspaper.'

'The Sanctuary? We used to go there before it was ruined. Haven't they done enough damage yet? They are so careless and greedy. We see expeditions here all the time. They make a supermarket of Kathmandu. I hope you will make that clear, in your newspaper.' She might have lost everything else, but she hadn't lost that tone. Crusading in the sixties, it was harrowed and querulous now. It had all been said a million times. But it forced him into defence, as if she still owned moral superiority. Neither of them had that; yet he felt a rush to justify. Then pity again when he looked at her. 'You're still fighting battles,' he offered. 'Does it get any easier?'

He flinched as she almost accused him of patronising her. The walls of her existence were so thin he could see inside. She thought better of it.

'It does. It becomes a habit. I don't care about winning. It's not the point.'

'Why – do you do this to yourself?'

'Ask your climbers.' A harsh laugh became a coughing-fit. 'That's their territory, isn't it? Mountaineering as a metaphor. What do they find up there in the snow? They don't bring anything back either, as far as I can see. Not even their rubbish.'

As she struggled to breathe, paper lungs tearing, Terry felt the astonishing proximity of death. He caught a flash of what the climbers found; life like a flame in the wind, the nearness of extinction, an illusion of control. They tested their limits time and again, reaching for exaltation, but it was a disease that devoured them, one by one.

Carla had begun to shake. It was an insistent vibration, as if a small engine, overstrained, was working loose. This was how she would go; the bones would rattle apart in the dry skin, and the tiny engine would spin dizzily out. What then?

She wanted to leave, but – she needed something. Money. Cruelty sparked in him, two wires touching, love and revenge.

'How long have you lived in Nepal?' he delayed.

'Forever. They threw us out years ago, but we keep coming back. We go to India in the monsoon.' She set her frail jaw, and the rapid words absorbed the vibration. 'We're illegal now since they changed the laws. We have to be careful at the border. That's why I ran from the house. We thought it was Immigration.'

Terry heard the sad wing-beat of a marginal life; barred from her country, barred from the cafes, barely at home in her body. And yet that 'we' suggested a migrant flock, made him feel unaccountably lonely, a refugee in his own life. This was the tribe he dreamed about. Lost, but sacred in their wandering.

'How did you find me?' She resented it. 'Jimmy, I suppose. I told him never to give my address.'

'How the hell did he know it?'

'He tracked me down. No, I tracked him down. I was in bad trouble. Jimmy always stayed in touch through friends – and he wrote, *poste restante*, every Christmas. We always picked the letters up, but we seldom answered. He knew there was someone there when they didn't come back. That was an answer in itself. Jimmy is loyal. My – Jeff – my husband, was in prison. You don't get out unless someone pays. Jimmy paid. He got an embassy onto it. Jeff would be there still. He would have died.

'He helped me too, cheques and food-parcels. I felt guilty in the end. I had to stop him. Why should he support us? I sent word we'd moved to India and wouldn't be back. How did he find the Nilgiri –?' She slumped back into a tense vacancy, her face hollow as a painted skull.

'Carla –'

She rose from the table on shivering limbs, took his bundle of notes and disappeared into the street.

'I'll bring more –' but she was gone, a whisper of wings.

He sat still a while. Rush-hour filled the street. Past and future merged within him. It was quiet in there. A shaft reached down into the darkness of his life. Time dripped, like blood, at long, slow intervals, and echoed later in the liquid depths. He heard himself grow old. When he left the cafe, he walked up Freak Street towards Durbar Square. Crowds shrilled and swarmed. He turned into Kumari's House.

The shadowed courtyard was enclosed in hidden space. He found a last banknote in his pocket and placed it on the plinth. It had no meaning in the dark, until a breeze fluttered it like a candle-flame.

There was a faint glow from a light within. A wistful silhouette leaned at the window.

A voice called and she melted away. Much later, she reappeared. In a blaze of desire he jerked the camera from its pouch and pointed.

The flash exposed a withered housekeeper, shocked eyes framed in straggling hair.

BLIND DATE

'You need a woman! I keep telling you –'

Henry leaned forward and winked his rural wink in a Dublin drinking-factory. 'Not a wife, mind. I'm not talking about a wife. Or a mother – A woman!'

Michael recoiled from the lewd eyelid. All over the place men were winking privately. A conspiracy of nods, a nodding-club. He wasn't a member.

In the late Sunday lounge Henry looked the full family-man. Early fifties, plump face, thin reddish hair, comfortably stout, tweed suit, signet ring, good gold watch. Out of place among the suburban lower-paid and the unemployed, their cheap suits and washed-out wives. The vulgar tie lying on his chest struck a wrong note – not a cancellation though – even if it was vulgar it was also silk. It contradicted the expression of the suit, shirt and shoes, and illuminated the meaty features from below with a sensuous, self-indulgent look.

Michael stared at the older man. It was true that he needed ... something. Somebody. At least Henry was no longer trying to sell him the rubber woman secondhand. Still, like everyone else in the lounge, Michael felt his blood moan with a relentless dissatisfaction. At the next table two young wives with faces so nakedly bare that the bones might break through the skin took matching gulps of vodka to appease their blood. They grimaced, patted their hollow chests, screwed up their eyes and reached for smouldering cigarettes. Armed, they turned on their round-skulled, moustached men and blew smoke at them like quenched fire-dancers.

Michael switched stricken eyes back to Henry. Too late to do anything, duck into the toilets, dash for the door. Two ... two ladies came heaving through the haze, squeezing between stand-up drinkers, bending around the seated, approaching with organised intent, and Henry waved a welcome while the other hand reeled in a lounge-boy. The tie came excitedly alive, fat lips smacked, he winked with every fold in his flesh.

'Stuck beside the "Ladies" Henry, knew where to look, didn't I? This is my friend, Bernie. She's from Belfast.' The voice lowed happily above Michael's head, and her heavy hand caressed the dandruff-trap of his collar. He turned slowly to the women, his vision congested as always by a sense of his own appearance. At a distance, to a passing glance, Michael had the gallant, dashing look – sculptured features, manly chin, modelled hair of an upmarket tailor's dummy.

So oddly cleancut was the image that the passing glance returned – and found the flaky skin, chewed lips and twitching eyes. Close up, his hair had a homemade appearance, as if each black fibre had been glued on individually with random spaces in between. It was, he knew, the kind of head found in drapery displays alongside kneelength woollen underwear.

The large, doughy woman, metallic blonde, mouth and eyes wide open, tilted him back for inspection. His dry lips stuck to his smiling teeth; he was afraid the strain would split the skin and fill his smile with blood. She smiled with ridiculous, unwarranted warmth.

'Sit down here, Eileen girl, what'll you have?' Henry had her by the plump cardigan somewhere along the upper arm, hauling her generous rump across his body to sit beside him. 'No, no – I'll get this one –' Michael was desperate to justify his presence. He'd got the last one too.

'Right, right, O.K. Let Bernie in there near you. What'll you have, Bernie? Michael's buying. You're in good company now. Michael, this is the famous Eileen I'm always telling you about.

'– Jim! Hey, Jim! Two large vodka-and-whites, another bottle of stout is it Michael? – give him a large bottle, Jim, he's going to need it – and I'll have a pint and a large Jameson – and hey, Hey Jim! Twenty Major.'

Michael peered at the blind date hunched on a stool beside him and his eyelids locked with fright. Six inches taller than himself and broad in the shoulders. A hank of black hair hung down either side of her head hiding her face except for the inner halves of two cold eyes, a bony nose, and a pout of lipstick smeared around a thin mouth. There was a sinister swipe at romance in the lipstick and the hair – danger dressed for a dance.

All around him Michael saw bone-brained, bullet-headed men sucking pints and loosening up their partners. Later on the earth would move – from sheer weight of numbers, if nothing else. He took a stuttering sip of stout. It tasted like nettle-soup. Guinness and smoke were as elemental to this crowd as water and air. Eileen sat opposite, her middle-aged skin so plumply pink it looked inflated. There was so much of her he couldn't take it all in. Henry could. His busy hands palpated the fluffy cardigan and tight slacks, checking she was all there. When he found nothing missing he concentrated on one large knee, massaging it as fondly as if it were his own. Vegetarian by nature, Michael shrank.

'Hiya, Bernie,' he hiccupped.

'Hi.' The corner of her eye glittered at him, a glass splinter. He recoiled. Eileen sensed stalemate and leaned across.

'Where are you from, Michael?'

'Sligo.' He tried to make it witty, 'Where are you from yourself?'

'Wait'll I see now, who do I know in Sligo? D'you know your man Willy at all?'

'Willy?' His heart sank. 'Willy who, Eileen?'

'Will-he-or-won't-he, Bernie! Willy Yeats, who d'you think?' Laughter rattled inside her padded frame.

Henry nodded in pleasure at the mention of poetry –

'I will arse and gonad, go to Innishfree ...'

'Or Ben –', she broke in, 'd'you know Ben, Michael? Ben – what's his name?'

Michael knew they always had you in the end, answer or not –

'Ben Bulben, that's it! D'you know him? He's a friend of Willy's?'

She took pity on his embarrassment. 'I'm from Roscommon myself,' by way of apology.

Michael considered, Even the crows carry lunches when they cross Roscommon. Too dangerous.

'Bernie's worse,' Eileen went on, 'May God in his mercy look down on Belfast ...'

Bernie ignored her. 'What d'you work at?' she attacked Michael.

'I'm – an accountant.' No one ever asked further. Accountancy killed questions.

'... and this yoke here,' Eileen knuckled Henry in a bicep, 'no one knows where he's from. The original man from nowhere. What's the big secret, Henry?'

'Oh-ho, now that'd be telling!'

Strange that Eileen didn't know either. Country people knew everything about each other, and revelled in it. Michael had nothing on Henry, just spots of local colour – the flushed pursuit of large women, and ties like panting tongues. There was probably nothing to him behind the shallow mystery he cultivated as an identity.

'What do you do yourself?' Michael tried Bernie again.

'Unemployed.' An accusation.

'What did you do before –'

'Knitting.'

'What – what kind?'

'Balaclavas. Paramilitary balaclavas.' The syllables rattled like hail-stones on tin.

'Did you – did you sell them?'

'Bags of them.'

'Over the counter?'

'Fella called to the door. Friday nights.'

'A terrorist. My God, what was he like?' It was the longest conversation he'd ever had with a woman.

'I wouldn't know. He wore a balaclava.'

'One of yours?'

'Damart.'

'Don't believe a word out of her,' Eileen advised, 'she told the Labour she used to knit Tricolours. There was no demand for them with the Flags and Emblems Act.' She tossed her head in scorn. Bernie's veiled eyes glittered. Henry winked, juicy lips smacking, 'Drink up! We'll go after this one.'

Rows of bleak houses, neither a city nor a suburb, a maze of concrete streets pushed blindly into the country, amber lamplight thickening the dark. Michael paid for the taxi.

'Enjoy the party, girls!' The driver's snigger was full of innuendo.

Henry danced Eileen across the waste-ground, tripping on her heels, shrieking. Bernie slunk along behind, and Michael carried the drink. Elation and depression wracked him.

He was being fixed up tonight for services rendered – and for greater dues to be exacted.

The account began in a dancehall, and built up debt over two years. Michael had been hiding in the "Gents" the first night. Henry crouched bow-legged in front of a bit of mirror, combing water into his foxy hair.

'Some talent here tonight, boy. Must be the moon brings them out. I'm after scoring big, and it's feck-all use to me. The one bloody night I'm skint. Be a sin to waste it, all the work I put into warmin' her up.

'Come here. I'll point her out and you take over. You'll score, no problem, don't worry about that. She's dyin' for it – the right man is all it wants, and the taxi-fare to lift her. Look over there, man, look – the big one in pink, says her name is Maisie –' he leered happily at that, 'what more could you want? Go on over and get stuck in. Jesus! –' he shook his head with noble regret, 'the one night I can't afford it! Come on anyway, I'll introduce you. Any name'll do; don't give your right one. Say I had to go in a hurry, the mother's dying or something. Don't say I was broke, money turns them on.'

Michael shrank in hideous terror. 'No! No! I couldn't – don't –' The sight of the warmed-up woman in pink clung him to the floor.

'Why not, man? You can't let a good thing go. You'd be doing her a favour. I've been sweetening her for hours. Can't help it, it's in the blood. I had to tear myself away, said I had to make a phone-call.'

The yearning patter was hypnotic, a tubby lecher with a red, razor-polished face. Out on the floor the woman wheeled in shortsighted, bewildered circles. '... the one night I can't afford it! You'll have to take her off my hands, or one of those gobshites'll be in ...' nodding contemptuously at the rows of upstanding countrymen, most of whom held important, muscular jobs in the building-trade.

'You can't let it go! Maisie –' He marvelled again, 'she's all yours. I saw you here before; you must have an eye for the talent.'

'Listen,' Michael was desperate, 'Listen! I'm here every Friday, but I have to go now. I'll lend you a tenner – you can give it back next week.'

Henry tore at the strap of his watch – 'Here, take this to cover the loan. It's worth a hundred any day –' The strap was stubborn.

'Not at all, not at all, I'll trust you. You can do me a favour some time.'

Not next Friday, but the one after, Henry re-appeared. He said nothing about the tenner, but he told Michael in carnivorous and gynaecological detail about the encounter with Maisie, whose name had changed to Dolores in the meantime.

Somehow they were partners in the success, and the relationship prospered, Henry taking the active role, the sleeping partner – while Michael invested nervously.

Tonight – a small, ugly house, half pebble-dash, half brick, the middle unit in a row of five. Two of its neighbours defied the night with lighted windows. Henry's house was not only dark, but the upstairs windows were curtainless black squares.

The key wouldn't fit. Henry peered, 'Bastards! Swine! Stuffed with matches again!' He seized a brick from the garden, smashed it through the glass, reached in and kicked the door open. Silence deepened in the neighbouring houses.

A torch clicked, lit a bare hall and naked stairs.

'Is it a p-power-failure?' Michael whispered.

Bernie laughed, the first sign of appreciation all evening.

'Didn't pay his bill. I wouldn't either for a dump like this.'

Henry fussed with bogus hospitality, octopus-arms bundling them into the front room. A jagged draught whistled through the broken pane. Eileen knew her way around. She cracked a match at the mantelpiece, and a hissing gas-lamp threw her squat shadow on the wall.

Henry pressed Michael and Bernie together, 'Don't mind the state of the place, I'm doing it up slowly.' Eileen bustled proudly, busy as a housewife with unexpected guests. The room was freezing; one threadbare rug on bare boards; the curtains were old sheets, dubious stains exposed. But the squalid room was entirely dominated by a brand new suite of furniture, a sofa and two armchairs, bulging proportions upholstered in plum plush with a frilly, white trim at the seams.

'Put a match to that, Eileen!' Chopped-up scaffold planks stood by the hearth, and the grate was full of newspapers and splinters. 'Make yourselves at home now,' Henry pressed drink on his guests and caressed the rump of an armchair.

'What d'you think, Michael? Nice? Bought it last week at the front door. Hundred quid, cash on the nail. Gave him seventy-five and a promise.' He pushed the back of the armchair and it sprang into a stiff, nasty-looking bed. 'The sofa makes a double. You could sleep half a dozen here!'

'They wouldn't get much kip with you,' Eileen grumbled.

'Not bad, is it?' Henry smirked round the room, 'rent-free with the job.'

'What job?'

Henry tried superiority on Bernie; 'Protection of the vacant family-home, a vital community interest in this age of vandalism.'

'Security! You're keeping squatters out. Squatters has a right to live too, you know –'

'Not in this house they don't!'

Bernie's glance scorched his possessions, 'I don't suppose they'd want to.'

Eileen's grip stiffened on a bottle. With her straw hair and fighting stance she could be standing guard on a hooped tent and smoky fire.

Michael made peace. 'It's a great place, Henry. How long are you in this one? You've done a lot of work on it.'

The redness faded from Henry's glare. 'A few months. They're getting it hard to give them away now.'

'A fine house like this,' Michael ploughed on, 'You'd think they'd be queuing for it –'

'They don't know what's good for them. They want palaces with free transport and shops giving food away. Do you know –' hands on her hips Eileen was proud of her social conscience, 'there's scores of good men like Henry minding the best of houses all round the place, and the Corporation can't give them away! And who's paying for it all? The taxpayer –'

'When did they start taxin' what you do?' Bernie kept one eye on the bottle, reaching for a weapon herself. For the sake of the furniture Henry disarmed them. 'Cut that out. We're here for a bit of fun. Who knows what'll happen yet –' He took a juicy swig on a bottle. Michael, copying, got the lip-suction wrong, and sour liquid dribbled down his chin.

'I must be three months here, anyway – I'm up to H in the phone-book, page 300,' Henry worked it out, 'that's two pages a day is a hundred and fifty days, thirty days in a month give-or-take – God! that's five months –'

'You've a phone here?' Michael was impressed.

Eileen laughed, 'He uses the phone-book for toilet-paper. He reads it too. It puts him in the mind for his puzzles and quizzes.'

'How's the writing, Henry?'

Bogus self-deprecation, 'Not bad. I'm trying to break into radio. Words and riddles and that. I'll try a few on you while I have you here. You're an educated man.'

'Fair enough; might as well be useful.' Michael swayed on a choppy sea of drunkenness, unnerving lurches in his brain. Ideas tugged at their mooring, chunks of identity crumbled away.

'Poor Henry,' Eileen sighed, as he lumbered upstairs, 'he takes this stuff terrible serious.'

Henry sat opposite his audience, opened a copybook. He shot his cuffs, fondled his tie, grinned nervously at Michael.

'Good evening, listeners –' The burning plank spat derisively.

'Good evening, Listeners! What are words but the raw material of communication, the threads we weave to clothe ideas? Curses, poems, weather-forecasts, jokes and prayers are all composed of words.'

Michael's brain and eyes glazed, but Eileen beamed approval, mouthing the mealy phrases. 'Words are the currency of the intellect, minted by philosophy and science, polished by poetry, spent by the common man.

'But let us, listeners, consider tonight, not the weighty works of

Shakespeare or the Bible, but the lighter side of language in a new panel-game called – "Word Play!"'

The dismal razzmatazz of his voice faded, leaving flecks of spittle on the velvet couch. Eileen clapped, brisk staccato in the silence.

A yawn bulged in Michael's throat. He clenched his teeth and glared fiercely at Henry until the yawn was about to burst a hole in the back of his neck. His jaws sprang open, a rush of gas brayed out. Tears squeezed down his cheeks. It was shocking – as if he had shouted at the Consecration. Henry crumpled. 'You don't like it …'

'Of COURSE I like it, Henry! I *love* it. The c-currency of the intellect! I *love* it. Go on, go on!'

'Well –' Henry hesitated in case there was more praise, 'I start 'em off with riddles. This one's a Shakespeare-play.' The special voice again, 'This fellow wouldn't open up to strangers; this fell-ow wood-ent –'

'Hamlet!' Eileen clamoured, 'is it Hamlet, Henry? Or Macbeth? King Lear? It's not Henry the Fourth anyway, nothing backward about Henry –' He turned on her with the full contempt of the male intellectual, 'It's Shylock, you daft eejit. Shy-lock!'

'He's not a play! You said a play. Didn't he Michael?'

'Not a play!? Not a PLAY?!? Isn't he the bloody Merchant of Venice, you daft –'

Insult reddened her, 'I'll get you, you bastard! Makin' a fool of myself for the likes of you!'

'Eileen has a p-point there, you know, Henry. You did say a play –'

'It's a trick-question,' Henry dismissed them irritably, 'we're not giving prizes away for nothing. Now the next round is a new idea. I'm still working on it. I say a sentence that ends in "he said" or "she said," and you have to fill in the adverb that suits the sentence. For ten marks. And you lose ten marks if you don't get it,' he threatened, 'so you can keep your trap shut, Eileen, you wouldn't know an adverb if it kicked you up the arse.'

'"I'm in a hurry," he said.'

'Quickly?'

'Good man, Michael, you're on the ball. "I'm in a hurry" he said quickly. "I could eat a horse" he said …'

'Hungrily? – Greedily?'

'No. Hoarsely! "I could eat a horse." he said hoarsely. Tricky one that.'

'"I'm trying to lose weight,"' Eileen interrupted.

'Are you?' Henry answered absently, 'don't bother.'
'"I'm trying to lose *weight!*"' she insisted obstinately.
Michael faced her unsteadily. 'Thinly?' She shook her head.
'Stoutly? "I'm trying to lose weight," she said stoutly?'
'No. I'm trying to lose it and I can't.'
'Oh, I see. Infatuatedly?'
'"I'm trying to lose weight!" she said indefatigably!' Eileen said emphatically.
'Undo – What!?' Henry was staggered.
'In-de-fat-igABLE! Not able to lose it! D'you not get it? Eejit!'
'Here's one for you, Eileen.' Michael glowed with excited alcohol. 'This is his wife to Henry the Eighth. That's a clue. "Your majesty is overweight," she said.
Will I tell you, will I tell you, you'll never guess? It's "unthinkingly." Cost her her head!'
'Why didn't you give me a chance? I nearly had it!'
'Here!' Henry broke in belligerently, 'whose programme is this anyway?'
'I have one! I have one!' Michael bounced on the couch, 'just one more. Please!' he begged. His head swirled with giddy intelligence, a cluster of bottles stood by his shoe.
'It's this late-night radio programme, see, and the D.J. reads a complaint from a young listener – "Dear D.J., why do you always play my favourite record after midnight?" he said.' Wild-eyed he leered at Henry, Eileen and Bernie in swaying succession, then exploded 'Disconsolately!'

Henry stamped upstairs, in a huff. The stippled ceiling shook. 'You trumped him,' Eileen explained. 'He'll be himself in a few minutes.'
'Always makin' excuses,' Bernie sneered. 'You think he'll marry you for it. He'd better – no one else will!'
'Who asked you, you tramp?' Eileen's ear was cocked to the room above.
'P-pardon,' Michael hiccupped, 'are you two supposed to be friends?'
Eileen considered the question wearily, slumped in the chair, even older than he'd thought. 'We work together. We live together. Protection, not friendship.'
'Eileen doesn't have a pimp. She's too proud. Hoping someone'll make her an honest woman before it's too late.'
'That's my choice. You haven't one because they won't touch you!'

'There was a woman burned to death by a pimp not long ago.' Bernie smiled a threat.

'Lord have mercy on us!' Eileen crossed herself.

The room whirled. Michael blanked out all sense and tilted towards sleep. A piercing squeal – 'Ha! Look at her. The tramp! Snuggling up. She has her eye on you ...'

He felt the coarse hair whip off his shoulder, and for a split second Bernie's red fingernails lingered inside his jacket pocket.

Her breath hissed against Eileen's vindictive squeals.

Cheap music accompanied Henry's descending tread.

> Two worlds apart;
> I was the Joker,
> You were Queen of Hearts.

He danced into the room, cheap tape-recorder cradled against his chest. 'Ladies and Gents! Take your partners Please, the next dance Please. An Old Time Waltz!'

He snapped the tape on and a pedal-guitar intro slurped through the crackle and hiss. Taped from a radio.

> The-e/stars/we-ere bright/la-ast night/in Galway,
> When you wrapped me in your charms;
> Tonight the bulb in your front hallway
> Lights a new lover to your arms.

Henry drew Eileen upright. The two bodies flexed together like intimate muscles.

'On your feet, boy!' Michael tried to stand to order – an obedient reflex, rising for the Gospel, the National Anthem. His coat strangled his knees. A fierce lunge, he forgot to straighten his back and found himself pointing headfirst at the fire. His thoughts were still sitting down. A lurch, and they passed him by, his brain grabbing clumsily at Bernie's body, while he skated on rolling bottles.

The wig – how did he know that? – swung across her face, the sour lips ... and a searing scar down the jawline, laced up with livid stitch-marks. It was covered instantly. He had to see it, verify. It was the sharpest truth in the world. It reduced everything to scar-tissue around it. He grabbed.

She slapped him. Darkness flooded his eyes. He slumped on something solid, head between his knees ...

'He's throwin' his guts up,' Bernie complained, 'can't hold his drink.'

'Off the sofa. Quick!'

Dumped on a stool, a bucket rattled at his ankles, head pumped up and down between his knees. His stomach erupted. Hot, harsh liquid spattered his hands and knees, splashed into the bucket. On and on. Knuckles on the back of his neck. He opened sticky eyes, stared into a coal-scuttle. Awed nausea at the quantity. 'Let me – let me up.' Trying not to taste his mouth. His eyelids were gummed together, acid running in his nose. Without taking her eyes off him Eileen opened her shiny handbag, held out tissues.

'Don't worry about it,' Henry reassured, 'a bad bottle. You're like a bilge-pump. Best ever I saw.'

'Bad bottle!' Bernie sniffed, 'no guts, more like!'

'No, I –' Michael retched, 'I –' disgusted with himself, 'I'm allergic to drink.'

'What!?' Henry was shocked to the core. 'God, that's a good one. Allergic to DRINK!'

'Yes. I am!' Suffering gave him the right to anger. 'I've damn good reason for it. My mother ...'

'Sssh. His mother –' Eileen rebuked the laughter.

'My mother, Lord have mercy on her, drank like a ... like a f-f-f-' he couldn't afford the fluent rhythm of profanity, '– Fish.' Their eyes slid away. Mothers were embarrassing – except to Bernie, who raised her bottle truculently to the dead woman.

'You don't *understand*!' Michael strained for sympathy, 'That's what has me this way.' The enormity of pre-natal fate swamped him in tears. He gestured fiercely at himself, rejecting the bloodshot eyes, white face, limp hair, and the gangling body. He saw it with disgusted clarity and wanted to be rid of it. It wasn't his *fault*!

'Before I was even *born* I was p-pickled in alcohol. That's a fifty-fifty chance of deformity before you start. How's that for odds?'

'Get a grip, man!' Henry pleaded.

He would not be stopped. He had a searing vision of himself as victim. 'That's right, 50-50. Half the little hoors come out defective. Russian Roulette before you're born. Genital damage, unitary ... urinary damage, brain-damage; it's all on offer. And no choice!'

'I didn't know anything about this for years,' he wailed, 'no idea at all. I knew there was something wrong somewhere, but not me and her, not us. She was supposed to protect me. That was how I saw it. We were alone, see, the pair of us, no f-f-f-f-father. He was – gone away. Dead, disappeared – I didn't know.

'I thought the smell off her breath was perfume, the way mothers are meant to smell.'

'For Christ's sake,' Henry hissed, 'knock it off.'

Michael was oblivious. He was telling it to Eileen. She was locked moon-eyed into his story.

'She died when I was eight. The house was coming down around us, fists at the door all the time for rent and foodbills and all she'd pay for was bottles of medicine. I used to shout at them, "Go away! Me mammy is sick with you banging on the door every day." I'd threaten them with a cap-gun.

'I was her hero, she said, she'd take me with her when she went. I didn't know where we were going. I got hungrier every day – I couldn't wait for us to go wherever it was …' His voice rose to a cracked wail. 'It wasn't her dying that crippled me – it was leaving me BEHIND.

'I wasn't at the funeral – I didn't know. I kept waiting, in my uncle's house, for her to come back and get me. I never even unpacked the little bag. I used to lie awake at night waiting, listening to the house creak with footsteps.

'One night the curtains moved in a draught and I ran to her screeching with joy. I broke the window with my skull.

'I held the curtains in my arms, like I used to dance with her empty dress, and the blood ran down my face – I thought I was crying blood. There was a smell of mildew and mothballs off the curtains. I knew everything in that moment. Everything was wrong – cold wind and rain outside, lies and broken promises, empty days and nights. Nobody comes back.

'I went to school in town, and the other kids caught on to me straight-away. I used to pee sideways, and I had to go about twenty times a day; except when it got blocked and I couldn't go at all. I'd turn blue in the face and swell up. They'd be poking me with pencils and rulers.'

He glared accusation at the bucket. 'I realised she hadn't l-loved me at all, she'd *ruined* me! I got the same smell off a few other people, I saw the bottles and I knew what it was – dirt and desertion.

'There I was, an orphan, running to the toilet every hour, and pissing round corners! And it was all *her fault*!

'Someone said she drove my father to an early grave worrying about her – and then I knew it was Him I missed all the time, and not her at all.'

Eileen stared open-mouthed, and he felt a powerful surge of elation. Getting his own back.

'Give us a break' Henry begged again, 'this is meant to be a party.'

'And h-how would *you* like to be born deformed?' Michael's indignation was fierce and simple. Eileen switched to Henry for his answer.

'So what did you do?' he groaned, 'It's not like that still, is it? I mean – you're a grown man now, aren't you? Well, Aren't you ... dammit?!'

'I had an operation. But it still twists when it's cold – very painful, I assure you.' Michael was overcome with dignity.

Eileen leaned over. 'Show us it.'

'Show you –'

'The bend in it. I never saw a bend in one before, did you Bernie? Is it like this?' She cocked up a fat thumb and wiggled it experimentally at the knuckle.

'Go on!' Henry had a glint in his eye, 'show us! I dare you!' Maybe there was a party in this yet.

Michael's lower lip trembled. 'Jesus, cryin' now!' Bernie sneered.

'At least you had a feckin' mother,' Henry argued. 'I never had one at all!' He saw the weakness in this, 'not that I ever knew anyway.'

Mouth and eyes full of quivering pity, Eileen swivelled, great arms branching towards him. 'Hush,' she soothed, 'hush, don't cry, don't cry. Sure, you have me ... Did she die when you were born, acushla, was that it? Musha, you poor divil, come here to me, alannah!'

Henry shoved her off. 'I don't know – and I couldn't care less!' He took a furious, compulsive breath and, to his own amazement, plunged in after Michael.

'I was like a lot of other poor fellas, dumped in a church doorway, or handed over to the nuns by some misfortunate skivvy washing pots in a convent.'

He struggled to get a grip on himself. 'They have it easy now,' he raged. 'Any young one gets in trouble can skip off to London, not a word said.' Henry had put a few on the boat himself. 'I was put out for adoption. No one took me. I was always a bit sickly as a child – you wouldn't think it now – and we used to get terrible sores from feeding calves. The nuns had to go behind the priest's back and bring in the seventh son of a seventh son to cure it. They were catching it themselves. I'd say it was the food did me in too.

'You can't beat mother's milk for nourishment. Very scarce in a convent.

'Anyway, in the heel of the reel they had to get shut of me, and –' he knew he'd gone too far to withdraw, '– and I ended up in an Industrial School at the age of seven.'

Eileen jerked under an invisible slap, 'Letterfrack?' A petrified whisper.

'LetterFRACK!' Henry cracked it like a whip. He seemed satisfied in a grim way, as if confession had relieved him physically.

Eileen went soggy with woe. 'Jesus, Mary, and Joseph! I'm back to that. You're lying to me! Tell me you're lying –

'The first boy I was ever friendly with, I'll never forget him, we used to play Tig in the yard, he got sent to Letterfrack for stealing. He was only an innocent little divil that meant no harm, ten years old and never mentioned again. As if he was dead! Like one of the lost souls, God help us! Purgatory, Limbo, and Letterfrack.'

'You never TOLD me,' she screeched at Henry, 'I thought –'

'She thought you had a rich family,' Bernie cackled. 'The black sheep, waiting to inherit!'

'Why would I tell you? It's hardly good news, is it? Look at you now! I don't even like to think of it myself. I never looked back until I passed through the place last summer on a mystery-bus tour. God knows what possessed me to go on that. Where could it lead only back to the past.

'My stomach was sick all the way out the road from Galway. I could taste the kip in the back of my throat. All it took was the rain on the bog to set it off again. I felt the rest of my life was a short holiday, and I was going back. I couldn't think of a single worthwhile thing I'd done in the whole forty years to save me. A few women – and where were they? I was on my own.' Henry's tone veered further into self-pity, 'Ah – I should have had children –' and then into self-righteousness '– by God, they wouldn't have ended up in any bloody Borstal!'

'When I got there I didn't even recognise the place. Full of Germans and Americans buying jumpers and bits of Connemara marble. I had to look for a roadsign to prove I was home. Never even saw the bloody barracks, if it's still there. I stayed on the bus when everyone else got off. Ten minutes was all it meant to them, a quick piss, but I gave ten years there. Ten years!

'I had a pint afterwards in Clifden to settle my guts – all I could think of was burnt porridge and mortal sin. Everyone else in the pub was American. Like a different century. If I tried to tell them what it used to be like they'd think I was raving mad. The young ones anyway. Some of the older crowd might remember, no matter where they came from; all the more reason why they wouldn't want to hear a word about it.'

'You should have told me!' Eileen warned bleakly, drawing herself up. Her eyes were bitter holes in the pink make-up.

'Aye, you should have told her! You should have said you had nothing instead of tellin' LIES. Yon wee woman wants respect and security, and what have you got?' Bernie surveyed the room again, added it up – 'Nothing! Eileen thought you were coming into money when the will is settled. I heard you as good as say it! Doesn't look like it now, does it Eileen – unless they're payin' compensation for a hard childhood; we'd all get a few bob then.'

'Shut your mouth,' Eileen snarled, 'I take a man at face-value, not like you, you tramp, you're only interested in the size of his wallet.'

'Nowwwwwww –' soothed Henry.

'It's true!' Eileen turned to him tearfully, 'don't mind her lies. I never gave a damn where you come from or what you have. As God's my judge, all that talk of orphans put the heart across me. Ye're like two children come back to haunt me.

'I had two myself, two boys – I should have told you that. I would have told you … Sure, we all had them then, we were young and innocent, we didn't know any better. There was no contraception, and the fellas wouldn't use it anyway; that'd be a sin. The babies went off for adoption, the way calves are sold, and that was an end of it. After the second I had the operation.' She paused in fright, clutched her heavy breasts '– but I can feel them here still, both of them, I swear. That feeling never leaves me! You're alright with me, Henry – I understand.' She gave him a solemn squeeze, and thrust out her jaw, to let the world know she had the moral victory.

Staring at her, Michael shuddered with hallucination. He saw her loose face gazing into sad, fly-speckled vacancy as she breast-fed Henry, his hairy body dressed in an old, cloth nappy and a rusty pin. They lay heaped together on an institutional bed, among rows and rows of babies in untended cots. Henry had a mother now.

'I – want – a – child!'

'Jesus-wept' – Bernie leapt away from Michael. He pounded his fist at the palm of his hand, and missed.

'I Want A Child!' he bellowed again.

Eileen shook her head, sad jowls swinging. 'Don't look at me, son. I can't help you. Sure I had the Operation.'

Michael threw a tantrum, drummed his heels on the floor, hammered his knees, 'I don't WANT any bloody Help! I want to have it MYSELF.'

Bernie hit him, hard and vicious, again and again, 'You – dirty – Pig!' Sober with pain, he fended her off.

'Wait a minute' Henry was thunderstruck, 'what did he just say?'

'I – want – to – have – a – bloody baby!' Michael mouthed each word deliberately, 'Myself! I – want – to – give – birth! Reproduce myself. Make a better job of it this time.'

'H-how!?'

'That's no problem. The technology is all there – organ transplant, insemination …'

Eileen bit her lip thoughtfully, 'It'd have to be a Caesarean,' she warned.

'But – but WHY?' Henry sounded as if Michael had proposed crucifixion.

'It's the only way to get total control, eliminate the gamble. Look at me and you, Henry – and thousands like us – abandoned, dumped, unwanted. But I know exactly what I want. The only cure for me is to reproduce myself. I know what I needed when I was someone else's baby, and I'm the only one who can guarantee to deliver that. If there's a mother involved as well, she'll hijack the child, or else abandon it. One or the other. And besides –' he asked Henry bitterly, '– where would I find a mother anyway? I couldn't even keep my own when I had one! Look at HER!' he pointed at Bernie with his wounded arm, 'Look at her! – beating me up after a few hours' acquaintance, what chance would I have against a mother? My own child's mother?' He thumped his stomach in a passionate *mea culpa* –

'When I have my own baby, I'll correct all the mistakes. Love, and Truth, Protection, Security – I'll give him everything he needs before he even knows he needs it … because I *know* what he needs!'

'Suppose it's a girl?' Eileen asked shrewdly.

'D'you think if they can organise my baby in the first place they can't fix something as simple as his sex?'

Henry blanched, 'How are you going to manage the – the plumbing and all that? You – you won't need the usual service, will you?' His party was really going haywire now.

'Not at all. I'll handle that end of it myself. A few eggs is all that's required for fertilisation, and the surgeons can supply that. They have their sources. No offence meant, going to a stranger,' he assured the ladies courteously, 'I'm sure you'll understand the need for anonymity – to avoid maternal claims in the future.' They stared at him goggle-eyed, and nodded slowly.

'The Church won't like this, you know,' Henry stroked his upper lip after a long silence.

'Not at first – but wait till they see the benefits! There's a lot in it for the Church. Self-perpetuation. Propagation of the priesthood without recourse to Eve – except for the ovum of course, and they'll get around that in time.' Michael jumped to his feet and strode around the room. His coat hung askew and his trousers were badly stained. He had the air of a major prophet.

'Listen – this is Messianic! It's the nearest you can get to Virgin-birth. The Church has a problem recruiting priests – this is the solution. Breed them from the stock they already have! Like royalty – a controlled line of succession, only twice as controlled in this case. No women: maybe the consecrated flesh might be hostile to the ovum at first, but they could get around that. Nuns might be acceptable.'

Eileen sat in deep thought.

'If it works,' she told Bernie sadly, 'there won't *be* any nuns. There won't be any real women either. This is the breakthrough the bastards were looking for. They'll put enough eggs in the fridge to breed the whole future of mankind, and then we'll be redundant – for breeding anyway. I'm gone already.

'Maybe they'll still want the other thing, or maybe they'll look after that themselves too. Worms are that way, aren't they? Then they'll do away with women altogether. Some tribes are at it since the world began, killing off babies to save on dowries. I'd say there was a lot of that down our way too.'

'It's a man's world, and no mistake,' Henry sighed complacently,

Bernie was on her high-heeled feet, crouching over him, viciously angular. She tore back her hair, thrust her face at him, crucifix at a vampire. He grunted in disgust, tried to look away.

'So you'd drive us out of business, would you? Leave us good for nothin' only layin' eggs, is that the way? See this –' Slicing the full length of her cheek, eyelid to jawline, the scar was a stitched-up snarl. She stabbed it with a crimson fingernail; it spoke to Henry.

'That's a souvenir of a man like you. A fat slob with a purple face and hairs in his nose and ears. He used to stand behind me in the back desk and put his hands on my shoulders. I thought that was nice – I wasn't much to look at. I went round to his house for a grind in Irish – *Tiocfaidh ár lá!*, all that shite – and I put my arms round his neck, an innocent wee girl lookin' for romance. He took one look at me – 'Jesus, I couldn't face that' he said. 'Turn round, I'll have it the other way!' There was a breadknife on the table ... I stuck him with it. He did this to me then with the same knife, trying to cut my throat. His blood caused an infection and made it worse. They took half my face off.' She rapped the scar and it rang cheap plastic, like a doll's face. 'He died of a heart-attack later, and I've no regrets. I done five years for that bastard, and I'll do it again.

'I have clients who like me like this. They want to be punished. I've plenty of practise at punishment.'

The crimson nails reached for Henry's throat – 'so don't give me any shit about a man's world.'

Eileen fell on her, screaming – 'keep your murdering hands off him.' Spitting and scratching, they rolled onto the floor. Henry, unsure of his strategy, alternated between kicking Bernie hard in the ribs, and pulling them apart. They were inseparable.

Michael backed towards the door.

'Well, goodnight all,' he whispered uncertainly, 'goodnight now. And – thanks, Henry. Thanks for the party. See you around.'

'Hold on!' Henry hissed. One last kick, and he tiptoed away from the struggle, 'Hold on, Michael, I'll come with you.'

CLIFF HANGER

Every warm Sunday crowds visit the car-park at Glendalough for the brooding scenery and monastic ruins. Tourists stroll the paths in leafy sunlight, separated from the landscape like an audience at a film. There is a sense of composed history and geology about the place. Imaginary monks and saints queue up at the ice-cream vans and Portaloos.

But the blind eye of the Upper Lake records time accurately, with the truth of a mirror. Time is in the still background, the mute skyline. Life flits across the glass, like an insect, without impinging on the deep reflection.

Not everybody stays within umbilical reach of the car-park. A mile beyond the lake, high above the narrow floor of the valley, there is a line of steep, grey cliffs. The granite glistens when the mica-flecks unite to reflect the sun. Every crack, every slab, every corner up there on the remote skyline has a name and grade, a detailed topography of holds. On any warm weekend climbers can be seen strung out below the rocky horizon like gaudy scraps of bunting.

One deep, blue Sunday a college club milled about at the foot of those cliffs, all sweating faces, strident mouths, parched throats from the gruelling slog up the boulder-scree.

There was a mess of ropes and climbing gear to be divided out among the novices. An air of hilarious incompetence prevailed, perplexed persons stepping into harnesses like bondage-straps, posing nervous questions about bowline knots and figure-eights, while a few of the expert – self-appointed – went about supervising the preparations, and especially paying intimate attention to the tying of girls' knots.

Mick Dowling had a special technique which involved brushing his knuckles across the victim's thighs and then in a low curve over the abdomen as he tied the rope.

Dowling certainly looked the part: burly, broad-shouldered, with a square-cut, rugged face, and an affectation of headbands and tight tracksuits. But if you took power-weight ratio into account he was considerably more meat than muscle, and would never make a dexterous climber. And if you knew a little about crags and mountains, it was obvious his experience didn't add up to much either. But shy, first-year students didn't know the Index from the Eiger and were wildly impressed when he showed snowy slides or waved to them from a rock-climb in Dalkey Quarry.

The only other third-year climber in the club was Vincent Barry, a silent youth with an inward air. He kept his distance from the club and its bantering intimacies.

Vincent was beginning to climb solo in the Quarry that year, lurching from one hold to the next on the impersonal granite that questioned nothing but his nerve. He was obsessed with the suspense, and surprise of solo-climbing, the excitement of placing his body in an apparently implausible position and extracting it safely upwards, with what he hoped was polished skill. But there was very little elegance in his diffident persistence, slouching silently on long legs in baggy clothing. He was often pointed out to new members with a kind of derisory pride as the club's Odd Man Out, the exception that emphasised their happy unity.

What Vincent needed was a determined climbing-partner, someone to challenge him, the kind of relationship where he would fight his way up a hard climb, knowing that if he didn't do it his partner would.

There were several of those teams around and Vincent envied their confidence and commitment. They did new routes, free-climbed old aid-moves, chattered in pubs about handjams and overhangs, miming moves in the air with an extravagant semaphore.

Ideally he should have climbed with Mick Dowling for their mutual improvement, but their natures were antagonistic. Vincent had no interest in Mick's extrovert style which involved nonchalant repeats of climbs he already knew well, where the leader's protection was as good as a safety-net.

Today at Glendalough Vincent was preparing to take a couple of beginners up Quartz Gully, a fine climb of middling difficulty. They were strong and fit, and he saw no reason why they shouldn't be capable of the grade. He distrusted the tradition that kept beginners on easy climbs until they developed an awed resistance to difficulty. His nerves bristled when Mick approached with an air of brotherly concern.

'What route are you bringing the lads up, Vinny? Have they done the easy slab yet?'

'I don't know whether they have or not. We're doing Quartz Gully.' Vincent's answer was sharp. He knew Mick was the sort who felt his own expert status was threatened by beginners who showed a lot of promise.

'Are you sure that's wise? Do you reckon they're up to Quartz?'

'They'll be fine,' Vincent snapped. His judgement was being undermined in front of the group. Mick shrugged easily and turned back to his own charge, capture-of-the-season, Janette Stirling, a striking, fair-haired girl who looked about seventeen until her cool voice and sharp, mature eyes cut deep into the observer's giddy pretension. She was twenty-two years old, had worked in Manchester for four years before coming back to College.

On a few evening meets in Dalkey Quarry with the club Janette showed a smooth command of technical rock, although she had no inclination to lead.

'I climbed a lot when I lived in Manchester,' she told her admirers in dismissal of her ability. 'We ... I ... used to go to the Peak District every weekend,' she added. Her listeners recognised romance behind that 'we' chopped off with a quick frown.

Vincent had been very excited by her self-contained poise as she followed his lead up the intimidating headwall of In Absentia but he could only nod and smile tightly in response to her thanks at the top. Then, as Mick appeared effusively on the path behind them, he turned away to coil the rope.

Mick had stood on the ground below while Vincent led the climb. He shouted up instructions to Janette about the moves and the holds, managing to demonstrate his familiarity with the route without having to risk leading it in front of her. Vincent raged silently as they walked back down the steps into the Quarry, Janette smiling affectionately at Mick who was sketching lavish moves in the air.

'I'll take you up a few good climbs in Glendalough'... Mick's gloating voice had churned up through the intimate dusk.

Eventually all the novices at the crag were teamed up with leaders. Some had already gobbled all their supplies, condemning themselves recklessly to a day of drought. The majority were doing the short routes at the base of the buttress, a popular group exercise with scope for ribaldry.

It looked as if no one was ever going to ask, so Mick announced to a sudden hush that he was taking Janette up ... Prelude and Nightmare! He put a kind of ghoulish emphasis on Nightmare. Even those who had never heard of the famous climb winding its protracted line up the full height of the main face were struck with the dizzy romance of it.

Vincent thought grimly that this would be at least Mick's seventy-seventh ascent of the route; he should be able to climb it blindfolded, and it was all big holds anyway; for all its impressive steepness the climbing was mostly straightforward, and even the hardest section at the start of the Nightmare pitch was over-graded. There was a lot of nonsense talked about Nightmare, Vincent thought, but it started on a big, flat ledge, even if it was two hundred feet above the ground. And that steep crack somehow gave people a sense of peril. But modern protection was so good that the furthest you could fall at that point was about six feet. Fair enough, it was a different story in the old days, but people were still cultivating myths and legends just to invest the bit of ultra-safe rock climbing they did with an aura of adventure.

He could imagine how Mick would milk the occasion for all it was worth, casually stamping his own image on the vertical landscape. 'That's Spillikin over there, the overhanging ridge. It's the hardest climb in Wicklow,' contriving the impression that he'd be off climbing routes like Spillikin himself if he wasn't nobly engaged in conducting Janette up routes he could climb in boxing-gloves.

Vincent was seething with frustration as he eased his charges up their climb with a discreetly tight rope. He desperately wanted to try Sarcophagus, one of the great classics of the crag, unmatched for quality anywhere in the country they said, even on the cliffs of Fair Head. The line looked fierce. Boldly direct up the main face, and then into a clean, pure corner flaunting its architecture like an angle in a church-steeple. From below it seemed to lean in blind rejection of human aspiration, and yet there was a thin crack in the back of that corner, handholds and footholds on the walls, and there would even be traces of black rubber where hundreds of feet had tiptoed towards what Vincent thought must surely be immortality.

He would have to ask Mick to climb it with him. No one else could. Mick hadn't done Sarcophagus either, but he wasn't likely to try it today. He wouldn't risk failing before an audience.

A breathless choking in his throat muffled the hope that Janette might offer to follow him instead.

After a couple of hours he descended to the festive base. Anyone who had a lunch was enjoying it under the envious supervision of those who hadn't. Mick and Janette were the centre of attention. Vincent couldn't understand how anyone with a voice so measured, so self-contained, could allow herself to be the focus of that circus.

'I reckon we've set up a record for the club, Vinny,' Mick greeted him with grinning satisfaction. 'Prelude and Nightmare in forty-seven minutes flat. We were really moving, man!'

'Great stuff,' Vincent responded absently. 'Listen Mick,' he dropped earnestly on one knee beside the lolling figure, 'what about Sarcophagus? Since you're going so well, let's give it a bash after lunch?'

He paused urgently, but his face – unused to expression – looked wooden.

'Sorry Vincent. I'm going up with Janette to do Aisling.'

'I suppose you're going to time that as well,' Vincent jerked to his feet in disappointed fury.

'Well, now Vinny,' Mick was indulgent, 'you have to admit three-quarters of an hour isn't bad for Prelude and Nightmare. I can't see you doing better.'

He was teasing; it amused him to wind Vincent up.

'I'll halve it!' snarled Vincent blindly.

'That'll be some trick!' Mick laughed, sitting up. 'How will you manage that?'

'Don't be silly.' Janette's scornful voice rang through the babble of exclamations as Vincent hurled away, stumbling ignominiously on the steep ground.

He rushed along the heathery base of the crag, sick with fury and fear as the challenge swelled from a defiant stab to a nauseous enormity churning in his stomach. His head tipped back and he stared up the wall reeling above him.

Where did it go – did he even know where it went? His eyes raked the blurring crag without recognition. Yells and running steps behind him, Mick's mates to the fore, the rest of them trailing.

His fevered vision raced down the boulder-field to the cool, enamelled lake and the distant track by the shore vanishing into the woods, away from this sickening mistake. He jerked his attention back to the brutal crag, and the track still hung in his eye with the diminishing dot of his own figure running along the edge of the lake.

Where was the start?

A ramp, wasn't it? He had climbed it two years before, on the safe end of a rope. The ramp, balancy, awkward, leading to a hard scrabbling pull up a steep slab. People sometimes hurtled twenty feet from those moves back down to the sloping ground ... and off to hospital, his mind exaggerated.

He was standing under it now, the rock utterly inorganic, shining with slick heat. Looking up he saw ledges gashing the face from side to side, promising occasional sanctuary. But the baked, bulging rock between them ...

The anxious spectators – a lynch mob – he thought, were almost on his heels, but he felt entirely alone. Through the panting and the babble of voices he heard the hostile thud of his own heart. Each beat had the crisp overtone of a shell under stress, a kind of brittle tick.

There was a bird piercing the air with a needle of song, another scraping its beak feverishly against a glass sky, and all around them, enclosing the voices, heartbeat, bird-sound, there was the waiting calm of a windy place on a still day.

His hands floated limply towards the rock, rubber fists in a nightmare fight. Before pulling into the first move he swiped in panic at the sole of each foot to dry off any grass-sap or cuckoo-spit that might subvert friction.

He hauled up on flaky holds, his fingers digging painfully into the rock, until his body was level with the tilted ramp. As he edged an agonised toe out onto its polished surface, his body tense, teeth clenched, fingers pinching the rock, he heard the first brazen shout.

'Ten seconds!' the voices yelled in unison.

The first beat of the blood-chant it seemed to him. His body stalled in mid-move. Heat rushed to his face and hands. Sweat beaded. Light flared on the rock, there was a buzzing in his brain. Bluebottles swarming on the Lord of the Flies.

Paralysed by the impression, he couldn't move, a skinny body hanging on awkward rock glaring its fear.

'Fifteen seconds, sixteen seconds, seventeen seconds ...'

Mick's loud voice penetrated his paranoia, an anxious entreaty. 'Come down out of that, Vinny, and don't be acting the eejit!'

He was moving again, traversing the diagonal ramp, toes shuffling on its outer edge, fingers clinging to the crease where it met the face, then a side-pull higher and he lurched out left onto a long foothold. He lay trembling against the short, steep wall that separated him from the ledges above. Stretching up to his full height he fumbled at the flat handholds, his fingers and forearms straining to lift the body that was making no more effort than a corpse to assist in its own elevation.

The thought of lifting his feet off the severe foothold and running his toes on friction up the exposed rock was unbearable. With his stomach curved in against the wall he strained helplessly, his fingers futile. Space gnawed at his ankles, and he shot a glance down at the narrow foothold for reassurance.

'One minute!' the chant brazened.

He had to lean out from the rock to get his feet up, but as his body arched the strain increased on his fingers. His toes kicked on to the gritty, holdless, rock. On sweating finger-tips he pulled viciously, shuffling his feet up, shifting his weight on to implausible friction, and flung one hand high to a better hold, greasy skin welding itself to the coarse granite.

Heaving his body higher – while his imagination flailed and hurtled horribly down the rock – he was pressing down now on the hand-holds in a mantelshelf move, right leg coming up inch by inch and scraping onto a foothold.

There was an audible release of tension below, a concerted sigh of relief which reached Vincent's strained perception as a menacing hiss.

'Two minutes thirty seconds,' piped a lone voice, callous with innocence.

The first hard moves were over and Vincent felt utterly drained. If he found that so hard, what chance had he higher up, on Nightmare? He was drained of tension as well. He knew he was safe: he was going to give up.

If he could have traversed off at that point he would, but the logical escape was a little higher, just before the start of Nightmare. There he could scramble aside and descend a gully.

Mechanically he ascended easy ledges towards the next problem. He was being funnelled upwards into a steep, inverted V in the cliff. He stood fifty feet above the ground, enclosed like a small statue in a rocky niche. His white shirt shone in the pocket of shadow. There was a piton in a mossy crack, the old-fashioned protection for the next move out left. He imagined the slender, nylon rope around his waist, clipped securely into that piton, and paid out from behind by a firmly anchored second.

He recalled a steep, blind move here, pivoting on a poor foothold with a hidden grip to swing around the edge of the niche. But there were handholds like gloves to reach after the first move. Get it over with! A moment of delicate balance, a fingery pull, and he had the good hold, fingers curled over the lip and then slotted as far as the knuckles.

A wall of clean rock hung steeply above him with a sense of friability where it had been scuffed bare of vegetation. It was split by a good, rough crack. Strenuous to start; he fixed his eye on a high handhold and launched himself vertically upwards, heart thudding, as the grudging holds multiplied.

A chorus of diminished voices announced the four-minute mark. They knew he would descend the gully.

He thought of athletes skimming over flat ground, a four-minute mile, five thousand two hundred and eighty feet. In four minutes he had dragged himself one hundred and fifty feet upwards, on his fingertips, to a narrow ledge with a gigantic flake of granite rearing behind it.

The absurdity of the comparison squeezed an hysterical giggle out of him. Four minutes and he was near the top of Prelude already. He could make the halfway mark in six or seven. At that rate he could finish the double-route in a quarter of an hour and make a total mockery of Mick. Why, a good climber – and he had no illusions about himself on that score – could probably solo Prelude and Nightmare in just a few minutes!

His brain swam as mental arithmetic took over from fear. Again he looked out and saw the sandy track by the lake-shore vanishing into the cool seclusion of the trees. This time he saw himself, not running away, but triumphant on the path. Victory bubbled in him. Another ten minutes could make him a hero. Not much of a hero, he understood. There were plenty of people who soloed incredibly hard climbs, and they didn't necessarily amount to much either. But heroism was all about who you needed to impress.

He didn't hear the five-minute call, if it was uttered at all, for he was working up the groove behind the huge flake. He reached the top of Prelude and its intersection with the escape route.

A pair of traditional stalwarts making their way up the gully stared in alarm at the pale spectre emerging from the top of Prelude, eyes set with belligerent intensity, face and hair slick with sweat.

'What's all the shouting about?' they demanded, with the nervousness of men who suspect that every crisis is bound to involve them. Wordlessly the apparition in baggy trousers and soaking shirt, shook its head and disappeared out rightwards to Nightmare Ledge.

Depending on a climber's confidence this flat platform in the middle of the steep wall is a small or a large ledge, combining an insecure or a safe stance with a fine or a frightening sense of exposure. Resolutely Vincent faced the crucial crack. His legs tightened and trembled as the short, fierce-looking problem reared over his ledge like a cleaver above a chopping-block. He realised in panic that he was viewing it like a novice.

An old piton protruded from the bottom of the crack and he grabbed it for security while he steadied his swimming vision. It seemed to twitch like a rusty nail and he jerked his hand away with a yelp of fear.

He forced himself to concentrate on the sequence of footholds at the side of the crack. He had seconded it once before and been carefully briefed. There was a hidden hold over the top, he recalled, but was it right or left ... or was that some other climb?

He dimly remembered a tense scrabble on the end of the rope before a small handhold swung him out onto a grappling traverse. He looked in horror down the plunging cliff to the boulder-field below. Experience dissolved in his brain, and rock became an insuperable barrier again. But there *were* holds, he berated himself frantically. Holds! He had climbed much harder rock than this with ease. On a rope! He tried to imagine it around his waist, reassuringly taut in case of need.

He saw himself instead, soft and wingless, trying to fly. His muscles slumped, helplessly.

A voice jeered from the horizontal past. 'Twelve minutes.' They were expecting him to slink sheepishly out of the gully.

Just another three minutes – he prayed in a pleading whisper. Three more minutes ...

He clenched the side of the crack in a fierce grip, trembled his foot up onto a flat hold. It was still reversible.

Sweating fingertips grabbed a good edge inches higher. He stepped up again. Still reversible.

His body hung out from the crack, suspended from flimsy forearms. Fear locked his fingers like vice-grips on the holds. He tried to step down, dared not dislodge fingers or feet.

Irreversible!

The roaring air sucked at his spider-life. Teeth grated in his head, eyes screwed in agony as if the bone itself were clenching shut. Ankles shuttled and rattled. It was up ... or off!

He kicked a toe higher in the groove, wrenched on his arms, flung his fingers over the top of the crack ... a curved edge, rounded, smooth, slipping ... He clung, his body an unbearable sack of lead, lurched his feet up again. Hidden friction lifted ounces off his arms.

Unlocking numbness, his fingers fled out of sight, scurrying desperately for the hidden hold. No feeling, but something hooked, held, hung. Hanging, he thrashed his right foot out and levered his weight in agonised jerks. And the angle burst back, burst like the door of a car-crash slow-motion seconds before the fuel explodes. Threw him out onto the traverse.

He leaned in a groove above, gulping with dizzy nausea.

About to faint he fumbled for a handhold to anchor his body as waves of blackness ebbed and flowed. He was convulsed with the savagery of the struggle. Foul images seethed within him, over and over, his body hurtling out from the rock, wheeling and tumbling loose-limbed in the air, trailing a long, curling scarf of a scream. The bloody climax among the boulders repeated with the insistence of a jammed projector.

Behind the persuasive lie, seducing him slowly into a swoon, he felt the liquid throb of his blood-system. His body was a single pulse, a soft bag of blood jellying its way up the jagged granite.

He swayed out from the stance, pulled himself back in again, pressing his chest against the cold, grey rock, nausea loosening his stomach and knotting his throat.

A tiny, bantering voice grew in his imagination: Do you want a rope Vinny rope Vinny rope ...

Mean little playground tune.

He was mesmerised by the brutal texture of the mica-crusted rock sharpening and blurring in front of his eyes as his body swayed to the cyclic rhythm of the images falling and re-falling in his mind. Minutes passed precariously as he balanced on the patient granite. Every harsh breath was a victory for survival.

He underwent a bitter, little death of the heart, and a slow unsteady regeneration.

Heroism, he learned, wasn't worth the fuss.

His legs were splayed apart across the groove, stiff and wooden as stilts. Every quiver threatened to topple him. He moved up slowly, hating the cruel, inorganic rock.

Long afterwards, he descended to base. There was no one there.

He collected his gear and went down through the boulders towards the track without a backward glance.

Mick was bellowing instructions to Janette from Aisling Arête. From the top of the crag they saw him diminish on the lakeside path to an incidental dot.

Vincent vanished from the club. He denied himself any curiosity about climbing, and never heard that he had started a crazy trend of time-trials.

A week later a well-known climber soloed Prelude and Nightmare in four minutes.

THE FOX

Michael Hayes threw himself full length on the ground as the mist broke away from the hillside. He forced his body tight against the heather. He bunched one fist under a gaunt cheekbone to prop his head. The other hand clenched a short machine gun, supporting it above the mire.

His thin face, ginger hair and beard were daubed with clay. Dirt smeared his clothing. His body was part of the landscape, a smudge on the wintry hillside. His head moved, eyes raking the limits of vision where the mist was thinning his cover. Grey rock, stunted furze, heather, and the peat-black gash of a stream. A clump of reeds trembled against the sky. No sign of life. He was lying in a hollow and the rim blocked his view down the valley.

There were hundreds of soldiers in the hills, helicopters coming and going through six days and nights. They must have caught the others; they wouldn't last a day in this muck. Three guards shot dead after a car-chase. Seán smashed into a bridge in Glenmalure. Lugnaquilla sealed off with rings of guns. They knew they had Michael Hayes surrounded.

He lowered his face onto his hand and closed his eyes. Verses in his head.

> Reynard, sly Reynard lay low through the night.
> They swore they would watch him until the daylight.
> Next morning so early the hills did resound,
> To the hooves of the horses the cry of the hounds.

A shudder ran through his body, wet denim plastered bitterly to his skin. After six days and nights the cold no longer reached his brain, senses disciplined to numbness. As long as it didn't freeze, or snow.

Waiting for the mist to lower again and let him continue crawling down the valley towards a road, houses, food. Not that he could surface within fifty miles of here. Every house baited like a trap, guns trained, dogs loose, but he must sustain the promise of heat and food within reach in order to go on surviving.

Swearing into the earth, concentrating his will, he demanded mist, darkness. It seeped across his mind behind the closed eyelids. His head nodded heavily, then jerked awake again with an electric jolt at the base of the skull. Fatal to doze. Images of the Bog-People, leather bodies dug up out of black turf, preserved over hundreds of years. To sleep now and resurrect in a glorious century, intact! Would the gun survive, or emerge as a rotten shadow beside him? He clenched the fierce muzzle for reassurance.

Michael Hayes bared his pointed teeth in a snarl of contempt. There were no resurrections, no second chances. A few miles away Art O'Neill died on a frozen hillside four hundred years before, stuck to the ground with frost; and all the years of imprisonment, the escape, the winter-flight through the Wicklow hills were a waste of history. Red Hugh survived that ordeal with frostbitten feet, and then threw the future away forever at Kinsale and Valladollid. Survival was the first law, and success the other one. Two hundred years ago, on the far side of this hill, Michael Dwyer stumbled out of a besieged cottage straight into the muskets of the soldiers to draw their fire, and let his companions escape. A hero or a fool? A corpse anyway.

> I am a bold undaunted fox
> That always could outrun the dogs,
> I made my home among the rocks,
> Between the mountains and the bogs.

He stiffened. Something on the hillside above. Movement flickering beyond the arc of vision. His finger slotted into the trigger-guard, his head swivelled an inch. Two big hares came bounding across the hillside a hundred feet away. He could almost feel the powerful hindlegs kicking the earth like heartbeats. But there was something wrong, a downhill grace, angularity. They were deer! a pair of deer, and at least a thousand feet away. He could distinguish a faint web of antlers swaying above a small, fine head. The illusion frightened and warned him. If he could see antlers at that distance then he was far from invisible himself. Why were the deer running? Someone on the ridge? He drew in his head and lay motionless.

High above, binoculars were trained on Hayes. He lay crucified on the trembling cross-hairs of a rifle-sight. The soldiers shivered with the waiting tension. At first they had thought Hayes was dead. Then the glasses picked up the slow, evil swivelling of the head that had brushed by them in the mist on the rim of the Barravore Valley. They watched the weapon as if it had a will of its own dragging the body along behind it.

A scuffle of running feet, and the terror of responsibility lifted. A colonel and a special mission squad came running low from the blind side of the hill. He threw himself flat on the ground, crawled forward to the rocks. He studied the body five hundred feet below for a motionless minute, and then wriggled back to the radio.

'... Target static. Location 053 934 ... Forestry within reach.'

It was obvious that, short of a bullet in the head, Michael Hayes would reach the trees if he was flushed out of the hollow. If he got in there with a sub-machine gun, men might die digging him out. If they flung a helicopter onto him now he would shoot it out to the death. And Hayes had to be taken alive. To stand trial. Those were absolute orders. A political imperative.

The radio drew a silent army into a closed circle around Barravore. A pair of ravens circled the valley, croaking raucously, refusing to settle.

The mist had melted away. A wash of pale sunlight seeped through the clouds and stained a distant hillside. Hayes lay among the reedy tufts of grass and heather, head moving an inch at a time. The gun was malignantly alive.

'I am a bold undaunted fox that ever yet outran the dogs ...' Michael Hayes was not his name. He took it from a song and gave up his own. One of the hunting-ballads where the fox was a hero on the run leading the hounds of the law a wild chase all over the country.

'Connemara being remote, they thought 'twas there I might resort;
As they were growing weary they thought they'd try Mayo.
In Swinford Town as I sat down I heard the dreadful cry of hounds ...
... But still their search was all in vain for Farmer Michael Hayes.'

Rotting on a hillside like a sheep carcass. Starvation had flushed him into the open this morning. Six days and nights in a sloping hole under a rock, lying twisted round a boulder, water flowing under his body and dripping down on him from the roof nine inches overhead. No use trying to escape at night, blundering into rivers, around in circles, until he hit a checkpoint or a tripwire. He moved out at dawn under cover of a thick mist, enough visibility to see ten or twenty feet ahead. Keep moving downhill, keep losing height. Follow a stream down and out.

The mist betrayed him on the open hillside. Blind hunger threatened to stampede him. They were waiting for him below, soup-kitchens steaming at the mouths of the valleys, wafting the aroma up into the hills. The army was poised to scrape him off a soup-wagon like a needle off a magnet. Rambling again; delirious. He opened his eyes and stared into the straggling vegetation inches away. Short, thin reeds, most of them snapped off at a yellow point, whether sheared by the wind or cropped by sheep. Clumps of withered grass, the roots almost washed out of the clay. As he stared at the grass his head moved slowly towards it driven by the blind volition of his belly.

Green-streaked mouths of famished corpses. Famine-victims eating grass. Textbook inspiration of hatred. They died spitting bile at their tormentors. He saw his victims lined up in a shadowy jury, red-streaked mouths open in the dark. And the three guards mowed down against the stone wall, dark bodies on the pale road, blood on the green grass. He knew there was no mercy in him. He nourished this savage freedom, knowing there was a world of his own kind.

He stared at the earth again. Green, spongy moss. The sharp tang of sorrel convulsed his memory. And the hint of honey in the clover tip. All the leaves and flowers the children nibbled. They had trained him in every aspect of guerrilla war, self-defence, ideology, propaganda, but no one ever thought of a bit of Botany. The moss was mushy, dense, vividly green. He pulled a soft tuft and it glinted wetly at him. He was reminded, with the force of a blow to the stomach, of lime-filling in a chocolate sweet. The image was too rich for his wretched gut.

The chocolates he brought first time he called. So many of his gestures were second-rate. His emotions had needed a different world. He couldn't accept that it might be more appropriate to change the feelings than the world.

She opened the box greedily and picked the soft ones, Turkish Delight, Strawberry, Lime. His stomach churned with revulsion against the self-indulgent probing of the bitten fingernail, and then the tight teeth, nibbling at the lumps of sugar. Giggling, she held out half a sweet to him, the sick green of the filling shining slickly at him. He shook his head – he preferred the hard ones. Margaret remarked that men always preferred the hard ones.

She had black, curly hair and white skin; she wore tweed and thick-knit wool. She was ideologically right. But in his fantasies he harboured a quick-limbed dancer in skin-tight silk.

The chocolates were melting in his brain and convulsions racked his stomach. A hunger-strike would be paradise to this wet, hunted extinction. He thought how she would have cried dutifully, an inherited affliction, as he starved with the dignity of a patriotic saint, in newspaper headlines, breathing away his life for the dream of a new nation.

But even then he had known there would be no new world. The truths were money, religion, and blood.

Live, survive at all costs. The triumph of the body. Thinking of Margaret, her inherited belief in sacrifice, his teeth recoiled in a bitter grimace from the pale flesh and the chain of bones stretching back through generations of dutiful suffering. There was nothing in that past but oblivion and decay. Michael Hayes was going to live.

He gripped the gun with ferocious fingers, dirty, bloodless talons. A law unto itself, its own physics and morality. So hard that the fingers could have been wreaths of mist.

He remembered the kick of the machine, its contemptuous power like electricity, lightning, death, the external forces that flogged the world. The three men hurled backwards against the wall, limbs flung, heads loose, jaws dislocated, as if a whip had caught the puppet-strings.

The Colonel watched over the body, without blinking. There were a hundred men in the valley already, and Hayes was still the only one visible. Fifty men had closed in from Cannow Mountain and the Table Track to the east. They were spread across the head of the valley. A troop was descending from the north through a deep gully at the end of the Barravore cliffs. Dozens more were filing up from below, concealed behind the dense streak of forestry that ran down into Glenmalure.

The ravens were giving it away. The Colonel longed to raise a rifle at the noisy, black rags and nail them to a silent sky.

Hayes listened to the squawking radar overhead. The day was bright as interrogation now. He tensed his nerves in a steely mesh to keep him pinned to the ground. Perhaps it was he who was keeping the ravens up? Circling above his body like vultures. He twisted his neck to glance up and winced with disgust at the pellets of sheep-shit beside his cheek. If he could catch a sheep … could he eat raw meat, warm and bleeding? He retched at the thought and his mind swam.

He pressed his wrist to his mouth and sucked hard, gnawing at the skin with chalk-dry teeth. A taste of turf, bogwater, his lips felt like cracked rubber.

You couldn't catch a sheep if you needed one. They were smart when it came to being stupid. Those stories of heroes surviving on fruit, berries, and wild meat – no man could live here without provisions.

Jack London told the truth, trying to kill the dog in the snow to warm his hands in its guts and save his own life. The dog kept his distance. The footballers eating each other in the snow. Catholic rugby-players. Plenty of meat on them. Communion and the Indivisible Body of Christ? It was dog eat dog up there, leave it at that.

Some of them got out alive.

Where was he going when he got out of here? None of the old reliables would hide him now. A dead policeman was like an anchor.

The dreamers would drive him out. No doubt there was a contract on him already. They would have to catch him first, and if he got out of this hole he could survive anything.

He wasn't trusted any more, they called him a "mercenary" because he staged a few jobs of his own. They'd come to that soon enough. Everybody came to it in his own way when the visions were threadbare. A man was supposed to retire quietly at that point and let another wave charge headfirst into history.

Maybe it was time to go home, take over the farm and settle down. Quit rambling the hills in all weathers ...

He knew a cleft in the ground in Sligo, a deep crevice in a rocky hill beyond Ben Bulben. Wiry mountain grass grew over the edges hiding the narrow slit from view. Sixty feet deep in the middle, and you could jump across the top of it. There was safety in the bottom of that. A little roof of poles and twigs covered with grass deep down, and lie under it as long as he liked. Forever.

Beside the mossy mound of old bones.

A day, five years ago, the sun blazing promises of a new world across the hillside, larks screaming revolution in the sky, Michael Hayes came hurtling down the mountain on a training exercise, blood pounding in his ears, pistons hammering in his chest, fitness flailing the spring air. Straight into a huddle of sheep behind a wall. They scattered in terror.

His own body seemed to hurtle through the air with the power of devastation, boots flinging mighty leaps off the springing turf, soaring over rocks, bushes, and tumbling walls. He marked down a panic-stricken sheep fleeing wildly ahead of him, its lamb cast off in a frenzy of fear, and he pounded in pursuit. Bleating wildly the fat sheep hurtled ahead of him, zig-zagging across the slope. Twenty yards in front it seemed to miss a step, skidded frantically and plunged out of sight.

He dug his heels into the turf, lurched sideways and threw his weight back against his flight. The skid rattled his knees cruelly, his legs shot from under him, and he landed heavily on his shoulder and hip, every bone shuddering with the impact. He rolled over and over down the slope digging his fingers into the earth until the thin bones bent backwards and threatened to snap at the knuckles.

He came to a halt on the lip of the chasm, headfirst, staring into the rocky depths. The sheep lay tumbled in a heap of wool at the bottom, stirring slightly. He pushed himself dizzily to his feet and looked back up the steep slope. Far above, the lamb was coming, at a run.

The Colonel tightened the circle again, pulled his men in closer. He suspected Hayes might be dying of exposure. He would prefer to carry out a bullet-ridden killer than an emaciated corpse cured by suffering.

There was a waiting arc of steel three hundred yards behind Hayes and pincer-jaws tightening from the front. He was at his most dangerous now. A trapped animal, nothing to lose.

That tent of skin and hair, lying in the muck on a frame of bones, with the space-age weapon beside it, was the shape of violence. Death, when it came, would be a storm of destruction.

Michael Hayes felt invisible eyes drilling into his back.

The bubble of air trapped in the valley was tight with tension. He was pinned below a snow-slope – a ski twisted under him – the creaking mountainside about to avalanche. Huge cracks and crevices ripped across the tilted ice. He tried to roll, but he was frozen into the snow.

Lying in a river-bed below a dam, a concrete cliff holding a deluge back; the dam breaking up, slabs of concrete flung out into the air, whale-spouts of water in the sky; the river rising. Move! He must move.

He understood at last why he was lying motionless on the side of the hill. Nothing to do with mist or camouflage. It was weakness, paralysis. He couldn't move.

He gathered the slack threads of his will, knotted them into a whip, and flogged himself up on his elbows. A blade of icy air sliced between his body and the ground. He had warmed up the patch where he lay, and the wind was plundering the warmth. He tottered dizzily to his feet, cradling the gun. Heavy as a jack-hammer.

The horizon reeled around him. He stumbled forward to the rim of the hollow and saw the trees.

The Fraughan Rock Glen! He cursed his blindness and his luck. A hundred yards further in the mist, and he would have been out now. The strength of rage flowed into his muscles. He began to run.

'KEEP HIM OUT OF THE TREES!'

Armed men poured from behind the forestry, rushed along the edge.

He was a dark blur of movement streaking along the ground.

One of the racing soldiers waved his rifle like a huge stick, shouting hysterically.

Hayes was going to get there first. The undergrowth of briars, and furze was fifty yards away. The soldiers twice as far. The machine-gun was flying over the rough ground as if the body it bore was weightless.

A soldier dropped to his knee, whipped the rifle to his shoulder, aimed between Hayes and the trees. The screaming shot stretched a line through space tight as barbed wire.

Hayes stammered his answer. Bodies jerked, and buckled to the ground. The manic rattle hammered against his ribs. He couldn't hold it straight.

The soldiers hurled themselves into the grass. A random streak of bullets raked the air.

There was a man still running, brandishing his rifle against the sky, screaming crazily. His mouth was wide open, his feet rose and fell in frantic strides. He was running away from terror in the very worst direction. He did not know how to stop.

The galloping boots and gaping mouth stampeded towards the gun, waded into the final trickle.

The scream died, the body toppled without a whisper.

The stuttering bullets stalled.

Tattered rags of silence hung across the glen, ripped by rows of jagged holes. From behind every single hole, from the dark side of that silence, a thin scream of violence poured into the still world.

Hayes lurched towards the forest and vanished among the trees.

The baying of the hounds was a howl for blood.

The valley shook as the flying horses thundered low over the ground, flailing the air. They landed in a huge circle around the wood, and the hills resounded to the amplified halloo of the huntsmen.

He slunk through the undergrowth, dragging his belly low against the earth, jaws open, trailing a dribble of white spit. He burrowed into a dense thicket, thorns ripping his skin. Turned within and listened. A frenzied yapping and snarling. The undergrowth burning with teeth and eyes.

A fresh clamour, howling and baying in front. He veered off to the left, but the trees thinned out.

He sloped back in, ears drawn tight against his skull, tail brushing the ground. He ran once round a small circle, and then stopped dead, facing his baying pursuers. He raised his snout in the air, and emitted a high-pitched howl of desecration. It cut through the trees and hung sharp and clear in the air above the hunt.

Trailing his scream, the fox ran straight towards the hounds.

STONE BOAT

It was once widely believed that the worst sin a priest could commit was to have a relationship with a woman. According to a popular folktale, there was a special hell in store for such a crime.

At sea-level in the great cliffs there was said to be a secret door. The woman and her lover arrived by boat. The key was in a fish's mouth caught without a hook. The woman sailed the boat away as the priest entered the rock. His footsteps patrol the darkness within forever.

The climbers brought excitement. The island always had tourists, but these were different. A new breed of bird, they came to colonise the cliffs.

I had known climbers in Dublin before I was sent over here. I tried it myself when I was younger, but I hadn't the head for heights. I was prised loose and lowered off. A pity. It seemed an ideal sport; intense enough to flare away the libido. I took to water instead, a solitary ocean-going swimmer. The salt and the cold cured desire.

On those urban days when storms arose I prowled the parochial house and dreamed of sin, red rose on a white blouse. It drew me in. The east was harvest country. Fall was inevitable, blossom to the blade. Then the stony road to an island parish. What have they done to deserve us? Our clay-foot tramp on their Atlantic rock.

My work here is not consuming. People are superstitious, but they are also healthy and independent. I exercise a priestly presence. My purpose is to swim the island completely round. A limestone pier dips in the tide below the village, a rusting ladder on either side. Down one, twenty miles around, up the other. It is my fate, my obsession.

I've done sections in summer, cleaving the water on a running tide to fetch up exhausted at the White Strand, An Trá Bán. The currents and tides seem insuperable, and there is a long stretch under the western cliffs where the sea swells on the calmest day. There is no escape there for five miles.

From dreaming headlands I search the water, ebb and flow, rip-current and tide-race, seeking their equation. I may have to tread water at Poll na Scadán, Carraig Liath, Aill an Ghliomaigh, until the water runs my way. I want no cover, but sometimes a currach will follow without seeming; drifting near me on the trail of pots. Under peaked caps silent faces watch.

I weave through the static on the trawler-radios; *'Seachain, tá'n sagairtín ar muir ...'*

The sea is my fate. It is another life. I must make the best of it. I choose it as I believe Saint Brendan chose, not a means to an end, but an element to launch the soul. Though I will never make an island of a fish's back and light a fire around its blowhole I am my own navigator. If it happens I will go down with my body. A doctor said I fall into the tide like a shot seal, that I have a death-wish and it springs from guilt. He may be shrewd, but he has no power. We alone have a cure – *Ego te absolvo* – but it is a poor illusion. It takes two to forgive.

Truth is arbitrary as a floating bottle, smashed in clichés on the shore. Hidden in sand it gutted me. Bloodied fragments flashed a truth: to still the flesh I need a sword, a symbol slashed across the spirit. I cut a drowned cross in the sand under the wave's edge with blood-rimmed glass. This is not psychosis. It is the heart making meaning instead of love. I was too close to the sea. It was all-pervasive, like war, pounding the beaches of my mind. I wallowed precariously, up to the chin in sway and temptation. I should not have been condemned to an island. But a desert, a forest, a mountain, a city, would have been the same.

Scorching a Latin breviary I walked along the beaches where the land dipped underwater with the weight of my presence. I was a sailor afloat on a table, racked with thirst. When I leaned towards the edge, it tipped me off among the sharks. On windy days, broadbacked in rusty black, I gusted along the shore, seagulls screaming overhead, as if something freshly killed was to be dumped.

When the climbers came the island lifted a little out of the sea. The first pair stayed a week, made miracles, and left. Like pilgrims they hardly spoke. I never heard their names. They climbed a lonely prow that sweeps up from the sea to prop the headland high into the sky. I swam that section for the first time then. Did they see a bull-seal lolling in the summer swell, a white collar under his grievous chin? I watched them, tiny figures on the overhanging rib, feet braced, tearing at the island with their arms. They would pull this pillar from under the rim, bring the island crashing down to pin me under, swallow me, as if I had fished that key too soon and entered the dreadful door. Abandon hope all ye who enter here. Watching, I revelled in wonder: could I climb out of the sea? Out of the grave? Out of hell? Like a jellyfish dreaming of hands, a current swept me three miles down the coast.

After the eagles the small birds came, then the scavengers. From novelty to nuisance overnight. They didn't see themselves like that. Even the illiterates among them felt superior to the culture of the island. It was hardly conscious; a condition of the colonial-nostalgia that rears them. All they saw were the very old and the very young. Everyone in between has abandoned the island, the country too. I do baptisms and funerals, no weddings.

They were a nine-day wonder themselves. Later, they were the circus that hasn't left. The glitter wore off and exposed the tawdry tricks. We learned how the ropes, the drills, and the bolts worked. We saw them fall off and swing, cursing, in a safety-net of preparation. There was not much magic. Tom Pháidín Tom, ninety-one, who had spent hazardous hours hanging on hemp gathering eggs across the vertical night-wastes of those cliffs attacked me as a raucous bunch passed his hovel,

'Bhíodar ag stracadh as Aill na nÉan inniu gan meas acu ar ubh ná éan. Ní dhéanfaidís caoga bliain o shin é.'

There were courteous exceptions, awed as much by human tradition as by geology. Ropes on their shoulders they surveyed the island like a ruined cathedral. But without the language they cannot see the walls and roofs, the pillars and luminous windows of a past that towers above the present. All they see are the pink and yellow bungalows, the plastic blight feeding on ruined stone. But the old structure is still there, shapes of light and air, arches hanging in psychic space, built of word and memory on an island-plinth, spearing the sky with the Michaelian M.

After six years I am still tracing its blind shapes in the minds of old men, feeling for foundations in their everyday lives. I hear the high line of a rampart hidden in a verse, a gargoyle grinning in a sneer. I catch a fading glimpse of marble in an inward eye. It's an illusion. This is not their vision, this Italianate pomp I was born with and cannot shake off. I am not a pagan no matter how hard I aspire. Except at sea. Swimming the western shore under the cliffs I look up between walls of water and know the island and everything on it, heaped up against the end of the world, is the last great altar to the setting sun. We know nothing yet. We live still, the entire world, in the prehistory of ignorance.

One autumn day without a future I walked the remote headlands towards Dún Beag. Weeks of violent weather had blown the climbers off the island. They had never come this far anyway. In the half-circle of the ruined fort high above the sea I planted my feet in windswept grass and leaned into the gale. Nothing lived in that storm, not even a gull. I smelled the salt of sorrow. It preserves this dead flesh. Slowly my arms lifted in submission to the west. They rose until the hands touched above. In big, black boots I rocked on the very edge of the continent. Sea-water rocked within me, tilting the balance.

I felt a quiet presence behind, tugging my attention. Paper was offered, like the page a begging child will press upon you in a city street.

The wind tore at the paper. The message was indecipherable, the language – even the letters – unknown. Exasperated, I turned it upside down: drivel. Then over. From behind, the trace was clear; I knew those bulging, bellied letters. Copied from some tablet, some ancient grave-stone. All the distortions of age and weather had been rendered as part of the text. I didn't understand it. It was older than the language I spoke. Turning, I recognised the short, fat climber ...

... short and fat, Johnny-Jump-Up, five foot five and thirteen stone. Bow legs, broad arse, no shoulders, neckless. Don't be fooled by appearance – in my mind I'm slim, suave, strong. I have the definitive style of my time. Imitators underline my perfection. I glide over ardent obstacles. My utterances are quoted –

But you won't have spoken to me. You are affected by external problems, pimples, boils, hairy ears, cross-eyes – no, no, mine, not yours! You think the sublime is only for the beautiful, and of course you are beautiful, aren't you? In your mind. When you lean back in some skintight position, perfection humming in your strength, and climb like archery on galloping horseback or whatever it is you do, you *are* beautiful. In your mind.

And so am I. You may have seen me at crepuscule, elasticating on unclimbed rock in my green jumpsuit like an adam's-apple straining for operatic pitch, or looking – that malicious girlie said – like a sack of frogs.

In the gold-and-purple throne-room of my heart I am no frog. Never Falstaff, but Prince Hal. Charming too, courteous, friendly, shy. For fear of rebuff I don't make first moves. When I fell off on your arrival, plumped among the boulders, I was not looking for the kiss of life, believe me – just stepping aside till you enquired 'Alright?'

'Fine, thanks. Fine!' I sang out. 'Abrasions only. Want to hold my rope? Hello! Hey! Hellooo?'

Participation was the wrong approach, but I wanted to belong. Then I saw your video and I resigned.

The first face spoke; 'For me it is the *move*. Hardness in a vacuum. Such difficulty that nothing else exists.' A grip of steel. His jaws steel-hard, ripping language into shreds.

The second wove seductive moves and words. Grace and elegance. Dancerly metaphysics. The body-language screamed IMAGE. And Image is about two things only; class and sex.

The third had nothing to say. He had been to an island. He showed a film within the film, to illustrate. Deserted corners, cracks, arêtes and overhangs. That was climbing. Rock. Not muscle, technique, image, point of view or scenery. The climbing, not the climber. Geology was its own commentary. The lines were pointed silently by a moving finger, the body pared to its extremity.

I left this barbarism, and fled to the west coast of an island off the western shore of an island way off the west coast of our island, where the cliffs prop the last arch of European sky above the rim of the western sea. I would achieve something colossal there, reeking of belief and transcendence, some outhung, suspended edge, prow of the great stone boat on which wise men fled to islands.

Exclusion made a thinker of me. Thought is outlawed in sport, confined to the asylum of the head. Philosophy is worse – banished to an inner island, without return. On a sloshing ferry I limped into exile. Shouldering through the ocean the tempest dropped, the island rose. I slipped ashore in Paradise, a wedge afloat upon the ocean. Not Napoleon, not Prospero, but, where the bee sucks there suck I. From frothing beaches the land climbed up and up and plunged so clean and sheer that a continent at least, perhaps a planet, has calved from this eternal shore.

But the athletes were already here, exponents of Image and the Move. I went to Aillanilla, forgotten corner of the island with its remnant of a fort overlooking blank, bleak cliffs undercut by time and the sea. Not for ordinary climbing; there is no place to start. I burrowed into the fort and lived on mushrooms, berries, eggs and dreams.

I'd seen the padre wandering land and sea. Like me he was alone. I envied the certainty of his solitude. A tall, powerful man, strong in the shoulders. Thatched with grey hair, his square face had stiffened before its time. The hooded eyes were not for looking into; they were the windows of an unhappy house but someone in there would never leave. Sometimes he wore the monsignor's frocked cassock and biretta, and I knew how unromantic the toga would have been. Stripped to black bathing-togs he had white, unused skin without body-hair. I think he oiled it. He entered the sea with severe purpose, as if he'd stepped on land for a few hours and was finished with that. The Great Silkie. The seal-man.

> He came one night to her bedside
> And a grumbly guest I'm sure was he,
> Saying "Here to thee's thy bairn's father
> And here for thee's thy nurse's fee."

Sometimes he stumped to my fort and stared at the sea from under a stormy brow. He understood the island like a prisoner knows his prison. I wanted to ask him questions; I didn't dare. Was this Prospero?

Aillanilla, the poet's cliff. I guessed at the story. Only a poet would be lonely enough for this barren place, no access down to fishing, no ledges for birds' eggs. He might have thrown himself from the cliff, behaviour popular with poets. Or was he pushed, to shut his mouth? These people had taken poetry seriously. Song and story is threaded through the island, in and out of caves and coves, laced around rocks and ruins, the vegetation of history. Time itself is bound in sheaves of words.

The solution-pockets in the rock are footprints of the past. A race of giants marched across new ground to build at the far end of their world. Behind them history erupted and cast their footsteps in its flow. It erased their memory, but their forts and footprints remain. Down the millennia the west wind blows through empty holes where meaning was thatched to shut this oblivion out. Geology claimed the footprints, tourism claimed the forts.

The climbers hung out in the village hostel and the juke-box bars. They rattled like starlings in the damp, windy weather. Meanwhile, I roped-down towards the churning sea, and there, on a vast grey wall clean as a page, carved into the island, I discovered *language*.

... Wind and spray attacked his paper in my fist. No message would survive this weather. A rumour in a storm.

'Where?'

His stubby finger pointed at my feet. I stood beside a rope, thin as a stretched nerve, disappearing over the edge. I stared in angry confusion at the cable that had brought a message up from the sea.

I recognised the climbing-rope and understood how apt it was that I had stood there, arms renouncing revelation, and he had given me his message. We reeled into the shelter of the fort. Within the whorl of a clochan his domed tent clung to the ground like a shell.

The letters had been roughly traced onto the page. Each character was about two inches high, confused in outline, as if the surface distortion of the stone had been sketched in by a copyist who couldn't tell text from background. Irritably I smoothed the paper and turned it over. The tracing came through behind, without the added detail, and I recognised the g, the t, the d. It was gaelic script, quite ancient.

What was it doing down there? How much was there? What did it mean? Did it answer me? We communicated first in sign-language, silently, eyebrows raised, hands measuring, pointing, as if human breath were redundant, not only in that wind, but in that place where everything was cast in stone. Then, getting to know each other, we resorted to language. He began in a hesitant, rusty voice, unused to talking. I examined his unprepossessing surface for dishonesty or fraud. There was none. Only insecurity and unease. I sat sideways in confessional mode staring out to sea and his story flowed.

... That wall seemed perfect, a surface flawless as canvas. It couldn't be climbed. I wanted to paint the sea on it, paint a reflection as clear as a mirror. The sea would go right through its open window and flow out the other side of the world.

The first time I went down I lost myself in the blankness. The day was calm but the swell washed against the rock. I was looking vaguely for fingerholds, toeholds, a climber's line. There were no good holds, nothing to engage more than a fingerprint. Then, in the centre of the wall, right in the middle, I found the marks; a maze of signs, ten foot square.

I thought they were fossils at first, those worm-casts written into Moher-stone, like the carving on an old tomb. I began to understand. Hanging on the rope I knew the island was speaking to me. Whether it spoke in air or stone, thundered aloud or whispered from the corner of its mouth, I heard nothing, but I knew it spoke in some ancient tone, and there on the rock was the text, and it meant absolutely nothing.

And yet – I had seen it before, words in wild rock ... The drone of the ordinary dissolved my reverie; the murmuring sea, the whisper of a breeze, gulls crying, blood in the temples. I stared into the alien letters, remembered mantras and the creak as prayer-wheels turned the world.

OM mani padme hum OM mani padme hum OM ... Om ... om ...
It was old. The edges were blurred on the flint-hard rock. I had seen
the carving and heard Buddhist mantras in countless expedition-films
from Tibet and Nepal; cliffs, rocks, boulders, thousands upon thousands
of exquisite stones, centuries old, heaped in hundred-yard walls
throughout the Himalayas. Against the soles of my feet this tight little
Christian island pulsed with an Asian heartbeat *OM ... OM... OM... OM.*
Who was he, the anchorite who had dwelt here among the ruins of
other mysteries, and left no trace in island-lore, no word in Robinson's
pilgrimage? How long had this taken to carve? I chipped with the spike
of a piton-hammer. After several blows the rock splintered incoherently.
A flake lodged in my eye. I had barely scratched the surface. It might take
months to shape my ragged name upon the rock.

His calm, copperplate characters hung there neater than print, as firm
and right as the grain of the rock. Although I understood nothing I knew
the nature of the mani-writing lay in that assurance. The monk found the
language in the rock itself and brought it to the surface. For the believer
faith lay at the heart of things. His task was to bring it forth. It would
transform the surface, and the observer, by its presence.

But these islands were the preserve of Christian saints. Their brand was
the crucifix and crown of thorns; yet, once upon a time, a man had come
from somewhere impossible and left a different truth behind. How had
he come? Above all, why choose the absolute obscurity of a sea-cliff? Was
the impact of the text in its presence under sun and stars, and not in its
meaning to others? Are we irrelevant? Or – here I felt more profoundly
afraid – was it left for an eye as wild and obscure as the missionary's own?

There might have been many monks wandering the medieval world –
disguised as poets, yes, of course – leaving language that links into an
irresistible testament to be revealed when it comes true. Was I eaves-
dropping on prophecy? I was further frightened, for predestination robs
us of freedom, and I imagined instead a Christian heretic, familiar with
dangerous creeds and banished here to this remotest shore of Europe.

Whether Buddhist, Christian, or poet, the practical question remained;
how had he written this? Had he levitated, or leaned from the deck of
some mystical ship and chipped? Had he abseiled? I visualised it; a pole
stuck out across the headwall, a makeshift pulley-wheel, a rope of hair
and fibre. A harness like a trouser-seat. The monk lowers himself hand
over hand into the weather, a rock counterbalancing his rope, and works

all day at his cruel labour of love, of faith, of penance, all day through sun and wind and rain, pulling up hand over weary hand at night to sleep in a hole in the rocks. Prayer made manifest.

Perhaps – hardest, most desirable of all – he had accomplished it in his mind, trained to believe so deeply that it achieved itself. I spun on my rope and stared out to sea through envious tears. Busy among the waves you swam by, and your wake made sense of the ocean ...

... I found it a healing concept. His readiness to believe the impossible uplifted me. He sought a greater role in human destiny than chance had allowed. The script was obviously Gaelic, not Asian, but I didn't tell him. I demanded the entire text. It was a spiritual order, not a request.

His strange eyes swivelled and bulged. The muddy irises glowed with golden mission. Perhaps his eyes weren't distorted at all, but sited for the widest range of vision. With all that lateral perception there must be a narrow ridge of blindness down the centre, so that he couldn't see what was in front of his nose.

Three days after the storm I swam past Aillanilla to view the text from below. In the centre of the grey wall he hung rapt as an artist, ten-foot sheets of print-out paper sellotaped across the rock. I saw no trace of writing, the distance was too great. Was he exuding something sticky from his own brain? The scrap he gave me was genuine, even to the extent of being innocently back to front – but it might have come from anywhere. He scrabbled sideways, unrolling paper, and I saw a fat arachnid spinning an arcane web.

No, he was a believer. I knew he was a believer, as I could never be – because he had missed the obvious detail in front of his nose. Down the wall ran a jagged stain from top left to bottom right, so long exposed to the sea that it was almost invisible, almost the same ageless grey as the rock where he worked. Perhaps it was only visible from a distance, visible to an unbeliever, but there was no doubt that at some far-off time a pillar with ledges and flakes had clung to this cliff and afforded a stairway down the smooth wall. Nearby cliffs supported huge, leaning flakes, and on sea-level terraces I had seen the roots of pinnacles toppled by storms. Squinting, I thought the stain levelled out under his heels for about ten feet in a ghost of a ledge. It was very faint, the trace of an old shadow. The pillar had hung detached before it toppled. When they finished their script they had taken poles and levered it away from the wall. It rumbled into the sea, they probably raised a roar, but louder still was the thunder of the written word challenging eternity.

He didn't see me below. I might have barked like a seal, or tugged his rope to hear the cracked note of a hermit-bell. I swam below the wall. It was completely undercut. The deep sea nibbled a long way in. There was no plinth for a pillar. The first break was a hundred yards away, where the low overhang ended in a sea-level ledge. There, a deep cleft that looked almost climbable split the wall above the ledge.

After dark he came to the parochial house, excited, ill-at-ease. Despite my calculated aloofness we were conspirators. The paper was unrolled in strips across the floor. He had seen too many films; he called the letters hieroglyphs. After three days we had half the text. The effort exhausted him; he got it back to front again. I was irritated. I wanted a full version in decipherable form. Already I could feel the meaning stirring in my veins.

I goaded him; the monk must have been a hardier breed – three days wouldn't achieve much with a chisel. But it wasn't the work that bothered him. He needed to climb. Something was stirring in his blood too. There were holds. They began with a foothold on the lip of the overhang. The rest were tiny, but they formed a sequence up the centre of the wall if ... I knew what he meant; if you believed in them. In breathless, technical hieroglyphs he explained there was no protection, nowhere for another climber to belay, unless he stood in a boat, and he didn't have a boat ... or a partner.

'You expect *me* to hold your rope above while you fool around climbing?'

He was shocked, wanted no such thing. He intended to do without a rope. His eyes had that foolish, golden gleam again.

He would abseil to the overhang, ten feet above the sea, step off the rope onto the foothold and climb from there. If he fell he would hit the water ... I realised he knew as little about the sea as I knew about rock.

'Can you swim?' No answer. 'What will you do –' I was frigid with anger, '– walk on water?'

That, as far as he was concerned, was my job. I wanted to punch him for his obstinacy. But a fist would sink to the wrist in him. I could have raised my hand in a blessing, that dismissive gesture only one move away from a slap in the face. He jerked his knees up towards his chest, a pulpy creature remembering violence, but within his softness there was a hard bargain; if I wanted the rest of the words I would have to swim.

A sharp wind blew against the swell and whipped up spray. Anger, salt in the blood, spurred me on. Long before I reached Aillanilla I saw him standing motionless on the rim. It was the silhouette of a standing-stone, a mooring-post, a permanence that could be marked on a sea-chart.

The wind and waves exhausted me. With stretches like this I could not imagine swimming the island round. When I reached the wall he launched onto the rope and slid to the overhang, his feet compressed like a dancer's in tight, stiff shoes. The rendezvous was too strange for greetings; I, black and white, with rubber lips, red eyes and hoarse lungs – he, a hoofed spider disengaging from the rope. It sprang like elastic, out of reach.

Limbs spread he lay against the vertical rock above me, one foot on a marginal hold. I could see the full expanse of his rubber sole. Nothing else held him but the friction of danger. I had seen the others adhere like this; I knew it was possible. Some of them were louts, so it was neither miracle nor magic – just a skill. But they were strong and slender, adapted like rock-fleas to their medium. This one was short, round, fat. Instead of those little goat's feet he would have been better equipped for his immediate future with frog's fins.

He brushed the rock with his left fingertips, sifted options, selected. His right toe lifted, scuffed, engaged. It couldn't be more than a pebble. He stepped up. From beneath I saw what he was doing – what the others had done on the prow below the fort; he was flying close to the face, flying so close that he brushed it in places. A flutter of fingers, a flick of the limbs, he moved up again. There were holds. Blinded by spray I couldn't see them. I could only guess at the play of forces braced against edges and wrinkles, the tension plucking at tiny flakes. His feet lifted. Water-logged, unevolved, I couldn't judge their weight. Were they light as chamois, or were they armies marching up the alps? His body hung out from the rock, a sacrifice to gravity, then it soared from its slump with the mystery of rebound.

I wallowed on my back, shivering at the icy slap of waves on my belly. What I saw was more than skill; the intention, the belief, were so intense that he generated movement on blank rock, spinning progress within himself. The stairway was long gone – I couldn't even see the shadow –

but he climbed as if it were still there. The act itself was not transcendent; he was a climber exercising experience and skill; as I accepted the progress I accepted the edges and flakes that made it possible. But the sea was black and hard as marble, he had no rope, and he could not have understood where he was going. *Om mani padme hum* ...

He reached an impasse. Antennae flickered, scanned the carving. I knew there were no holds there; any roughness would have been chipped away to smooth the page. Nothing there but the letters, and he knew they weren't holds.

Eager – a child's hand raised – he reached into the labyrinth for the meaning. *Om mani padme hum.* I should have told him. His fingers gripped, tightened on the invisible, he lifted the intent of a foot – and fell.

Fell? Falling, I thought he would drop feet first towards the sea. But he was thrown – hurled violently back by a jolt, a shock of incomprehension. He spun sideways in the air; as he passed the overhang his head struck the blind blow of a hammer. Stunned, I didn't hear the splash. But there were two of us in the water. His black hair streamed towards me, staining the water red. A hundred yards away, the ledge; there was no rope hanging.

I had ordered him to place one in case of accident. I could leave him, unconscious, on the ledge while I swam off, or haul him up from above. He had his own means of climbing a rope if he was conscious. But there was no rope. It would have been a failure of belief, a safety-net? Perhaps he didn't have a second one.

I seized him under the arms, turned him over. His face was grey, and slack as rubber. Water dribbled from his mouth, blood bubbled in his hair. One arm clamped around him I flailed blindly on my back. He drooped against me like a corpse. A grim embrace. He dragged me down, down into the water. Sinking, there was nothing random in my memory; and no remorse. I thought of all the hours my arms embraced you, forbidden woman. Throughout that long, slow drowning my soul reclaimed you. It will never let go.

Inch by inch the overhang passed overhead. The cliff was opening to receive us. I kicked and fought until the ledge loomed alongside like a harbour wall and I gaped up into the cleft. Time and again I jammed him against the rock, willing him to float, climbed out to find he had drifted out of reach and was sinking. A final effort coincided with a wave.

I knew resuscitation, the kiss of life. Before I began that grisly embrace

I heaved him into a sitting position, propped up his chin … *In nomine patris et filii* … I hit him a stinging slap across the face. He choked, dribbled, stared at me, one wild eye askew. The lid closed to shut out what he saw.

Fallen angel? Grey flesh quivering in garish garb he looked like a dissolving jellyfish. His failure confirmed the impossible. I would never swim full-circle now. Whether to survive or to escape, I climbed that fifty metre chimney, barefoot, naked. Gravity was a tidal current and I fought every vertical inch. He came up hours afterwards. I had transferred the rope from his abseil. I watched him climb the mouth of the groove, back and feet braced against opposing walls. I had squirmed as deep as I could within the cleft where the sharp rock bit into my flesh.

He stayed in the parochial house for a week. My housekeeper nursed him. I had never thawed her widow's chill, but she warmed to him. She called him Friar Tuck. I saw him as a half-drowned Buddha. Pale and bloated he squatted in an armchair while I chipped grimly at the text.

I extended two full-length mirrors edgewise on the floor and propped the tracing opposite. I worked from the reflection, distracted by my own unshaven face lurking behind the letters. Glossaries and grammars littered the floor. The outline of many letters was in doubt. If I copied down the text I seemed to define words in my mind. I avoided such concrete acts to keep the poem fluid until it hardened of its own accord.

There was a constant feeling of energy frustrated, a fever like sugar burning in the brain. My temperature soared, I felt an overpowering urge to rip back my sleeves and cool my veins in the mirror, plunge to the elbows in its current where I would surely find the invisible shapes dropped there centuries ago. In the middle of the night I would start awake from a buzzing dream, drowned in sweat, and order – implore – him to go down again to verify. Some of the sketch-marks could be accents, or they might be incidental scratches. A dot or a stroke changed everything. The broad vowels floated in and out of shape like spots before my eyes. One accent and a flatter arc could make the difference between Bod and Bád for a serious example.

He was coarse enough to say that only a celibate would confuse those. Celibacy, I responded drily, is a moral intention, not an act of castration. We are normal men. I felt a near-irresistible urge to talk, to confess to this detached figure. But I knew that, without remorse, it is useless to confess. I could not regret a single embrace of our lost love; not one moment of our entire year stolen from my vows could I renounce. And I swear, Evelyn, if you would take me again, as you swear you will not, I would leave everything and go. The more I scraped at the mute surface, convinced that it could speak to me from the past, the more I needed to pour forth this language of my own. I shut my teeth against my tongue and laboured. I had to make a single chisel of my mind, but it rattled like a jackhammer.

He sailed on a stone boat and dreamed an island; that much seemed certain. It was an image of transcendence. I didn't quite translate it; it came like revelation. But he was pursued. By whom? By whom? The island turned to stone. Good or bad? Miracle? Disaster? He sailed alongside – to shelter? to hide? – leaned from the deck and carved. Why?

Faoiseamh ní gheobhad ... No respite from weeping rock ... or keening sea. Never? Not even light after darkness? I needed the final lines, for redemption or despair.

Buddha would not descend. He was finished with this – waiting to leave the island. He would wander east, to Asia. The mani-stones had laid a grip upon his soul. And there were mountains too. He was at peace with a new dream.

He taught me to abseil, gave me a gift of his rope. I learned on the fort, a twelve-foot descent. As the line poured slowly through the alloy knot I walked down the prehistoric wall and felt no qualms. I was eager to begin the slide into the sea. At noon, my head full of translations and tides, without a whisper of prayer, I crossed the rim of the island.

He blessed me with farewell. I saw myself reflected in his mute appraisal; sea-plump and hairless, smooth skin blotched with blackened bruises, black togs, black rubber tight upon my skull ... the brain and crotch were already seal, the skin was turning. Amphibious! Shock rippled through me as a shot explodes in blubber. But no one is fully human, no one is entirely man.

Below me, vertical rock, horizontal curve of the sea, severe dimensions for a distorted soul. Today I would swim around the island, thread that ellipse in the angle between cliff and sea. If anyone saw me now, a renegade, sleekly naked, striding down Aillanilla on a strand of coloured string, casual as a demon on a broom, I would be shot. 'We saw a seal at the salmon-nets, your honour.'

When I reached the centre of the wall I didn't recognise the inscription.

I had an image chiselled in my brain. But these marks were not incut as I expected; the letters were carved in relief, a weave of bewildering ribs raised like Braille upon the rock. We had never discussed that detail. I placed my fingers on the first line and urgently penduled along. It made no more sense than a row of fossils. I swung back left, fingers still in touch. There it was:

> I sailed on a stone boat … I dreamed an island

I found it, felt it clear as my own signature; thought too of the shipwreck – the Titanic's number in reverse reflecting Antichrist in code. Was it the boat that was made of stone? Or was it the sailor? Dully I probed for the real words now, not for images:

> Adrift in a boat … made of stone … I dreamed an island

I knew how it felt to have a heart and soul of stone.

Around the raised letters the rock was natural – rough and weathered. It had never been chipped nor the level lowered to pronounce these words. Swinging wildly in mid-air I felt the cord tighten. The whip cracked. It was not reversed. It was written from within the cliff.

The final lines. I knew already. Written in darkness he spoke of sun. The last day sailed west and she went with it, crossed the horizon, and faded.

> *Aonraic. Oíche shíoraí*
> Solitary. Night forever.

JOHANN

The door opened. A figure in a shapeless tunic shuffled through. The long corridor was dimly lit. Johann guided himself by touch along the wet wall. After every dozen steps his hand scraped across another iron door. He added a name heavily under his breath. Some of the names were foreign but he pronounced them all with the same guttural resonance.

At every hundred paces a bulb shone in a wire cage. Lichens festered around the weak lights. He stamped his feet on the stone floor and clapped his palms roughly, applauding the illusion of heat. He breathed deep to prepare for effort.

Grey hair and beard fringed a thin, physical face. The straight nose, sharp jaw, jutting brows were reminders of aggression, but all the strength had drained away in the furrows of age and neglect. He stooped away into the shadows still naming absent names.

Johann smelled a hard, clear night outside the walls. The air had the dry sting of frost. No wind. Nothing to blind the sky. He was running out of names, or repeating himself – Wallenberg for the second time – Raul – pausing at the broken door; but that was years ago, and someone else had been there since, a man with a sharp, bitter language – English, he thought. He was gone too.

He turned a corner and saw the window ahead. Breathing quickened to a rasp and his palms skidded impatiently across nameless doors. The small opening high in the wall shed a square of barred light on the floor. He flexed his muscles and jumped clumsily to hook the grille. His bones vibrated with effort as he hauled himself up till his face was level with the light. It was night in the outside world and the stars struck cold and deep into his eyes.

He had timed it precisely. No watch, clock, or calendar, no sense at all of minutes, hours or days, but he could judge moonrise and sunset to within a hairsbreadth of the horizon.

He saw the blade of a crescent moon skimming exquisitely up the ridge of a mountain, slicing an icy arrowhead out of the sky. Once a year the image was immaculate, the silver scalpel paring the exact silhouette until it reached the tip of the icy triangle, and paused for the downward stroke.

He never stayed to see the moon escape into the sky. He had always dropped to the floor and returned to his cell to dream of the moon slicing back to earth along the other edge of the arrowhead. Others had brought him to this window when he needed a vision to survive. He recalled a line of men here on a clear night, queuing to celebrate an accident of beauty. Wallenberg had seen it first – the man with the power to interrupt nightmare.

The mountains endure. The first time he met Wallenberg he stumbled past the thin, pale man in a corridor. The Swede brushed aside his own guard, an obedient shadow, and laid a detaining hand on Johann's shoulder. The mountains endure. What shocked Johann, and drew him back to a kind of sanity where he questioned things again, was the sound of his own language, his own dialect, in the foreign mouth. It was as if he had spoken himself. The mountains endure. Afterwards, he was never sure if that was what he heard, or if he had simply understood by touch what Raul had meant to say. Perhaps nothing had been said at all. The mountains endure. The message carried an inescapable conclusion: in spite of this. In spite of suffering.

The guard materialised again and Raul Wallenberg moved on, but as always he was in control and it was the guard who was marched away.

There were windows for other seasons – dawn in the funnel of an eastern pass, alignments of Orion's belt. But the men were all gone and Johann kept the vigils alone. They were the measure of his existence.

Sometimes the sky was sullen on this special night – it was a long time since it had been clear. But the past too was obscure. He could seldom remember who was the victim and who was to blame. The knife-edge of the horizon re-opened the wounds, and the cold night was full of revelation.

He knew immediately his strength had withered. He was shuddering with effort. Once he could hang by his bent arms, from the first phosphorescence to the final radiance. Now it had barely begun and he was sinking already, his feet scrabbling on the rough wall. Desire welled in his heart, a hunger for magnificence. Darkness slid inexorably up the mountain, and the windowsill eclipsed the moon.

Closing his door he lay down on the iron cot, having arranged the grey blankets to avoid the holes. Heels together his bony feet stuck straight up. He folded his hands across his chest and closed his eyes.

Johann concentrated on the midnight mountain. He plundered his dim resources to bring the shape to life. He summoned colour from distant meadows, olive uniforms, a blue-eye in a Judas-hole, to melt the long darkness into summer light. He tried to build a blaze from the brightest moments. Desire fanned the dull edge of memory. Colour was refused! His skull ached with effort. The bleak triangle of ice bulged within the bones. It was rooted in the glacier, locked into the pointed angle of the sky.

Five hundred metres above the glacier the ice funnelled through the first rock-band. From below they could no longer see the Major Ice-field above the rock. They knew it was there, the upper half of the wall, swept by avalanches spouting from a rocky chute that might – or might not – penetrate the summit overhangs.

In the middle of winter they stood below the mountain, three young men on the edge of a first ascent. The icy wind was the breath of time and place. Two pairs of eyes, cold behind wire spectacles turned on him – your idea, lunatic. You go first.

Responsibility was the worst burden. It unbalanced Johann's heart in a way the heaviest rucksack never could. He stiffened himself. He was ready. His arms and shoulders, his chest, were powerful – swelling with strength. His booted feet were confident as hooves.

He looked up. Here, at its narrowest point, the bergschrund formed a shallow ice-cave. The lower edge of the slope jutted out across his head. He reached up with the heavy axe and struck a lazy blow. Sparks of ice flew from the glancing pick, and the shock of impact shook his bones. The others winced, shifted their eyes back down the valley. Snow-covered mountains stretched beyond the furthest limits of vision. Home was ten hours away.

Johann looked again along the great crevasse dividing the glacier from the face. There was no other way across. He removed his gloves, knotted the rope around his waist and threw the coils to a reluctant pair of hands. His fingers throbbed with hot, impatient life. They were immune to the weather. He was twenty-five, and ready.

Again he swung the axe. Anton and Boris ducked for fear of shattered steel, but the pick drove deep into the brittle ice. He released his grip on the singing handle, took a loop of cord and swung it high in the air. It dropped around the head of the axe. No one spoke. They heard the wind polishing the face. Johann beckoned and pointed. Boris stepped forward, handed him his axe and crouched on the narrow ledge. He clasped Johann around the knees and lifted. Seizing the buried pick Johann thrust his boot into the hanging loop. The axe jerked, tilted, the handle slammed against the ice, held by tension only. Johann's lips peeled back from his long teeth. Leaning backwards he swung the second axe at full stretch. It slammed into a tight fissure that split the rim of the overhanging ice. In the same motion he hauled on the handle and kicked off the loop below. He swung out, lunged for the second pick and heaved again. Crampons thrashed against the ice, his body lifted till he was level with the lip and pushing down on the buried steel. He jerked one hand loose and chopped a fist into the icy crack above his head – a salute to the unknown.

That was someone else Johann watched from his grim pillow. He felt no connection with the brain and blood flailing against gravity long ago, pulling towards his future. He could not feel the force of being there. He might as well have crouched with Anton and Boris on the freezing ledge below, robbed of retreat, watching in horror as the rope twitched out another ten metres, then the blunt triumph of anchors in the ice – his voice coming down to them like a stranger's, stripped of feeling in the bitter air.

'Come up!' He hauled them onto the face.

The wind tore at their clothes, rejected them.

Sometimes butterflies were blown up from the valleys and plastered to the ice. Only the tides of avalanche, the explosion of a storm was worthy of attention here. The white triangle of the mountain billowed around them, the wind cracking in its frozen canvas. They were sailing into an unknown winter.

All the way up the ice, two days of hacking steps and hauling ropes, they pleaded for retreat. Boris short and squat with bristling hair, his bare face begging like a hedgehog. Anton strong and stocky, weak in the will, his eyes outraged, a student out of his depth. Johann ignored them. Even when the cloud cleared and they imagined the chimney-smoke in the valleys. It was easier to go up than down, he said.

The gully did not lead to the summit. It died out among overhangs of rotten rock. He spent hours up there probing with frozen fingers while they sheltered below and begged him to succeed. Easier now to go up than down.

He failed.

He got them off in a day-and-a-half retreating down the face with a single axe between the three, ravaged by frostbite and defeat.

Anton and Boris never climbed again. They joined the army and went away to die defending two square metres of muddy snow.

Johann lost the will to try again; he had strained his courage in a single effort. No one suspected. His were pragmatic people to whom any success was an accumulation of attempts. They had problems of their own. War was coming closer.

For a while Anna seemed to cure him of defeat. Perhaps she drove the symptoms deeper. She arrived on holiday the summer after his attempt, the year before the war.

She wanted to climb while it was still possible. She could pay a little for the privilege. An old guide at the station said gallantly that he would take her himself if only he had the strength. He recommended instead a young man – a powerful climber – convalescing from a bad experience.

Anna stood firmly outside Johann's house while he stammered in the dark doorway. He was filled with confusion, unable to look her in the face, dimly aware of a woman almost as tall as himself whose smooth, brown skin was utterly exotic compared to the freckled complexions that he knew. At first her blue eyes and wide mouth were friendly, pleased to have found the right house. She explained her purpose in the cultivated accent of the lowlands. Her voice reminded Johann of the radio, the intelligence of far-off places and events. It was not the climbing that presented problems but what he would *say* to her all day.

He mumbled an excuse about farm-work and started to withdraw. She wore a yellow, sleeveless dress, one hand in a side-pocket clenching with annoyance. The colour shimmered before his eyes and her voice was distorted by a pulse thudding in his head.

She turned aside and looked angrily at the mountains around the valley. He looked at what she saw and the familiar view was completely changed, swimming in the sky, as if he was a child staring at it with his head between his legs.

'I was told you were available,' she said accusingly. 'I can pay. And I'm fit – if that's what you're worried about!'

She kicked the ground with impatience. Johann's voice shook, lapsing helplessly into dialect as he made the arrangements.

During the first day's walking in the sunshine her resentment relaxed, and gradually his shyness gave way. She was a little older than Johann but her manner was not superior. Her shirts, breeches and boots were well-worn and she seemed strong and independent. She had no need of a guide at all. Johann thought her perfectly capable of walking the mountains on her own.

'Walking!' she laughed. 'I came here to climb. When do we start?'

Johann had never climbed with a woman before. Usually they hired the older guides who patronised them and kept to easy ground. It had never occurred to him that anyone like Anna would take the slightest interest in real climbing. He had always thought of it as an achievement of muscle and sweat. He had imagined beauty as meek and passive, self-protecting. He took the dawns and sunsets, the silent spaces, casually for granted. They were aspects of the weather. But it excited him constantly now to see these ordinary things through Anna's eyes. It was like a conversion of the senses, a refinement of reality. He realised he was deeply proud of the mountains and proud of his achievements. Proud but anxious – everything was changing and under threat.

Anna sang, laughed, ran without losing breath, on the high tracks and easy ridges. She was fascinated by Johann's work and education. Her own urban background she dismissed as irrelevant. There were clashes. She seemed to think his dialect and accent quaint as if he had chosen them for effect. She laughed in disbelief at his rebel politics. To restore his pride he hinted at membership of the separatist guerrillas. They would come into their own soon, he promised fiercely. He could not be drawn further on the subject.

After three days' walking he took her climbing. Rock, ice, ropes, pitons, a complete performance. She was easy to teach – hungry for a change of angle and elevation.

The dull earth reeled away beneath their feet. They entered an exalted state.

Lying on the iron cot in the dark Johann leaned inward towards the light he had released. His eyelids fluttered and the harsh breathing softened, fanning the dream to a blaze. Bright, sun-coloured days, red rock between the green valleys, the blue sky, and the white snow, came sliding up from the dark – from beyond the edge.

Holding his breath against excess desire he watched the radiant landscapes flicker, fade, and resume. He was waiting now, preparing to dissolve over the edge of disbelief into ecstasy, but already he was afraid of the horizon, of where he would arrive on the other side of memory. This hovering between delight and terror recalled the heat trapped in the colours, desire blazing in the blood. He remembered the rage for suffusion of the senses, stifled by dread.

The sunlight soured, laughter ripped through the dream. Beneath him, Anna's heavy hair swung loose. Sweat poured down her face. Her head was thrown back, smooth throat stretched, a pulse hammering below her ear. She looked up to him, pleading. She dangled from a handhold on a steep wall, emptiness below her, and he sat overhead helpless with laughter, ridiculing her reliance on the rope.

'Tight!' she screamed, and he pulled it tight until the line bit deep into her skin.

He could not stop the terrible laughter; it was strength asserting itself. He was still rocking back and forth, hating himself for it, as she collapsed weakly on the ledge, her confidence drained away in the reek of sweat. She allowed him his assertion as if it was a temporary right to be dealt with later. The breathless air was hard with light reflected from ice, water, mica. In the aftermath of cruelty Johann sensed his own transparency.

He helped her up, apologising, on the verge of strange language. Anna grimaced, looked at him, measuring his embarrassment. She leaned across and kissed him, in mockery, a salt kiss like a bite across the lips.

The climbing was easier above. They ran like partners in a dream, faster and faster for the sheer release of movement, the spirit flying while a conspiracy raged in the blood.

Days flared past. They scrambled on warm ridges and pillars, slept on starry ledges, dropped down to the village like parachutists for food and wine, and vanished again for a second week of celebration. Johann observed the code – propriety and safety. It was his last defence.

The villagers saw them wander in, hair bleached to straw, faces burned, the intimacy of height and silence in their eyes. They whispered to him that he deserved happiness but he must not get carried away. His eyes turned absently aside to search. Had he heard the news, they insisted: the armies were coming again? It was time to leave the mountains, to hide the harvest, to organise. His face lit up as she strode along the street towards him. The neighbours looked at her and shook their heads. They were afraid for Johann. He had endured pain and hardship; he was a special young man with great strength, but he was too single-minded to understand loss.

Crossing a wide stream in the mountains Anna slipped on a wet stone. There was no danger. Cursing, she floundered in the icy water. Again Johann was overcome with involuntary howls of laughter. She was helpless, falling again and again, unable to keep her feet. Her clothes clung to her body. He stumbled across to help. She wrenched powerfully on his arm and dragged him in. The water was glacial, agonising.

Shocked to hysteria they crawled out on the grass, and wept with laughter, their eyes locked together. The sun was plunging into evening. Anna sobered suddenly. Started to shed her soaking clothes. A moment of hypnotised silence and Johann began to strip. The wind quickened, she moved towards him. He recoiled. The smooth legs, the brown face and neck, were part of a stranger's body, ice-cold, unknown, pale as snow from the shoulders to the thighs.

Trapped in the dream, approaching the dark shore. Memory swept him along. He struggled to withdraw but he was caught in the grip of the truth. Johann was running slowly through his brain on rubber legs pursued by Anna's terrifying laughter. The laughter was hurt and childlike, sharpened by the shrillness of betrayal.

Anna went home. She wrote immediately, preoccupied with the chaos in the south. Life in the city was under siege.

Johann didn't answer.

He no longer knew what was restraint and what was failure. He stalked alone in the mountains balancing his future on his finger-tips, testing fragile rock with the weight of his existence. He caught glimpses of the White Sail brooding remotely, threatening the return of winter.

Work forced him back to earth. He reaped acres of grain single-handed, refusing assistance, and stored it in the foothills. Within two months war was underway, conscription in the plains, the disaffected fleeing to the mountains. The population swayed like seaweed with the tides from the west and then the east and back and forth in the ebb and flow of influence. But resistance hardened in the mountains. The separatist movement gathered strength. Patriots from all over the country – some of them mountaineers – flocked to join the partisans.

Johann hurled himself furiously into the organisation. He was admired for his accomplishments and courage, to his secret shame. He burned to justify that respect within himself. Overnight he became leader of the local unit, arms and men, some of them climbing comrades, at his disposal.

On a wet September evening just before dark Johann stood at an upstairs window waiting to hold a meeting. It was as if he had been posted there. The weary shape approaching in the street must be imagination, but his heart was thumping so hard he couldn't breathe. He jerked back out of sight.

Cropped hair, wet and plastered to her skull, face thin and white, shadows in the eye-sockets. The shoulders were slumped and she wore grey, anonymous clothes. The difference proved her real.

But it couldn't be! Wild evasions sparked. Her sister? He saw the real Anna lying in bomb-debris, blood in the corner of her mouth. 'Find Johann. Tell him I ...'

He slammed his back against the wall.

Anna knocked at the old guesthouse across the street. Her knuckles hammered among his heartbeats, and went on hammering when she stood back. She squared her shoulders to the closed door with sudden authority. Aunt Zelda opened it a few inches, shook her head through the gap. Anna's hands lifted towards her. Reluctantly the door opened wide enough to admit her.

He knew he had seen her, but he could not believe it. Johann watched the house till midnight. Even in the dark he could imagine every detail – the ornate woodwork he painted for his Aunt Zelda, the bowed roof that might refuse another winter, the split grain of the front door, the hinges he replaced last year. His mind clung to the shapes of things, fought clear of meaning. The outlines of the ancient village sagged together in the dark. Pain creaked beneath the surfaces of objects and events. That night he lay entirely sleepless – Anna, the movement, mountains, Anna ...

The eiderdown smothered him. He knew Anna would have no trouble sleeping. She was like that. He threw off the cover and lay shivering in the cold.

On the iron cot in the cell Johann's knuckles clenched in the same frenzy of desire and rejection.

This was not memory. It was re-experience! As always he had broken from the dark into brief sunlight, and then crashed on into deeper darkness beyond.

He saw exactly how Anna's hair had swept up from her clear forehead, curling and twisting thickly, and the tiny scar below her right cheekbone where a mole had been removed. He saw the long lobes of her ears and the way her top lip clung to her teeth when she was tired or thirsty.

But Anna was no longer in a room across the street. Anna was thirty years away. And her eyes – looking up as she climbed towards him – were not the soft blue of alpine flowers. They were the colour of icy water reflecting the sky.

He was headlong on his way to learning everything he had always known.

In the morning he hurried along the street. Worn cobbles, cracked black timber, houses decaying with their occupants, the whole village crumbling into the earth.

She carried Zelda's egg-basket. Accepted already.

'Johann!' she bubbled with unreserved delight, 'Johann! I thought you'd be away! My God, I didn't know you. It's the … it's the beard!'

Emotion thundered towards utterance, but the words froze. His hand jerked up to the hair itching his face. He had lost control of expression, his mouth smirking and his brain helpless to stop it.

'I don't have time to shave now,' he mumbled.

'So I hear! You must be very busy. Organising.' She gazed in admiration.

He gave a sharp, melodramatic frown. 'What do you know about that?'

'Zelda told me of course. She's very proud of you. You're going to save the whole country it seems.' She was laughing at him.

'Zelda remembers me from the summer,' she continued happily. Johann caught a flash of the closing door, the imploring hands.

'She says I can stay awhile if I work for my keep. My money's no use to her, and anyway there's nothing to buy. '

Johann said nothing. He sensed a hollowness without knowing what it was. She chatted away gaily, flashing glances at him, then lifting her head to the clouded mountains beyond.

Sudden determination focused her. She looked around quickly. An old man smoked in a doorway, gazing at the weather over the rooftops.

'Johann, I came to help! It's – nothing to do with you – you'll be glad to know. I just want to be part of whatever's going on up here.'

Her tight hair was greasy. There were blemishes on her skin, and the sunken cheeks emphasised an awkward nose. He had never seen her plainness before. Deep creases of fatigue between her eyes. The mystique had vanished. She was ordinary now, like a local woman. Less, even. They had substance behind them.

He saw Zelda's basket again. It was heaped up with precious brown eggs, worth a fortune. She was carrying it exactly as Aunt Zelda did, exactly as his grandmother had carried the same basket, looped over an arm and resting loosely on her hip. He had never been trusted with it. He would break an egg at every step. Anna was at home already.

'Why did you come back?'

He meant it to sound curious, flattered even, but it came out as an insult. Her chin lifted under the impact. He felt the force that distinguished her.

'I like it here. That's all. It's beautiful. I feel I know the mountains.' Her eyes dropped and he suspected mockery. 'Thanks to you, I suppose.'

But she looked vehemently south. 'I had to get away – as far away from all that as possible.' She faced him, just as she had faced Zelda at the door.

'Don't make me unwelcome, Johann, please. I have nowhere else to go.'

Anna could not be kept out of the resistance. Nothing balked her determination to belong. Within weeks she was attending secret meetings, sitting quietly at the back in a long, black coat borrowed from Zelda. She was careful not to offer opinions, though Johann could sense her mind working like a hidden clock in the room. She had regained her colour and her face was keen with a nervous urge to serve.

Her presence hypnotised and horrified him, like mountain roses swarming with bees: absorbed, seductive and dangerous. When she was in a room, no matter how crowded, Johann felt isolated from the others, as if – between them alone – they shared a powerful mystery; but when emotion surged forward he found the barrier again – the very idea of her. She was beyond him. He did not know how to reach outside his limits.

Anna was only one of the new faces. Some had been frequent visitors but they remained outsiders. Those who remembered her from the summer idyll saw her at first as Johann's girl; they were amused by the distance at which he kept her, as if he was trying to disguise the fact. When they teased him he showed a vicious streak of authority and stunned them into silence.

Johann believed passionately in the need for revolution and an independent mountain-state. It was the only way to preserve their lives from dilution. The mountain-farmers believed not only in defending their land but in reinforcing private ownership. They let the idealists say what they liked as long as their speeches added up to that.

There was very little they could achieve yet. The military had not penetrated that far, and showed no sign of doing so. There was a comfortable suspicion among the local men that the area would be ignored. It was too awkward, too poor. Who wanted it? The visiting partisans were happy to keep it that way. They saw no need for provocation. They were fed and sheltered. They spent pleasant days in the mountains storing food and weapons against the day when Johann's plan might come into effect.

He was determined to make that day happen. First they would provoke an all-out attack, then retreat into the high mountains to fight on their own ground. His strategy was to lure the enemy through key passes to be ambushed by pockets of guerrillas overhead. Calculated explosions would cut off retreat and reinforcements. Avalanches could be arranged. The campaign was planned to act as a flash-point, rousing a passive people to widespread rebellion.

Anna was in the mountains every day building up the supply-dumps. Good-humoured, resourceful, she was becoming a popular focus in the village. Her reputation as a climber grew and she was careful not to challenge anybody's pride. She was indistinguishable from the others, even in the rowdiness she cultivated to hold her own. Scornfully Johann thought that, if she could, she would have grown a beard. He never missed a chance to deny her hold on him.

He was living on the run – from his own imagination more than any threat – bearded and spectacled, moving from house to house with a rifle and a box of books. He suppressed his passion and it tormented him. His zeal for revolution grew as the winter hardened. It was the mission his life hungered for. He stood for hours above the village, staring out towards the valleys and the captive plains. Behind his back the mountain leaned over the horizon.

Weekly briefings became harangues. Revolution must be taken seriously! It demanded secrecy and discipline. His lean face had become hard and drawn. He raged that the police knew every single move they made. Why not invite them to the meetings to save the trouble of informing?

He organised a number of ambushes to capture arms, detonated some explosives; suddenly, two of his men were killed in an attack on a barracks. One was a bizarre outsider who had been certain to kill himself anyway, but the second was a neighbour, dull and slow-witted, whose death hung over Johann's head. The others were even more convinced of the need for caution. Thoughtfully they continued training and stockpiling in the mountains. When the village ran low on certain provisions these were carried back down again. There was little else to do in the winter snows. Events developed a strange quality, somewhere between farce and nightmare, fuelled by quantities of potato-spirit.

Another ambush, another death. The taste of resistance was turning sour. Anna confronted him in a candle-lit attic where he sat speechless with obstinacy. She stormed in wearing the long, black coat and an air of delegated challenge.

He was alienating the community that supported him, she began ... Johann jumped to his feet, shouting. Whose community was it? His skin tightened to an ugly ivory.

She tried to argue. What was the point in attacking with inadequate weapons and numbers? Was it violence for its own sake?

Johann was enraged. They understood nothing that was going on. It was the evidence of guerrilla presence that kept the military out.

Anna retorted that the only evidence was three dead comrades.

The plane droned through the darkness, turned abruptly as if it had strayed north and realised its error. A parachute drifted towards the snow. As he watched it drop like a foreign seed on their moonlit mountain Johann chilled with premonition. He had received a rare, coded briefing in advance. His men ran forward and bundled up the silk. Johann strode stiffly towards the stranger.

Jean brought greetings from the separatists of Western Europe. His contacts were impeccable and he came with the warmest recommendations from Johann's superiors further south. He was being lent to the movement because of his experience in alpine combat. His mission was to liaise with local groups and instruct them in new techniques.

To Johann this was evidence on the one hand of the importance of his area; on the other, it was interference with his command. Jean could neither be ignored nor absorbed. His manner had the wide-awake ease of self-sufficiency. He stood inches taller than Johann and his spare frame was wiry with muscle. A ready grin invited acceptance, but without the smile his face was hawk-sharp with a hard, energetic mouth and eyes hooded against speculation. His age was uncertain – the weathered skin too tight to wrinkle, too hard for youth. Only the clear, grey eyes gave a clue; when measuring Johann's welcome they cooled and hardened with old experience.

But his arrival galvanised the flagging group. Some members had lapsed, discouraged by Johann's emerging politics, others had disappeared to join the army. Now the faithful felt an official sense of purpose again. Recognising the hungry urgency of their mood Jean quickly made it clear that he did not deal in impetuous action. He was here to help with long-term strategy, and to learn the language – he grinned agreeably through his mangled phrases. He believed, not in outnumbered defence, but in undermining occupation. He understood from his previous briefing that it would come to that – if enemy expansionism continued. Johann noted the easy grasp the stranger had of complex terms despite his language problems.

'Our aim,' he contradicted bluntly, 'is to prevent occupation in the first place!'

Jean's eye wandered, without any obvious sense of irony, around the room taking in the numbers present, dwelling on them individually with abstract assessment. Johann was about to explain hotly that they were only a fraction of the available support, but he realised the other man knew all the details already and silence knotted between them.

Jean wore an ice-axe emblem on his lapel. He had been a mountain-guide at home before the war. Complimenting the local mountains he asked about the prominent face he had seen in the moonlight of his arrival. His fingertips met in an elegant point and his palms leaned apart at the wrists enclosing a sharp triangle of air.

It was climbed of course, he presumed delicately. Often? Implying that it would be a slur on local talent to think otherwise. Johann ignored him, continuing to list items in an inventory.

Jean pressed again, deliberately.

Embarrassment forced others to answer together.

No, they admitted with unexpected shame, it was not actually climbed. The ridges yes, of course, but that face ... well, it was probably impossible! Rubble falling down it all the time. And bloody steep – far steeper than it seemed!

But Johann here – they smiled at him hastily, patching the atmosphere – Johann tried it once. He spent three days on it in winter, and if that wasn't enough ...

The explanation faltered again. Jean flashed a smile of approval at him, but Johann wasn't fooled. He smelled the superiority behind the respect. The gallic tribute of those tight jaws meant nothing. The tall man was sitting easily on the edge of a table, his tunic open, one leg swinging affably, thick black hair with startling flashes of grey pushed back from his aquiline face. He was waiting. Johann felt his skin grow clammy in the cold room, frustration forced out through his pores. He wanted to say coolly; 'the rock up there is rotten, too rotten to climb!' and dismiss it then. At once an excuse – and a challenge. But in spite of himself he growled abrasively, 'you'll have to wait till winter to find out!' Smarting with resentment he turned back to his notes. 'If you're still here!'

Jean showed no sign of departure. He was as captivated as a tourist by the pretty villages and the wild mountains. Everything here, he said, reminded him of his own area before it was developed. Billeted at Zelda's he told stories of the war at home – over now and won – marvellous stories, livid with blood, ice and courage, tales of ambush and attack, of white eagles and silver foxes skiing down the mountains to annihilate the enemy. He took no credit for gallantry, reflecting instead a wry sense of self-ridicule. When they wondered breathlessly why he wouldn't stay at home and savour the peace, he laughed and admitted he preferred the excitement of a just cause. The movement, he said, was world-wide now and his war would not end till theirs did. His listeners felt the warm fraternity of struggle.

But for the time being it seemed Jean was more interested in exploration than resistance. One shoulder was hunched slightly higher than the other, sharpening the angular attention of his head. He was recovering from a bullet-wound and he needed a lot of exercise to restore his strength.

'No use getting into a fight without the strength to win,' he shrugged.

Apparently unaware of the effort they had cost he dismissed Johann's hoarded weapons as 'catapults and spears.' He had a trick of relying on language difficulties to offer innocent insults. He would organise an air-drop of arms as soon as supply-lines were set up. Meanwhile lie low and keep fit! There were comrades abroad eager to help when the time came.

Keeping fit meant climbing everything that had not yet been done in the mountains. Jean hardly ever repeated an existing route regardless of its excellence; he was interested only in pioneering, even if the new line was inferior to an established climb.

Johann knew the name of this attitude from his textbooks; it was imperialism! To his utter fury Jean innocently handed him details of every new route, neatly written out with the date, the grade, and the time taken. The standard of difficulty was consistently high. He obviously inspired confidence because none of those who climbed with him ever mentioned fear when they discussed the routes, maliciously he thought, in Johann's hearing. He was the only one who resented the agreeable foreigner. The others were confused by the vehemence of his hostility. It couldn't be on account of Anna: Johann went out of his way to underline his total detachment from her. He answered her frigidly when necessary, never using her name or looking directly at her. Sometimes it seemed to the others that she was teasing him, tricking him into confrontations.

They competed eagerly among themselves to climb with Jean. There was glamour in a first ascent, even if it was an unappealing couloir they had never noticed before. But Anna was his preferred partner. She was the only one who spoke his native language and had an international sense of events. And she was talented – lighter and faster than most of the others. She would never challenge for the limelight either, for Anna had compromised her independence. Fearing to antagonise the men she had become an habitual second. This had developed into an assumption of inferiority. Anna had let it happen as the price of absorption into a male community.

Johann spent the year doggedly trying to build up his support. He became increasingly politicised and caused a split in local feeling. He argued now that independence would not be sufficient in itself. They must aim towards a state that was absolutely true to the traditions of the mountain people, a state impervious to corruption by outside cultures. Exclusive nationalism.

He was not alone in his ideas, neither locally nor on a larger scale, though he was unaware at first of the echoes. Soon covert rallies were being held in an effort to build a political wing to the movement. Johann and others travelled widely, urging the need to break with the neighbouring country that had diluted their history and identity for so long.

Only through national freedom could they find the strength to resist the totalitarian invasion already devouring their neighbour.

For a while Johann found relief in his new crusade. He was standing on a rough platform at a village festival on the far side of the mountains listening to speakers of his own persuasion arouse the audience when he first became aware of opposition to what he thought was absolute – almost genetic – truth. The hard blue sky, the festive costumes, the dark mountains, clustered farms, and the intent listeners, were identical to the features of his own home. Character was shared like a language by that small select group – his people! Theirs was a unique identity. And though a long way from home Johann was known here, both as a partisan and a mountaineer. He was astounded therefore to hear voices heckling a local speaker. It was as if they contradicted the rhythm of his blood, challenging the very nature of his feelings.

How, the hecklers demanded, did the platform think a handful of mountain farmers could maintain a separate existence without the support of that country which virtually subsidised them at the moment with employment and trade? It was pure fantasy, they yelled, a fairy-tale, an impediment to progress.

Thunderstruck, Johann saw many of the audience nod and smile with furtive complacency as if their own ideas were being voiced. A moment later he found himself at the front of the platform shaking with fierce conviction. He addressed the objections, denouncing them as treachery. He sketched the evils of invasion and tyranny, the subjugation of a proud race, confiscation of the tiny fields, collectivisation on behalf of factory workers in foreign cities. Had they no pride, he exhorted, no will, no sense of destiny? Did no one realise there were more important things at stake than material wealth – which would be robbed from them as soon as they succumbed to it?

The true issue, Johann asserted, was national identity, the noble spirit of the people. It was a cultural value which could only be preserved in determined isolation. And its propagation was their sacred charge.

'Without identity,' he challenged fervently 'without soul, without language, without the old and tested way of life, the way that is hard but simple and pure, our children will be impoverished beyond slavery, beyond starvation!'

Johann's harsh voice ignited the emotions he had aroused. The crowd flared with patriotic passion. He offered them answers: discipline, courage, self-determination. They must stand now and fight! Fight for the future in the name of the past!

He raised his arms in the fascist salute, his eyes rose fervently above the tumult, and the barrier of mountains blocking the whole horizon echoed their isolation from the outside world.

But the opposition at home to the new doctrine was not so easy to quell. Johann was no longer a hero or a prophet there. The force of his faith made it impossible for him to understand how anyone but a traitor could attack it. It was as if he discovered poison in a mountain stream. In the intervals between his travels he tried to increase the guerrilla activities of his unit. The response was sluggish; there was an uneasy cohesion now between politics and militancy. Johann knew they badly needed weapons for the coming struggle, but there was no further mention of the promised airlift, and Jean contrived to be away when Johann was at home.

The older people favoured his politics, but not his violence. Resistance was fine when it meant firing off the odd shot from a safe ambush to preserve their self-respect. But they were not willing to be sacrificed for a lost cause.

There was raw dissatisfaction among the younger men.

Tradition robbed most of them of any rights to the land that passed from patriarch to eldest son. They sought a focus for their discontent. The neighbouring army, already at war, was an uneasy option. It was hard to decide whether or not they were actually occupied by a country of which they had been part for centuries.

But surely, they had a common enemy now in that totalitarian expansion threatening to engulf them both?

The Movement, popular at first, was losing its grip on them. They had no place in its emerging politics, and there was no clear direction for guerrilla action. In the intervals between seasonal work they enlisted their frustrated energy in the mountain cult. Jean and Anna were the focus of this disaffection.

The summer passed in a blaze of inflamed emotion and autumn brought the first high snows.

Rationing increased the disillusion in the villages. Suddenly there was harsh resentment of any mouth without a justified claim on food. It became apparent to Johann that people cared more for bread than brotherhood. He denounced the failure of patriotism. Some of his men were forced out of their billets, and he had to impose authority for the first time over his sullen neighbours.

On a freezing afternoon in midwinter footsteps hurried up the ice-encrusted stairs to the loft where Johann was studying. He glanced up impatiently, expecting the woman who brought his food. Anna stood in the doorway, the promise of a smile offered in exchange for a welcome. Behind her the outside world was a blinding rectangle of snow and icy light. He smelled the cold air invading the room, withering the quiet shadows.

Anna's cheeks were rubbed to a bitter glow by the wind, and her eyes were bright and nervous with excitement. In spite of the savage draught ruffling his papers Johann felt his cramped heart expand towards a source of warmth and instinctively he tightened his limbs against the urge. He noticed that as usual his feet were numb with cold. His eyes returned to his book. The print was meaningless and he shut it slowly with an imitation of reluctance that appalled him. Giving her no chance to speak he rose unsteadily to his feet.

'Anna' he ordered heavily, 'you will have to stop this nonsense in the mountains. There's work to be done here! You're giving bad example ... making it impossible for me.' Anna recoiled in angry surprise. 'Don't blame me,' she snapped. 'You create your own problems!' Then she laughed and rolled her eyes at his idiocy, refusing to take her own anger seriously either. The old fashioned, local clothing she wore should have placed her firmly under his command, but her expression repudiated him. His knuckles clenched with anger and the realisation that she would never respect his authority. Without her approval he had no respect for it himself.

'What do you want?' he snapped frigidly. 'I'm busy.'

Anna glanced at his books with ironic disdain. Following her gaze Johann flushed. He felt how precarious his world of intelligence and inspiration must seem, balanced on a few battered, uncertain texts.

'I came to tell you something important!' Anna burst out. Her voice shook with excitement, animosity forgotten. She pointed through the black, timber-beamed wall, her finger stabbing the shadows with determination.

'Johann, tomorrow we're going up ... to climb *that*! The Spearhead!' The whimsical name spat at him from her glistening lips. She stamped once on the dusty floor then looked him straight in the eye with tense anticipation. Her lips stayed open in a fixed smile full of white teeth.

Johann heard himself laugh. It was the first time in months. It scraped from his throat and fell helplessly into the room like a dry coughing. The absurdity! He felt the weather – the deep snow, the abysmal cold – tighten in his head sharpening his defences. The impregnability of the mountain was assured. 'Who...' he demanded contemptuously '... is WE?'

Anna ignored the insult but the tension in her jaw increased. Without changing her expression she was no longer even faintly smiling. She put strong, roughened hands on the table and leaned towards him. Johann saw her knuckles trembling, almost felt the vibrations through the timber. It was the nearest he had been to her since they climbed together and he was shocked again by the difference in her face. She was never what he expected. The constant shifts, not just in style but almost in substance, bewildered him. It was impossible to know her. He saw the hard, naked flesh of a face from which romance and luxury were pared away. It was not a woman's face – to be calculated with emotion – but the cold visage of an antagonist.

She swallowed deliberately before she spoke, determined to carry out some intention though the reason for it had already deserted her.

'We wanted – we *decided* ...' she corrected coldly '... to ask you to come with us, since you had the ... *courage* to make the first attempt. We thought it *right* ...' She was underlining words to whip him with the absolute failure of the idea.

Johann's breathing locked in his throat. He floundered in angry confusion. Were they mocking him? He knew Jean would never have thought of asking. The gesture was entirely Anna's. Did she mean something by it, or was she tying to make a fool of him? She must have known he would refuse. He had no idea what to think, but he was already answering with grating sarcasm. 'It's madness! Dangerous lunacy. He will not succeed.'

He thought of the gaping bergschrund, the ice stacked above it like a limestone overhang. His lip curled. 'He won't even –'

She was turning on her heel, the heavy dress flaring with fury.

'Anna!' his voice barked impulsively, 'Wait!'

She turned, charged with hostility. Seeing the expression on her face he was terrified by what he had achieved. The shock detached him briefly. As his mouth struggled for the truth he felt – for an instant, within himself – a dark, silent opening. It was a displacement between feeling and words, and within the gap he felt a poisoned response flicker towards emergence. It belonged neither to emotion nor to reason. It was beyond his control. If he could hold the awareness long enough to ...

'Anna! Don't go!'

Not what he meant. It was an order, not a plea.

'Why not?' she sneered scornfully, tossing her head. 'What is it to you?' The moment closed over, sealed with an instant scar.

'There's a *war* on, Anna!' he retorted furiously. 'A war! Out there!' He stabbed his finger in the opposite direction.

'We must dedicate ourselves to the Resistance. We can't take any other risks. The mountains will wait.' He stumbled – mountains waited for destiny, not for individuals.

'Don't you understand?' he demanded desperately.

'I understand *fear* when I see it!'

It was said with the contemptuous clarity of the obvious. He knew what she was going to say in advance, and knew she was right. The real shock came from this sense of foreknowledge.

'Fear?' he raged. 'Fear!' His fingers tore at his face in denial. The long, wooden word gagged his tongue, '... responsibility!'

Choking with fury he glared at her. 'I have nothing to be ashamed of. I did my share in these mountains when that was the thing to do! Anyone will tell you that!'

The need to hurt was naked on Anna's drawn skin. 'Not any more, Johann,' she hissed. 'Your reputation has run out. I'll tell you what they're saying now – that you've lost your nerve and you won't admit it. That you're trying to hide behind politics. That you want to be a hero but it's always someone else who has to pull the trigger.' She stamped her foot viciously with each accusation, 'and they're right! They say it would be better for everyone if you gave up playing politics and went back to climbing mountains. At least you knew something about that – once.

'I've just offered you a chance to prove them wrong. It wasn't easy to come here like this – but you turned it down. Like everything else! I thought if you took a break from your ... your patriotism you might recognise it for what it is!'

She took a bitter breath and plunged on, enraged by an echo. 'You dare to tell me there's a war on! Me! As if I didn't know more about war than you ever will.

'What do you think drove me back here?' She pounded the table furiously. 'When I got home after that self-indulgent *holiday* with you I found out all about war, very quickly.

'And it's got very little to do with discipline and sacrifice! And plans, and patriots, and guns.' She snorted with outraged contempt. 'You ought to have joined the real army, Johann. You'd love all those games. They'd have made you an officer – you're fool enough. Maybe there's still time!'

Johann said nothing. He didn't move. He knew he was seeing Anna clearer than ever before. And with a sharp, almost sensual pain he saw himself too, reflected in her contempt.

'But that isn't war, Johann. That's only the sound of it. War is invisible. It starts long before the armies face each other. Real war is a disease … a civilian disease.

'It's hunger, curfews, disappearances, midnight arrests, torture, people too frightened to talk to each other. The kind of terror that power, and death, feed on!'

'That's what I found when I went home. Maybe it was the same before I left, but I didn't notice it until I felt the peace up here. Then I saw war raging like an epidemic – a fever – in the people around me. They were rotten with disease. I knew it would take bombs and guns and soldiers to burn it out. And death!

'It was incurable by then. Too late to do anything: you either get infected, or escape.

'So I came back here! I thought it was cleaner in the fresh mountain air. The disease hadn't reached here yet, and you dreamed of keeping it out. Such an innocent dream! I laughed at it first when you told me; then I had to come back and help, in spite of … of everything, including you. But whatever innocence you had here is dead now – and you've strangled it, Johann. You've strangled it!'

His mouth opened to protest, a black gap in his silent face.

'You don't believe me, Johann, you don't know what I'm talking about yet. But it's you! – you and your disciples who did it. You're full of hatred and fear, and it's infecting everything you touch. Look at the people around here! Your people.

'All the warmth and humour and trust is gone. They're at each others' throats now. They don't even know why. It's all disguised in slogans – who's a fascist, who's a red, who ….' she blessed herself sarcastically '… who's descended from a Jew. It's a dirty little war of ugliness and suspicion and you're fanning the flames in the name of freedom! You don't even see it yet, you won't recognise it till the blood spills. And it will be the blood of your neighbours, and they'll get nothing for it – not even pity or respect.

'It has to come to that now, because the disease is gone too far. Maybe even then you won't understand – you'll think people should be sacrificed for principles. As long as you're around to enforce them afterwards.

'Listen to me, Johann! You were born here, but you've forgotten everything. There's a world of difference between dreams and reality and everyone else knows it. You don't!

'They think first with their blood, their bones, and their bellies. You're thinking with a box of worm-eaten books before you even use your brain.

'They don't give a damn for an independent mountain-state. A ghost republic bathed in blood. They know they'd starve if they tried to stand alone. That's all that matters!

'Listen to them if you still don't believe me. Listen to them – when they don't know you're there. They can't say it openly. You've got a few fanatics behind you now Johann, and it's dangerous for anyone to contradict.

'The only supporters you have are men with a grudge against reality like yourself, and that's the most lethal support of all –

' – That's the disease!'

The final words came as fiercely as if she tasted blood and spat it back. Johann remained motionless. His only hope lay in the dignity of silence. Between the phrases of the attack a cold internal voice advised him to have her shot – to do it himself. He shivered with desire and revulsion, imagining his comrades in the Movement – dedicated men, strong and peremptory. They eliminated opposition before it interfered. They were committed to an ideal and fierce in its pursuit. There was no other way.

He saw them now as they had assembled the week before – the national revolutionary committee – himself the youngest member, and a sudden jolt of distrust questioned the row of heavy faces and the sharp, shrewd eyes. They lived on a constant level of violence. For the first time Johann understood he would not choose to be involved in an ordinary world with any of them. He examined the faces individually with bitter disillusion. Some were there for the thrill of reckless conspiracy; some were honing private ambitions to settle on the day. The rest, like himself, were puppets of their own emotion.

In an awful, undermining way Anna was right. There was no support.

He felt the confused and suffering weight of the people dragging down his dreams like paper flags into a mess of blood and snow.

Johann stared back into Anna's glowering eyes.

'Are you finished?' he asked quietly. He knew she was not. The sharp teeth were ready to rip him again.

But he had recognised with a shock of identity a familiar echo in Anna's voice. It was the resonance of hysteria and it came from the same dark displacement he had discovered in himself a few moments before. Anna too was on the very edge of control, torn between opposed convictions. She had come back here to fight – now she had lost her nerve, and taken refuge in mountaineering with its imitation of courage. And she too hated what she had given up. Johann had gone the other way; briefly they had passed each other by, their voices were entangled and still tearing apart. Johann found himself transparent with bitter lucidity. Anna's attack, fired by her own crisis, had exposed him to the bone. He felt no temptation to argue his case, to justify himself. There was nothing to say. Anna had echoed his own hidden awareness with unerring accuracy.

He knew he had chosen impossible politics, and used violence to punish reality when it did not conform. And yet, despite the absurdity, he had no choice. There would be no alternative soon except to lie down and rot into their own soil. He felt dimly that struggle was still a valid end in itself – but only for the undivided, the incorruptible.

'At least you knew something about that, once!' Briefly the echo reassured. But he had reached a point in mountaineering when his nerve would take him no farther. He had to live with failure at that point, or else push himself – and his luck – farther than he dared. He did neither. He turned his back and hoped the mountains would have changed before he looked again. Johann admitted all that. It was obvious, and he brushed it impatiently aside.

But passion was a different thing. It was a constant crisis. It bulged within him, livid, unmentionable, a physical condition. He could never come to terms with that.

Anna waited, unappeased. When he fell in love with her, tumbling into an impossible obsession, he had feared her sophisticated standards and refused to face them. He had cut himself off, agonisingly, rather than risk any further failure.

He knew now that that was the ultimate defeat. Self-inflicted! Beyond anything else, he hoped she did not guess what he had done to both of them. He was determined to keep that secret at any cost. He had never given the slightest clue to his feelings.

'Are you finished?' he asked again, unsteadily. Anna shook her head slowly, deliberately.

'No! I came to tell you something else. I'm leaving, Johann! As soon as that climb is finished. Jean is right; it's the only thing left here, and I'm going as soon as it's done.'

She was leaning towards him – not to approach, but as if to push him away. And yet he heard her words from a long way off. He felt her hot breath on his face and smelled a faint sting of alcohol. Awful certainty stabbed him, jealousy before any emotion. 'You ... you're going away with Jean!' His voice wailed and broke.

'That's none of your business!' Anna retorted angrily. 'Don't play the wounded lover with me, Johann. It's too late for any of that. You had your chance!'

He was staring at her in open-mouthed anguish, his face unmasked. Anna laughed harshly. 'Oh yes, I know what you're supposed to feel, though sometimes I doubt it. Zelda told me about you months ago.

'I suppose I was meant to come crawling to you on my knees again. Well, if you couldn't tell me your own feelings – whatever they were – I didn't want to know. You killed mine deliberately anyway. Whatever inadequacy you're cursed with you took it out on me.' She drew a deep, vindictive breath. 'Let me give you a bit of advice, Johann! What you feel is not love. It's self-pity!

'Well I'm sorry but I can't waste any more sympathy on you. You've done too much damage already.'

She drew further away in distaste, shaking her head at the stricken face that gaped at her, bone-white and betrayed. Her voice dropped to a cold, even tone of withdrawal. 'You disappoint me Johann, and that's the reason why I'm going. But you've disappointed a lot of others too, and they have to stay here. That's why I'm telling you this; I'm trying to do something for them before I go!'

Stripped of secrecy Johann's resistance collapsed. In its place there was an eerie, detached calm – pain stretched to a pitch that his mind could not admit. He felt his heart hammer loud and loose in his chest, as if it had torn away from a powerful enclosing pressure. The released heartbeat was so strong he felt his body twitch and jerk. In a moment the shock would diminish and the overwhelming pain return. In the interval disembodied reason functioned coolly. He could not let her go, or existence would always feel like this, unendurable, inescapable.

He backed unsteadily into the dark loft, retreating before Anna's hatred. Shards of plaster crunched beneath his boots. Reaching the solid resistance of a wall he focused painfully on the waiting face blurred by silence and shadows. He had watched her from this distance at every meeting. He could not remember a single thing he had ever said or done that did not revolve secretly around her presence.

She was still there. Waiting. A question stirred in him. It was almost a joke the way it crept into his numb vacancy and he felt his horrified lips twitch. Did she intend a miracle of reconciliation? Or was she bent on his total destruction?

The two possibilities were the furthest extremes of optimism and despair – and though he knew which was true he knew also that an illusion of hope was essential to him.

The light seeping through the snow-banked window was waning fast. The loft was thick with shadows. Anna's white face drifted in the darkness. The anger on the dim features was indistinguishable from grief, or pain, or loss.

Johann was convulsed suddenly by guilt, as if he had struck her brutally. It passed and left a sense of clear, tragic pity in its wake. He was not the only victim! She was waiting because she had nowhere else to go. Obviously Jean only wanted a temporary partner. He would be gone as soon as it suited him, and gone alone. The mountain was not a destination for her either – it was an act of defiance. She thought that if she reached the impossible summit she would come down somewhere else, somewhere completely different.

But the notion of the mountain terrified him. He saw the pointed roof of the loft rear above her, the apex lost in shadow, a prophecy filled with threat.

If she simply went away he would still have hope, but he knew with certainty that departure to the mountain was final. It *had happened before*.

He moved impulsively towards her. Anna straightened and jerked back but his hands beseeched her.

'Anna don't. That mountain is not ...' he struggled for words '... not what you think! Leave it alone, Anna! Let him take someone else. It's too dangerous!'

The warning tumbled passionately from his mouth – but she heard him say plainly: You're not good enough.

Her pale cheeks reddened and she threw back her hair furiously. 'How dare you tell me what to do.'

Johann ignored her protest. He knew where he was now. He felt the wound in his consciousness opening again, a blind gap widening quickly as memory pushed through the darkness towards recognition.

He was breathless with urgency. It had happened before. He had to stop her. How to begin?

'Anna – remember the medal I had … the International Expedition! I gave it to you!' His voice was quick and impetuous, almost a wail. He had never spoken like that before. Crying for attention.

'Everything went wrong.' His hands were close to his face, hovering.

'I couldn't believe how big the mountains were. These –' he shook his head fiercely at the walls, '– these are only miniatures!'

'What are you trying to say?' Anna broke in impatiently, 'You did nothing, did you?'

'No,' he admitted, 'I did nothing, – but not for the reasons you think. The expedition was cancelled. It was a disaster.

'No,' he rushed, forestalling her, 'I wasn't involved. They wouldn't let me.'

'They wouldn't let you? What kind of nonsense is that?'

Johann spread his trembling hands; his voice was tired, incapable of anger. 'Anna, four women died in a blizzard a week after our arrival. Is that enough for you?'

He saw furious resistance on her face but he went on flatly. 'The first female team to try anything so high. They couldn't wait to hurl themselves at it. I was in base-camp all the time. They wouldn't allow me on any team because I was too young. Not even the easy ridge-repeats.' A sullen shadow passed across his face.

'It was my own fault. I was sixteen, I passed myself off as twenty and they found me out. It was too late to pick someone else from our province so they put me on base-camp duty. Kitchens and latrines, working with the porters; it was a punishment.

'The other climbers ignored me. Some treated me like a servant, especially since I came from here. They pretended they never heard of our mountains, they made stupid jokes. But the women understood. Especially Vera! They understood why I wanted to be there – no matter where I came from.'

He put his hands to his face and spoke through his fingers.

'I think I knew beforehand that something had to happen. She was the best person there, and she was living those days at an incredible pitch of anticipation.

'She used to show us pictures of her children. She had a daughter my age; she said I'd have to meet her.'

Anna's eyes were narrow with suspicion. 'Don't give me a sob-story!'

'No. No! It's the truth. I didn't feel ... It's not what you think.'

'They went up in poor weather. No one else was doing much, just acclimatising, but Vera and Arlova were full of confidence. It wouldn't be a hard route – just an enormous snow-climb.

'I was with them when they left for the walk-in. I helped Vera put her rucksack on. I couldn't believe the weight of it! I couldn't have carried it to seven thousand metres, or even five! But she just shrugged it on and walked away, waving to everyone.

'She was walking backwards, laughing at us all, waving for a camera, and I tried to imagine they were coming down to meet us after the route shouting in triumph. But she was getting farther and farther away and the laughter was growing thin, and she stumbled a bit and had to turn her back on us.

'The weather broke two nights later and it never really cleared again. It snowed right down into the valley, into the summer meadows where the flowers were growing the day before. Every night was like another door locked behind them. The porters said they were the worst storms in twenty years. Even in base-camp the winds were so fierce that tents were completely destroyed.

'We wanted to go up after them – not just me, but most of the others. Maria's husband was in the camp, but the authorities wouldn't let us move. They said it would be suicidal, the mountain was avalanching over and over again and the winds were impossible. I would have gone anyway, and so would the others. Everyone loved them. We knew there was only one hope – that they might have reached the summit and dug snow-holes before the worst of the storms. Tents would be useless in the winds. If they were in snow-holes they might survive to traverse the mountain in a lull and descend the west ridge. But they couldn't have enough food to endure the storm and then the long descent. I remembered the weight of Vera's sack and I wasn't so sure.

'There was almost a mutiny and a rescue-team was allowed to leave base-camp. They crawled along under the storm for two days and then began the ascent of the West Ridge to meet the women on their way down. I begged to go, but they wouldn't listen to me.

'The weather cleared a little and they were able to climb. But they met nobody on the ridge. The higher they went the more hopeless it was. Finally they knew they were just a recovery-squad.

'You can't imagine what it was like for the rest of us below, no word, no hope, nothing to do but wait for the worst, and all the time inventing some impossible escape. I still couldn't get the weight of Vera's rucksack out of my mind. I told everyone she was carrying spare food. I was determined to believe it. But they said if she was carrying that much weight then she was in even greater danger from exhaustion.

'It wasn't food … The rescue-team found them on the summit. They had to dig. They were wrapped together in one tent, buried under thick snow. The whole bundle was already frozen into the ice, and the rescuers had to hack it loose with ice-axes.'

Johann paused. Looking over Anna's head he confronted something invisible; 'and do you know what they did then? They were too exhausted to bring the bodies down. Do you know what they did?

'They wrapped them in the tent, tied it with a rope and pushed them over the East Face. I still can't believe it, but that's what they did!

'They thought the bodies would disappear, like a burial at sea, but they came all the way down to the lower slopes – three of them. The canvas ripped and three of them came down. 'They sent me out with another team to help bring them in. I don't know why they did that either – my God, we were all too young!

'Maria's husband came with us, and examined them one by one as we lowered them onto the glacier. But she hadn't come down. He was hysterical with grief. They had to restrain him physically from starting up the face. He wasn't even a climber. He blamed himself for letting her go.

'Vera was the farthest away. She almost looked alive. Asleep or something. Her skin was so cold and hard it was unmarked. Her rucksack was there too. It was still heavy. I opened it. There was a big camera in it – an old fashioned one – to prove they'd been on top I suppose. It was smashed to bits.

'All the pictures of her children were in there. And a picture of her husband. He was much older than Vera. And there were flags: from her club, her city, her province. But there was no food.

'I found a diary in the top of the sack while they were carrying her down. There were entries for every day of the climb and they got shorter and shorter as time ran out. Pages with no dates, no times, just a clumsy scrawl as if she had gloves on, or her hands were numb. Messages for her children and people I'd never heard of. She didn't know where she was towards the end, no mention of the snow or the storm, just vague things she wanted to do. And then – a last page that said the others were all asleep, she had done everything possible for them and ... and soon she would sleep herself. It was like a lullaby, as if she were singing a lullaby!

'At the bottom of the page the writing cleared with a great effort – the pencil dug into the paper – and she wrote:

'We are sorry we have failed you.'

'Can you imagine that?' Johann whispered to Anna. 'They thought they had failed us, us!'

He took a shivering breath and exploded. 'It was OUR failure! They were too important. We should never have let them go!'

Anna flinched. Her head jerked back. 'What right have you,' she hissed, 'to decide what anyone else should do?'

Johann was jolted brutally into the present. He stared at her dizzily, tears blinding his eyes. The rage of loss was so bitter he could have struck her to release it. He could say nothing. Nothing! The air was frozen finally between them, his heart ticking towards explosion. In five seconds, four, three ... he would shatter. She turned abruptly and left the room. The door slammed. Boot heels hammered down the wooden stairs.

Johann stood in the darkness. He held his breath, straining for footsteps returning on the stairs, like heartbeats from a dream of death. But there was silence everywhere, and he exploded in slow, unbearable grief.

He followed them when they quit the smothered valley for the white mountains. Away from the village Jean and Anna clasped hands briskly and swung along together oblivious to the extra shadow they cast in the early light. Anna was teaching Jean a song and she laughed helplessly at his total elision of the guttural. Their voices chimed thin and faint in the muffled landscape. They moved fast on the frozen snow-crust, skimming across the drifts as if on skis.

Johann struggled grimly to stay in range. His muscles were weak and stale, and the icy air burned in his throat. He knew every step of the path, knew exactly where he could move unseen and when to hang back. But he was invisible to them; they were sealed in their own rapport. It was exactly how Anna had been with him at first.

Soon they left him far behind. Already his boots, stiff from disuse, were gnawing his heels. The heavy rifle slung across the rucksack chafed his shoulders cruelly. He carried it for –

Certainty burned in his brain. Last week three of his best men had been ambushed in action by the military police. They had barely escaped with their lives. Johann had worked it out grimly last night, grief and humiliation hardening together into revenge. Someone was spying. He stalked Jean, like a wounded hunter.

He lost them in the afternoon when the memory of tracks had faded away, and the rocks, the streams, the great reefs of moraine, were sunk without trace under frozen waves of winter. He stumbled to a halt at times, against a bank of snow, to gnaw some bread and cheese, churning it around in his mouth. His stomach rebelled against it, and finally, after struggling up a steep slope he threw it all up and left himself utterly raw and empty, at the mercy of the landscape. The sky, the ice, the crackling air, the rock-scars like chipped enamel on the white faces, closed in to crush him in the grip of a monstrous, mineral world.

Traversing the endless plateau, skirting its ridges and rifts, he no longer thought of where he was going. He would travel until he dropped. He was conscious only of a determination to go on – on to some conclusion. Not to be beaten by default.

The pain of betrayal and the rage for revenge, were dimmed by exhaustion and cold. But there was never any doubt of his direction. He had not seen the mountain all day – it was hidden by intervening peaks – but it drew him with irresistible force.

There was no twilight. Darkness fell like an abrupt decision. It seemed to come from within his brain, a dismissal of the white wilderness.

Hours later a stark moon rose and lit the glacier. The way stretched wearily on, up into the shadow of the spear-crested cirque. Once he saw a light twinkling cheerfully ahead, but it was a bright star rising over a ridge. He climbed a buried icefall to the upper glacier, and a grunt of relief acknowledged the easy step. It was normally a steep, unstable obstacle; but now the heavy, solid snow made everything possible. It would have been a good time to climb.

There were familiar peaks on his left and right. Thin, tapering spires, dizzy junctions of rock and air, he had climbed them all before, addicted to their altitude and grace. Now they were stony shadows, scraping sparks off the black sky.

He could not recall warmth under a blue heaven, could not remember sunlight blazing on bright rock, nor remember a time without this dark taste of ice and pain in his mouth. He was drunk with displacement. Someone he had known – close and lost as a dead twin – had revelled in those jubilant walls and kept the memory when Johann fell away into confusion. As if he had slipped from some golden morning far down into this hideous dark, he flashed past all his attachments, saw how they were linked and lost. He had loved these mountains and been rejected, had loved Anna and been displaced, had loved an idea and left it in ruins behind him in the valley.

Jagged splinters of the past tore his memory from within. And the cold weight of the rifle dug deep into his back.

Casually he broke through a crust of snow into a hidden crevasse. Instinct jerked his body into a whiplash and he saved himself. As soon as he was secure on the rim of the chasm he cursed his recovery. Then the hallucinations began. He stumbled into villages of sérac and shadow that returned to ice with such poisonous derision that he doubted whether reality existed anywhere. All he wanted now was sleep; isolated houses – some with doors, windows and smoking chimneys – drifted up from his subconscious, jutted cruelly into the landscape. And for a long time the traitor was behind him, pursuit reversed, and Jean was filling in his footprints to erase him from the surface of the snow, so that the further Johann walked the less he existed. He dodged, weaved, and sometimes he doubled back to shake off his invisible pursuit. But Jean was deadly. He had a year's practice in trailing Johann!

When he reached the little hut on its rock-island near the head of the glacier he almost dismissed it as another mirage. It was caked with frozen snow. Only the shape was visible in the shifting night, an ice-enamelled box drumming with silent tension. Together they were asleep inside.

The logic of arrival returned him to his senses. He saw a grotesque image of himself shambling through the dark towards inevitable contempt. He could not bring himself to approach the door and whimper for shelter. He had rights here. He remembered the building of the hut fifteen years before, the first time he had come this far into the summer mountains riding a mule with a load of planks, then trotting behind his father's long steps across the glaciers. The hut was hammered together from pine planks. His father and his uncle were two of the carpenters who finished it, hanging the heavy door at the end of the third day's work. The following year they were conscripted and never returned. Now the hut looked as if it had absorbed its origins. It seemed to have grown from its own powerful root under the snow, and the door and windows were indistinguishable from the dull bark of the trunk.

He thought of kicking the door open and announcing he had come to join them on the climb.

An image of two drowsy heads on one mattress regarding him with horrified contempt dragged a grunt of humour up from his bowels. That he should come to this!

It was obvious that he couldn't climb tomorrow: he could barely walk. He was at the limit of endurance now, but it would be a greater humiliation to reveal that jealousy had driven him there. He had no faith now in the moral superiority of revenge. Guilt was too complex to be resolved by execution. He dreaded the icy cave, the old bivouac nearby. It was like deliberately entering a grave, but dignity forced him down. There was a flat space there under a boulder. He had cleared it himself long ago, and built the overlapping walls to shelter it on the first day the men were erecting the hut. He crawled in now and spread out his coat. He pushed the frozen rifle down through a sleeve and dragged a heavy sleeping bag on over his clothes. The gun lay awkwardly beneath him, but he fell instantly into an icy sleep.

... Under the blankets on the iron cot Johann lay wide awake in his cell, dreaming, dreaming. The details were perfectly clear; the heavy boulder crusted with icicles, the black hole in the snow-drift. And the wooden box nearby, containing all that anyone could ever desire – shelter, warmth, food. Jean was inside with Anna, and he was outside.

How much was true, how much reserved by memory, no longer mattered. Reality had no witness except himself. He was outside.

But there was a quickening of cold new emotion in the old man's brain this time. A trickle of judgement, clearer than revenge. It stirred like blood released from a long freeze.

He knew that somewhere guilt must emerge this time, like the bones and the rags, the buttons, the teeth, and the rotting leather that dribble out at last from the snouts of glaciers.

Voices outside the hut woke him slowly. Consciousness drifted up through drowning waters. A gulp of icy air. Self-discovery sharp as nausea. Cold shudders racked his body, convulsions racing through his frozen limbs. He clenched his teeth against the spasms, and all the shivering came to a rattling focus in his jaws. He opened his eyes and felt the black weight of the boulder pressing down inches above his blind face. He almost cried out in choking terror.

They were leaving for the mountain. It was still pitch dark and he had slept at most three hours. If he had lain unconscious any longer he would never have recovered. Footsteps rang past the bivouac. Not the faintest crunch of snow under the boots. Anna's voice was strained and brittle. She spoke the foreign language but her fear was obvious. Jean's response was low and toneless, like water running under ice.

Johann crawled from the bivouac and stumbled towards the hut. It was a desolate sanctuary, the blood-heat had leaked away, and the bare walls and roof enclosed a solid cube of night.

He shook with advanced exposure. Heat was crucial. An ashy spark in the wood-stove! He built it up into a reckless furnace, plundering the emergency firewood, splintering the wooden spoons and breadboard.

He rooted frantically for food. They must have left him something! He refused to believe he was invisible to them; they must be as involved in his presence as he was in theirs. Not a crumb! He boiled a jagged lump of snow-ice. The hot water seized his stomach with violent cramps. Blood returning to the frozen toes and fingers brought the agony of amputation in reverse. At this stage of exposure he knew revival was harsher than decline. He writhed before the stove, an animal in crisis.

The mattress lay neatly rolled against the wall, feathers sprouting from its cover. He rocked back and forth moaning with recovery and stared at it in a desperate attempt to ignore the increasing pain. When he lost control he beat his frenzied fingers into its bulk forcing it to absorb his anguish. The coarse texture and rusty pattern responded with a gush of memory like an explosion of feathers. A matrimonial mattress long ago – he was dangerously close now to the source – it had slipped down the scale of comfort until finally exiled here. He remembered it swaying up the track, outrageously loaded on a mule's back, firewood slung across it, and they rushed to tilt the mattress every time the mule's tail lifted.

Deeper still he seemed to recall it – not this one but exactly the same – in the vicinity of childhood, in a hushed dark bedroom, before it went down to Aunt Zelda's house after a funeral.

He hurled it flat on the floor fumbling and tearing for its secrets, as if something might reveal how close they had been last night. Feathers drifted up around him like snowflakes, but the past was silent and absorbed. With detached horror he saw himself crouch in wild unreason over the battered mattress, cursing, and clawing – and yet he knew that somewhere behind the pain he was bitterly, irreducibly sane, like a man driving himself into a drunken frenzy to blind the unforgettable.

Long after dawn he left the hut and followed the last curve of the glacier. The mountains were carved out of solid daylight, with smears of darkness where the rock showed through. He turned the foot of the final ridge and looked straight in at the blank triangle.

Breath seized in his throat. Three hours at most and the two black dots were one third of the way up already. Johann could measure them moving – the white bulge of the rock barrier sliding away below them. It was time accelerated, like seeing an hour-hand move. He shook his head in stupefaction. It must be an illusion: choughs flying up the face. They could never have got so high!

A second shock. They were moving together. No belays. Thirty feet of rope between them as if they were walking up a snow-slope. But this was an ice-wall. Insanity! At that angle if either slipped they were both whipped off instantly.

Johann had spent a whole day's climbing to reach that height – three hundred metres up the face. He had bivouacked just above that point. Every metre gained had meant a step cut, holds hacked in the glassy ice with the blunt axe, a ledge chopped at every twenty metres, ice-pegs battered in, the others dragged up skidding and scrabbling on the grey, winter glaze.

His stunned brain slowly absorbed today's conditions – eyes dazzled from within as he understood the glowing face. Instead of winter water-ice – the colour of lead and as hard as glass – he saw breathless, brilliance clinging to the face. Fresh snow … Snow! The huge triangle was lightly, evenly plastered.

Johann gouged his incredulous eyes, The north-facing ice was too steep, too smooth, to hold snow like that. It sloughed off in powder avalanches immediately after a fall.

But Jean and Anna were still moving. Even as he gaped, the rock-barrier slipped another ten metres below them. They had stepped up through it on a rib of snow, as if bare rock had never existed there. The recent weather flashed through his mind. A storm three days ago. But the effects of that should have avalanched immediately! Then the temperature had dropped to an abnormal low. The day of Anna's visit the village was creaking in the grip of a savage freeze. Then bitter, windless weather. Yesterday evening the temperature had seemed beyond the extreme – he had put it down to his thin blood, the loss of heat from a raging heart. But he understood now! Extreme conditions had frozen a crust of snow to the ice-face overhead. Crampons and axes bit firmly into it. But it was no more than inches thick and already thawing. The temperature was shooting up this morning. Johann broke into a frantic sweat at the consequences.

He realised he was watching something new in mountaineering – new by local standards. A gamble on opportunity and speed. Where he had waited for stable conditions, however hard, and then inched his way upwards, Jean had seized transition and was flying towards the top. He had a few short hours between the snow-ice and the avalanche. But surely he had misjudged it. Surely he was a day late!

A thousand metres, angle sixty-five degrees, temperature minus ten and rising, eight hours of daylight left. Three hundred metres climbed. Johann worked it out numbly. They could do it. Barring accidents.

But an accident was guaranteed. Inevitable. He could not believe the mountain would submit to calculated treachery.

Standing on the smothered glacier looking uselessly upwards, Johann saw his last ambition being cheated from him. He had meant to climb the mountain when the war was won. It was a pledge to self-respect, made in subconscious silence in case it could not be redeemed.

Barring accidents! The insistent thought had the conviction of evil in his brain, a primitive mix of curse and prayer.

But if Jean failed, Anna was doomed. That rope was the ultimate intimacy, even more than the mattress.

The face was angled away from the heat of the day – until this afternoon, when the last rays of the setting-sun would breach the summit-cornice. They must reach the top before the thaw.

A rush of awful contradiction squeezed venom from his heart.

The deliberate curse echoed around the silent cirque, gathering force and resonance as it hurtled from wall to wall, crashing and booming between the summits, a voiceless roar hammering at the frozen lid of the sky.

The vengeful breath retracted and sobbed in his throat. There was one thing stronger than hatred. He could not bear to lose Anna. She was a hostage on the mountain. Jean had robbed him now of his last resorts of hope and of revenge.

Helpless rage ignited him. He dived against a smothered boulder and dragged the rifle from his back. White-tipped fingers clung to the icy steel. He screwed a telescopic sight onto the barrel, a clumsy range-finder – two lenses and a focus. No, he did not intend to shoot! He could not execute Anna.

The weapon gave a vacant sense of power, something to control. And through the powerful lens he could watch her crawling up the face. Towards what conclusion?

Weaving with weakness the cross-hairs searched the shining snow. The smooth stock against his trembling jaw, the solid rock and ice under a sliding elbow – he knew he was the only weak component in a hard machine. The sight lurched, picked up a blurred figure, long and thin as an insect, limbs working busily. His fingers stumbled against the trigger and withdrew. The rope led downwards. He lowered the barrel to find her. A terrifying thought kicked from the polished wood into his skull. Bullets would not be necessary! The sound of gunfire alone would trigger an avalanche on that shivering face.

She was unrecognisable in helmet and bulky clothes. For one exultant moment he thought it was someone else, a legitimate enemy on his terrain. But her movements, the angle of her head, the action of her arms, were undeniable. Anna had not adapted to ice with the smoothness she showed on rock. Ice took confidence beyond technique. Johann felt a stab of simple surprise; there was something wrong. She was fumbling, climbing without rhythm. He had expected to witness excellence. Instead she was visibly slowing Jean.

He felt his tension release a surge of sympathy. He understood the fear she felt up there, making her kick too hard and flail the axe into the ice behind the snow. It was not just fear of avalanche and the frail snow-crust, but a sense of the overwhelming enmity of that wall. The exposure undermined the imagination. Jean knew nothing of that, the inhuman vacuum sucking at the soles of the feet. There was nothing in his head but time and motion.

Still Johann couldn't believe they had climbed so high – a third of the face in three hours. The bergschrund alone ...? He whipped the barrel down the face, found the black crevasse and followed it. Magnification was unnecessary. With the naked eye he could see the mass of old debris heaped up on the glacier below, ice-blocks supporting a tongue of snow that bridged the bergschrund and reached onto the face. He remembered the bare, overhanging ice, the rattling axes, his skin sticking to the steel, the wildest thing he had ever driven himself to do. He focused on the spot. A ramp of ice-blocks loomed through the glass. The myth was buried and Jean had strolled across it stripping Johann of his main achievement.

Barring accidents!

The telescopic sight crept up along the snow, found Anna again. Her legs continued to kick and lift, arms threshing like a swimmer caught in a current. He made an effort of will and attached her to himself, focusing the glass carefully to increase her safety, as if he were tightening the rope around her.

He opened the other eye beside the barrel and reeled with the strain of split vision. She was still there, working jerkily upwards, safe within the hazy cameo that pinned her to the face. But there beside her, far, far away on an unbearable expanse of white, two tiny black spots crept beyond control against the rising light. He felt the sun swinging south, rolling towards the rim of the cirque, blazing already onto the glacier behind him. His heart pounded in panic and Anna dissolved in his sweating eye-socket, distance sucking her away into its vacuum.

He shut the murderous eye of exposure and drew her back into the rim. The tense cross-hairs meshed against her body like a safety-net.

Through the long, melting morning he lay flat on the rock, his head on his rucksack, rifle pointed at the face. When he blinked his eyes stayed shut and he fell instantly asleep for seconds at a time. Waking, he caught her again and again as she faltered, the rope twitching impatiently at her waist.

Trickles of snow were pouring down the face now. The southward slopes creaked and settled behind him. When he glanced fearfully at the sun-clogged snow, it shone with a slick, creamy gloss. But the face was still in shadow.

They were over two-thirds of the way up. Anna rested frequently, slumped against the steepness. He breathed slow and deep, sent strength along the line of vision. Sometimes she was lost in spindrift – streams of powder sliding from above. Once she disappeared for so long that he screamed and waved his arm clawing the curtain aside.

And there would now be stones shooting from the summit as the ice peeled away from the rotten rocks. He could not see the missiles but the air around her was charged with menace. She was difficult to pick out now, even through the lens, a limbless dot on broken ground.

The great rock-bulge below the last ice-field glowed ethereally as the sun swung towards the west ridge. Light trickled softly onto the face down the ramps and gullies from the summit. The mountain gleamed with a vicious grace.

He knew Jean thought nothing could stop him now, ladders of sunlight lowered to lift him to success.

What did Anna feel? Pain and the futility of pain? Doubt and dread? If she knew the stories of the first attempt then she was expecting the real trial overhead.

Johann had never explained what was up there, on the rusty tip of the spear. The rock was steep and rotten, the ridges beyond reach and impenetrably corniced. He offered no excuse beyond his own weakness. Conditions must be worse today, a treacherous scum of snow on the crumbling rock. Squinting, he saw the cornices foaming in the sunlight.

Jean was starting the crux now. He was at the foot of a gully, halted at last while the second dot crept up to him. What did they say to each other? He strained to understand. Anna was beyond speech. They were taking a belay at last, where there was nothing solid enough for support or attachment.

Johann saw the position as if he stood there with them, crowding for space, Boris and Anton slumped weakly on the ledge beside his feet, black lips and burnt-out eyes. A rough groove reared out of the ice, splitting the last rock-step. It was full of congealed rubble, fragments of red rocks stacked overhead, shifting and smearing at the touch. The poison on the point.

He had hammered an ice-piton straight into a loose seam in desperation and still there was no security. In a moment of lucid fantasy he saw himself climbing on sea shells and broken crockery.

Twenty metres higher, out of sight of the belay, an overhang sealed the groove. To right and left bloated red rock bulged. No way of knowing what lay above, how much climbing, how hard or dangerous. The one thing he knew for certain was the function of this gully.

It was a snow-spout and a stone-chute.

Johann leaned out below the overhang. A fall must drag his comrades off the ledge; they could never hold him now. He was entirely alone, surviving for three men. He mustered a surge of courage, a snarl of faith.

Stepped up and leaned out again, fumbling below the rim of the over-hang … a jutting block to grab; if it held, swing free and launch, lunge for something secret behind the lip.

His mouth moved, inventing holds, cementing them in place. A foothold shifted under his sagging weight. He had found the crux of his existence and it was a gambler's choice. The wrong decision now and he would be dead and a double-killer. Johann backed off.

Jean had no such choice. The slopes below him creaked and rippled with tension.

Anna swayed at the foot of the gully. She was invisible to Johann at last, but he knew exactly where she was, her head bowed against the rubble, wet rope useless in her hands, her face transparent with exhaustion. She no longer knew who was climbing above her, why she was condemned to be here.

Johann rubbed his eyes in anguish for her. He heard the rumble of his fingertips against his skull. Under a rush of pressure the eyelids burst open.

White light burned into his brain, rebounded through his mouth. The summit was erupting in a storm of powder, the cornice pouring white lava down the gullies. The mountain shivered softly, brilliance seething and streaming down the blind triangle. The snow-slope burst in billowing waves, surging, sliding, sweeping. A huge pulse drummed in Johann's head, darkness screaming from his mouth. A wooden club kicked against his jaw, butting and recoiling over and over again. He squeezed the frenzied trigger at the serene avalanche, and the rifle hammered tiny nails into the thunder.

The old man closed his eyes. Barely breathing he lay in darkness. His memory was empty. The white wave had erased the black pinpoints of pain and cured the long, sharp scrape of their ascent.

The past hung within him, a clean, grey triangle, steep and unin-habited. He lay at the apex, looking down. Levitation was as simple as desire at last – no ambition to impede or challenge it, no emotion and no witness.

He saw the great spillage fan out from the base below. Like milk boiling over, a pleasant stir of recognition. It flowed out towards the glacier and slowly seized solidity – swelling the river of ice. Shimmering clouds hung in the air awhile, then cleared like morning mist.

Johann was in no hurry now. He had thirty years at his disposal.

He embarked on a rhythm of cold content, allowing the rubble to settle softly in his mind. The snow merged with the underlying ice and slowly melted into the glacier to make room for the next avalanche and all the falls to follow. He almost slept on the cot, turning sideways and drawing his legs up under the blanket.

But try as he might to retain the ease of passion spent he could not erase the two small mounds together on the ice below. A thin cover of snow persisted over them, a blanket on a distant accident.

Later, there were voices near him. The gun was levered from his hands. He was lifted roughly and carried against his will. He had no desire to be taken down, jolted across the ice on a rope-stretcher. He lay sprawled in warm darkness then and molten liquid filtered down his throat. He was aware of his hands and feet being massaged, but it seemed as senseless as polishing timber. When he opened his eyes he found the wood-stove floating in a haze beside him, the wooden floor, the striped mattress under his cheek.

He looked up into ambiguous eyes. His lips struggled to offer the most important truth. His tongue was useless, but the words slid up from his chest, already shaped like nuggets of ice.

'... they got nowhere. Just over the bergschrund when the cornice fell. Madness!' He buried his face and dissolved in genuine grief.

He was carried down to the village. And two days later soldiers swept the valley. Their information was precise. The hard line partisans were hunted down. Some were shot on sight.

Johann was held for interrogation. There was no attempt to save his fingers and toes. They were amputated in case he died too soon.

Deranged with pain, torture revealed nothing but hatred. He was obsessed with one thing only – Jean's treason! He had the final proof, too late. As soon as their agent was dead they had moved in and cleaned up.

A thin, sharp-eyed officer with weak hands and a lateral approach took over the interrogation.

'Marceau?' He raised his eyebrows coolly at Johann's ranting.

'No, no, you've got the wrong spy there.'

He crossed his boots with polished satisfaction, smiled and knifed him with her name.